THE ART OF THE GAME

KAYT MILLER

Editor: Hot Tree Editing

Proofreading by: Hot Tree Editing

Formatted by: Kayt Miller

Graphic Design: Book Smith Design booksmithdesign.com

Original Cover Art: Paige Knotts

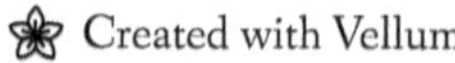 Created with Vellum

Bedhead

Redhead

Deadhead

FarmBoy

Game Changer

One of a Kind

The Virginia Chronicles

Our of the Blue: The Flynns Book One

Mick'sology: The Flynns Book Two

Vested Interest: The Flynns Book Three

The Importance of Being Ernie: The Flynns Book Four

The Importance of Being Kennedy's: The Flynns Book Five

Quirky Girl: The Flynns Book Six

The Art of the Game

Lainie: The Palmer Sisters Book 1

Agatha: The Palmer Sisters Book 2

Sadie: The Palmer Sisters Book 3

Cortland: The Palmer Sisters Book 4

Keely: The Palmer Sisters Book 5

Violet: The Palmer Sisters Book 6

Molly: The Palmer Sisters Book 7

The Portrait Painter

Hopeful Romantic (Coming soon.)

Thanks to Margie Dill (Coming soon.)

CONTENTS

CHAPTER ONE

REGGIE

"YO, DUDE. THIS YOUR ART?"

Dude? My shoulders slump at those words. I know he's talking to me, and I can only imagine why he called me dude. People. Listen up. Women can have short hair and still be women. *Geesh.* I slowly turn toward the deep voice to confront what I assumed would be his face. Not the case here. Instead of a face, I'm looking at some massive guy's chest. I scan up, past the widest set of shoulders I've ever seen, to a face too beautiful for a man, let alone one built like a brick shit house.

He blinks at me. "You're not a dude."

Ugh. Men. That statement really gets my ire up. "Really, genius? You don't think so? I mean, I've got short hair. But I've also got these," I say, placing one hand on each of my large breasts. "Confusing, right?" God, sarcasm is awesome.

The Neanderthal smirks at me. "You're definitely *not* a dude," he says, nodding at my chest.

Jerk.

Jerk or not, he's hot. I'm afraid to look at him too long for fear I'll start to climb him like a damn tree. I wonder if he's proportionate. *Stop! I can't think that way.*

I start to turn away, you know, so I don't turn to salt, as he says, "Wait, dude."

I turn back and raise an eyebrow. I guess I can see how he would mistake me for a guy. I'm not dressed very girly for the opening reception of my thesis show. I'm wearing my typical tee, ripped jeans, and most comfy Birkenstock sandals covered in layers of clay dust and muck. Why dress up? The only people I know here are classmates and a professor or two. My folks, especially my dad, would never make the trek here for this, so I didn't bother telling them.

"Sorry. It's just... you're wearing baggy clothes, and you were turned away so I couldn't see those," he says, pointing to my girls. "And your hair *is* really short."

It is short. I like it that way. Right now, my hair is in sort of a pixie cut, but I've let my bangs grow out so they hang long enough to hit my nose. I love it because it's easy to work with every day. In the morning, all I have to do is wash and go. The only thing dramatic about my hair is the color. I've dyed my mousey-brown hair platinum blonde, creating a more dramatic look.

His hair almost hits his collar, so I ask, "Yours is pretty long. Does that make you a chick?"

"I'm all man, sweetheart," he says with a beaming smile.

A smile that makes me nearly pass out from the complete and utter gorgeousness of it. He's got straight, white teeth surrounded by full lips. The day-old scruff of his beard isn't thick enough to hide the dimple on his left cheek, thank goodness. Holy hotness, Batman, this guy is too good to be true. I chew on my lip ring nervously, nibbling on the black metal ball against my lip.

No matter how smitten I am, I can't let him get away with saying that crap. "Typical. You sound like a sexist idiot when you say shit like that."

"I'm not sexist. On the contrary, I'm a firm believer that women are far superior to men." He winks.

"Ugh, this is about sex, isn't it?" I roll my eyes.

Ignoring my question, he asks, "So. Reggie? Is that your real name?"

"Yeah? Why?"

"Your name is *Reggie*, and you're giving me shit about confusing you for a guy? You're dressed like a guy, and you've got a guy's name. Unless your real name is something like Regina. Is it Regina?"

"Nope." I shake my head. I'm not telling him my real name. Why should I? I reserve that honor for only my closest and dearest.

"You're not going to tell me your name?"

"No." I sigh. "What do you need, uh...?"

"You don't know who I am?"

I blink at him. Should I know who he is? Placing my hands on my hips, I jut a leg out for extra sass. "Should I know you?"

It's his turn to blink. "No, I guess not." He meets my stare for a good ten seconds. "It's Carter."

"Okay." *Finally.* "Carter, you wanted to ask me something?"

He runs a massive paw through his shoulder-length mane of dark auburn hair—so dark you could get away with calling it brown, but I'm an *artiste* so I notice subtleties like that.

"You did these?" he asks, pointing to one of the eight large clay sculptures.

"Yeah. These are mine. You wanna buy one?" I give him my own smirk. No one ever wants to buy art at a student thesis show, let alone stuff like mine—abstract clay pieces that no one understands. Hell, even my professors don't really get my work.

"Maybe. I like that one." He points to my favorite piece, inspired by my best friend, Kai. The only one in the show I'd never sell.

"Not for sale." I turn once again and get three steps away before I feel a warm hand on my upper arm.

"Reggie, wait."

I look down at his hand on my arm and freeze. He's not squeezing me or hurting me. It's just that I'm struck by the sizzle that's running down my arm to my hand. I wiggle my fingers, trying to stop the charge. "What is it you need, Mr. Carter?"

"Carter. My first name is just Carter, and I want you to come home with me."

I know I must have blushed right then because he gives me a small smile. "Not for *that*. No offense, but you're not my type."

"Wow, why would I take offense to that? You're not my type either."

"Why? Because I've got a dick? You gay?"

"God, no, asshole. Seriously? Get over yourself. You think I have to be gay *not* to be into you?" I grumble as I pull my arm from his grasp. "This conversation is over. You're rude, and I don't like you anymore."

"You liked me before?" he asks with an arched brow and that stupidly gorgeous smirk.

"I liked the fact that you were interested in my work. But now you're just discourteous."

Carter chuckles, and the sound rumbles through my body. Oh, hell. I don't need to be attracted to this hunky jerk face. *Be strong, Reggie.*

"Look, Reggie. I bought a house, and there's an art studio on the property—"

"Property? You rich or something?"

"Or something. Anyway, there's a studio with a bunch of clay shit, and I don't know anything about pottery. I need someone to look at it and tell me what's what."

Clay shit? Blaspheme! "Where is this 'property'?" I used air quotes. Had to.

"South Barrington."

I let out a slow whistle. "Whoa, South Barrington? You *are* rich." South Barrington is, by far, the fanciest, hoity-toitiest suburb of Chicago. "You've got to be caked."

"Caked? I've never heard that one before."

I shrug. Yeah. I'm cool with the hip urban dictionary stuff.

"Will you come out there and look at it?"

I get that deer in headlights expression. I can feel my eyes bug a little. "What?" I screech a little too loud.

"I said—" He clears his throat. "—will you come up to South Barrington and check out the clay studio?"

I gulp. "Why me?"

"Why not you? This is your thesis show, yes? And you're getting your MFA in ceramics, right?"

"Uh, yeah." And damn proud of it.

"You know how to use the oven things and the wheel things?"

"Of course." I roll my eyes. No self-respecting ceramicist would *not* know about the oven things and the wheel things. Assuming a confident and possibly smug expression, I peer up at the tallest guy I've ever seen, "What's in it for me?"

"Well, if you don't have a car, I can have one pick you up so you won't have to hassle with transportation up there."

I make that come-hither motion with my hand that says, *What else?* "And?"

"I'll give you five hundred bucks."

My eyes grow large. So large I feel like my eyelids have hit my hairline. Sweet. That's rent. Hell, yes. But I need to be cool here. "Maybe. When?"

"I'll be out of town this week. What about a week from tomorrow?"

That's a Sunday. It's the only day next week that I don't work one of my jobs. "Sounds good."

He reaches into his back pocket and pulls out his phone. "Give me your cell number."

"Why do you need my number?" Okay, *duh*. I know why he needs it, but I said it. It's already out there. I've gotta go with it.

It's his turn to roll his eyes. They're very green. I'd go so far as to call them Windsor emerald if I were painting him. Not only are they a rich grass-green hue, but also they're surrounded by thick, long eyelashes. Why do guys always get those long eyelashes? It's not fair. "I need it so I can give you *my* number. You know, so we can communicate. I need an address to send the car to as well."

"Right." I take his phone from his hand. "What's your pass code?" I can't enter my number if it's locked up.

He thinks about it for a second and then says, "Sixty-nine, sixty-nine."

"Jesus." I roll my eyes. Hard. Then mumble, "Ass."

Unlocking his phone, the first thing I see is a picture of Carter wearing only board shorts, no shirt. I feel my panties melt just a tad. *Hubba-fucking-hubba.* My momentary lapse into an erotic fantasy of Carter ends as soon as I see the woman standing next to him in the photo. She's a gorgeous blonde woman in a white bikini, if you can call it that. It's made up of string and three tiny triangles, two cover her nipples, and one covers a no doubt hairless hoo-ha. She's tall. At least she looks tall from the picture. Her head reaches this guy's shoulder. Looking at me compared to that, I'd guess I'm about five inches shorter than her and about seventy pounds heavier.

"Wow, this must be your type then?" I turn the phone to show him. I know he knows what picture is on his home screen, but I show him anyway.

He shrugs. "Natalia. Yeah, she's okay."

Okay? She's more than okay. She *is* hot. And even though I'm strictly into the male of our species, I shrug. "I'd do her."

"I thought..."

I know what he thought. He thought I was straight. I am. "Figure of speech."

I add my name and number and shoot myself a quick text, then give his phone back to him. "I sent myself a text, so I now have your number."

"Right. Send me your address. I'll text you the time you'll be picked up. Don't text me like some random. I don't have time for useless chitchat."

"Well, as long as you don't do the same to me. I'm busy too."

He chuckles, and it makes my lower half hum like a hive of bees. His voice is delectable.

"Hey! I am." I've got a million part-time jobs. Plus, I'm still writing my thesis.

"Sure. No worries." He smirks. "See ya, Reg."

"That's Reggie. Not Reg."

"Right. See you, *Reggie*."

I wave like a dork as he turns to leave. I watch him go because, well, I've got a hoo-ha too. Jesus, the man is a work of art. He's got to be six-five or six-six. Most of his height comes from long legs made of thick muscle. His jeans look bespoke; like they were made for his body. They'd have to be. He's massive. A guy like that can't just walk into Walmart and buy jeans, for goodness sake. Hell, *I'd* make him some jeans if it meant I could get up close and personal with that high, tight ass... and if I could only sew. I let out a soft, slow whistle as I watch him walk out the door of the gallery.

What the hell am I doing? "Shake it off, Reggie. That man is way out of your league."

CHAPTER TWO

REGGIE

"WHO'S OUT OF YOUR LEAGUE?" asks my best friend in the entire world, Kai Apatu.

"The guy that just walked out. Did you see him?"

"The big guy with the awesome head of hair? I wonder what kind of shampoo he uses. Did he hit on you?"

I scoff. "No. Of course not. A guy like that would never go for this," I say, pointing at the My Little Pony tee with the whole gang on the front, including Rarity, Pinky Pie, and my personal fave, Rainbow Dash. The words "Ponies Forever" are printed above them in glittery letters. It's *awesome*.

"Of course he would. You're adorbs, honey. He was hot. I'd do him."

Okay, when I said the same thing earlier about Carter's woman, I was just kidding. When Kai says it, he means it. Although, that guy, Carter, isn't the kind of guy Kai usually goes for. Sure, that guy was pretty enough but Kai has a type and Carter was definitely not it. Actually, the two men remind me of one another. They're both massive, you know, tall and thick. Except Kai is beautifully native Hawaiian, the lucky bastard. Some would call Kai bisexual. Others might say pansexual or omnisexual. Kai doesn't discriminate. He's just *sexual*. He likes people, and most people like Kai. He's jovial and sweet and kind of hot. I can't think of Kai like that, though. He would be like my baby brother if I had a six-foot-four, two-hundred-and-eighty-pound baby brother. Damn, can you imagine giving birth to that? Ouch!

"Damn straight, I am." I snicker. I don't really have much confidence in myself when it comes to the opposite sex. I'm not a virgin or anything. I've slept with a few guys here and there, but nothing ever meant anything or was ever long-term. For years, my focus has been on school and my art, plain and simple.

"Seriously, what'd he want?"

"He wanted me to go home with him."

Kai nearly spits out the sip of spiked punch he just drank. (Yeah, I spiked it.) "And you didn't go? You're such a damn fool, Vivien."

Confession. My name is Vivien. Vivien Reginald. I hate my name, which is sad because it's kind of a cool name. I used to love it because my dad chose it, naming me after Vivien Leigh. You know, from *Gone with the Wind*? My dad loved, or I should say *loves*, actors and actresses. Hell, he's trying to become one right now. He left us when I was thirteen and moved to the Big Apple to live out his dream of starring on Broadway, leaving my mom to raise three kids, ages seventeen, thirteen, and eleven. *Who does that?* Anyway, he cursed us all with stupid actor names. My baby sister is Grace after Grace Kelly, and my older brother Dean is named after James Dean. I still can't figure out why my mom went along with that. It's not like they're terrible names. It's just, in retrospect, they suck.

"Well, shocker alert, Kai... he didn't want me for sex. He wants me to look at some equipment that was included when he purchased his mansion in South Barrington."

"You said so much just now, but I'm going to focus on his

equipment," Kai says, giving me that creepy eyebrow-lifting thing.

"Ceramics equipment, perv. Apparently, the previous owners left some shit there. He wants me to tell him what's what."

"When?"

"Next Sunday. He's sending a car."

"He must be loaded."

I shrug because it seems like he might be, but it's hard to say. "No idea."

"I wish I could go with, but I'm working all day Sunday."

Eye roll. Kai doesn't really work. He doesn't have to. Instead of working, he gives painting lessons to older, genteel (i.e., rich) ladies from around the city. He's sharing his gift with the world. He says it's his way of painting it forward. Get it? *Painting* it forward?

"'S okay. I can go alone. I'm a big girl." Sadly, in more ways than one.

"Promise me you'll text me every twenty minutes."

"You never check your phone during your lessons. I'm not doing that. It's a hassle. I'll text you when I get there and when I leave. If you never hear from me again, you'll know something happened to me."

"Great," he mutters. "That's so not a good plan."

"It's all I got, Kai, baby." I reach up and pat his cheek. "Who loves you, Kai?"

"You do, Viv."

"That's right. *I* do." And I do. I literally love the man like crazy.

CHAPTER THREE

ON SUNDAY MORNING, I find myself sitting on the front stoop of the crappy apartment building that houses the crappy two-bedroom apartment I share with three crappy roommates. I wait outside so said roommates don't question me about where I'm going and what I'm doing.

Oh, who am I kidding? It's eight thirty in the morning. They're all still asleep, since they partied well into the morning, and probably won't be up by the time I get back from the burbs. It's how they spend most nights, since none of them have to work or take out student loans. Their tuition and living expenses are paid by their parents. I pay them cash every month, which they then pocket for "fun money." You know, for booze and stuff. Fun money for me pays for food and bus fare. Yeah, they suck. I'll be paying student loans off for the rest of my life.

I shake my head. I can't think about that. I graduate in less than a month. I need to enjoy life now. Adulting will happen soon enough.

Thankfully, a big black town car pulls up in front of my

building. A man about my dad's age, so I'd say in his late forties, steps out wearing a dapper suit and tie. "Reggie?"

"That's me." Jumping up, I grab my hobo bag and hop down the four steps to the sidewalk. "Hang on." I pull my phone out of my pocket. "What's your name?"

"Edward."

Of course it is. "Mind if I snap a pic, Ed?"

"As you wish."

Wow, it's like I'm in some fancy British movie, except he's not British and who'd want *me* in a movie? "Thanks. My best friend wants to know who I'm with since I'm going alone."

"Understandable. I have daughters. Safety first."

I jog to the back of the car and snap a picture of the license plate. I send both photos to Kai and hop in the car.

Edward gets behind the wheel, then looks back at me through the rearview mirror. "Are you hungry? Mr. Corcoran told me to pick you up some breakfast if you're hungry."

Mr. Corcoran? Oh, Corcoran must be his last name. "Sure. Drive-through is fine. There's a Starbucks on the next block."

"On every block, miss." He chuckles.

I'm not sure I'm digging being called "Miss". "Just call me Reggie."

"Very well, Reggie."

He finds a Starbucks with a drive-through, and I order a breakfast sandwich and a venti coffee with steamed milk. Yummy.

The drive is quiet, with Edward focused on his job. I could read, or... "Hey, Edward?"

"Yes, miss? I mean Reggie."

"Do you drive Carter all over the place?"

"No, not exclusively. I work for a car service, but he has my direct number when he needs a lift to the airport and for things like this."

Things like this? I wonder if he drives lots of women up to his swanky mansion. I can't ask Edward that, though. That'd be rude.

In less than an hour, thanks to no traffic on Sundays, we're pulling up to a set of massive iron gates that look to be about twenty feet high. I watch as the gates open slowly. As he pulls through, I crane my neck to get a view of the property—and it is a *property*. The front yard is massive. The driveway looks like it's about as long as a football field. When we round a corner, I gasp. "Holy shit."

Edward chuckles. "Indeed."

I blink a couple of times, making sure I'm not seeing things. Carter Corcoran is definitely loaded. His house is ginormous. I stare at all the architectural details, wishing I'd listened in my History of Architecture class. Then I'd be able to tell you more about the design. What I can tell you is that the driveway turns into a circle as we approach the house. In the round, grassy area in the center, there's a large fountain with some kind of ugly-ass mermaid spouting water from her mouth. Edward stops the car right in front of the entrance. I watch him open his door, but I stop him. "I got it, Edward."

He turns back and smiles at me. "As you wish, Reggie." Wow, he's such a nice guy.

I step out of the car, looking up at the front door. It's covered with a portico or roof that sits two stories above the porch. Four Greek-style columns hold up the portico. I recognize the style of Greek columns as Corinthian. Wow, I do remember some of my history. There's a set of steps leading up to the door. I count fifteen of them as I take them one at a time. When I look left, I see a garage that has at least four doors. Beyond that is more driveway paved with brick that looks like an area for additional parking. I peer right and can't even see the end of the house. It's that big. "Wow. I wonder how many bedrooms are in this place."

A deep voice responds, "Six. Six bedrooms, fourteen baths."

I glance up, spying the source of the voice. He's looking even hotter than he did a week ago, dressed down in a pair of sweatpants and a T-shirt.

"Only six bedrooms?" This house looks big enough for about thirty bedrooms.

"The main house is twenty-two thousand square feet."

"The main house?" I squeak.

"Yes. Come on in. I'll show you around."

I step into the foyer and nearly pass out from the scale of the place. It's so massive, even Carter is dwarfed by it. "Do you have a bunch of kids or something?"

"Nope. No kids."

"A wife?"

He smirks. "No. Are you interested?"

I remember that smirk now. "No, *geesh*, Carter. I'm just trying to figure out why a youngish man like yourself could (A) afford a place like this and (B) need all this space for just himself."

He shrugs. "It's an investment. I got a good deal."

I nibble on my lip ring. I know this nervous habit is not attractive in the least. "What? It was on sale for two million?" I laugh.

"Something like that."

I blink at him, thinking about his response. He bought a house worth millions as an investment? Who does that? I follow him into a large room with floor-to-ceiling windows overlooking a yard that could fit a few more houses this size. There's a wide deck and just beyond that an Olympic-size swimming pool. Even further back is a lake or pond or whatever you call it, and back even more, it looks like a tennis court.

"You play tennis?" I ask, turning back to look at the rest of the room.

"Nah."

Nah? "Well, maybe you should learn." I don't know why I care. I guess I think it'd be a shame to waste it. I look past him and see a gorgeous fireplace surrounded by large stones so big that I'd call them boulders. In front of the hearth is an over-stuffed sectional sofa that could probably seat twenty regular people or ten Carters. A television the size of a car is mounted above the fireplace. Everything in this house seems to be jumbo-sized. Bookcases on either side are filled with books, movies, and pictures. I step up to the photos and see some with Carter. The first one shows him standing behind an average-size set of older people—parents, I'm guessing—and what looks like three siblings. He looks a lot like his brothers. They're hot too. In another photo, Carter's with six or seven other guys, all about his size. In yet another one, he's wearing a blue football uniform. The photo looks like it was taken by a professional.

"You played football?" I ask, looking at more pictures.

"Still do."

"At your age? Are you on some sort of park system senior league?"

He chuckles.

I don't know why it's funny. Illinois has some great parks-and-rec organizations that host sports leagues, have aquatic centers, and such. I should know. I grew up in Elk Grove Village, about twenty miles from here. My mom always had us in leagues and activities. It probably kept her sane having the three of us "busy."

"You still don't know who I am?"

I turn and blink. "No. How was I supposed to figure that out?"

"Google."

I shrug. "I don't have time for googling strange men."

I think I take him off-guard a little bit, because he nearly chokes trying to hold back laughter. Gathering himself, he says, "It's okay. You don't seem like you're into sports."

I take offense to that. "I'm into sports. I like sports." I just don't participate in any. Well, I walk a lot. Does that count?

"I play football."

"I think we've established that." I roll my eyes and turn back to the photos, bending down to see one of him standing on a stage, holding up a blue jersey with a number one on the back. I feel him move closer before I hear him. Pointing at the photo, he says, "That's me as a first round draft pick for the New York Giants."

"As in the professional New York Giants?"

"One and the same."

I stand up and look around the room. "Now this all makes sense. But why did you buy here if you play in New York?"

"Because I'm from Chicago. My family lives here. It's my home."

"Do they live in the burbs too?"

"Nope. They are city dwellers. To find a property large enough with a lot this size, I had to move out here. Besides, I'm sick of the city. I like it quiet."

I get up on my tippy-toes to pat his muscled shoulder as I step past him. "I get it, old man. I totally get it."

"I'm not old. I'm twenty-five."

"That's older than me."

"By what? A year?"

I shrug. I'm just fucking with Carter. I'll be twenty-five in six months. It's just fun to tease the big guy. "Where's this art studio?"

"Right this way." Carter leads me through a large set of

French patio doors onto a wooden deck that spans the entire back side of the house.

I stop for a second to take in the view of the pool, lake, and surrounding land. "How many acres do you have here?"

When I hear nothing, I look over in time to see a set of stairs down and the top of Carter's head as he descends. I quickly jog to catch up.

He's waiting at the bottom, looking a tad impatient.

"I'm coming."

Smirking, he mumbles, "That's what she *always* says."

I stop. "No. You. Didn't."

He chuckles. "I did. Sorry." He looks sheepish. "Habit. I'm around big, rude guys a lot. But that's no excuse."

"No worries. I'm not some wilting lily."

"Shrinking violet. I think you mean shrinking violet."

"Whatever. Same difference."

Shaking his head, he rolls his eyes. "Come on. It's over here."

I follow him to the west side of the property to what looks like an average-size house. It's all on one level with two doors that face the big house. He approaches the door closest to us and turns the knob.

Pushing the door open, he waits for me to walk through first. "This is it."

I step over the threshold and stop in my tracks. "Holy shit balls."

"Is that a good 'holy shit balls' or a bad 'holy shit balls'?"

I don't answer because I think I've died and gone to fucking heaven. "Good. A very good holy shit balls."

The room is vast. I turn three-hundred-and-sixty degrees to take it all in. When I look up, I see the room has a loft space that looks set up as a reading nook and workspace. There are a couple comfy-looking chairs, a drafting table, and a shelf chock-full of books. On the main level, the room is filled with everything you'd ever need to become a professional clay artist. Everything. I don't know where to start in the space, so I turn left and make my way to the wall closest to the door. I meander around the perimeter to check out each station or section in the room, stopping in the area designated just for wheel work. I look back and see Carter walking behind me, watching.

I point and say, "Those are potter's wheels. You throw pots, bowls, plates, and vases on those."

Carter nods.

There are two different pottery wheels, an electric wheel and a kick wheel. Further down are shelves filled with powdered chemicals for creating glazes. There are also shelves holding premixed glazes. The wall between is pegboard covered with small colored tiles. "These are samples of glazes." I pull one small tile and turn it to read the back. "This gives you the name of the glaze and its firing temperature." I point to the numbers zero-five. "That means this is a low-fire glaze." I scan the wall, taking it all in. "There are about two hundred glaze samples here." I look back at Carter, who's running his hand through his hair.

"Don't worry about learning everything right away. Baby steps."

He nods and gives me a small smile.

Moving on. Shelves on the other side of the room hold boxes of ready-to-use clay along with containers of powdered clay and additives like grog, sand, paper pulp, and nylon fibers. In the center of the room are three long tables made for hand building and anything else you want to use them for. "Wow, Carter. This place is amazing."

"There's more." He walks past me to the back of the room and opens another door. "I think these are kilns."

"Kilns. Plural? As in more than one?"

Carter nods and waits for me to step into the room first. "Holy mother of God, Carter. You've got to be shitting me."

"Is it good?"

I just stare at him. There are four kilns of various sizes and functions. The smallest one is made for glass slumping and has a programmable thermostat on the front. "This one is for glass. I've only done that a couple of times, but it's cool."

"That makes sense. I wondered what all this was for." He opens a cupboard door for me to see it's filled with sheets of glass in every color and texture. There's a shelf filled with frit, or crushed glass, and several shelves with glass molds.

The other kilns in the room are electric kilns, one larger than the others. I point to them. "These are meant for pottery."

"Okay, so what are these for?" He opens yet another door, this one leading to the outside.

I follow him out and gasp. "I'm literally speechless right now."

"What are they?"

"That one"—pointing to the smallest of the large outdoor kilns—"is for Raku."

"Whatever that is," Carter mumbles.

"It's a traditional Japanese process that produces pottery with an iridescent finish. It's labor intensive but worth it."

"And that one?" He points to the largest kiln, which looks like a vault with an arched roof. There are steel supports on all four corners and more secured around a thick door that slides on a track. This kiln is encased in hard firing bricks.

When I slide open the door, I see it's thickly lined in more firing bricks like it's in a cellar. I smile. "It's a salt kiln. You can do all sorts of cool stuff with glazes in that thing." I look around for the gas needed to operate both kilns. "There should be propane or natural gas for these two."

He points to another door on the side of the building, then walks over and opens it. "These it?"

I gulp. This place is a fully functional art studio made for a real artist. "Whoever lived here before must have been a professional artist. It's weird that they left this all behind."

"I can look at my paperwork to see who owned it before me, but the reason it's all still here is because I asked them to include everything here in my offer." He points to the building that houses this amazing studio. He steps into the grass, adding, "Okay, Reggie. There's a large pit dug out over there." He points at the yard near a line of trees. "Is that for pottery too?"

"No. Way." I feel a little breathless now. This place is unbe-fucking-lievable.

"Way."

I giggle at his old joke. *Wayne's World.* I jog out to the hole. Carter follows. Squatting over the hole, I tell him. "It's a wood-fired earthen kiln. It's an ancient process. I've never done it before, but I'd love to." I turn to see he's squatting beside me. "So, what're you going to do with all this stuff? Are you going to sell it or something?"

"I'd like to learn how to use it."

"*You* want to use it?" I know that sounded bitchy, but come on, he's a football player.

"Yes. I like art. I've been painting for a long time. I enjoy it, but I'm interested in other things. This studio is the main reason I bought this place."

"Serious?"

"Serious," he deadpans.

"So, are you going to take classes? There are probably some places around here to do that."

"I hadn't gotten that far. I wanted to know more about the equipment first. But I'd prefer to have someone here to teach me."

"I bet you would, Richie Rich," I say as I slug him on his shoulder with enough force to push him off-balance.

"Shit, you're strong for such a little thing."

I blink, then smile. I'm far from little, but it's nice hearing it.

"Come on. Let me show you the other half of this house."

"Don't tell me there's more studio space?"

"Nah, it's an apartment."

I have to jog to keep up with the man. His legs are twice as long as mine. On the north side of the building, he opens another door.

I walk through and gasp. "No. Way." I turn to Carter. "This is nicer than my folks' house." I'm referring to the house we had before Dad rode off into the sunset, because the house after was a crap-shack apartment.

I walk into the open-concept kitchen/dining/living room and see it's furnished with a midcentury modern sectional, chair, and coffee table. The dining room has a drop leaf table in a honey color and four chairs that match. I walk back to a completely updated kitchen. There are stainless steel appliances and a countertop made of some type of stone. I run my hand over the top of the cool surface.

"Quartz," says the big man, watching me intently.

"Ah, of course. I watch *House Hunters*. Quartz is where it's at, baby."

When Carter chuckles, I feel it vibrate through me again, leaving my body sort of tingly. He turns away and walks into the living room. I watch him go because, again, I'm a woman. It's then I really take notice of his clothing. He's dressed very casually in flip-flops and sweatpants that should be outlawed in seven countries, since they hang low and highlight all the important parts, like his ass and thighs. I can't even think about his other bits. He's also wearing a Chicago Bears T-shirt that should also be a crime to wear since it's so tight on him I can make out his abs. And the Bears? Doesn't he get into trouble for wearing another team's gear? I follow him down a hallway.

Pointing to a door, he says, "That door leads to the studio space, so there's direct access."

I nod as we walk further into a large bedroom with an adjoining bath that I can only dream of having one day. There's a tub *and* a shower, separate from one another. Beyond that is a walk-in closet that would hold my clothes and all three of my roomies' clothes. The bedroom is huge as well, no surprise. A king-size bed with a canopy sits in the middle of the room, against the back wall. Two nightstands, a tall dresser, and a long dresser with a mirror rounds out the room. There's also a padded bench at the end of the bed. What the hell is the bench for? I stare at it a few seconds, contemplating one of life's great mysteries. Hmm, I guess one could use it for putting on and taking off socks. I shrug to myself; it's the only purpose I can think of for something like that.

"How many bedrooms are in this place?"

"Just one, but there's another bathroom down the hall." Carter points toward the entrance to the studio.

"Amazing."

"You like it?"

"Uh, yeah. Who wouldn't?"

"Good." He looks down at me like he's trying to figure something out. Those two lines between his eyes are obvious. "Well, I've made us lunch. Let's go back up to the house and eat. I'm starving."

Me too. Looking at my phone at the time. It's a little early for lunch, but I could eat. "Sure. Great. Sounds good."

CHAPTER FOUR

REGGIE

HE WALKS out of the bedroom and through what I guess you'd call the front door. Jogging up the steps to the deck, he stops at the patio door. There's a keypad next to the entrance.

"You have to punch in a number to get in and out?" I'm not sure why I'm surprised. This place is massive and I bet it's a target for jewel thieves and the like.

"Yeah, and this one keeps activating whenever the door shuts. I've gotta call the company. So if you need to get in while you're here, the code is sixty-nine, sixty-nine."

I roll my eyes. "Of course it is." It's the same as the one on his phone. "You're such a perv."

"Not a perv, babe. My jersey number is sixty-nine."

"Seriously? Did you pick that? And aren't you worried someone will figure out all your passwords?"

"No."

"No?"

"Nah, it's been my number since high school. Can't change it now. I'm superstitious about my number."

"Oh, right. I get that." I don't get that. I'm the least superstitious person on the planet because luck is what you make of it. I follow him inside to the kitchen and plop my ass down onto one of the barstools that surround his breakfast bar, as he pulls things from the fridge. I don't know why it surprises me. "You cook?"

He looks offended. "Of course I cook. I'm not without skills in the kitchen"—he arches a brow—"and elsewhere."

"You had to go there, didn't you?"

He shrugs. "Told you. I'm around idiot guys all the time. Sorry. No excuse. I'll be on my best behavior from now on."

As Carter chops lettuce and vegetables, I listen as he talks about his job. I never knew there was so much to professional football. Even though it's technically the off-season, he still has to work out every day, watch films, study playbooks, and meet up with coaches in New Jersey every other week or so. That's where he was all last week.

He serves lunch on the large deck overlooking the lake that is not a lake. It's a pond, according to Carter, but it is named Lake Adalyn. I stand corrected. And confused.

When I ask him if he enjoys playing football, he shrugs. "I do. I'm good at it. But I look forward to a time when I don't have to do it anymore and I can just concentrate on other things. Things I enjoy."

"Like art?"

"Yeah. Painting makes me feel centered, if that makes any sense," he says chuckling.

"I get that. Are you going to let me see some of your work?" While I want to see it, I'm nervous it will suck and I'll have to pretend I like it.

"Sure. After lunch, I'll take you to my studio."

"You have *another* studio?"

He chuckles again, and you know what that does to my lady parts. "I've set my stuff up in one of the smaller bedrooms."

Must be nice to have so much room. "Cool."

Lunch is delicious. Carter has made us big salads with lots of veggies and grilled salmon. You'd think I'd be a nervous Nelly eating lunch with a man like Carter, but I'm surprisingly relaxed. The guy is easy to talk to and he seems to be the same around me.

As I pick at my salad, Carter tells me about his goal of starting a foundation related to the arts. "A lot of ball players try to give back to their communities. I've wanted to start something, I just don't know where to begin."

"I can see how that'd be a challenge. But I bet there are people out there who know how to do it. A consultant or something?" What the hell am I talking about? I know nothing about consultants.

"My buddies have given me a couple of names. I just..."
"What?"
"The mandatory team workouts and pre-season are going to start soon, and that will take over my life. I want to get this thing off the ground soon."

Even though I don't know this guy, I feel sure of one thing. "If anyone can do it, it's you." I reach out and pat the top of his hand that's resting on the table. A sizzle runs through me with just a touch. The guy is electric. I pull my hand away and pick my fork up and pretend I'm eating.

Carter eats and talks. He spends a good bit of time telling me more about the foundation he wants to start that would fund after school art programs and grants for art supplies for teachers in Chicago. He asks me lots of questions about the kinds of classes I had to take to get my MFA and about my goals and dreams. I guess a professional football player would know a lot about those. Besides that, I can tell how passionate he is about art, so it made it easier to relate to him, since I'm just as passionate. I'm so comfortable with him, I end up telling him more about myself than I normally do. Truth? I'm not used to telling a complete stranger so much. Carter's surprising me, and that scares me. He can't be *that* perfect. Right?

After lunch, I follow him up a grand set of stairs to the second floor. As we climb, I find myself at eye level with his beautiful, round ass. Since he's wearing sweatpants, I can tell you for sure that his bottom does *not* jiggle. His buns have got to be rock-hard. My hand twitches with the need to test that theory. *Down, girl.*

"Here we are," he says, interrupting my impure thoughts. Damn it. Pushing the door open, he waits for me to walk in first.

If this is one of his small bedrooms, I'd like to see his big one. *That's what she said.*

This room is literally the same size as my entire apartment. I think I need to accept that Carter's house is big all over. I wonder if he... *Stop it, Reggie.*

"Right over here, Reggie." Carter is standing beside a wall of windows that overlooks the lake, er, I mean the pond.

I walk over and stare at the canvas resting on an easel. "You did this?" My mouth is hanging open. I'm sure it's really attractive—not. I snap my mouth shut and stare. It's a landscape painting. I look out the window again and then back at his painting. "It's amazing, Carter."

I glance up at him and see something I haven't seen from him yet. He looks nervous. Unsure. "Seriously, it's amazing. I love how you used such strong contrasts of light and dark and complementary colors like red and green, blue and orange, in unexpected areas. I also like how thickly you painted. It reminds me of the way Vincent Van Gogh used to paint."

"I saw his work at the Art Institute. I liked his brush strokes and his vivid colors."

"Me too. It's too bad he was so misunderstood when he was alive, huh?"

"I read that. Dude had issues."

I giggle at his simple but true analysis of Van Gogh's sad, short life. "True dat."

Carter startles me when he throws his head back and laughs, hard. It makes me giggle just listening to him. So, I do. Uncontrollably.

He squeezes my arm. "Damn, Reggie. You're hilarious."

That's me. The funny fat girl. "Anyway, what else have you got?"

"In here." He crosses to a door and pulls it open. Inside are vertical shelves built with narrow slots to store canvases. They have the same thing in the painting studios at school. "Were these shelves here?"

"No, I had them built. I didn't want anyone to see them."

"Why not?"

"This is my secret. Only my family knows. And now you. Which means I don't want you to tell anyone about any of this. It'll end up being on *SportsCenter* or some shit, and I don't want that."

"You think an awful lot of yourself, don't ya?" I snicker.

He arches a brow. "Google me. You'll see."

"I'll put it on my to-do list. Now, show me what else you've got." I walk past him into the closet and peek at each of the painting cubbies. "You've got a lot of work in here."

"It's pretty much all I do when I'm not doing football shit. It relaxes me."

I pull out a painting that looks different from the one on the easel. It's a painting of a woman's face surrounded by swirling colors and patterns in blues, purples, and deep reds. It's obvious no one has taught him how to draw a face in proportion, but it isn't important on this painting because I can see the emotion throughout. "Did you know her?"

He blinks, surprised by the question. "Uh, yeah. Casey Hart. She was a... a friend of mine. She died in a car accident when I was in high school. A drunk driver T-boned her when she was on her way home from work."

God, that story sucks. "You must have been close. I can tell it's personal from your use of color and brush strokes."

"We were." He pauses. "I'm surprised you could see that. I..."

"I really can. You what?"

"She's really the reason I want to create this kind of foundation. I want to name it after her."

"Wow, that's so cool, Carter. Her name was Casey?"

"Casey Hart. H-a-r-t."

"You could call it something like Hart of the City Foundation since you want it based in urban areas, starting with Chicago." I look down and see a sketchbook and pencil. "May I?"

"Sure." He steps closer.

"You could do something with a painting palette as the background of the logo and then small h, big A, little r-t for the name. So something like this: hArt of the City Foundation."

"Yes. That's it." His big hand moves up to squeeze my upper arm again. Looking into my eyes, he smiles, "That's exactly what I want. I knew you'd get me."

He knew I'd get him? Clearing my throat, I move back to look at the painting. "This is good. I love how you use color. I bet you do it instinctively."

"I guess." He shrugs and arches a brow, giving me a sly smile. "Never had one lesson."

"Ferris Bueller? Nice."

We needed a little comedic moment. He sensed it too. It got really heavy before. I step around him to go back into the bedroom. "If you paint like that without a lesson, I bet you could make some cool stuff with clay too. That is, if you want to learn." I smile up at him.

He smiled back shyly. "Thank you, Reggie. That means a lot to me. I think your artwork is really good."

"Thank you, kind sir," I say with a curtsy. After a quick tour of the rest of the house, I find my way back to the front door. Edward and the town car are waiting for me. I turn to face Carter. "Welp!" I say with a clap of my hands. I'm nervous now for some reason. "Thanks for lunch and for showing me around."

"Yeah, thanks for coming up."

"And, um, thanks for showing me the studio. I'm glad you're going to keep it. I know it's none of my business, but it would be a travesty if you dismantled that amazing clay studio." Shit, I've thanked him like thirty times. I'm so socially awkward. Shoot me.

"I'd like to use it. Even if I suck at it, I want to try."

"Good." I smile, turning around to face him right before I start the descent down from his front portico. "Glad to hear it. You really are an artist at heart."

His eyes grow round in surprise. His mouth opens then closes again. He's trying to say something.

"What?" I want to know.

He steps toward me. "I've got a proposition for you."

Oh, shit. He's propositioning me? "Uh-huh?" Yes. I sound skeptical but also a little excited.

"What if you lived here"—he points down—"and helped me with the foundation?" He must sense my shock because he adds, "I mean, look how fast you got the concept of the foundation, about Casey. Shit, you nailed the logo in one shot."

I blink at him, eyes fluttering rapidly. "You want me to live here? I can't afford a place like this," I say, flailing my arms around. "Not even when I'm an adult will I be able to afford this place."

He chuckles again, and my nipples peak. Damn him and his sexy rumbling chuckle to hell.

"Well, you wouldn't have to pay me anything. Plus, you could use the studio whenever you wanted."

Whenever I wanted? I feel my panties get a little wet. What? Clay is sexy. "I..."

"You could give me clay lessons when there's time too."

I blink again. I feel like passing out, so I stay quiet.

"And... you can use everything to make your own stuff."

That's it. I'm going to pass out. I start to tip backward, but Carter wraps big hands around my upper arms. "You okay?"

"I think I've died and gone to heaven."

Chuckling once again, he asks, "So, is that a yes?"

Sighing, I close my eyes and lay my head back. "I don't graduate for another month." Not to mention I've still got to finish my stupid thesis.

"That's fine. You can move in when you're ready."

"And I have to work."

"Why?"

I stare at him like he's an idiot. "I have debts. Student loans will come a-knockin' at my door soon."

"Ah, I see." He slides his hands from my shoulders, and I feel sad about it. His hands were big and warm. "I'd pay you to spearhead the foundation."

"How much does spearheading something pay?" *I mean... spearhead the foundation?* I don't even know what spearheading something entails.

"I'm not sure what the going rate is for something like that. Let me ask around, and I'll let you know."

"Sure. Okay. Maybe." I'm currently a bartender, a waitress slash short-order cook, and a data-entry operator. If worse came to worst, I could probably find something around here to supplement my income. "Let me think about it." Because I don't know the first thing about spearheading let alone doing that with a foundation. I step down to the driveway just as Edward steps around the car to open my door.

"Text me when you decide, Reggie."

"Will do. Thanks for everything. Lunch was great."

Carter gives me a small smile and a wave. "See ya, Reggie."

I wave back as the car starts the hour-long trek to my neighborhood where my crappy apartment is in the crappy building with my crappy roommates. Now that I've seen how the other half lives, my place seems even crappier. The only reason I live with them is because it's cheap. But let me tell you, sharing a room with a girl who snores like a chainsaw is for the damn birds.

Resting my head on the seat back, I replay the events of the day. There were some really surprising moments. First and foremost, that clay studio. I'm drooling just imagining what it'd be like to work in that space. I could get some serious work done, maybe get some exhibits in a gallery with the end goal of being a full-time artist. I snigger out loud as Edward peers at me through his mirror.

"Miss?"

"Call me Reggie, please. And I'm fine. Ignore me."

Edward chuckles. "Let me know if you'd like to stop anywhere. Mr. Corcoran said I'm at your service today."

"Wow, that's nice of both of you. But I need to get home. My thesis isn't going to write itself."

"Indeed, Reggie."

On the ride home, my mind keeps running through the day. It shocked me how good his paintings were. It's too bad I can't get Kai to look at them. That's his major, painting. Kai's a first year in the MFA program at SAIC. He's really talented. His work is all figurative and hyper realistic. He appreciates all genres, though. Yeah, he'd be an ideal person for Carter to talk to. I'll see if I can work that out.

At some point in the hour-long drive, I must have dozed off, because I feel a warm hand nudging my shoulder. "Reggie?"

I look up and blink. "Edward?" I feel moisture on my chin, and heat rushes to my cheeks. I drooled. I quickly wipe it away and sigh. I'm just glad Carter didn't see it.

Edward smiles but says nothing.

I could get used to this. I like Edward. And Carter? Well, what's not to like?

No, I will not let myself get all gooey-eyed over Carter Corcoran. It'd be a waste of energy. *Remember the blonde in the skimpy, white bikini, Reggie.* Yeah, I'll just gird my loins and concentrate on my goal of being a real artist.

CHAPTER FIVE

"SO, what're you going to do? Are you going to take the gig with Mr. McHotty?" asks Kai as he sips his blueberry martini.

I wipe off the counter in front of him, pretending to work. My boss here at the bar is sort of a hard-ass when it comes to chitchat. I shrug. "I want to. I mean, you should see the studio, Kai. It's every ceramicist's wet dream. And I need to work—I need to make money. My student loans are going to come due before I know it, and they're going to be massive." I sigh, taking another swipe at the bar.

"I know, hon. It's not fair. Did he tell you how much he'd pay you?"

"Yes, but I'm embarrassed to say." Carter sent me a text last night with a number. The salary was startling.

"What? Did he lowball you?"

"No. He named some ridiculously high sum, and I talked him down from that."

Kai's head drops to the bar top. He bangs his head against it a few times.

"What?"

Looking at me sympathetically, he reaches out and takes my hand in his. "You, my dearest friend, do not know your own worth. I'm sure whatever he quoted you was average pay for the industry."

I roll my eyes. "Yeah. That's what he said, but it was insane. I have no idea what I'm doing, so I need to work up to earning that. I wouldn't feel right taking the man's hard-earned money for doing a job I know nothing about."

Kai tsks. "For shame, girl. He got himself the deal of the century."

Kai is loaded, or I should say his parents are loaded. They're in the hospitality industry in Hawaii. That means they own fancy hotels—plural. They give Kai and his little sister, Kalani, anything they could ever desire, but he's not a snob about it, at least not to me.

"You can't change history. You need to focus on the future, and the future is with Professor Sexy."

"Professor Sexy?" I giggle. "Kai, I'd be shocked if he finished college. Don't a lot of those guys quit college to play professional sports?"

"He graduated."

"How do you know?"

"I googled him. Carter Corcoran. Six feet, five inches, two hundred and seventy pounds." He places his palm next to his mouth and stage whispers, "*All muscle.* He graduated with honors from the University of Illinois."

I scoff. "What was his major?"

Kai rolls his eyes. "History."

"Hm, well, that's interesting." I move to my right and wipe down a new section of countertop as I listen to Kai.

"He was taken in the first round of the NFL draft by the New York Giants, but it was widely known that he was hoping to play for the Bears, his favorite team since childhood," Kai says in a smug kind of way.

"Shit, how do you know all that?"

"I told you. Google. Plus, I read some articles on some of the sports websites."

"Wow, Kai. Tell me. What's his favorite color?"

He shrugs. "A guy like that? My guess would be red."

"Why red?"

"Red is hot and S-E-X-Y."

I giggle again. When I hear a voice behind me, I wince.

"Jesus, Reggie. Could you do something other than wipe off that one spot? You're going to rub off the varnish."

"Sure thing, boss."

"Oh, and since all you've done tonight is stand there and shoot the shit, you're closing now."

"Dammit!" That means I won't get out of here until after two in the morning. I turn to Kai. "I *effing* hate this job." I point behind me. "And that asshat."

"I heard that, Reggie. Don't piss me off more than I already am. I know you need this gig."

"Sorry, Pete." Not sorry. Pete Jones is a thorn in my side. He's never liked me. Hell, if he didn't need me desperately, I'd probably never get shifts here at the Chipp Inn bar, an old dive bar in the Noble Square neighborhood. I look around the place and roll my eyes. "God, it's dead. I hope it picks up. I need tip money."

"What do you expect for a Monday night?"

"I don't know. My life sucks," I say, sounding a lot like Eeyore.

Kai throws back the last drop of blueberry goodness and drops a twenty on the bar. "Keep the change, sweetie. I'll see you tomorrow?"

"Yeah."

"Give that offer some real thought, Viv. It'd be free rent, right? If so, you'd be able to use your extra money for those pesky loans."

"Yes, he said rent free." It's almost a deal I can't refuse.

"Well, if nothing else, there's always stripping," Kai says with a wink.

"Yeah, like anyone would pay to see this." I point at myself.

"Lots of people would pay to see that, Viv. You're gorgeous."

I toss the wet bar rag at Kai. "Stop teasing me and go home before I get canned."

"Fine. I'm going. Love you lots, Viv."

"Love you too."

I'm turning to help one of our regulars when Pete yells at me. Again. "Fucking finally, Reggie. Jesus, do some work for a goddamn change." I hear him mumble something like "lazy bitch" but choose to ignore it. Pete's an asshole, and nothing's gonna cure that.

By the time I drag my sorry ass home from the bar, it's after three in the morning. That gives me three hours to sleep before I have to get up and get to class. I'm a teaching assistant, TA, in a freshman class called Ceramics: Wheel-Throwing Fundamentals. It's a good thing I don't have to think about what I'm doing there. I can be a total zombie and teach that class. I fall face-first onto my twin bed and groan.

"Jesus, Reggie. Shut the fuck up. You sound like a damn moose when you come in late. Have some manners."

Okay. That speech came courtesy of my roommate from hell, Mona. Or should I call her Moan-*ah*? Her boyfriend is in our room, in her bed, four nights out of seven, and let me tell you: she's not shy or quiet. I need to hold my tongue though. I don't want to get into it with her. She plays dirty. The last time I argued with her, my favorite pair of Birkenstocks went missing. I suspect they're at the bottom of Lake Michigan by now. Bitch.

"Sorry, Mona." I pull myself up to the top of my bed and shove my pillow under my face. I can't get comfortable because I've got shit in my jeans pockets. I reach down and pull out the measly pile of tip money from one pocket. If Kai hadn't tipped me twelve bucks, I'd be screwed. I reach into my back pocket and slide my phone up to my nightstand. I must have bumped the button because it lights up, revealing a text I didn't know I'd received.

"Oh, my fucking God, Reggie. Turn that fucking light off and go to fucking sleep before I hold your fucking pillow over your face until you die."

Jesus. She's scary as hell. I sort of believe her. I quickly turn down the light on my screen and read. A text from Carter? I check to see when he sent it. Only an hour ago. He's up late.

Carter: Hey, it's Carter. What did you decide?

I start to respond just as Mona growls, "Not enough, ass face. The light is fucking blinding."

Holy hell, I hate my roommate. I need to get the hell out of this place.

Me: I'm in. I'll call you tomorrow to talk about it.
Carter: I'll call you. I'm busy all day.
Me too, jerk face. Maybe this isn't such a good idea.
Me: Fine. Night.

I shut off my phone, plugging it in to charge for the night, then lie down and sigh.

"Jesus. *Finally.* You're so inconsiderate, Reggie."

"Sorry." Well, sorry she woke up. The only time I like her is when she's asleep.

I get no reply from her and no response from Carter. Closing my eyes, I fall asleep before I can give it another thought.

CHAPTER SIX

"HELLO?" I whisper as I hunker down in the hallway outside my class.

I don't want my students to see me on the phone. I have a strict no-phone policy in my classroom. Students with their freaking phones have turned out to be the bane of my existence, let me tell you. Kids today will do nothing but stare at their damn phones all day long. By the time I'm done demonstrating something, they look at me with blank stares. But this is different. I had to answer this. It's Carter.

"Hey. It's me, Carter. I've only got a minute between meetings. When're you moving in?"

"No clue. The commencement ceremony is on May 13. Not like anyone will be there for it; I'd just like to go through with it." That is, if my thesis is finished by then. Ugh, writing sucks. "But I've got to be out of my current apartment by the end of May. I need to give notice on all my jobs." I sigh. So much to do.

"All your jobs? How many do you have?"

"Three. Well, four if you count my teaching assistant gig at school." I get some tuition covered if I teach a class each semester.

"Wow. Okay, it's April 24 today."

"Yes, it is."

"Smartass. What if you moved in on May 19? I could have movers at your place in the morning and—"

"I don't need movers. I don't have much."

"A pickup full?"

"Yeah, probably." Since I don't have a pickup, or any kind of car for that matter, I have no idea how I'll get my stuff there.

"Okay, I can get a pickup lined up. Be at your place by eight and have you moved in by noon. How's that?"

"Hang on." I pull the phone away from my ear to access my calendar app and scroll through his proposed dates. A chill of excitement runs down my back. I type in the information. Bringing the phone back up to my face, I say, "Yeah, that all works."

I'll just have to give notice the first week of May. Pete at the Chipp Inn will be thrilled to see the backside of me. I'll be glad to see the backside of my data-entry job. Talk about B-O-R-I-N-G. It's at a major insurance company in the city. I work second and sometimes third shift, which sucks big-time, and all I do is type names, social security numbers, birth dates, addresses, and phone numbers into their database. It sucks.

The job I will hate to leave the most is at the Palace Grill restaurant where I wait tables and make pancakes when they're desperate for the help. *They'd have to be. I can't cook. At all.* The restaurant is old, with a retro interior that's very cool. The owner, Sandy Lathrop, is a huge Chicago Blackhawks fan, so the place is all red and black. Plus, it's filled with Hawks memorabilia and fifties-style dining tables and has a counter with red stools running the entire length of the narrow building. The Grill is best known for its breakfast, since it's only open from six in the morning until two in the afternoon. The best thing on the menu, by far, are Sandy's giant cinnamon rolls. I always get one on my Monday, Wednesday, and Friday morning shifts. But it's the people I'll miss most of all. Everyone is jovial and hardworking. I feel myself get teary-eyed thinking about leaving.

I hang up with Carter and walk into my classroom in time to see every fucking one of the little bastards on their phones. I slam my hands on my hips and glare.

The biggest slacker in my class seems to be the bravest when he mutters, "But, Reggie, you were on your phone."

"That call was... none of your business. Put. The. Phones. Away." I watch them sit motionless. "Now." That gets the precious angels moving. The thing is, throwing clay is messy stuff. There's water and clay goop all over the place. Your hands get covered with ooey-gooey clay, so they're getting it all over their fancy phones. "Not to mention the clay will ruin your phones." *Idiots.*

CHAPTER SEVEN

REGGIE

SITTING IN WINTRUST ARENA, I look to my left and right at my classmates lined up to receive their diplomas. It's an auspicious moment in our lives and one I'll look back on fondly —and monthly—when the bill for my student loan comes in the mail. I don't know why I bother worrying about it. It is what it is. Sure, many of the students who attend SAIC can afford it, but there are quite a few of us in the same boat. I often wonder why I did this to myself, going in debt just to earn an art degree, but then I remember how much I love it. I've always loved making art, and I went into this consciously. I can't picture myself doing anything else. Hell, I don't even mind working multiple jobs as long as I can keep doing it.

When they call "Vivien Jayne Reginald," I groan at the use of my entire name. I've kept my first name to myself, a secret, pretty much. Some of my professors know because it's on their class list from the registrar's office, and Kai knows it, of course. I blabbed to him one night over too many glasses of three-buck Chuck. No matter, they just shouted it out to a few thousand people so it's out there in the universe now. It's not going to stop me from walking across the stage and smiling brightly at the president of the college. Hell, I'll probably never see any of these people again anyway.

I hear Kai scream my name from somewhere in the arena. He's my only guest for this thing. I didn't bother telling my dad. He'd never have made the trip from New York, claiming it was either, one, too expensive, or two, he's got a shot at a role in a play or a commercial and just can't right now or some shit. As for my mom? She would have come, but I told her I was skipping the actual graduation ceremony. She went to my undergrad commencement, so that's good enough. Besides, I think she was relieved. She hates driving down into the city.

God, I'm so nervous as I walk across the stage in front of all these people, but I smile like an idiot anyway because, damn it, I'm proud of myself. I just earned my fucking MFA, people. That's awesome! We shake hands, the prez and me. She tells me "congratulations" as I take my diploma from her and exit stage left. I open the leather booklet and see it's empty inside. I knew it would be. This thing is just a fake—a prop. I'll get the real one when I get the final approval for my thesis paper.

Ah, my thesis paper. The thorn in my side. I worked my ass off on that thing, and in the end, I'm pleased with it even though I researched one topic and it morphed into something completely different two-thirds of the way through. I wrote about people who made art later in life. You know, like long after college had ended; that sort of thing. When I searched for people who'd put their desire to create on the back burner, I discovered it had been primarily women who waited. I understand why that happened. They'd wanted to wait until the kids were raised or to retire. But what was curious was that this hadn't impacted men in the same way. There were far fewer men who waited for the timing to feel right. It made me think about my own father. He just up and left us when we were young to pursue *his* artistic dreams. If my mom had any dreams or goals early on, we didn't know about them. She kept those things to herself. *She* waited. Now that her three kids have all flown the coop, my mom is involved in a writers' workshop back in my home suburb. In the end, the topic was fascinating. I hadn't meant for it to become a feminist kind of paper, but if the shoe fits.

As I walk down the steps to the main level, I hear Kai again. "You rock, Vivien!"

I blush and roll my eyes. I love my friend but damn, he embarrasses the shit out of me sometimes. When my feet land on solid ground, I return to my seat and look up into the stands for Kai. I wasn't able to see him before the ceremony, so I've no idea where he is. I scan the audience, back and forth, and then back suddenly. "Holy shit. It can't be. What is *he* doing here?" I blink a few times to make sure I'm not hallucinating because Carter Corcoran is sitting next to Kai and he's smiling—at me. *Shit buckets.*

I give him that gesture where your shoulders hunch and the hands go out like the *Huh? What are you doing here?* kind of gesture. You know the one?

I see his chest move up and down and know he's laughing at me. When he does the same gesture back at me, I'm totally confused. To his right, I look at Kai and give him stink eyes.

"How did those two end up sitting together?" I say aloud. Who cares if my classmates think I've lost my marbles.

CHAPTER EIGHT

CARTER

HER NAME IS VIVIEN? I watch her walk across the stage, grasping her diploma along the way. It gives me time to check her out. She's not wearing a cap and gown like most of the graduates. Instead, she's wearing a dress that reminds me of something Marcia Brady would wear. You know, from that old sitcom *The Brady Bunch?* The dress is short, hitting her about midthigh. It's got long sleeves that end in white cuffs and match the white collar. Those are noticeable because the dress is a dark color. Blue? Black? It's covered in what looks to be brightly colored flowers. She's too far away to say for sure. My eyes scan down her short legs to see they end in vintage-looking shoes. They've got a short, thick heel on them, and they're white too. It's not a look I'm accustomed to. The women I meet usually wear shoes with four- or five-inch spikes for heels. They also wear dresses from this decade.

As she walks to the edge of the stage, I scan her again. She's chunky, that's for sure, but it's a good look for her—kind of hot. She's pretty. Stunning, actually, with her platinum blonde haircut, which is shorter than mine has ever been. Ordinarily I think short hair is a bad idea for a girl, but it looks good on her. It's probably because she's got such a cute face with her turned-up nose, freckles, and big brown eyes. Or it could be because of her lips. I'd call them plump. They sort of match the rest of her, full and luscious. Damn, my heart beats a little faster just thinking about her mouth and that sexy-as-hell piercing. The way she nibbled and tugged on that thing when she was at my place screwed with my head. I need to knock that shit off. Thinking about her like that is a bad idea. *Very* bad.

I shake my head. What's wrong with me? I've got Natalia. Not that things with Natalia are serious. They're not. Natalia and I just fuck when we're both in town. I take her to team functions sometimes just to have someone on my arm. She loves that shit. It gets her "exposure". Her picture ends up in magazines and shit which is all she wants. To be famous.

When she's here for modeling gigs, she'll stay in my condo downtown and I'll meet her there. Then she's off again to do her modeling and shit. It's the perfect setup. I'm not ready for anything serious and definitely not ready to get married. Besides, I can't see myself marrying someone like Natalia. She's too hard, too rigid. And she's expensive. I'm a generous guy, I've taken her shopping a time or two—you know to get her something to wear to a dinner or an awards thing. But I can't do that shit anymore. I'm sending the wrong signals. She's not a long-term kind of woman. When I picture the mother of my children, it's not Natalia. It's someone more like Reggie, or should I say Vivien? I wonder why she doesn't use that name? It's perfect for her. And damn, that name is hot, like some kind of sexy starlet from the fifties. My dick likes that name too. Shit, I've got to stop. Reggie's my employee and tenant. Or she will be soon. No good can come of my overactive libido getting in the way.

After the ceremony that lasts about two hours longer than I thought it would, I hang with the big guy, Kai. I didn't know him, but he recognized me from the art show. Apparently he's a friend of Reggie's. I wonder what kind of friend? I hope "friend" doesn't mean they're together. I clench the bouquet of roses I bought for her so tightly, I think I hear one or two stems snap. I growl internally thinking about Reggie, er, Vivien, fucking that guy. He seems nice enough, and he's good-looking, I guess. I can't wrap my mind around why I care if Reggie and this big dude are together. I just don't like the idea.

"Hey," says a winded Reggie.

I watch Kai wrap her up in his thick arms. Not as thick as mine though.

He says, "Congratulations, babe. I'm so proud of you."

She smiles up at him.

I'm waiting for them to kiss, but she turns to me.

I smile. Handing her the dozen yellow roses, I say, "Vivien?"

She takes the flowers, shaking her head. "Thanks. I knew that was going to happen. I go by Reggie. My name is Reggie."

"Got it." I nod. It's a damn shame but I get it. Honestly, I'm not sure I can keep calling her Reggie. "Congratulations, uh, Reggie." I want to hug her. I want to reach out and wrap my own muscled arms around her. But I don't.

"Thanks." She fidgets on those weird shoes.

I look down and see they are, in fact, old. The white patent leather is cracking in some places.

"So, Carter?"

"Yes?" I look down at her face and feel my heart pound in my chest. I like it when she looks up at me like that. It gives me all sorts of ideas. But, I shouldn't go there.

"Why, um, why are you here? Do you know someone who's graduating today?"

That's a good question. Why *am* I here? "Yes." I stare at her lips, then back up at her eyes. "You."

"Me?" She flutters her long, dark lashes that cover her pretty brown eyes. "Why?"

"You said no one would be here, so I thought I'd come lend my support. Besides, my meetings ended early. I was bored." Not true. I've got a shit-ton to do up at the house, but I kept picturing this nice girl going through this momentous occasion with no one to watch her, to congratulate her. I should have known her boyfriend would be here. Damn it.

"Oh, right. Of course. Well, thanks for coming." She nods and turns back to Kai. "Ready?"

"Sure, babe." Kai turns to me. "We're going out for an early dinner. Care to join us?"

I look at him, then at her. If my eyes don't deceive me, I'd swear she just gave Kai a dirty look. She doesn't want me to go to dinner? "Sure. Where are we going?"

"Carter..."

I look at Vivien and wait for her excuse. "Yeah?"

Shaking her head, she gives me a weak, fake smile. "We're not going anywhere fancy. You probably—"

"I'm not a fancy guy. Where are we going?" I ask again.

"Pizza," announces Kai. "Giordano's. It's Viv's favorite."

Wait, *he* gets to all her Viv?

"Which location?"

"The one up on West Eighteenth," responds Kai quickly, probably so Viv, I mean Reggie, can't argue.

"You guys got a ride?" I ask, knowing Reggie doesn't have a car.

"I've got a car. Viv and I'll meet you there in an hour."

I check my watch and note the time. "Meet you there at five?"

"Sounds good." Kai takes her hand in his, tugging her along. "Come on, Viv. Let's go find my car."

She giggles and looks up at me. "He can never remember where he parks. He's a dork like that."

I chuckle as they walk away and stare at her ass in that dress. It's shorter than it seemed up on stage. If she bent over, I'd get to see everything. I growl to myself. *Knock it off, Carter. She's taken, obviously. Taken by the only other guy in the place that could compete with me.*

CHAPTER NINE

REGGIE

"OH MY GOD, Kai. Why'd you invite him?"

"Why not? He's hot. I want to watch him eat breadsticks."

I giggle and slap him on the arm. "You're disgusting."

"No, I'm not. I'm a realist. And I know damn well that you want to watch him eat breadsticks too."

"Do not."

"Do too."

"Asshole."

"Bitch face."

"I'm not a bitch face."

"You can be."

"Only when it's shark week."

"Your menstrual cycle has no bearing on your bitchy days."

"Does too," I grumble. "Asshole."

"You might as well get to know him. You're going to be shacking up with him."

"Am not."

"Are too."

This conversation is going nowhere. "Let's just find your car, jerk face."

"I love you too, Viv."

That reminds me. Carter knows my real name now. Ugh. When he said it, my panties got all hot and bothered. I could just picture him moaning my name.

Shit! Stop it, Vivien. That's a waste of time and energy. I need to focus on my goals. Yeah, focus on my career goals.

CHAPTER TEN

CARTER

I GET to the restaurant fifteen minutes early. When the host dude recognizes me, I request a table at the back so I'm not hassled by fans.

"Right away, Mr. Corcoran."

Even though I play for the Giants, lots of people remember me from my college days, and many of them know I'm a Chicago kid, born and raised. Some give me shit for not playing for the Bears, but I had no choice in the matter. I was drafted by the Giants, and that's that. Don't get me wrong, it's always been my dream to play for my Bears, but that'll have to wait until my contract is up with the Giants in a year. Maybe then my agent will be able to get me home.

When I'm seated, I order a draft beer and pull out my phone.

Me: Got a table upstairs in the back.
Reggie: K. We'll be there in twenty.
Me: Want me to order you guys any drinks?
Reggie: ...

Reggie: Kai wants a Cosmo.

Me: And you?

Reggie: Water

Me: Okay. See you when you get here.

I wait for a response but get none. What else would she say to that? I order the drinks and read through the menu as I wait.

"Excuse me. Are you Carter Corcoran?" says a feminine voice.

Oh, here we go. Prepared to give my canned response, I look up into the eyes of a gorgeous brunette and smile. "I am." I stand, because I'm a gentleman like that, and hold out my hand. "And you are?"

"Kelly." She flutters her lashes at me. "Kelly Baker."

As discreetly as possible, I scan her body. She's tall, slim, and wearing a tiny pink dress. I see a flash of red near the floor and surmise she's wearing red shoes. She's hot. "It's nice to meet you, Kelly Baker."

She simpers and licks her glossy, red lips.

Damn, she's the entire package.

Just as I'm about to get to know Kelly a little better, the new blonde in my life steps up to the table, jams her hands on her hips and glares, then smirks. "Hey, Carter? How's it hangin'?"

It catches me off guard. It's not often a woman asks me how I'm "hangin'." I start to laugh, then throw my head back and laugh some more. "Shit, Reggie. You're hysterical."

"Yeah," she grumbles. "I know."

I look back up at Kelly, who's staring at the back of Reggie's head with pursed lips and a scowl. Her expression tells me everything I need to know about Kelly Baker. She's gone sort of stiff as her eyes stare daggers at Reggie. "She's with you?" she asks snottily.

I say, "Yes." Looking at the two women side by side, there's no comparison. Vivien, I mean Reggie, is far superior to the leggy brunette. Even with Reggie's diminutive build, there's something about her that sparkles. Her beauty comes from within. I can see it, and I barely know the woman.

At the same moment, Reggie scoffs, "No."

I'm pulled from my thoughts by Reggie's rebuff just as Kai appears. The three of us are at a standstill. Both women are staring at me. Both look angry.

What just happened?

"Yo!" says Kai, a tad too loudly. "What's going on?"

"Well, who are you?" coos Kelly. "Do you play football too?"

"No, honey. But your shoes are *divine*."

Divine? Huh? He likes her shoes. I stare at Kai. Nah, no way. He's into Reggie. I can tell.

Kelly looks down at her shoes and then back up at Kai, beaming. "Thanks. Got them on sale at Saks. Aren't they great? And *sooo* comfortable."

Reggie plops down in her seat, muttering, "It seems we've got a fourth for dinner." She sounds upset. "*My* graduation dinner, and there's now a fourth person." Yep, she's upset.

Maybe I shouldn't have intruded on her celebratory dinner. It's too late now. I'm already here. "Kelly isn't joining us. She just stopped by to say hello." I look over at her and see disappointment in her eyes. "Isn't that right, Kelly?"

"Right. I recognized him and wanted to say hello. Have a good dinner." She turns on her spiked heels and returns to her table. She's sitting with another woman, older but dressed in much the same way as Kelly. Same hairstyle, same makeup, same look of irritation on her face. If I had to guess, I'd say mother and daughter. Mother and daughter who set their sights on the rich athlete. It happens all the time.

"So, what's good here?" I ask as I sit down. I've been here a million times, but I feel like breaking the ice that's now covering our table.

"You've never been to Giordano's? I thought you grew up in the city," Reggie says, looking shocked.

"I've been here. It's just been years."

"Wow, that's sad. I feel sorry for you, Carter."

Ignoring her comment, I look at my menu. "So, what are you two getting?"

Kai says, "I'm getting a medium deep-dish with pineapple, bacon, onion, and artichokes."

I watch Reggie shiver. "God, that's so disgusting, Kai."

Kai shrugs. "It's my favorite. Sue me."

"I will. For loss of appetite."

They both snicker at her joke.

They have an easy banter that for some reason pisses me off. "What are you getting, Reggie?"

"Oh, well, I'm getting the small Greek salad."

I wait for her to tell me which pizza she's getting, but she says nothing more, picking up her glass to sip her water. "That's it?" Is she on a diet? She doesn't need to be. Her body is curvy in all the right places, but I guess she could be. I'm used to women like Natalia only ordering a side salad and merely picking at it. That can't be right. I'm pretty sure Reggie eats like a normal person.

"Don't go there," Kai sings.

"Go where?"

"Don't try to figure her out. She's as stubborn as a mule."

"Am not," Reggie says with a pout.

She's cute when she pouts.

"You are too, Viv. This is supposed to be a celebration. You can stop being so frugal and get more than water and a side salad. I'm buying."

"No way." She crosses her arms in front of her, forcing her chest up and out.

Damn, she's got a great rack. Clearing my throat, I look at my menu again. Let's try this. "Reggie, what's good here?" I nudge my head toward Kai. "I'm with you about the pineapple pizza."

Reggie giggles and moves her arms down from the defensive position. She also smiles at me for the first time today. She's got a beautiful smile. Her teeth are straight except for the slight gap between the two front ones. Why, suddenly, do I want to run my tongue over that gap? Shit. My dick is alive and kicking. When she speaks, I do my best to concentrate on her words rather than on the lip ring and her full lips forming words.

"If she splurges, Reggie always gets the six-inch pan with spinach, mushrooms, and green peppers," mumbles Kai behind his menu.

"Oh, are you a vegetarian?" I ask, looking over at her.

"Ha! No. But you're funny."

"Well, that pizza sounds good to me. I like vegetables on my pie. If I order a large, would you eat some?"

I'm trying to get her to eat pizza. Now that I know she's attempting to be economical, I'm doing this to help her out. I'm buying. I always buy. The difference between now and any other time? Usually everyone *expects* me to buy. Reggie doesn't. It's refreshing.

I peek up at Reggie over my menu and see her blushing. "Will you eat some?"

She shrugs. "I guess. But don't order that because of me. I'm happy with the salad."

"I like vegetables." I love meat, but I can get that anytime. "It sounds good to me."

"Okay. Sure. I'll have a piece."

"Great." When our server returns, we order our food and spend the forty minutes it takes to bake the thick pizza talking.

"Carter?"

"Yes, Vivien?" Did you see what I did there? I used her real name.

"Do you mind if we talk to Kai about your secret passion?"

Holy hell, she didn't correct me. Maybe I've got the green light to start calling her by the sexy name. Wait. What did she say? Secret passion? Oh, my artwork. "Can he be trusted?" I ask with one eyebrow raised. I'm seriously asking.

She turns to Kai and gives him a stern expression. "If we tell you something, you can't speak of it to anyone but us." She points to me and back to herself.

"Of course. What do you take me for?" Kai sounds offended. Turning to Reggie, he snaps, "Dish, bitch."

"Okay, Kai. Here's the secret." She leans forward to whisper. "Carter is a painter."

"I'm trying to be," I interject. I'd never give myself that title. At least not yet.

Looking only at me, she says, "Kai is an amazing painter, Carter. He'd be a good person to give you feedback on your work." She pulls her phone out. "Hang on, I've got some pictures." Scrolling through her phone, she stops, then holds the phone up in front of my face.

I stare at the most realistic painting I've ever seen. "This is a painting?" I blink. I take the phone out of Reggie's hand to get a closer look. "It looks like a photo."

Kai shrugs. "I'm into photorealism at the moment."

"Wow." I look at him. "I'm a novice, but I'd love some advice." Without thinking, I slide my finger over the photo assuming there will be more, but that's not what appears. Nope. Not at all. Instead of a painting by Kai, it's a photo of Reggie. A photo of Reggie wearing only black lace panties and a white cotton bra that can barely contain her tits. It appears she's taking a selfie in front of a mirror. Her body is turned, twisted, providing a glimpse of some side boob and one fucking stellar ass. Whoa, Reggie's got curves for days. I knew she did, but seeing her in the flesh, literally, puts forth evidence of the veracity of my claim. I'd give her an A+. I feel the phone being pulled from my hand. When Reggie sees which picture I was ogling, she turns bright magenta but says nothing. Smart girl, because I'd love to talk to her about that photo.

"Sure thing, bro. I'm sure I'll be up to your place to visit my girl here," he says, squeezing her shoulder. "I'll check them out sometime."

My girl? Maybe I was right before. Maybe they're together. Why does that irritate the fuck out of me? I want to ask, but it seems impolite. And none of my damn business. I've got Natalia. My shoulders slump a little. "Sure. Anytime."

When our food arrives, I dig right in. I'm starving. I'm always starving. I'm working out twice a day now and burning more calories than I was a month ago. Granted, deep-dish pizza isn't the best food choice for me, but this is a celebration, right?

When the check is placed between Kai and me, I reach for it, but Kai grabs it first.

Reaching across the table, attempting to take it from both of us, Reggie growls, "No, I'm paying for my own food. I knew this was going to happen."

"No, you are not," snaps Kai, obviously annoyed.

Right or wrong, I'm going to jump in here. "No way, it's your graduation. You're not supposed to pay for your own graduation dinner."

Sighing, she sits back down, placing her napkin on the table. "Fine. But I'd like to state, for the record, that I don't like it. I know you're both loaded, but that doesn't mean I need macho men paying for the poor defenseless girl's dinner."

"Defenseless," scoffs Kai. "In what universe?"

"You know what I mean, Kai. I don't need to be 'taken care of,'" she says, using air quotes.

"You know I hate air quotes, woman. Stop it!" Kai hisses. "They're uber annoying."

"It's why I use them as much as possible," Reggie snaps back.

It's like they're siblings instead of sexual partners. I fight like this with my brothers and sister, but I've never had that kind of interaction with a woman. *Well, maybe Casey.*

Kai says, looking cross, "I'm paying for everyone's dinner."

"The hell you are," I snap.

I watch as Reggie stands up from her chair, grabs her purse from the back of the only empty chair at our table, and turns to leave.

Kai mutters, "I invited you, Carter. I'm buying."

"But I'm the grown-up here." Sure, I'm older than both of them, but not by much.

Kai's expression grows stormy. I may have pissed off the big man. Oh well.

We both turn when we hear Reggie's voice. She's stopped at the table with the woman from earlier. "They're all yours." She points her thumb back at us. "Have at 'em."

"Seriously?" squeaks the brunette. Kelly? Was her name Kelly?

"Seriously," Reggie deadpans. "They're too high maintenance for me today."

I watch as Kelly stands up. I quickly stand and pull Kai up by his sleeve. "Let's both throw down some money and get out of here."

"Deal."

We each toss down a wad of cash and step out and away

from the table. "Thanks for everything," I say as we pass our server. "Money's on the table."

"Carter?"

I turn in time to see Kelly following, then raise my hand for a shake. She looks at my hand like it's an alien, but places her cold hand in mind. "Nice meeting you, Kelly."

"You too." She's pouting, and it's not near as cute as Vivien's pout earlier.

Why am I torturing myself over Vivien? She's taken. Or is she?

I follow Kai down the steps to the main level of Giordano's and ask, "So, how long have you two been dating?"

He stops in his tracks and turns slowly. "Who? Me and Viv?"

"Yeah."

He takes hold of my wrist, pulling me along until we're near the hallway to the bathroom. "You like her?"

Yes. "No."

"You do. You like her."

I shrug. "She's cool. She's funny."

"She's beautiful."

"She's attractive, sure."

We stare at each other.

"You *like* her," Kai repeats emphasizing the word.

"Does that bother you? Is she yours?" He *is* acting very territorial.

"Mine?" he chokes. "Vivien belongs to no one."

I'm confused. It's irritating. "Spit it out, dude. Are you a couple or what?"

"Or what."

"So, you're not in a romantic relationship with her?

"Nope."

"Why do you get to call her Vivien and I can't?" That issue is truly perplexing.

Kai takes a deep breath. His eyes soften. "You have to earn the right to call her Vivien. She'll let you know when or if that time comes."

Well, she didn't correct me earlier so....

I think that's all I'm going to get out of him about that. "Is she seeing anyone else?"

"She has terrible taste in men, so thankfully, no."

I nod at this revelation. Does that mean if she likes me, I'm bad for her? *Stop it. That's too many irrelevant questions, Carter.*

My thoughts are interrupted by a thick finger poking into my chest. "But she's my bestie and I'd kill for her, so watch your step, Mr. McHotty. Hurt her and I'll maim you."

Jesus. *Mr. McHotty?* "I'm not going to do anything to her. I was just curious."

"Sure you were."

"You fight like brother and sister. I just thought it was strange."

"Right." He rolls his eyes.

"I'm seeing someone." Someone I don't really like very much. I can't talk to her about things that are important to me. Namely art. Sex and shopping is all she wants to do. "Informally," I add.

"Vivien isn't someone you'd date 'informally,'" he says, using air quotes. I thought he hated those things.

"Look, I just wanted to know about you two. She's going to be living with me."

"On your property. Not *with* you, right?"

"Same thing."

"Uh, no it's not."

Jesus, this guy is confusing. One thing is crystal clear, however: Vivien is single.

———

KAI LEFT me standing by the bathrooms after our little talk about Reggie. I used the facilities quickly. When I step outside the restaurant, Kai and Reggie are huddled together in deep conversation. Wait! Is Kai telling her about our talk? If he is, should I be angry? Relieved? Fuck. This girl confuses me.

I interrupt them. "So, now what? We going out?"

They both turn to look at me, confused expressions on their faces.

"No. I've got to work tomorrow morning. Early," says a smiling Vivien.

"I'm free," says Kai with a smile. "We could go get a drink somewhere."

Why is he looking at me like that? "Um, well, I just thought we'd be celebrating Vivien's accomplishment. With Reggie."

I did it again.

"Sorry. No can do. I'm working at the ass crack of dawn at Palace Grill. I need my beauty sleep," she deadpans.

She didn't correct me. I'm going with it. I'm calling her Vivien until she tells me to stop. This just may work.

"You're already beautiful."

"Oh, you…" She slaps me on the upper arm and blushes.

I embarrassed her? Don't tell me she doesn't see how pretty she is?

"I've gotta go, guys." She points to Kai. "I'll see you tomorrow." Turning to me, she points but then drops her hand. "And I'll see you next Saturday."

"Saturday?"

"Moving day." She looks confused. "Right?"

"Oh, right. Moving day." I didn't forget. I was just trying to be cool. Trying and failing. I'm sort of losing my mojo around this girl. I feel like I'm in high school again. I've got a little crush, I think.

"Okay. Good. I thought you forgot."

I shrug. "No. I didn't forget. I'll see you on Saturday, Vivien." I lean down and kiss her soft, round cheek. "Congratulations."

The flush of pink on her pretty face is such a turn-on that the front of my pants tightens. *Down, boy.*

"Thanks, Carter."

Nodding, I head over to my Land Rover, slide in, and watch Kai and Reggie get into a cerulean-blue Mercedes SUV. Shit. Kai must not be hurting for cash. That car can run upwards of ninety grand, if it's loaded. I should know; I almost bought one.

CHAPTER ELEVEN

VIVIEN

THE KNOCK on the front door of my apartment is loud—loud enough to wake my roommates. Well, one roommate. The other two are out of town. I was trying hard not to disturb Mona. I even packed up my stuff and put it in the living room last night. Well, most of my stuff is out here. My bed is still in the room. Mona is going to be pissed off about that, but I'm not leaving it behind. I had to buy a new one when I moved into this place. Beds are damned expensive. Even though I won't need it at Carter's, I'll need it eventually. I won't live at Carter's forever.

When the knock sounds again, I quickly grab the doorknob before Carter can repeat the racket. I wrench the door open, and just as I'm about to say, "Shh, Carter," I see a guy who looks sort of familiar. "Oh, who are you?" I say almost breathlessly because, whoever he is, he's beautiful.

"Well, hello," he says, leaning against the doorframe in a Joey from *Friends* kind of way.

I'm half expecting him to speak in a thick New York accent and add, *How you doin'?* I wait for him to answer my question first, a hand on my hip.

"Clinton. Clinton Corcoran. You must be Vivien."

Why did that sound like something James Bond would say? And speaking of James Bond, Clinton Corcoran could probably play the part. He's classically good-looking. He's got the same dark hair and green eye color as Carter, but he's not as tall as his brother or as bulky either. That's not to say the man isn't built. He's got leaner muscle than his sibling, which is highlighted by the tight gray Chicago Bears tee he's sporting.

"Yes, I'm... No. It's..." I lose my train of thought as another man steps up behind Clinton. This one is tall. And he's sort of blond. My mouth goes dry as I do my best not to check him out. My heart is going pitter-pat at the sight of him. I must look like a damn fish gasping for air as I try to speak. "...Reggie."

"Johnson Corcoran." The blond god says as he reaches out to shake my hand. "It's nice to meet you, Reggie."

Why do I have the urge to take his hand and place it on my left breast?

I shake my head to get the naughty thoughts out of my mind. "Same here." I'm dumbstruck. How is it possible that there are two guys who look like they could be on the pages of *GQ* standing at my door? "Where's Carter?"

"Right here," he says as he steps up behind Johnson. "I see you've met my brothers."

Make that three guys. I look at all three hunks. Johnson's taller, not as bulky as Carter but close. "You're all named after presidents?"

"We are, indeed. Our sister is Kennedy," says Clinton.

I laugh. "My siblings are all named after actors from the fifties. Dean for James Dean and Grace after Grace Kelly."

"Your name is Reggie? Which star was that?"

"Never mind." I'm not going there right now. "Come. In. Please," I say, sounding like C3PO.

"Is Kai here?" Carter asks as he looks around the apartment.

"No, he's on vacation with his parents and sister. It's okay. There's not much, as you can—"

"Jesus fucking Christ, you fat fucking bitch."

Great. That hate-filled outburst came courtesy of Mona. I turn to my left as she steps into the living room. She hasn't yet seen the guys.

"I'm so fucking glad you're moving your lazy lard-ass out of here. I'm sick of you coming in at all hours and leaving *soooo* fucking early in the morning. You're so inconsiderate, you— Oh, well hello." Now, she's seen them. "Reggie? You didn't tell me we had company." She flutters her eyelashes at the three men and coos, "Oh, my goodness. And look at me. I'm not dressed for company."

No, she certainly is not dressed for company. Hell, she acts like these guys are here for *her*. She's wearing a thong and a tiny tank top that can barely contain her moderately sized boobs. That's it. But don't read anything into her remarks—she walks around like that all the time. She's not shy. And why would she be? She's got the body of a supermodel. Life is so unfair sometimes.

I glance over at the three hunks by the door and expect to see their eyes bugging out at the sight of her half-naked body, but what I see is, well, it's not that. They're looking at her, yes. But they aren't staring at her like she's hot—instead, they seem sort of pissed.

Carter speaks first, turning his head to me. "You let her talk to you like that?"

I shrug. "I don't *let* her do anything. She is what she is."

"Yeah, a bitch," mutters Clinton.

"I'm in agreement there," says Johnson stiffly.

I shrug. "It doesn't matter. I'm moving out today."

"Whoa, dude, are you Carter Corcoran?"

I look over at Mona again to discover the origin of that question is her idiot boyfriend, Donald. He's standing behind Mona in only his tighty-whities.

"Jesus, don't you people wear clothes?" asks Clinton.

Mona looks back at Donald. "Donny, go put some pants on. No one wants to see you like that."

I'd love to say the same to her, but the fact is that lots of people would want to see *her* like that.

"Reggie, what needs to go?"

Carter has taken charge, thank goodness. I'd like to get the hell out of here. I point to the luggage and boxes sitting just to the right of the doorway. "I've got this stuff and my bed." I move to the area with about fifteen small boxes. "These are my ceramic pieces. Fragile."

"Right. Let's put those in the back of my SUV. We can load the bed and any other stuff in Johnson's pickup," Carter says as he bends to pick up the first box.

"Can I help?" asks Donald as he steps out into the living room in a pair of red plaid flannel pajama pants.

Like it's planned, all three Corcoran brothers simultaneously reply, "No."

I giggle and sneak a peek at Mona. She gives me the same evil eye she's perfected in the year I've lived here, then her expression changes and she turns to the guys. She's eye-fucking the Corcoran brothers. When the three men take the first trip down the steps, I turn to pick up my suitcase.

"I can't believe you're friends with Carter fucking Corcoran," says Donald with awe in his voice.

Before I can reply, Mona says, "You've been holding out on me, Reggie. Friends tell friends when they've hooked up with guys like that."

"No, I haven't been holding out on you, because we're *not* friends."

"And whose fault is that? You're always working or making ugly sculptures."

Ugly sculptures? She's a photography major who only takes pictures of brick and concrete. Truth. She graduates with her undergrad in photography at the end of the summer. Her senior exhibition is entitled *Step by Step; Brick by Brick.* I'll give you a minute to absorb that one. Before you ask, yes, it will consist entirely of eight-by-ten photos of bricks and different kinds of steps. Granted, she shot them at different times of day and varied weather conditions, but that was the only interesting part about it. And she can thank Claude Monet for the idea. Hell, I take better pictures with my phone. Yes, I'm being catty.

Mona continues harping. "And you're never here. And when you are here, you sleep all the time, and you barely speak. You're weird as fuck too. Even with all that, if I knew you had those guys hanging around, I would have tried harder."

I roll my eyes as I step out into the hallway. Just as I'm about to walk down the first step, I hear the door slam behind me. "Shit. My keys are in there." Hopefully, she'll open the door for me. I'm not holding my breath though.

"Give me that," says a deep voice. Clinton.

"Oh, okay. Thanks." I hand him my suitcase and turn back to try the knob. Locked. I knew it would be—it happens automatically. I knock. When no one opens the door, I knock again. "Shit."

"What's going on?" I turn in time to see Carter step up on the top step.

"I'm locked out."

"But your roommate is in there."

I look up at him and roll my eyes. "She doesn't like me."

"So." He nudges me aside and knocks on the door loudly. "Open the door." His deep voice vibrates in the small hallway, then he raises his fist and pounds on the door. Good thing it's solid wood. "Open. The. Fucking. Door."

It's wrenched open by Donald. "She told me not to do it, but I couldn't leave you hangin', bro."

So, Donny could leave *me* hanging but not Carter? God, that's messed up.

"I'm not your bro, and your girlfriend is a bitch. You could do much better."

Donny shrugs. "Pussy's pussy, man. Am I right?" he says, holding his fist up in midair, waiting for Carter to do the same.

He'll have to wait because Carter left him hangin'. Priceless.

Donny gives up waiting and punches Carter in the arm instead.

"No, that's not right. And touch me again and I'll get Clinton to kick your ass."

I want to giggle, but I don't. "You don't punch people?" I ask, smirking.

"Nah. I'd get a bunch of shit from team management. Probably get fined by the NFL too. No, thanks."

By now, Johnson and Clinton are both back up to take another load downstairs, so Carter says, "Show me where your bed is, Vivien."

Why did that put sexy thoughts into my head? *Show me your bed, Vivien.* Ooh, that sounded nice. Hell, I didn't even mind it when he said my name. Yes, I've heard him use it several times and for some reason, I haven't felt like correcting him. Hearing it said with such a deep, raspy voice has made me realize it's not so bad—being called Vivien. I can only imagine what it'd sound like in bed.

I shake off my impure thoughts and lead him down the hallway to my bedroom. I open the door and see Mona standing completely naked by the closet. *Her* closet. A closet she refused to share, claiming she'd lived there first (which is true). Therefore, I had to use cardboard boxes that I kept under my bed for my stuff. Plus, she forbade me from *touching* anything in her closet.

She looks back over her shoulder. The minute she spots Carter, she turns, deliberately displaying herself. Flaunting everything. Next, she places her hand over her mouth and says, "Oh my God, Reggie. I'm naked here. You could have knocked." Then she giggles.

Ignoring her obvious ploy to get at least one of the Corcoran men's attention, I say, "I need to get my bed."

"Well, geesh. Let me get dressed first." She reaches out and grabs her sheer robe.

Geesh? The woman talks like a fucking sailor. "Geesh" isn't ordinarily in her vocabulary.

I stare at her robe and sigh. Yes, it's completely sheer. She slips it over her body, tying it around her tiny waist. I'm not sure why she bothers. You can see *everything*.

Releasing a frustrated groan, I yank the top mattress off and set about dragging it out of the room. Carter takes it from me and hands it to Clinton, who is now staring at Mona.

"You should get dressed," Clinton mutters. "We don't want to see all that." He picks the mattress up with one hand and leaves the room.

Donny peeks over Clinton's shoulder. "Woman! Get some clothes on," he shouts, then releases a cackle that makes the hair on the back of my neck rise. He's a weird little guy.

Stomping her foot, she spits more vitriol my way. "I can't wait until you're gone, Reggie."

"The feeling is mutual, believe me."

I help Carter with the box spring as Johnson enters the room. "Jesus, woman. You ever wear clothes?"

Sputtering, Mona steps around everyone and out of the bedroom.

"Guess not," Johnson grumbles. "Chicks."

"Yeah... chicks," I add with a giggle. "I'm not going to miss her. Not one bit." I look up at Carter. "She's evil. She stole my favorite Birks, my favorite jeans that were soft and comfy, my prized Police concert tee, and a stuffed cat my dad gave me when I was thirteen." It was his parting gift as he drove off to seek fame and fortune. "That last one still stings."

"Why did you put up with it?"

"Because it was cheap to live here, and I don't like drama."

"Ah, I see." He bends down to grab the bed frame. When he pulls himself up to full height, he moves closer to me. I watch him smile and see his dimple appear. God, it's beautiful. "Well, you don't have to put up with her anymore. You're living with me now."

We hear a screech and turn to see Mona. "You're moving in with *him*?"

Just as I say, "No," Carter says, "Yes." He also slides his arm around me, pulling me into his big body. "We're trying to keep it on the down low."

"No way. You can't be with *her*." Mona points at me.

I watch as he bends to place the frame back on the floor. His now empty hand wraps around my back and turns my body around. I gaze up at his beautiful face. It can't be avoided. Before I know what's happening, his other hand slides behind my neck. He's bent down, an inch away from me, smiling like an idiot. Oh, I get it. He's fucking with her.

But shit gets real the second he presses his lips to mine. *Sizzle. Zap. Pow.* That's the sound of the electricity running through me. I'm sure it's just me. He suckles on my piercing and nibbles on my lower lip until I open my mouth to say something like, "Oh, hell yeah!"

His full lips close over my bottom lip. When he gives my lip ring a gentle tug, I moan. What? I can't help it. It's a sexy move.

I think the moan was a bad idea, or a really good one, if you're in my place. So, yeah, a *fantastic* one. He pulls me in until we're plastered together, turns his head, and takes the kiss to the next level. He slides his mouth over mine, and I feel our tongues touch. Then it sweeps in and out like we're having mouth sex. Hmm, I guess we are. I wrap my arms around his neck and pull myself closer to him. I shouldn't be doing this. It's a super-duper bad idea. I feel a warm palm slide over my left ass cheek, then a squeeze. That's it. My panties just melted.

"God, gross."

Carter and I pull away from each other. I'm in a complete daze forgetting all about Mona. I turn to see Clinton and Johnson staring at us. They don't look grossed out like Mona does. Actually, they're both smirking. Why they're smirking, I've no idea. I gather myself and step away from the kissing bandit.

As I pass Mona, she hisses, "It'll never last. He'll get tired of your fat ass."

"Probably. But it'll be fun while it lasts." I know there's nothing going on with us. He was just doing that to annoy Mona, and I appreciate it. I appreciated it so much that my legs are now wobbly. I grab the doorframe on my way out of my old room and, turning to Mona, say, "If you happen to find any of my missing things, could you let me know?"

In the living room, I scan the space. I know there's nothing of mine out here. I never spent any time there. I look over at the kitchen and gasp. "My cereal." I've got a brand-new, unopened box in the cupboard. *I can't leave that behind!*

I make my way to the small galley kitchen. Reaching up, I open my one and only cupboard. Inside is a nearly empty jar of peanut butter, a sandwich bag holding a few crackers, two cans of Campbell's chicken noodle soup, and my box of Cap'n Crunch, the breakfast of champions. Okay, that's a different brand. I should have said *my* breakfast of champions. And the lunch and dinner of champions. I eat it all the time. I eat it with milk or without. I've eaten it on ice cream, on top of donuts. I would eat it here and there. I'd eat Cap'n Crunch anywhere.

Snickering at my own Seussian silliness, I get up on my tippy-toes to grasp the box. I don't remember putting it up that high, but I was probably in a hurry and tossed it up there. Grasping the edge of the box, I pull it out. It's light. Too light. With the box on the counter in front of me, I see that what was once an unopened box is now opened, and from the weight, I'd say it is nearly empty. I pull open the top and peer down. *Who the fuck ate my cereal?* These people make me insane. I feel hot tears gather in my eyes. They know I don't have money for food. They know this is all I eat when I'm home. They know how much my cereal means to me. So, why? Why would they eat my food? I look over and see Mona leaning against the wall.

"Donny ate some of your cereal. I hope you don't mind."

I do. I *do* mind. Holding back tears, I'm about to launch into a rant when I see Carter come up behind Mona. "This your stuffed animal?"

"Oh, my God. Meow Meow Kitty!?" I squeak the second I see my stuffed cat. "Where was she?" I take it from his hands and pull it to my chest and squeeze.

"In the closet in your room." He holds up a grayish-black tee. "This your tee?"

It's my Police T-shirt I've had since I was in middle school. It was also my dad's. I borrowed it one day and never gave it back. It's at that perfect stage in a T-shirt's life when it's soft but not worn out. "Yes. Was it with the cat?"

Carter nods as Johnson steps into the kitchen holding a dark-green plastic tub. I recognize it. It's Mona's. She's got several in the same color. I look over, peering inside, and see it's got all of my missing things inside.

"Hey," Mona spits. "That's mine."

She tries to take the tub out of Johnson's hands, but he holds on to it. I step closer and see my Birkenstocks, jeans, a necklace I thought I'd lost at the bar, and the set of house keys I misplaced. The roommates charged me thirty bucks to replace them. I'm seething inside. I mean, first, she lets Donny eat my cereal; now this. But I swallow down the anger. I won't get sucked into Mona's games. I won't give her the satisfaction.

"Yeah, that's my stuff."

Holding on to the tub, Johnson walks out of the kitchen, through the living room, and out the door.

"I need my tub back," Mona snaps.

"Nah, I think we'll keep it," says Clinton as he follows Johnson.

Sputtering, she turns to me. "B-but that's last season's color. If I have to replace it, they won't match."

The guys ignore her and it's amazing.

"Fine. Good riddance, fatty."

I see Carter's mouth is drawn tightly into a straight line. From my spot, I also see his fists are clenched.

"Yeah, well, the feeling's mutual." I will not give her the satisfaction. I step around her and follow the guys, dropping my key on the side table as I exit. I turn back in time to see Carter speaking to Mona. I don't know what he says, but I watch as her face turns from tan to visibly white. I don't wait to find out what was said. I descend one flight of steps, then feel Carter catch up behind me. His hand touches my lower back as he says, "I'm glad you're out of that toxic place, babe."

"Me too, Carter." *Me too.*

CHAPTER TWELVE

CARTER

WHERE DO I begin with all of that shit back at her apartment? I'm glad Vivien's out of that place. If her other roommates are as toxic as Marcia, or whatever the fuck her name was, then we saved her the torment. Jesus, women like Marcia back there are scary as shit. I feel sorry for the dumbass dating her. David? Doug? Oh, screw it. Who cares? I'll never see them again. I hope.

I'm looking in the back of my SUV at the boxes filled with her ceramic pieces. I open a small compartment on the side, above the wheel well, and grab several bungee cords. Securing one end to the metal ring mounted on the side, I stretch it across to the opposite side of the back end, essentially making a seat belt for her fragile art. I check my work and decide I need to pull the bungee tighter. After I feel confident, I shut the tailgate and turn, almost running smack dab into her. She's up on the curb while I'm down on the street, so she's several inches taller than usual.

"Is that okay?" I ask, pointing back to my car.

Without warning, Vivien wraps her arms around my neck. "Thank you."

I chuckle. "No problem. It only took a few trips. You don't have much shit." I pat her back gently. She smells fucking amazing.

She's still wrapped tightly around me. "No, that's not it." Pulling away but keeping her hands on me, she looks into my eyes. "Thank you for that, yes. But I mean thank you for finding my cat, my stuff, and for standing up for me back there."

I feel her hands on my shoulders, and I like them there. They feel natural. "Why didn't you stand up for yourself? She's pure bitch."

She pulls away slightly, and I miss her touch. "Because I don't care enough about her. I learned a long time ago not to waste my breath on people I don't like and who don't deserve my energy." She's now standing a foot away from me.

I liked it better before, when she was closer. "Makes sense." I look into her eyes and smirk. "That must mean you like me."

"Why would you think that?" She says smugly, with her arms crossed over that gorgeous chest of hers.

"Because, in the short time I've known you, you've never let me get away with anything." It's true. Even back at the art gallery where we met, she didn't pull any punches. "Anyway. It was no problem. I'm glad to help. As for finding your stuff, I had a feeling she had it in the closet."

"I should have searched there, but she forbade me from touching anything in her closet, and I wouldn't put it past her to have a nanny cam in the room." Reggie rolls her beautiful brown eyes.

Since we're making confessions, I need to say it. "Sorry about the kiss back there." *Not sorry.* "I thought she needed to get knocked down a peg or two."

The truth is, I've wanted to kiss her since that day at my house. Seeing her so excited about the art studio made me horny as hell. Besides, her lips are fucking plump and pink. Who *wouldn't* want to kiss them? If we hadn't had an audience, I could have kept right on kissing. Funny. I'm generally not into kissing. It's a means to an end, if you know what I'm saying. But with Reggie, the minute our lips touched, I imagined kissing her for hours.

When Reggie blushes, I smile. "No problem. No biggie." She fidgets, placing her hands in the pockets of her cut-off jean shorts.

It's then I take notice of her outfit. Why I didn't notice before is beyond me. She's wearing a white T-shirt with her college logo on the front. It looks dirty, but it's probably stains from art stuff. I scan down her body to check out her legs. They looked good in her dress last weekend, but these shorts are better. *Way better,* because they're short. So short, in fact, I get a true glimpse of her full thighs. Thighs I'd like to see wrapped—

"*Welp.* Ready?" she asks as she steps off the curb. "Am I riding with you?"

Riding me? Hell, yes, I wish she was riding me. I nod. "Let's hit the road."

CHAPTER THIRTEEN

VIVIEN

THE RIDE UP to South Barrington is quiet except for the radio. He must have satellite, because we listen to a television sports station all the way. He asked me if I minded, and I said, "No." It's his car. The driver gets to pick the music; at least that's what my dad always.... Anyway, it's the rule.

As the announcer talks about football, I hear them mention Carter's name. "Isn't it strange to hear them talk about you like that?"

He shrugs. "I'm used to it." He looks over at me and gives me a shy smile. Something I remember seeing in his painting studio. "It was really bad during the draft. I wasn't the number one overall pick. Defensive ends are never the first pick, but I was in the top five, so that was a big deal, I guess." He shrugs again.

"Defensive end? So, you play defense and you stand on the end?"

Carter chuckles in that rich, deep throaty sound I've come to love. "You still haven't googled me?" He looks a little surprised. "Yeah, that's pretty much it."

"Aren't you kind of skinny to be a defensive guy?" I know enough about football to know those guys are huge.

"Skinny? I weigh two-seventy," he says, looking offended. "I'm not a lineman. I've got to be leaner since I run around a lot, chasing the bad guys."

"You sound like a cop."

"Sometimes I feel like a cop." He winks. "Actually, if football didn't pan out, I was going to apply to the police academy."

"Really? That sounds cool. Dangerous, but cool. Especially in Chicago. Or would you have moved somewhere else?"

"No. Chicago's my home. I'll come back here permanently after football is over."

"And make art?" I'm not smirking or joking now. Art is serious business to me.

"I hope so. Not that I'll be a professional artist like you or anything. I just plan on spending my free time making art."

"Sounds awesome." A dream come true. That's not going to be how it works for me though, and I'm fine with that. I'll work odd jobs, maybe even try to land a teaching gig just so I can keep making art.

———

THE TRIP WENT FAST since we didn't have to fight weekday rush hour traffic. Carter stops the car in front of his giant gate. Grabbing the phone from his pocket, he hits a button, and the gate opens. "When we get inside, I'll download the app for the gate on your phone so you can come and go as you please."

"That's cool."

"It is. You can use it like this, or if you're home and expecting a visitor or pizza delivery, you can just use your phone. There's also a camera so you can see who's at the gate before you let anyone in."

"Wow. They think of everything," I say, not in the least sarcastically. It's true. Technology is pretty amazing.

Carter smiles. It's beautiful. "They sure do."

"Can Kai have this app thing? He's going to want to visit, and he's sort of a spontaneous kind of person."

"Sure. I'll need to program the password for him. Next time he's here, remind me."

"Will do, boss," I say as I salute him.

Chuckling, Carter pulls through his gate at nearly noon. It only took four hours to move my stuff out of my old place and drive it up to my new home. Actually, maybe I'm all moved in. I look over and see the pickup Johnson drove is almost empty. My bed is still in the back, but my luggage and other small stuff are gone.

"It looks like the guys beat us up here. We'd better go make sure they're behaving themselves."

I follow Carter into his house and see my luggage on the floor next to the kitchen breakfast bar. Johnson and Clinton are already lounging on the giant sectional sofa, watching the humongous television set and chewing. I peek over the back of the couch to see what they're eating. I'm starving.

"You want some pizza, Reggie?"

"You guys already ordered pizza?" Carter asks. "We couldn't have driven that slow."

Clinton smirks. "I called Pizza House on the ride up. We swung by to pick up a couple pies on the way."

Wow, it smells so good. I shouldn't, but I do anyway. "Sure. I could eat. But let me pay you guys back. I owe you for helping me."

"Nah, we're good," says Johnson. "Clinton used a two-for-one coupon."

"Oh. Are you sure?" I feel terrible. "I really want to—"

"Vivien. It's done. You can buy some other time. Okay?" Carter says, grabbing a slice.

"Fine. But I *am* getting it next time."

"Absolutely," adds Johnson as he takes a big bite.

"You'd better get some now. These guys are animals. There won't be any left," Carter says holding out a slice for me.

I cross to the coffee table to pick up a napkin and the slice of deep dish pizza that looks like it's got every topping imaginable. No matter. I'm not picky. I bite into the buttery pan-style crust, squeeze my eyes shut, and moan, "Mm, God. So good."

When I open my eyes, all three guys have stopped chewing and are staring at me. "What? Do I have sauce on my face?" I wipe at my chin and around my mouth.

"No. You're good," says Carter in a husky voice.

"Yep, you're good," mutters Clinton.

I move to an overstuffed armchair in deep brown leather just to the left of the sofa. Sitting down, I'm nearly swallowed by the thing. When I scoot back, my legs and feet end up sticking straight out like I'm a toddler in an adult chair. I giggle at the notion. Bringing the pizza to my mouth, I look over and see them still staring at me. "What?"

Carter replies, "Nothing."

Shrugging, I take a big bite of pizza and hope there will be enough left to have a second slice. I need to fill up since I don't have food for my new place right now. Hell, I don't have a lot of things—no car, no food. Damn, I'm sort of screwed. I should have planned better.

I'm pulled from my thoughts when a slice of pizza appears in front of me. It's attached to a giant muscly man. From my vantage point, the pizza is level with his, ahem, man parts. I refuse to look. It'd be a bad idea to imagine what Carter Corcoran's package looks like. *Bad. Idea.* But I do it anyway. He's wearing jeans that are pulled tight over his massive thighs. I scan up a tiny bit and see they're tight in other places too. Either that or he's packin' some heat behind the zipper. If you know what I mean. The other thing I notice is that they're loose around his hips. I bet if I lifted the edge of his shirt, I'd be rewarded with a mighty fine set of abs.

"Viv? You gonna take this pizza or what?"

Here's my chance. I could stop him and his "Viv" right this second. But why? I look up at him and see a sexy smirk. My guess is he just saw me ogling his goodies. Great.

"After we eat, we'll move your stuff to your place and then run to the store to get some food."

Oh, I don't want to be a pain in the ass. "It's okay. I—"

"I need food too, so it's no big deal."

Blinking rapidly, I smile weakly. "Okay. Yeah. Thanks."

"No problem."

I quickly finish my pizza and then wiggle out of the chair, escaping the fluffy vortex I was sucked into. I end up rolling onto my stomach and scooting out backward. Talk about awkward. Once I'm on land again, I hear snickering. When I turn, Clinton is laughing his ass off, and Johnson is chuckling as he says, "Nice dismount, Reggie."

"Oh, fuck off," I grumble. I know it's not nice, but I'm embarrassed, and when I'm embarrassed, I have a tendency to say mean stuff like that. It must have been pretty funny, because Johnson throws his head back and laughs as hard as Clinton. I stomp to the coffee table and grab the empty pizza boxes up into a stack I can carry with one hand.

"Oh, hell, Reggie. You're damned amusing. I'm so glad Carter found you and brought you home."

"Jesus, Johnson. I'm not a fucking stray kitten he found on the street."

"Oh, I beg to differ," mumbles Johnson.

Clinton jumps into the fray. "And Carter's kitten has claws."

"Hardee-har-har. You two are *soooo* hilarious." I do my best to give them my angry face, but I can't hold it, so I giggle instead.

The Corcoran brothers are funny. I hope I get to see them more often. I could use a laugh now and then.

I pick up the dirty napkins and other trash and place it on top of the pizza boxes. As I turn toward the kitchen, I hear a click-clacking sound. When Johnson grumbles and Clinton mumbles, "Fuck," I turn toward the sound, confused. That is, until I see the source of the click-clacking. Shoes. And not just any shoes. These shoes are about four or five inches high, bright pink, and look painful as hell. Said shoes are attached to long legs that are barely covered by a tiny black dress. It's sleeveless and very low cut. It's so low cut, I can tell she's not wearing a bra. I've seen her before, but I can't remember from where. I blink a few times, trying to remember.

"Natalia? What the hell are you doing here?" Carter looks unhappy about his visitor. He's just returned from the kitchen, and his hands are on his hips, his brows furled. "I told you I was busy all weekend."

"*Well*, hello to you too, *Carter*."

Carter says nothing.

"Darling," she simpers—changing her tune from snappy to syrupy. "I needed to see you." She scans the room and spots the brothers, and her nose scrunches up like she just smelled something bad.

Now I get Johnson's and Clinton's responses. She doesn't like them either.

Natalia's smoky eyes make their way to me, and the scrunched-up nose turns into more of a sneer. "Who are you?"

Before I can respond, Carter says, "The new housekeeper."

The new *what?*

Natalia sneers. "Housekeeper? She looks like a homeless person."

I gasp at the insult. I sure as hell hope Carter defends—

"She just got here today. She hasn't even moved into the servants' quarters yet."

Servants' quarters?

"Cut her some slack, Nat. She wanted to get to work right away." He turns to me with a pathetic pleading expression on his handsome face. I guess I'll play along—for now. "Isn't that right, Vivien?"

Oh. Hell. No. He doesn't get to use my real name in *this* context. It dirties it all up. Worse than my dad did when he split. I feel my face flushing hot. I know it's now pink. Moisture is collecting around my eyes. Angry tears, people. Believe me. I know he wants to keep all his art stuff a secret, but damn it. What the hell did I get myself into? Do I have to pretend to be the maid whenever *she's* around? No way.

I gather myself and, with a shaky voice, respond, "I couldn't wait to get to work." When her back is to me, I give Carter my dirtiest look. It says everything I need said.

Turning back to me, Natalia looks me up and down. "You obviously need the money," she sneers. "I hope you don't think you're going to dress like that."

"No, *ma'am*. I'm not going to dress like this." Yes, I am. You b-i-t-c-h.

I carry the pizza boxes into the kitchen, drop them on the counter, pick up my luggage, and head out the patio door. From the deck, I can take the stairs down to my new home, because if I don't leave, I'm going to punch Mr. Carter Corcoran right in his beautiful face.

Before I cross the threshold, I hear, "Excuse me. Vera?" says Natalia. "You can't just leave the garbage on the counter."

"Natalia, leave her alone." That's Carter attempting to put an end to this. Well, he didn't try hard enough.

"She's not much of a housekeeper if she just throws the garbage around," snaps Natalia.

"She's new. She'll get better."

I'll get better? I'm starting to think this move was a mistake. A big one.

CHAPTER FOURTEEN

CARTER

I FUCKED up turning Vivien into the help. I can see it from the look on her face. She's fuming. I don't blame her, but *shit*. I was just trying to think on the fly. I made a mistake giving her the code to the gate. No matter. Natalia wasn't supposed to show up here. The only time I've ever let her come to the big house was when I first moved in and didn't feel like driving or having Edward take me to my condo in the city. That's where she stays when she's in town. She's got a key, and the management company knows she's allowed to come and go as she pleases. Isn't that enough for her?

What I don't want is Natalia thinking this is more than it is. We're not in what you'd call a traditional relationship. We use each other when it's convenient. That's pretty much it. She agreed to it. But she's crossed a line by showing up here unannounced today. I should have turned off her access to the gate. I let it slide because she's never *just shown* up before. The thing is, I don't want to make a scene in front of my brothers. I know they think Natalia is a nightmare, and I tend to agree with them, but she's been in my life for over a year now. Our arrangement worked for both of us, or so I thought. Now, I'm not so sure. No. I'm positive. It's no longer working. Not for me anyway. Now's not the time to end it, though. I'll need to do it privately. I'll meet her in the city. Take her out to dinner someplace nice where we can discuss the end of our arrangement.

"Carter? Carter!"

I blink and see Natalia snapping her fingers in front of my face.

"Are you even listening to me?"

"No."

Natalia's angry expression washes away in seconds as she sidles up to me, rubbing her tits on my arm. I'm surprised they haven't popped out of that dress by now. It's a strange thing to be wearing at one in the afternoon. It's like she's going clubbing or something.

"Carter, *wuv button.*"

Oh, here we go. Baby talk. "Yeah." I hate baby talk. It makes the hair on the back of my neck stand on end.

I hear a gagging sound and watch as my brothers get up from the sofa and walk over to Vivien's few remaining belongings. Johnson picks them up, and they both exit through the same door Vivien used to escape. The looks on their faces tell me everything I need to know. Disappointment. In me. Johnson mutters, "Later, *wuv buttons.*" Yeah, I deserve that.

Ignoring my brother's rebuke, Natalia continues her play. "I missed you," she coos like a porn star. One of her hands slides down to my ass while the other one wraps around my neck. "When you said you were busy, it made me so sad." Her lower lip sticks out in a pout. "And horny," she breathes into my ear.

Okay, horny I get. I'm horny most of the time. I never seem satisfied. "Oh, yeah?"

"Yeah. Tonight, I'm going to do some naughty things to you."

"Tonight?"

"Tonight. Right after I get back from shopping." She flutters her eyelashes at me and turns her head slightly tilting toward me. It's weird. Like she's trying to tell me something—hinting at something. When I don't react, she sighs then holds her hand out, palm up. Oh. *That's* why she's here. She wants to go shopping. With my money. I made a mistake a couple of months ago. I handed her my credit card and let her shop on my dime one afternoon when I had shit to do. Now, I've become a source of funding for her.

Fuck. I shouldn't give it to her, but if I do, she'll leave and I'll have time to think and apologize to Vivien about the whole housekeeper bullshit. I reach into my back pocket, pull out my wallet, extract my black credit card, and lay it in her palm. She turns on her heel and heads out the front door.

"Toodles," she chirps as she exits.

Relieved she's gone, I toss the trash into my recycling bin and then wipe down my counters and the coffee table in my family room. After things are cleaned up, I follow the path to my brother's truck, but it's gone. I stop at my SUV to unpack her artwork but decide to see where she wants to store it first. I follow the path from the driveway out to the guest house. The front door is open, so I walk inside but see only Johnson on the couch, with the TV remote in his hand. "Where's Vivien?"

"She and Clinton went out."

"Out?" *What the hell does that mean?*

"Yeah, out." He turns back to switching channels.

"Out?"

"Jesus, dude. Yeah. Out."

I sit next to Johnson and sigh.

"You fucked up back there," he says, giving me the side-eye.

"I know."

"She doesn't seem like the kind of girl who deserves to be slighted."

"Who? Natalia?"

"No, dipshit. Natalia's a shrew." He lets out his own sigh. "I'm talking about Reggie. After seeing her with that bitch of a roommate, I have a feeling she's someone who puts up with a lot of shit from people. Otherwise, she would have punched you in your ugly face for that bullshit back there." He rubs his palms over his face. "You basically called her the help."

"Yeah? Well, you just met her. Don't pretend to know what she thinks and feels." Johnson's such a damn know-it-all.

He releases a whoosh of air, then turns to look at me. "Look. The girl has a wounded look in her eyes. And we all saw how her roommate treated her. Now, your fucking nag of a girlfriend is going to do the same damn thing? It's bullshit and makes you just as bad as her bitchy roommate."

"Hey!" I raise my voice at my big brother. "I didn't say anything disparaging. And Natalia's not my girlfriend. I don't have a girlfriend."

"Natalia's not your girlfriend?" Johnson has a grin on his face. "Awesome."

"It's casual."

"Does *she* know?" he smirks.

"Yes." *No.* "Maybe." I growl. "I don't know."

"No matter, you let Natalia talk shit to Reggie, so you'd better make things right."

"I will."

"As for Reggie not being your woman, she should be. She's cool as hell." Johnson turns to look at me. "She reminds me of Casey."

That's it. There's been something about Vivien that seems so familiar, so good. "She does." I hadn't put my finger on it until Johnson said it. "She's a lot like Casey." And the thought scares the shit out of me. I'm going to have to process this new information.

Nothing more is said. We both stare at the television, but I pay no attention. I've got to think. I fucked up, and I have to figure out how to fix it.

CHAPTER FIFTEEN

VIVIEN

"THANKS, Clinton. I appreciate you taking me to the store," I say as I push my cart out of Super Target to the pickup truck.

"No problem. It was fun. I've never shopped with a chick before. Well, besides my mom, but that doesn't count."

"No?"

"Nope."

"That surprises me."

"Why is that?"

"Because you're a hot guy. Don't you have a girlfriend?"

He smiles at my compliment. "I had one in high school. I got burned, so now I just do hookups."

"I get that." Because I've been burned. Countless times. "Someday you'll meet someone you'll want to grocery shop with." I nudge him in the shoulder.

"Well, I had fun with you, Reggie. Or is it Vivien?"

"No. It's Reggie, and if you call me Vivien again, I'll have to mar that pretty face of yours." I say with a laugh.

Clinton chuckles, and it's a nice sound but doesn't do the same thing Carter's does to me. I don't feel it down to my lady parts. I sigh in defeat. I need to forget about any sexy-time thoughts with Carter now that I've been relegated to servant status and we're no longer on a level playing field.

"Carter calls you Vivien."

I roll my eyes. "I can't get him to stop." And I like it when he says my name.

Clinton adds, "I know what Carter did back there hurt your feelings, but I think he did it to protect you."

Yeah, right. "How so?"

"Because Natalia is a vindictive bitch. If she thought you were anything other than the help, she'd be gunning for you."

"But why? I'm not a threat. Look at her."

"Oh, *you're* a threat."

"No way. I'm just here to help with the foundation." And to use that amazing studio.

"Oh, dear, sweet Reggie. You've no idea, do you?"

"About what?"

He places his hand on the cart to stop the momentum. "You're the marrying kind of girl."

Rolling my eyes, I reply, "Uh, no I'm not. I'm never getting married." Nothing good happens in marriages. People leave.

"Well, regardless. You're the kind of girl a man holds on to."

I snicker. I can't help it. "No man has tried to hold on to me yet." Not even my own father.

"You'll see. I'm right. Just give it time."

I push the cart hard enough that he's forced to release it. This entire conversation is making me uncomfortable and, frankly, angry. "I'm not here to snag a husband, Clinton. Jesus. I'm here to work. That's it."

"Sure. I know. You've got goals and dreams. I see that. You're a fighter and a hard worker. I respect that."

Releasing an exasperated breath, I push the cart to the end of the truck. Clinton's sweet, but I don't trust free, unwarranted compliments.

With Clinton's help, I put my bags in the back of the truck. On the ride home, I've calmed down enough to apologize. "Sorry if I was bitchy back there. It's been a long day, and I'm tired."

"No problem. I get it." He smiles at me from the driver seat.

I smile back. Clinton's a good guy. I wish I felt something for him. He's someone more my speed. If I felt something other than friendship, maybe I wouldn't think about his big brother so much.

———

"HONEY, WE'RE HOME," Clinton announces in a high-pitched voice as we enter my new place.

Johnson and Carter must have been sleeping, because they jerk awake.

"What?" Carter says, jumping up.

"He said we're home," I say as I plop my few grocery bags on the counter. I didn't buy a bunch of stuff. I can't afford it yet.

"You went out with my brother?"

I roll my eyes. "He took me to get a few groceries."

"I thought I told you I'd take you."

Clearing my throat, I attempt to gather myself. "You did, but I figured you'd be busy. Besides, 'the help,'" I say with air quotes, "doesn't usually go shopping with her boss."

"About that."

"Yo, dude," interrupts Johnson. "We're out of here. Later, dude. See ya, Reggie."

"Bye, guys. And thanks!" I shout.

"Yeah, see you assholes later," Carter says, distracted.

I turn my face enough to see his. "You were saying?"

"Huh?"

"You were about to explain why I'm your new servant."

"Servant? You're not my damn servant."

"Don't be dumb, Carter. That stuff back at your place was ridiculous. Why did you have to make that up? Are you afraid of your girlfriend or something?" It seems like it. "I know your art is a secret to everyone except your family, but couldn't you think of something else? Anything?"

"She's not my girlfriend."

I blink. She sure acted like a girlfriend.

"We just hook up sometimes."

"Wow. Does *she* know?"

He chuckles. "My brother asked me the exact same thing. But, yes, of course she knows. Our thing is casual." He sighs as he sits on one of the two barstools at the breakfast bar. "I'll talk to her about you. I'll figure out something. I just don't want her to know about me and the art stuff." He looks into my eyes. "She wouldn't understand."

"Okay." I'll let him sort out his stuff with her.

I turn to put my few groceries away. When I turn back, I see the door closing behind him. I lean on the counter as it clicks shut. Damn. He's gone, and I feel the loss of him. Ugh. What am I doing here? My feelings are getting involved, and that's a bad idea. I need this job right now. I need this job more than I need a man, that's for sure.

CHAPTER SIXTEEN

CARTER

"CARTER?"

I roll away from the annoying sound.

"Carter. Wake up."

"No," I mumble sleepily.

"Yes. Wake up. Where's Vera? I'm hungry."

"Vera?" *Who the hell is Vera?*

"Your new housekeeper. I'm hungry. I went downstairs, and she hasn't even made the coffee yet. You need to fire her fat ass."

I blink awake at her words. Looking up at her, I see she's wearing one of my Chicago Bears tees. I don't like it. She's going to jinx them. "She's not fat." *She's got everything in all the right places.*

She blinks at me, and I can tell she's already got makeup on. *When did she do that?*

"She's huge, Carter."

"No, she's not."

Ignoring my rebuttal, she crosses her arms over her fake breasts. "Well, you need to call her and get her over here to do her job."

Groaning into my pillow, I know I've got to put an end to

this charade about Vivien, but I fell asleep early, before Natalia got back from wherever she was, and wasn't able to set the record straight last night. And I can't fix it right this minute because my morning brain is fuzzy.

"Fine." I reach for my phone and hit the name Reggie in my contacts. It rings several times and goes to voicemail.

"Voicemail." I drop the phone onto the bed and attempt to sleep again. Just as I'm getting into sleep mode, I hear Natalia.

"Vera? Are you still asleep? This is Natalia. You need to get over here and make me breakfast."

Oh, shit. She must have hit redial. Vivien's going to kill me.

"Get over here now, or you're fired."

I hear the phone flop down near my head and I wince. Not in pain, not yet. Soon though, because Viv's definitely going to kill me.

I sit up reluctantly. "You can't fire her. You don't have the authority."

Natalia arches her brow at me. "Oh, yeah?"

"Yeah."

Her arched brow softens, and a smile appears on her face. Moving toward me like a feral cat, she crawls up onto the bed. Her palm rubs me right on my morning wood.

Shit. I'm horny. Natalia and I didn't do anything since I was asleep and too damn tired, which is fine with me. It feels wrong. Plus, I'd have thought about Vivien the entire time. Hell, this whole thing is wrong. I shouldn't be enjoying Natalia's hand that is now reaching into my boxer briefs. When I see her mouth open and her tongue appear, I know she's going to give me head. I lie back on my pillow as she gets closer to my dick, thinking just one blow job won't hurt, but the closer she gets, the more uneasy I become. Nope. Can't do it.

I start to roll away from her but her grip is firm. "Tell me I can fire her if I feel like it," Natalia says in a husky voice, poised right above my hard-on.

"Huh?" I'm distracted, not really listening to her.

"Tell me," she snaps.

I can't. I sit up and roll off the bed, my dick so hard I need to finish myself off. "No." I walk into my bathroom and start up the shower. I'll just jack off in there.

Natalia follows me. "No?" she squeaks.

"No. You can't fire her. She's not *your* employee." She's *mine.*

I step under the spray and soap up my hands. Washing quickly, I reach down and grasp my cock. Natalia is watching me with her mouth agape. I close my eyes and stroke myself, pumping harder and faster until I finally release. Come shoots out onto the glass wall, and I watch it get washed down the drain.

I sigh in relief. "Damn. I needed that."

When I look up, Natalia is gone. "Fuck." She's probably downstairs giving Vivien hell.

CHAPTER SEVENTEEN

VIVIEN

I'M LIVID. Why, you ask? Well, I'll tell you. It's because I was woken up at an ungodly hour—okay, so it's eight in the morning, but it was early considering I didn't get into bed until after three last night. I wanted to unpack, check things out. Try the potter's wheel. You know?

So, when I was rudely awakened by a phone call from a bossy woman, I thought I was back in my apartment with Mona. It's bullshit, actually. Carter asked me to move in here to run his foundation. Instead, I'm here playing pretend housekeeper for a woman who isn't even his girlfriend. At least that's what he says.

After I hang up with the harpy, I slide out of my comfy king-size bed and walk over to his McMansion. I don't change my clothes, I don't brush my teeth or hair, and I don't put on a bra. Nope, they get what they get.

I enter the stupid code into the keypad by the back door and enter the kitchen flipping on the light switch. Having no patience for any of this, I look through his cupboards, slamming doors as I go. When I find the cupboard that holds his cereal, I pull out the closest box and toss it on the counter. I find the drawer with the silverware and the cupboard with the dishes.

Pulling out two bowls, I pour the cereal up to the top. Next, I wrench open the fridge and pull out a gallon of milk.

"Whole milk? Who drinks whole milk?" I mutter.

I add milk to the bowls, stick a spoon in each, and do my best to catch the pieces that fall to the counter, nibbling on the ones I can't save.

Sliding the bowls to the other side of the breakfast bar, I announce to no one, "Voila. Breakfast is served."

"What is that?" The prissy Natalia points as she comes around the corner wearing a Chicago Bears T-shirt. That's it. Nothing else. Her hair looks perfect, and does she have makeup on already?

"It's breakfast."

She points a red nail at the overflowing bowl. "That's breakfast?"

I shrug. "It is in my world."

"B-b-but they're carbs."

"Yeah. So?"

"I can't eat carbs," Natalia screeches, outraged.

Damn, she's dramatic.

I watch as Carter sidles up to the bar wearing sweats and a tight Nirvana tee. "Hey, Vivien."

"Vivien? I thought her name was Vera?"

"I prefer Reggie," I sneer, looking angrily at Carter.

"Carter, tell this... this person I can't eat carbs. If I did, I'd look like *her*," she spits.

"This person," I say with air quotes, "is right here. Tell me yourself. Oh, wait, you already did. And there's fruit in there. See?" I hold up the box of Fruity O's. "It says right there. Ooh, and look, it's whole grain," I say as sarcastically as I can. I turn to Carter. "You're a gazillionaire and you buy Fruity O's? I think you can afford the real stuff."

"I like those better. The Os are bigger."

I look at the pink O in my hand. "Hm. You're right." I toss it into my mouth and crunch. Yummy.

"Are you going to let her talk to me like that?" Natalia screeches, bringing our focus back to her. "She's the goddamn help!"

"Actually, Natalia, I've been meaning to clarify."

"Clarify? What do you need to clarify, Carter?"

"She's not really the housekeeper."

"Not really the help?" She glares at me. Damn, her eyes are scary like that. .

"She's more of an assistant and house *sitter* than house*keeper*."

I watch the exchange between Carter and Natalia with rapt attention. Carter finally came up with a better story. Assistant and house sitter? I like it.

"An assistant? A house sitter?"

"Sure. So I've got someone here when I'm gone. Every one of the guys on the team has an assistant and house sitter combo."

"They do?" That seems to make her take notice.

"Yes. She'll keep me organized. Plus, house sitters keep my home safe and secure."

Natalia mocks, "But she'd never be able to fight off an intruder. Look at her. She's all flab."

"Uh, excuse me?" It's my turn to screech. "I'm in *great* shape." Not. But I have to defend myself somehow. This woman needs to get over herself.

"You're kidding, right?" She looks at me with a fake, arched brow. "I bet you couldn't run a mile."

"Natalia," says Carter angrily. "Leave Vivien alone. This is none of your business. You're not even supposed to be here."

"B-but, baby," she whines.

"No. I've had enough of this, Natalia."

Finally. The man has some backbone, but I don't think I

should be listening to this. It's none of my business. I slowly turn and tiptoe out of the kitchen.

As I make my way to the patio door, I hear her whimper, "Enough of what, Carter?"

"Of *everything*."

"But, Carter!" she whines, then sniffles.

"Please don't cry, Natalia." Carter's voice sounds monotone, robotic, like he's said that statement a million times. Perhaps he has.

Shit just got real. I speed up my pace to the door. I can't listen or I'll start to feel sorry for her. I'm a sap like that. Natalia is acting just a tad pathetic, but she doesn't deserve my sympathy. Not from what I've experienced with her thus far, anyway.

CHAPTER EIGHTEEN

FROM THE CORNER of my eye, I see Vivien sneak out of the kitchen. It's probably best. This conversation with Natalia isn't going to be pretty.

"But, Carter..."

"Natalia, I think it's time we end things."

"No, Carter." She sniffles. "Why? Are you seeing *her?*" she snaps, pointing out the door Reggie just exited.

"No, I'm not. She's my assistant and house sitter. That's it. I've only known her a few weeks. She just graduated from college, and she needed a job."

"B-but how'd you meet? Is she someone's little sister or something?"

I should lie and say yes, but I won't. "Craigslist. I advertised on Craigslist." So, yeah, I lied. I couldn't very well tell her I was at her art show. That'd make her ask too many questions.

"Craigslist?"

"Yes."

"That's stupid, Carter. Craigslist? She could be a criminal."

"I had her investigated. She's fine." Okay, since I already

lied once, I might as well keep it up. Right? My shoulders slump metaphorically. My mom would be so disappointed in me.

"So then why are you breaking up with me?"

I sigh as I sit down on the stool next to her. "Because. This thing with us has run its course. I'm not looking for a girlfriend, and you aren't looking for a boyfriend. Right?"

She blinks and whimpers, "I'm not your girlfriend?"

"No. We just hook up."

She blinks, her fake lashes fluttering like butterfly wings. When wetness appears, I brace myself for the waterfall I'm sure is fake. I've never seen her cry for real. It's always been for effect. "We j-j-just h-h-hook up?"

Okay, maybe it's real. She's really sobbing now. Be strong, Carter. "Yes. You knew this going in. We talked about it."

"That was a year ago, Carter. We've been exclusive for a year."

My turn to blink.

"You haven't been faithful?" Her sobs turn into full-on bawling.

"I haven't been *un*faithful. We'd have to be in a relationship for that to happen." Seriously, besides my kiss yesterday with Reggie, I've been completely monogamous.

She jumps down from the stool and runs up the steps.

I should follow her. I really should, but I think she needs a few minutes to gather herself. I decide to eat my cereal first, you know, before it gets soggy. Then I start on Natalia's bowl. Don't want it to go to waste. Mm, I love this shit. Sugary cereal is the bomb. When I finish the second bowl, I set them both in the dishwasher. Wasting more time, I wipe off the counter. With nothing else to delay me, I start up the steps. Slowly. Soooo slowly.

My room is dark when I enter. I reach for the switch but hear, "Don't turn on the light."

"Okay." She's got my blackout curtains pulled shut. All I can see is her dark silhouette. "Listen…"

"No," she says, clearing her throat. "Don't say anything else. Let me say my piece, then I'll leave."

I sigh. "Fine."

Her dark shape turns. I know she's facing me. "You're a fucking asshole, Carter."

I want to say uh-huh. But I remain quiet.

"While I remember talking about our relationship initially, I assumed things changed when you gave me keys to your condo."

Oh, shit. "About that—"

"Shut up. Let me finish."

Oookay.

"As I was saying. I assumed things changed when you gave me the keys. I shouldn't have expected anything from you other than your cock, I guess."

No, she shouldn't have.

"You gave me gifts."

"For Christmas."

"Where I met your family."

"Oh, that's right."

"And then there were gifts on Valentine's Day, asshole. What was I supposed to think?"

"I'm sorry if things were confusing for you, Natalia." Shit. I sent her a box of Omaha Steaks for Christmas. I sent everyone a box of Omaha Steaks for Christmas. It's more efficient to buy in bulk. *Jesus.* Meat does not a relationship make. As for Valentine's Day? I sent her candy and carnations, I think. They sure as fuck weren't roses.

"God, you're not going to let me finish, are you?" She's standing now.

I watch her bend down and reach for her shoes. She slips them on. Walking to the chair in the corner, she grabs her dress.

When she stops in front of me, I can finally see her face. There's mascara running down her cheeks. She looks kind of crazy.

"Fuck you, Carter."

Stomping past me, she makes her way down the hall and down the stairs. I follow. When she gets to the front door, I've got to say something.

"Natalia?" I say softly.

She turns, and her face isn't as angry. It looks hopeful. "Yes?"

"My T-shirt. You're still wearing my shirt." Don't judge. It's my favorite Bears T-shirt. I need it.

And there goes her hopeful expression. She drops her dress and the purse she got from somewhere, reaches down and pulls the tee off, and throws it at my face. "There. Happy?"

I am, but I keep my mouth shut. She picks up her dress and purse, and I watch as she steps out my front door in nothing but her hot pink heels. She's not even getting dressed? She stomps to her car, and I can't help thinking she looks sort of hot doing that. Then I shake my head.

She stomps back toward me. I'm prepared for a slap, but that doesn't happen. Instead, she reaches inside the door to grab her shopping bags. Which reminds me.

"Natalia?" I'm about to ask for my black card back but think better of it. I'll just call and cancel it. It'll be easier that way.

She whips around to glare at me. "What?"

"Nothing. Never mind."

Scoffing, she marches to her two-seater convertible, tossing the bags into the passenger seat. She hops in, starts the engine, and whips around my circular driveway, past that ugly-as-fuck fountain. I've got to get rid of that thing. I hit the button for the gate to expedite her departure, making a mental note to change the password to the gate, and watch her ride off into the sunset, completely nude. "She's gonna get a ticket," I say, shaking my head as I go back inside. Pulling my phone out of my pocket, I shoot a text to my agent and attorney to ask him to cancel the card and get the condo keys back from Natalia. I'll give her a couple of weeks to find another place but that's it. See? Done.

I know what you're thinking. You're thinking I'm the biggest asshole in the world. But I was always honest with her. I never felt like Natalia was my girlfriend. Apparently, she wanted more from me, but I couldn't give it. Not to her. Maybe I did give her a couple of gifts, but they meant nothing. That assumption is on her. All I know is I can't keep sleeping with Natalia when all I can think about is the curvy artist living next door. That's not fair...to Vivien.

Vivien. That name suits her far better. When I hear it, it makes me think of a classic beauty. She's definitely a Vivien. I don't get why she doesn't use it.

CHAPTER NINETEEN

VIVIEN

BACK IN MY NEW APARTMENT, I do my best to keep busy so I can stop thinking about what happened at the big house. Did they break up, or are they making up in his bed right now? I have no right or reason to be hopeful. It has nothing to do with me.

I keep busy by cleaning the kitchen and bathrooms. I snoop in cupboards and closets. When I discover a front-loading, stackable washer and dryer, I nearly orgasm. I've got laundry facilities? That's like discovering there really is a Santa Claus. I never have to lug my shit to a laundromat again. *Halle-fucking-lujah.*

Once those rooms are clean and I've got a load of laundry going, I eat a bowl of Cap'n Crunch for lunch while I lounge on my big sofa. Flipping on the television, I see I've got cable. Scrolling through the list of channels, I note I also have those paid movie channels. "This place has it all."

The television has a DVR and OnDemand. Awesome. I click his DVR to see what kinds of things Mr. Corcoran likes to watch. I scroll through the list and snicker. Among the '80s comedies and sports movies lies porn. Lots and lots of porn. I search the titles and snicker some more. *Edward Penishands?* He watched that? I read on. *Tropical Stormy, Forrest Hump, Bootylicious, and TITanic.* That last one makes me laugh out loud. There are more listed, but I've seen enough. For now, anyway.

I turn off the TV and move into the kitchen to wash my bowl and spoon, prepping them for supper. I look around the room and think a to-do list is in order. I really just want to go work in the studio, but I need to unpack and at least begin researching how to jump start a nonprofit foundation. I swallow a lump. I'm nervous. The guy barely knows me, but he trusts me to spearhead his foundation.

"No pressure, Viv," I mutter.

Oh, hell, when I did I start referring to myself as Vivien?

At the kitchen counter, I pull out my laptop and start with Google. I type in Carter Corcoran. When I hit Enter, the page fills with images and sites dedicated to information about the man himself. I gape at the extent to which the internet has paid homage to him. I scroll down the list of sites and click on a Twitter account called: Carter Corcoran Fan Club. I become a follower. I might as well. I've already got my panties in a twist over him. That makes me a fan, right?

After reading more trivia about Carter, I clear the search and type, How to start a nonprofit foundation. I hit Enter. A list of sites appears with information on my new job. There are ten websites to look through. I scan a few, jotting down notes, and save the search to my favorites.

"Phew, that's enough for one day." I chuckle at myself. I'm ready to get my hands dirty.

I make my way into the studio to check out the three small pots I made on the wheel in the middle of the night. It relaxed me—the sensation of smooth wet clay spinning in my hands is the most blissful feeling on the planet. To me, anyway. I grab some white clay without grog, easiest to throw with, and set to work. I feel like making some tall pieces. His kick wheel is smaller, so I'll be able to stand when I need to pull the pot up. Clay ready, I center it on the wheel and wet the clay. Using my hands and the spinning momentum, I draw the clay up and out. As I'm about to push inside, I hear a voice.

"I thought I'd find you in here."

Startled, I accidentally hit the side of the clay, making it tumble down. "Shit, Carter. Don't sneak up on me like that."

"Sneak up? The door slammed. You must have been lost in it."

He gets it. How the process of making art can draw you in. "Yeah. I was."

"Can I watch? I'll be quiet." He winks.

"Sure. I'll talk you through what I'm doing."

"Okay." He pulls up a stool until he's right next to the wheel.

He's so close I can smell him. Earthy, musky, manly. Delicious. Shaking my head, I do my best to focus on the task at hand. "You're going to get clay on your clothes."

He shrugs, so I start. As I work, I tell him what I'm doing, making sure to teach him important terminology along the way. If he understands the basic terms and processes, teaching him will be easier. When I'm done, I've created a vase about eighteen inches high with a slightly fluted top edge. I explain to him that I'll work on the vase more when it dries. "That's called leather hard."

He nods. "It won't break?"

"There's always that possibility. If I let it get bone dry, it's more likely to break. After I'm done, I'll let it dry completely, and we'll do a bisque fire."

"What's that?"

"It's the first firing, before glaze. But there's also the option of underglaze. I could use that before I bisque fire."

"What's the difference?"

"Appearance, and you can often get better details if you use underglaze. It all depends."

"There's a lot to this. Am I going to be able to learn it all?"

I laugh. "Of course, but we'll start at the beginning and see where it takes us."

He smiles until his dimple appears. "I'd like that."

"Okay, well, it's set." I stand up from the wheel. "Let me clean this up, and you can try it."

"Cool."

An hour later, Carter is one frustrated hotty. "Goddammit. Why won't this thing stop wiggling around on me?"

"You don't have it centered. You've got to have it solidly placed in the center of the wheel. Otherwise, physics takes over."

"Physics?"

"Centrifugal force."

"Well, the fucking force isn't with me."

I giggle, but when Carter glares at me, I stop. "Here, let's do it together." I reach my hands out and place them on the clay. "Put your hands over mine."

I feel like we're reenacting that scene from the movie *Ghost*. When he places his hands on top of mine, that zinging sensation works its way right to my nipples. The damn traitors.

Ignoring my impure thoughts, I say, "I have to use my upper body strength to force the clay into submission. See how I press my arms into my sides. That gives me support and stability. Next, I want to press the clay down onto the bat." I point to the plate the clay is spinning on, then add water to the clay. "That way I can get it to really stick. We need a good seal." I show him how to press the clay up into a tall cone shape. "We're pulling up the clay and need to keep adding water so it doesn't stick to our hands." Adding more water, I show him how to use his hands to center the clay by pushing it back down. We do this several times until the clay spins perfectly. "Okay, now. It's centered. Let's see you make something."

As he works, his face is so serious he looks almost fierce as he battles the unruly clay. I talk to him as he works, and he does as I instruct. By the time he's finished, he's made a bowl.

"Cereal bowl." He beams. "I made myself a cereal bowl."

"You did. It looks amazing, Carter. Congratulations on your first clay piece."

He stands up to his full height and wraps his big, muddy arms around me. "Thanks, Vivien. That was cool. I think I'll try it again."

"All right, I'm going to head home." I chuckle. "I've got a new job to start tomorrow. I don't want to be late for my first day." I wink at him, feigning confidence.

"Oh, right. We need to get started on the foundation." Carter almost looks disappointed.

I hesitate before leaving. "You want to start right away, don't you?" I hope so. I need the money.

"Sure. We'll talk about it tomorrow. How's that?"

Talk about it? What's going on? "I've already made a list of things to do."

"Before you start that, let me make some calls, babe."

Babe? Calls? I'm confused again. I shrug, "Whatever. Just let me know." I march to my door. Home in less than a minute. The shortest, most awesome commute in history.

———

A SHOUT WAKES me from a deep sleep. I blink, trying to get my bearings. I'm still not familiar with my new digs. This bed either. It's like a big fluffy cloud and so frigging comfortable I think I fell asleep as soon as my head hit the pillow. I keep still to listen. It was probably just a dream.

When I hear noise coming from the other side of the wall, from the pottery studio, I stiffen. Releasing air, I realize it's probably Carter. Sliding out of bed, I check the clock. "At two in the morning?"

Stepping into the hallway, I open the door to the studio. Carter is still sitting at the wheel.

"Carter?" I say sleepily.

"Oh, shit. Did I wake you up?"

Yes. "Sort of."

"Sorry. I was just excited. I finally made something by myself."

I walk over to him and look down at the wheel. It's another bowl. A large bowl with very irregular edges, but it looks sort of cool like that. "I like it," I say, smiling. I pat his shoulder. "You did great, Carter."

He turns to me with the biggest, brightest smile yet. "It took me forever, but once I got the centering part figured out, it worked. You're a great teacher, babe."

Babe again? It must be just something he says to everyone. "Aw, shucks. You're embarrassing me, Carter."

Turning his big body away from the wheel, he looks into my eyes. "I'm serious, Vivien."

I meet his gaze. "Thanks, Carter. You're a good student."

That's the way we stay for a good fifteen seconds. Just staring at each other. If I weren't half asleep, I'd think it was uncomfortable, but since I am, it isn't. What it is, though, is turning me on.

His eyes have moved south down my neck, hesitating at my breasts, then down to my feet. "Nice outfit."

I shrug. "It's what I sleep in."

"I like it."

Okaaaay, I'm waking up now.

His eyes have made their way back to my chest, then up again. "I *really* like it."

So, yeah. I'm braless. No surprise. Who sleeps in their bra? It's not like I'm wearing some kind of slinky lingerie. I'm not. I'm wearing a black tank top and gray shorts. Nothing special, but Carter seems to like it.

"Thank you," I mumble, because I'm trying to end this awkward moment. Crossing my arms in front of me self-consciously, I add, "It's late. Shouldn't you be back at the McMansion with your girlfriend?"

I don't know why I said that. I think it's my roundabout way of asking about earlier today.

"She's gone." Standing up from the wheel, he wipes his hands on his shirt, pulling it tight against his flat abs as he goes.

"Oh."

"And she was never my girlfriend."

"Was?"

"Was. I ended things."

"Oh."

"Yeah. Oh."

He steps closer, and I back up. He takes another step closer. I step back. My breathing has picked up. "Carter?"

"Yeah?"

I step back once more but stop when my back makes contact with something solid. I look over my shoulder and see it's one of the large wooden tables. "What're you doing?"

Pressing his body against mine, he places his arms on the counter on either side of me. He's warm. "Honestly, I don't know what I'm doing."

Clearing my throat, I attempt to gather myself. "You don't?"

He shakes his head. "All I know is I can't stop thinking about you."

"You can't?"

He shakes his head again. "That kiss. Back at your apartment."

With a breathy voice, I respond, "Yeah. That was a good kiss."

"Just good?"

"Yeah."

Carter chuckles in that deep, rich sound that makes my body come alive. "Well, I don't want you to think my abilities in the kissing arena are mediocre."

"At best." I smirk. I feel sort of empowered. This guy, this man, is way out of my league, but for some reason, he's attracted to me.

Carter's hand has moved from the counter on my right to the back of my head. He's swirling his thumb around at the base of my neck. God, it feels good. Gathering myself, I need to stay focused. His lips get close to mine as one of his palms finds my ass. I breathe in his scent. It's normally manly and musky, but now you can add the smell of earth, clay. It's an aphrodisiac for me.

Carter's hand leaves my neck and joins his other one on my ass. He squeezes it like he can't control himself. His long, hard dick is digging into my belly. The sensation of his hands caressing me is making me wet and needy. I want to climb him.

"That is a bad idea," I mumble. Because it is. He squeezes my bottom again, and I have to concentrate. "Definitely. Bad idea."

His forehead touches mine. Sighing, he says, "We shouldn't?"

"No, probably not."

Carter still has one big warm hand on my ass, but his right

hand moves up my back, running up and down in a soothing way. I'd love to tell him to stop, but I can't. He leans down and kisses the tip of my nose.

"You're beautiful, Vivien. Inside and out."

I know I should punch his pretty jaw for calling me Vivien, but the way he said it, akin to a whisper, so personal and sweet... I embrace it. From his lips, I love hearing my real name.

CHAPTER TWENTY

VIVIEN

I MUST HAVE HIT the snooze on my phone alarm fifty times, because now I've overslept.

"Damn it!" I wanted to get up bright and early so I could get a jump start on the foundation. I look at the clock and see it reads 10:32. "Shit."

If I hadn't lain awake until four in the morning thinking about Carter and our almost kiss... I was honest when I told him it was a bad idea, but I was hella disappointed when he agreed so easily. We ended our moment by agreeing to be friends. *Just* friends. Ugh. I'm always just a friend.

Rolling out of bed, I make myself a bowl of cereal, gobble it down, and jump in the shower. I need to hurry. I bet Carter's been up for hours waiting for me to get my lazy ass out of bed. Out of the shower, I rub the towel over my short hair and finger comb it. Done. Wiping off my body, I dress in a T-shirt dress I bought at Old Navy on super clearance. I slide on some flip-flops and am out the door in no time.

On the deck at his patio door, I take in the view. "So pretty." I breathe in the fresh air and smile at my new life. "Not bad, Viv. Not bad at all." I knock on the glass pane of the patio door and wait. Yes, I know the code, but I'm reluctant to just go in without knocking. What if he's walking around naked? Oh, shit. That'd be a sight to see, wouldn't it?

I knock again and wait. Rolling my eyes, I type in his jersey number twice and wait for the beep. I turn the knob and step into his open plan kitchen, dining, and great room.

"Carter?" I say in my normal voice. I take several more steps in and call louder, "Carter!"

When I hear nothing, I move up to the kitchen island. "Carter!" I start to pull out a chair to sit down when I'm startled out of my skin by Carter at my back.

"What's up?"

"Jesus, you scared the crap out of me. Where'd you come from?"

He steps around the kitchen island to stand in front of me setting down a huge binder with the Giants logo on top.

I let my eyes wander up his right arm and nearly choke from my gasp. *Whoa-fucking-whoa.* Carter is wearing only sweat pants. That's right, ladies, no shirt. His stomach looks like it's carved from beautiful marble. Michelangelo would so dig this guy. But that's not the part that has my panties practically melting off. No, it's not that he's shirtless. It's his face that made me moan just now. It's because... oh, God, I can barely contain my vibrating lady parts. It's because he's wearing glasses. And not just any glasses. *Nerd* glasses, ladies. Holy crap. I can die happy now. The only thing that would be better than this is if the pants were gone. But even then, it's not necessary. So, in conclusion, let me just say that I will never see anything or anyone as beautiful as this man right here, right now.

I look at his face and see him smirking. He caught me. I might as well tell him. He should know it's like my fricking kryptonite. So, I do. "Holy shit, Carter. You look hot in glasses."

Chuckling, he holds the frames like he's going to take them off.

No. Please no.

"Yeah? You like them?"

"I do. Any red-blooded woman or gay man would."

He looks to his right, then back at me. "Natalia hated them."

"Yeah, well, she's an idiot." I'm staring, sure my eyes are bugging out of my head. *Attractive, Viv. Real attractive.* I've got to get the hell out of here before I try to lick those glasses off his face. Time to change the subject. "I knocked."

"Sorry, I was in my office." He nods down at his binder.

"I'm ready to start work."

"Work?"

"Yes. The foundation."

"Oh." He runs his fingers through his hair. "About that."

Uh-oh. What's going on?

He looks at me sheepishly. "I'm not ready. I need to make some calls first."

"Carter, I need to work. I've got bills to pay."

"I'll start paying you today." He reaches around to his back pocket and pulls out his wallet. "How much do you need?"

This is *not* how it's supposed to work. Correction. This is not how it's *going* to work. I'm not a freeloader. I won't take money from this guy for doing nothing. "I haven't done any work. I haven't earned any money." I slide off the stool and stand with my hands to my sides.

"Consider it an advance."

"No."

"No? Why not?"

I need to keep my irritation at bay. He doesn't know me, so I can't expect him to understand my reluctance to take money I haven't earned. Money I don't deserve. Sighing, I place my hands on the edge of the counter. "Look. If you're not ready, I'll just go get a part-time job until you are. I won't take your money until I'm doing something to earn it."

"That's ridiculous."

"No, it's not."

"Yes, it is. Call it a retainer, then."

"I'm not an attorney."

"Kai was right."

I raise one eyebrow, waiting for his next words. I hope he chooses them carefully.

"You're stubborn as hell."

I cross my arms over my chest. "So?"

I watch as Carter crosses his own arms, mirroring my defiant stance. The pressure from the move has forced his biceps out so they're even bigger than before. "So, you'd rather job hunt than just wait a day or two for me to get my shit together?"

"If need be, yes."

He lowers his arms and places his hands on the breakfast bar. Leaning forward, he smirks. "I'll make some calls today. We'll start tomorrow."

"Fine," I say with a small smile.

"Fine." He nods. "In the meantime, my brothers are coming up to hang out by the pool today. They've requested your presence. Apparently, you're more fun than me."

"I think I've got some room in my schedule. Let me know when they get here."

He looks up at the clock hanging in his kitchen. "They'll be here in less than an hour, so go suit up."

"Yes, sir." I salute. "And make those calls. I need to work."

"Aye, aye," he grumbles.

I leave through the patio door and head down the steps, all the while wondering where the hell I put my swimsuit. Yeah. I know—first world problems.

———

OKAY, I've got good news and I've got bad news. You want the good news first? I found my swimsuit. The bad news? I bought it about thirty pounds ago when I thought I'd start lap swimming for fitness. I release an internal snort at that ridiculous notion. So, yeah, I've got a swimsuit. It's one of those racer-back ones that was tight when I bought it. It's supposed to fit tight to your body for more aerodynamics. (Internal snort number two.)

I step into the legs of the thing and pull, getting the openings to midthigh, where it stops. I tug on the straps until the leg holes make it to the right locations. Now, here's the tricky part: getting the damn swimsuit over my big butt and ginormous boobs. I grasp the sides and start to wiggle back and forth. When I've got it pulled up to my waist, I accidentally let go. I hear a loud snap and seconds later, pain. OMG, it hurts. A lot. I bend at the waist and regret it because I can't breathe. Breathing is important.

Standing up, I look down. My body is pouring out of the suit. It has pushed my stomach up and out, giving me the muffin top that ends all muffin tops. I turn to gaze into the mirror and I'm torn. Should I laugh or cry? Laugh. I choose to laugh. I look like a balloon that someone has squeezed in the middle, forcing both ends to fill with air to near-bursting. The leg holes are so tight, I think I've lost feeling in my extremities. My lady parts are dangerously close to being squished, making me concerned I won't be able to have children, let alone use those parts for fun. *It's not worth it.* I grasp the suit at my waist and push down. I've started sweating, which is making this thing stick to me. I dig my thumbs between the suit and my hips and push again. Wiggling frantically, I'm finally able to get the damn thing off.

"Stupid swimsuit." I'm tempted to throw it away, but I

distinctly remember it costing me a pretty penny. Once it's off, I toss it behind me. "Now what?"

I decide my only option is to wear clothes to the pool. I step up to my dresser and find an old bra I can wear under a tank top. Digging through the drawer that holds my shorts, I find a pair of athletic shorts. They're tight too, and short, but at least I can breathe in them. It'll have to do.

CHAPTER TWENTY-ONE

CARTER

STANDING in my kitchen choking down a protein drink, I hear a knock. I walk to my front door expecting to see Johnson and Clinton. As I open it, I say, "You don't have to knock, ass—" I stop midsentence when I see her. "Natalia? What're you doing here?"

"Carter? It's nice to see you too." She steps around me and through my foyer to my living room. Sitting daintily on the big leather chair, she crosses her long legs, making her already short skirt slide up further. Placing one hand on her knee, she gestures to the sofa nearest her.

I step into the living room but don't sit down. There's no need. She'll be leaving any minute. "What can I do for you, Natalia?"

Standing up, she moves toward me. "I came back to give you another chance."

Another chance? "That's big of you."

"Well, I don't think I'd put it that way. There's nothing big about me." She titters. "What I mean, or what I decided, is that it'd be a shame if we weren't at least friends."

"Friends?" She wants to be friends? Men and women can't

be friends. Well, at least those who are sexually attracted to one another can't be friends. It's a fact.

"Of course. We had fun together, didn't we?"

I give her a disbelieving stare. I wouldn't call our arrangement fun. I wouldn't even call it satisfying, to be honest. Sure, the sex was okay....

"I mean outside of bed, silly," she says with a giggle. "We had fun at parties and such. I'd hate to lose your friendship. Don't you feel the same?"

She's now less than a foot away from me. She's been slowly slinking closer as she speaks. Her hand reaches out and rests on my forearm. "I don't think our arrangement had anything to do with friendship, Natalia." I mean, I hang with my friends. I *like* my friends. There's not a lot to like about Natalia's personality.

"Arrangement?" she says in a pitch higher than normal. "Relationship. That's what it's called when you *date* someone for over a year." She practically spits out the word *date*.

She's still angry. I get it. "Semantics."

"Carter, you don't think we can be friends?" Her voice has softened to nearly a whisper. It makes me feel guilty. "Or is it that you're unwilling to try?"

It's definitely the second one, but I can't say it. There's something about her expression. Vulnerable. She looks vulnerable. Sincere. Can Natalia be sincere? I think not. My theory is she realized my card was canceled, so now she's back. Ben, my attorney-slash-agent, let me know that part of the process had been completed last night. Before I can respond to her claim, the patio door opens and Reggie steps in wearing the tiniest tank top and shorts I've ever seen.

"Jesus," I mutter.

"Oh!" Vivien squeaks. "I didn't mean to barge in."

"Sure you didn't," sneers Natalia.

Viv looks from me to Natalia, then back to me. "I'm sorry to interrupt." She turns to leave just as the front door flies open.

"Pool party!" yells my baby brother from the front entry. "Where's the beer?" When he steps into the living room, he sees the three of us. "Oh."

Johnson pulls up behind him. He seems to choose to ignore whatever is going on with me and the two women. "Are we swimming or what?" He turns to Vivien. "Hey, beautiful. Ready to swim?"

Reggie beams at my big brother, and it pisses me off. "Sure. Let's go."

Ignoring Natalia and me as he passes, Johnson says, "Clinton, grab the beer from the fridge." He follows her through the patio door, yelling, "And some chips. I'm hungry."

CHAPTER TWENTY-TWO

AWKWARD. That's what I'd call this supposed pool party. I'm not sure what's going on with Carter and Natalia, but she's here, in a tiny red bikini. She must have known about the party. How else would she know to bring a suit?

I look down at myself to see my makeshift swimwear. None of the guys have mentioned it, but Natalia has made some offhanded remarks about my tank and shorts when the guys weren't around, like, "Couldn't find a swimsuit in your size?" and "I think there's a Lane Bryant in the Arboretum mall. I'm sure they'd have your size there."

Number one, Lane Bryant is a great store. I've purchased many a sexy top and jeans at that store—on the clearance rack, of course. I'm not caked like Mr. Moneybags. And number two, whenever she says shit like that, all I want to do is punch her in the throat. Is that wrong? Yes. But, I don't care. She's got no right. I'm nothing to her. Sure, Carter tried to kiss me last night, but we both decided to be friends. Friends with no benefits whatsoever.

"Hey, Reggie. Get in. The water's nice and warm," Clinton says, bobbing up and down in the deep water.

"Sure. Why not?"

"I know why not," mutters Natalia under her breath. "As soon as your white tank gets wet, they're going to see all that flab."

Yeah, she's sitting next to me. She plopped her boney ass down as soon as she stepped onto the pool deck. Getting away from her is reason enough to get in the water.

I move to the edge of the pool and dip my toe. I wouldn't call it warm, but it's not freezing cold. Just then, I feel myself being launched forward, right in the pool. She pushed me. That bitch pushed me. I frantically swim to the top, gasping for air. Water went up my nose, causing my eyes to burn. Damn. It hurts. I blink the water out of my eyes in time to see Johnson standing over Natalia. I can't hear what he's saying since I've got water caught in my ear canal. Shaking my head side to side, I finally free up one ear.

"She could have been hurt. Hell, we don't even know if she can swim."

"Oh, don't be so dramatic. She's big. She'll float."

"You're such a rude bitch," snaps Clinton from the edge of the pool. "Why are you even here? I thought this was bro time."

"Clinton," growls Carter. "Not now."

I look over and see Carter sitting on the edge of the pool not far from me.

"You invited *her*." Natalia points at me. "She's not a bro, unless I'm missing something."

I look over at Carter, who remains silent. But Clinton doesn't.

"She's more woman than you'll ever be."

"Thank God for that. If I got *that* fat, someone shoot me."

"No problem," grumbles Johnson. "Let me get my gun."

"Enough!" shouts Carter. "Natalia, if you're going to be a bitch, you can leave."

I turn back to her. This is like a soap opera. She sticks out her bottom lip in a pout. "Carter, baby, I was just kidding."

"Don't pout, and definitely don't call me baby. We're friends. Remember? Just friends."

Well, damn. Just like he and I are *just* friends.

"Come on, Reggie. Let's go sit in the hot tub," says Clinton as he swims up to me. "You okay?"

"Sure." I swim over to the steps near the in-ground hot tub. As I step out of the water, my shorts pull down slightly. I grab them to keep them up. Turning toward the hot tub, I see Carter. His hands are covering his face. I also hear him mutter, "Jesus."

He must still be frustrated over everything that just happened. I look up and see Clinton and Johnson staring at me. "What?"

"Nothing, doll. Nothing," says Johnson with a chuckle. "Let's hot tub."

I take three steps down into the warm bubbly whirlpool and moan. I hear Carter again. "Jesus."

"What's wrong with him?" I say, pointing my thumb backward.

"He's a dumb shit."

I look at Johnson. "That's why he's muttering to himself? Because he's a dumb shit?" It makes no sense.

"Pretty much," agrees Clinton. "Come here, beautiful. Sit by me."

I scoot closer to him and sit right in front of a jet. "Oh, God," I moan. "That feels amazing." I look up and all three men are staring at me again. "What?"

"Nothing," Clinton and Johnson say simultaneously.

I shrug and sink down further. It feels so good. That is, until a skinny leg steps into the water. What the ever-loving...

"I thought I'd join you boys."

"Great." I think that was Johnson. Hard to tell with the noisy motor of the whirlpool.

Carter follows close behind Natalia. As she scoots to make room for him, he moves past her to sit next to me. Her scowl does not go unnoticed. By me, anyway.

This pool party is so *fun*. That was sarcasm, by the way.

CHAPTER TWENTY-THREE

CARTER

THE POOL PARTY IS A CLUSTERFUCK. Natalia ruined it for everyone. She's always been like that at group events. She hates the WAGs (wives and girlfriends) of my teammates. She only seems to be able to befriend men, as if she's jealous of the women and in direct competition with them. Don't get me wrong, I'm not excusing her for all the shit she said to Vivien today. (Yeah, I heard most of the barbs.) I'm not. It's bullshit.

Before she leaves, I pull her aside and tell her my feelings on the matter. "Natalia, if you're serious about being my friend, then you'll leave Vivien alone. She's just working for me. She's not a threat to you."

I don't think I said it right, because she slithers up to me, wrapping her arms around my neck in an attempt to kiss me, and says, "What a relief. For a second I thought you found her attractive. But, I should have known you'd never go for someone who looks like the Stay Puft Marshmallow Man."

I take her wrists in my hands and pull them down, gently. "See, right there. That's completely uncalled for. Just because she's not model-thin—"

She scoffs. "Not even close."

Sighing in frustration, I release her hands, step up to the front door, and open it for her. "Natalia. My friends don't say those kinds of things about other people." Especially people like Vivien.

"Fine." She slips past me. Turning, she gives me a flirty wave. "Call me."

No. I'm not going to call her. "Take care." I hope that's enough. What else do I need to say?

My brothers left an hour ago, and Vivien went back to her place. I take the steps up to my studio two at a time. I need to paint. I'm frustrated and confused. Painting always relaxes my mind. I search for a new canvas and choose one that's about twenty-four by thirty-six inches. I move the easel around until I'm facing the windows. My view of the studio is directly in front of me, but I'm not going to paint the landscape today. No, today I'm just going to paint. I don't care if it looks like anything. I just want to smell the oil paint, feel it move beneath my brush, and let myself go.

Once my palette is ready, I pick up a golden-brown color. Just like Vivien's eyes. I'm not sure why that thought came to mind, but it did. Next, I sweep up a glob of light yellow, like her hair. It's actually darker than her platinum locks, but it'll do. I continue to work that way, thinking of colors that remind me of her. Pink for her lips, black for that tantalizing lip ring, and red for passion. Her passion for art is one of the sexiest things about her.

When my canvas is covered in paint, I set the brush down and stare. It's abstract. Colorful, like the woman I just met who has changed me somehow. It's like she's given me permission to be creative. My family has always supported me in whatever I was doing, but not until now have I felt that being an artist was okay.

I take that back, Casey made me feel that way. Hell, she's

the one who inspired me to try it in the first place. So, since she died, Vivien is the first person to make me think it can be a bigger part of my life.

I leave the canvas out to dry as I clean up my tools and paints. All of a sudden, I'm starving. Hell, when was the last time I ate? I make my way downstairs and pour a bowl of cereal. Stepping out on my deck, I watch the sun going down in the distance. Turning to look at the studio, I notice a light on inside. She's working too.

———

I OPEN the door to the studio and see her standing at one of the long tables doing something to a hunk of clay. It almost looks like she's kneading dough.

"Hey," I say as I approach.

"Hey, Carter," she says, grunting as she presses the clay onto the table.

"What're you doing?"

"Wedging."

"Wedging?"

"Yeah, you do this before working with clay because it forces out air bubbles that could be caught inside."

"Air bubbles are bad, I take it."

"If you have an air bubble in your clay and you fire it, the pressure will build up inside the bubble and pop or explode once it gets to be too much."

"Wow. That's kind of cool."

She stops moving and looks at me. "Not when you've spent two weeks on a piece, it isn't. It pretty much shatters everything. Putting it back together is not possible."

"I see." I'd hate for one of my bowls to blow up in the kiln. I'm damn proud of them.

"So, you want to work on the wheel again?"

"Nah, show me something else."

I spend the next hour learning how to use something called a slab roller, along with the process of scoring or scratching up the clay and adding slip or liquid clay so I can attach two pieces of clay together. She explains how clay shrinks as it dries and brushing slip on the clay and scoring it keeps the two pieces together. I get it. It's like gluing stuff together. By the time she's done with her lesson, I've attached shapes I cut out with cookie cutters to a square piece of clay—a tile. It looks sort of ridiculous, but I understand the concepts.

"You could attach shapes to your bowls from last night. They're both still wet enough to do that."

I look over at my first bowl sitting on a shelf. "No, thanks. I want to keep them as is." I smile at her. "I like 'em."

"Me too. You did great on the wheel."

"I think I prefer that over this," I say, pointing down at my tile.

"Well, then focus on the wheel for a while. You can make more bowls, plates, cups, and vases. Stuff like that." She shrugs.

"Cool." Wiping off my hands, I return my unused clay to the airtight bag.

I watch her work on her own project, using only her hands to form the clay into thin snake-like pieces. In the hour since I got here, she's turned those snakes into a really cool vase. She's using slip and scoring too. Her process is much more time consuming and way more interesting than my tile. She's so engrossed in her work, she doesn't even realize I'm staring at her. Or the fact that she's got a glob of clay on the tip of her pretty nose. Her hands are covered with the stuff too, but so are mine. It's a messy medium to work with, but it's almost therapeutic, that feel of wet earth between my fingers. I take a moment to really look at her. She's wearing her college tee again. Now it's going to have even more stains on it, but that's part of making art. It's messy, like life can be, which is weird because my life is all about structure, routine, rigidity. Art is the antithesis of that. Just like Vivien's the antithesis of my usual woman. Not that there's anything wrong with that. There's not. As a matter of fact, I've never felt so at peace with another person, especially a woman. Not even my family. Hell, I've never been with a woman who could stand to ruin her nails.

Reggie's different—layered and interesting. One minute she's giving me sass about *earning* her money rather than taking it; the next, she's quietly making something beautiful.

"Can I ask you something?"

I'm pulled from my thoughts by her voice. "Sure."

She's stopped working, observing me instead. "Did you invite Natalia today?"

"No. She showed up uninvited." *Should I say more?*

"She had a swimsuit."

"She had extra clothes in her car after a photo shoot, including that suit." I look at her. "I'm sorry about today, Vivien. She was especially cruel to you."

Her face turns pink. "I don't care about that. I'm used to women like her. Just..."

I wait, but she's hesitating. "Just what?"

Looking down at the table as she plays with lumps of clay, she says, "Next time you invite her to stuff, could you let me know? I'd like to avoid her if at all possible. Don't misunderstand. It's none of my business who you hang with or date or whatever; I don't mean that. This is your home. I'd just prefer not to interact with her." She's chattering quickly like she's trying force the words out as fast as possible.

"No."

Her head rises quickly. "No?"

"No. I mean, yes, of course I'll let you know. I didn't know she was going to show up. She wants to be friends. But, we're not dating. Hell, we never 'dated,'" I say with air quotes.

"Oh. Like I said. It's none of my business." She's no longer looking at me. Avoiding eye contact is more like it.

"Now can I ask *you* something?"

She shrugs.

"When she was saying all of those bitchy things, why didn't you stand up for yourself?"

She stops working and meets my gaze. "Carter, I'm essentially a guest here. I didn't feel comfortable making a scene."

"But..."

"But nothing. I told you once that I don't bother with people like Natalia. She's not worth my time and energy. It wouldn't make any difference anyway. She's going to say what she wants to say. She's your girlfriend. I learned a long time ago that crying and whining about life is pointless. Nothing will change people like Natalia. People still say and do mean things. It's just a fact of life."

"First of all, she's not my girlfriend," I growl. I'm getting damn tired of people saying she is.

"Then why didn't *you* say anything?"

"I did. I asked her to stop being a bitch."

She rolls her eyes. "Okay. I guess you did." She's wedging more clay on the table.

Damn, I'm getting turned on watching her create. Clearing my throat, I say, "I think I'll head home. Thanks for the lesson, Reggie."

"No problem. See you later." She keeps her head down, focused on her work.

"Sure. Later."

CHAPTER TWENTY-FOUR

VIVIEN

SLEEP ESCAPES ME, so I call Kai. He's a night owl like me, so I know he'll be up after midnight.

"Hey, Viv. How's it going at the McMansion?"

I laugh, and it feels amazing. I miss my bestie. "Good. Confusing. Weird."

"So many adjectives there, sweetie. What's good, what's confusing, and why is it weird?"

"Carter is confusing. He tried to kiss me again."

"Again? You're keeping things from me. You'd better spill, bitch."

"Oh, right. You've been gone, remember? But, yes. He kissed me in front of Mona."

"You mean *Moan-ah?*" he says her name with a moaning sound.

Snickering, I say, "One and the same. When she got a look at Carter and his brothers, she—"

"Brothers? How many? Are they as gorgeous as the man himself?"

We've gone off the rails. He's no longer interested in the kiss since I mentioned brothers. "Two brothers. One older, one younger. Johnson is the older one, and Clinton is—"

"Johnson? Clinton? Are they all named after presidents, or what?"

"Their sister is Kennedy."

"Keep going. Describe them. In. Detail."

I laugh again, lying back on my pillow. Kai is perfect. He always knows what to say to make me laugh. "Johnson is the oldest. He's taller than Carter, blondish, with leaner muscles but he's still built."

"What about his face? Cuter than Carter?"

"He's cute. Definitely. His face isn't as angular as Carter's." I know he'll get what I'm saying. He does portraits. He looks at people's faces all the time. "He's really nice and quite a flirt."

"He was flirting with you?"

"Well, he's a flirt. I suspect he flirts with everyone."

"What about Clinton?"

"Shorter than the other two. He's adorable. His face is softer but still gorgeous. I could see your sister liking him."

"Kalani is too young to date," he says in a stern voice.

"She's in college. She's nineteen. Stop being a mother hen."

"Whatever. So, tell me more."

So I do. I tell him about my apartment, the studio, and the pool party from hell.

"I haven't met her, and I already hate her," Kai says.

"You'd love her shoes."

"Don't care. Anyone who talks to my Viv that way is dead to me. Manolo Blahniks be damned."

I tell him about the kiss in front of Mona and the almost kiss in the studio.

"He's got the hots for you."

"He does not. We're just friends."

"That's not my impression after he asked me about you at Giordano's."

"Huh? What happened there? I was with you the entire time."

"No. You went outside after one of your 'I support myself' tantrums."

Oh, yeah. I did. I stay quiet so he'll tell me more. I can't believe this. Is it possible that Carter Corcoran likes me? You know, *likes* me likes me?

"He pulled me aside and asked if you and I were dating."

I release a scoffing-slash-coughing sound.

"What?" He sounds defensive. "I'd do you."

"Kai. God, you're such a perv."

Ignoring my comment, he tells me about their conversation at the restaurant.

"I can't believe you didn't mention it before." It doesn't matter. Carter is two things: one, out of my league, and two, just my *friend*.

"You were busy. I was busy. You know now. He wanted to know if you were seeing anyone. And I told him no. I said a few other things, but you get the gist."

I don't even want to know what else he said. It doesn't matter. I know Kai's got my back. He always has my back.

After more gossip about SAIC and some mutual friends, we hang up, but not before I say, "I love you, Kai."

"I love you too, Viv. Sweet dreams, beautiful girl. Talk to you soon."

"Come up and visit soon."

"Will do. Mwah." He makes the kissing sound on his end.

Kai is just what I needed to clear my head, and I finally fall asleep after two in the morning. He keeps me grounded. On track. No matter where I've derailed.

WHEN I CHECKED in with Carter this morning, he told me he had to work out, then had a conference call with a trainer or something. We're supposed to have our first official work meeting at two o'clock. That's when I decided to get out of the house for a while. I'm getting kind of stir-crazy. It's also when Carter and I got into another argument. He thinks *I'm* the stubborn one.

"I'm going to run some errands, then."

"Where're you going?"

"Mall and around."

"How're you going to get there? The mall's at least eight miles from here."

"Bus." I shrug. "Or Uber if need be." Those are expensive though. "Until I get a scooter or something."

"A scooter? You're going to ride a scooter in the winter? Besides, I've got cars. Take one."

"No, Carter," I say, exasperated. Hands placed defiantly on my hips, I add, "You've got to stop."

"Stop what?"

"Henpecking, being high-handed, you know... bossy." *And stop trying to give me stuff.*

"I choose to ignore that last statement. I've got an old car—"

"No."

"Why not?"

"Because."

"Because why? Damn, you're stubborn, babe."

"Am not."

"Are too."

"I am *not*, Carter. It's okay for me to be self-sufficient. I don't want to rely on anyone. I'll just be disappointed."

"In me?" He seems saddened at my statement.

"No. I don't know. Maybe." He's flustering me. I feel my cheeks heat.

He shrugs. "No worries. If you change your mind, keys are hanging on the back hook by the entrance to the garage. Car's in there. 2006 Nissan Altima."

"That *is* old. For you."

"It was my first car. Drove it all through college. Her name is Alma."

"Wow, super creative name, Carter," I chide.

He shrugs. "It fits."

"Fine. If I change my mind, I'll consider taking Alma for a spin."

"I've also got a new Mercedes SLC class. It's—"

I quickly interrupt before he can say more. "No, thanks. I'm fine."

As I turn to leave through the front door, he calls, "Vivien, be careful. Remember to use the app for the gate. I programmed everything in there for you. And call me if you need me."

"Thanks, Carter." My hand on the door, I add, "I appreciate you checking on me." I really do. I don't remember the last time a man cared about me. Well, Kai. He's the exception.

"No problem. See you this afternoon."

Plopping my ass on a bench at the bus stop, I check the bus schedule again. I've got twenty minutes. Since I've got time to kill, I grab my phone and open up the Notes app to make a list. "I need to open a bank account somewhere nearby, and I'd like to check out my neighborhood." Bitch face mentioned a mall, so I think I'll check it out. I'm about to put my phone away when it hits me: "I need to call Mom. She has no idea I even moved." God, I'm a shitty daughter.

She answers on the second ring. "It's about time you called me, Vivien."

"Oh, sorry. I've been busy getting settled."

"Settled? Where?"

"South Barrington."

"South Barrington?" she squeaks. "Where in South Barrington?"

"What? You want the address?"

"That'd be great. I can Google-map you. I don't like not knowing where my children are living. What if you needed me in the middle of the night? I wouldn't even have an address for you. Anyway, what the heck are you doing there?"

"It's a long story."

She sighs heavily.

"I got a job."

"Oh? A teaching job?"

"Not exactly. It's related to art, though." *How do I explain the foundation? Carter wants to keep it a secret for now, anyway. He won't be able to keep it a secret for long.*

"In South Barrington?"

"Yeah. I live in the guest house, next to a majorly amazing pottery studio. I'll work from home."

"Who do you work for?"

"You don't know him."

"*Him?* Please tell me there's a *her* too." *Okay, here's the thing with my mom. She's gun-shy when it comes to men, thanks to my dad, so it makes sense that she'd pass along that fear to her children, to her daughters in particular. In her words, she "doesn't want to see us get hurt." Too late. If she had her druthers, all three of her children would be single for life. Ironically, she wants grandchildren. I don't know how you could have one without the other. Immaculate conception?*

"No, there's no *her*. Well, not technically. He's got a friend. She's a her." *Wow, way to talk, Reggie. She's a her?*

"Who is this man?" There's worry in her tone.

I pause to figure out a way to explain.

"Vivien?"

"Mom, there's nothing to worry about. He's not appealing in the least."

"Is he old?"

"Older." Than me. "Yeah."

There's a pause on the other end of the phone.

"Mom?"

"Oh, sorry. My mind wandered there for a minute. So, when can I come see this new place?"

"Soon? I'm just getting ready to start my new job today. As a matter of fact"—I see the bus approach—"I need to get going."

"Vivien Jayne."

Uh-oh, she only says both names when she's getting serious. Or mad.

"Yes?" I release a sigh.

"Tell me his name."

I'd growl in frustration but that will only encourage her. "Carter Corcoran."

"Thank you. I've got friends from my writing group from that area. I'll ask them if they know him."

"Mom?" I hear myself whine.

"Don't 'Mom' me. I need to know you're safe."

"I'll text you the address."

"You know I'm not good at the texting, Vivien." She sighs. "Fine. Text me the address, but call me for everything else. Leave a message if I'm busy."

"Sure thing."

"And Vivien, I'm going to plan a visit to see your new place soon. I'll bring dinner. How's that?" she asks tentatively.

"Sure. Just let me get the hang of things. Give me a week to get settled."

"Okay, honey. That sounds..."

"Mom."

"Oh, sorry. Yes. Let's do that. We need to get together. Have a chat."

Chat? My mom doesn't *chat*. Well, she does. Of course, she does. Everyone chats. It's just, when Mom says chat, it means she wants to *talk*. About something. Something unpleasant. Because if it weren't unpleasant, she'd just tell me now.

"Okay, Mom. Gotta run. Can't be late on my first day."

"Right. Love you. See you soon. Send me that address right away so you don't forget."

"I'll do it as soon as we hang up, Mom. Promise. Love you too."

Great. Now I'm freaked out about whatever it is Mom needs to tell me. "Shake it off," I mutter as I start a new text.

Me: My new pad: 17 ½ Star Lane. South Barrington, Il 60010

Mom: Thank you, sweetheart. I'll sleep much better knowing where you live. <3

Oh, yay. Mom's learning how to do emojis? I thought she said she didn't do "the texting." I slide my phone into my hobo bag as the bus hisses to a stop in front of me, then step on board, placing my money into the slot. Taking a seat in the front, I watch the stops pass one by one until I reach my destination.

CHAPTER TWENTY-FIVE

I CHECK my watch for the third time. "She'll be here any minute."

"I hope she's not going to be late like this a lot," Julia Mayfair says as she pulls her laptop from her bag. "There's a lot to do to get this off the ground. Punctuality is one of my must-haves."

"I know. She's not—" I hear the patio door open, then close. "In the dining room," I shout.

When Vivien crosses into the dining room, she looks at me, then Julia. "Oh, I didn't realize you had company. Should I come back?"

"Nope. This is Julia Mayfair. She's here to get this foundation off the ground."

"Oh." Vivien looks a little confused as she glances at Julia, then gathers herself quickly, stepping into the room.

"Let's sit down at the table." I hold a chair for Julia, and as I move toward Viv's, I see she's already seated.

Before I can ask her what's wrong, Julia says, "Now that we're *finally* all here," looking at Vivien.

Viv looks up at me. "You told me two o'clock."

"I did?" I thought I said one thirty, but I'm sure she's right.

"Yes." She crosses her arms and leans back in her seat.

I recognize the move. She's pissed.

Ignoring our back and forth, Julia continues. "Carter, you've told me something about your idea for the nonprofit you'd like to start." She leans down, pulling out a black binder with my name on the cover. Wow, she's efficient. "I've outlined the steps to start this venture." She looks at Vivien, then back at me. Viv still looks unhappy. With her thin brow arched, Julia adds, "You and I can go over this privately, if you'd like."

Does she sense Viv's irritation? "No. Let's do it now. I want Vivien to hear this too."

"Oh, well, if you insist." She opens the book and hands me a copy of the information. Since I'm sitting across from Vivien, she can't see what I see. I slide the papers to the center of the table and turn them so we can both read them.

"Vivien, would you mind taking notes of the meeting?" She looks at Viv with a smile.

Sighing, Viv leans forward. "Do you have paper and a pen?"

"Of course. *I'm* always prepared." Rummaging through her briefcase, she pulls out a leather-bound legal notebook and a fancy pen. "There you go. Next time, please have materials ready to work."

"Gee, thanks," Viv deadpans.

"You're very welcome. Okay," Julia says with a sigh. "As you can see from the bulleted list, there are several things we *must* do right away."

I read along the list as she says each aloud.

- Develop strategic goals and business plan.
- File for state and federal tax exemption: 501(c)(3).
- Get an EIN or tax ID number.
- File for charity solicitation registration.

- Develop a marketing strategy including logo, website, and other media and graphics identifiers.

I interrupt Julia. "I'd like Vivien to work on the logo." I turn to Viv. "Is that something you can do?"

"Sure," she says, never looking up at me.

"Oh, are you a graphic designer?"

"No." Viv finally looks up. "I'm a ceramicist."

"Oh, well, perhaps we should—"

I interrupt her before she can say we should hire someone else. "She's an artist. She'll do a great job." I want Vivien to create the logo.

Julia smiles. "Oh, well, that's great. One less thing to think about. Let's continue. We'll need to set up a corporate sponsorship program and develop a fundraising strategy and events."

"What do you mean by fundraising events?" Viv asks. "Carter doesn't want—"

Julia holds her hand up, halting Vivien midsentence. Placing that same hand over mine, she tilts her head in my direction and smiles. "I think you need to trust me on this, Carter. You don't want this to be funded entirely from your own money. It's a nonprofit. People love to donate to charities, especially if they get to meet a handsome athlete when they do." She squeezes my hand and returns to her list.

I look up at Viv, who has her eyes back on the papers in the middle of the table. I want her to look at me so she knows I appreciate her effort to defend my feelings as they relate to the foundation. We've talked about my vision for the foundation. She knows I hate formal fundraising shit; being dressed like a penguin and acting like a show pony is not my cup o' tea. I know it's a good way to raise money, having attended my share of events for other guys on my team. But, any kind of fucking fancy-dress, monkey-suit-wearing bullshit is a hard no for this foundation.

My thoughts are interrupted when Julia continues with her list. "Recruit and train a fundraising team. Enlist the help of a grant writer." She turns to me. "Carter, I've written several grant applications, so I'd be happy to do that for you as well."

"Okay." I have no idea why writing a grant takes a special skill set, but I'll just take her word for it.

"Great." She shuts her folder. "Carter, let's have lunch tomorrow. I'll start the nonprofit paperwork with the state and feds today. We can hash out the rest of it tomorrow."

I look over at Vivien. "Can you meet for lunch?" I'm not sure why she couldn't. This is her job now.

"Carter?" Julia says.

Viv sets the pen on top of the legal pad and slides it back over to Julia. "Sure thing, boss. Are we done here?"

"Yes, I think so?" I look at Julia, who nods.

I watch Vivien stand up and make her way out the patio door.

"Carter?" I feel a hand on my forearm. "You should really consider hiring someone else. That young woman doesn't seem, well, like the right fit."

"I want Vivien." I hear my own voice say the words, and it's raspy. I'm so confused about her. She seemed angry just now. Did I do something? I can't read her, and I want to. I really want to be able to read her. "I want Vivien to do it."

"She was late."

"No, not really. She was right, I told her two."

"Time is money, Carter."

I think she just deliberately ignored my defense of Vivien. "I know."

"This job requires dedication." She pauses. "And experience." She pauses again. "Think about it." Julia pats my arm again. "I'll see you for lunch tomorrow."

"Sure. Twelve thirty?"

"Perfect." Her hand slides down my forearm, and when it reaches my hand, she squeezes.

I turn and walk to the window as the door shuts. Running my hands through my hair, I close my eyes tightly. I'm at a loss when it comes to Vivien.

"I need advice." But I've no clue who to talk to about her.

———

"WHAT'S WRONG?" asks my sister Kennedy as she answers my call.

"Nothing. I just thought I'd check in." *And ask for advice from a woman.* Kenny will know what to do or at least advise me about Vivien.

"You never call me. Something has to be wrong, Carter." I hear loud noises in the background. My sister is a general contractor leading a team of guys for Flynn Construction in Chicago, building everything from homes to office buildings. She's amazing. A tiny dynamo. (She's short, in case you didn't get that.)

"No, it doesn't. I call you." I pull my office chair out from behind my desk and sit down.

"You text occasionally about family stuff. Wait, are Mom and Dad okay?"

"You'd know before I would. You live a mile from them."

"Whatever. Spill. I've got like ten minutes before I have to go yell at someone."

"Anyone in particular?" Her husband Ernie works on her crew sometimes. They met at work and he fell head over heels for my sister. Her? Not so much. I think he grew on her; either that or he was extremely persistent.

"No, not Ernie. He's working on a home reno with his brother, Ed." She sighs as the background noise diminishes. "All right, I'm in the trailer now. Talk."

"Fine. It's about a girl. A woman."

"Natalia?" she grumbles.

"No. Her name is Vivien. Well, she prefers Reggie."

"Oh, I've heard of her. She's working for you? Johnson and Clinton have a thing for her."

Goddammit. They'd better not, I growl inwardly. "No, they don't. They like her, but it's not a goddamn 'thing.'"

"Don't get testy, Carter. So, what is it you want to ask me?"

"I like her, but she's confusing."

"Uh, okay. Well, women confuse men, Carter. That's the way it is. Tell me what you like about her? What makes her special?"

Where do I start? "She's beautiful."

"Naturally."

I'm not sure if that's a jab or what, but I continue. "She's smart and funny. She's an amazing artist and teacher. She's already taught me how to use the potter's wheel. I made two bowls so far."

"Cool. I guess I know what we're all getting for Christmas." She laughs. "What else?"

"She's easy to talk to, and I feel more myself than I have in years."

"Johnson mentioned that she reminded him of Casey."

"She does. They don't look alike, but their personalities are similar. Vivien's stubborn as a mule just like Casey."

"She sounds great. I can't wait to meet her. When are you going to bring her home?"

"Maybe you'll meet her at Mom and Dad's anniversary party?"

"You're inviting her?"

"Of course. She lives here. Besides, I want her there."

"As your date?"

"I don't know. I think I need to take things slow. She's different. I don't want to blow it."

"Oh, my God. You *love* her."

"Love? No, Jesus, Kennedy. I *like* her."

"Does she know you *like* her?"

"I kissed her."

"And?"

It was amazing and hot as hell, but I'm not telling my sis that much. "It was just to make her ex-roommate jealous. I wanted to kiss her again, but we decided it'd be best to just be friends."

"You friend-zoned her? Oh, wow. Why?"

"Because we're going to be working together. It seemed... appropriate at the time."

"I get that. Ernie and I had to figure that out too, since we worked on the same job site and I was his boss. But we did work it out. Lots of people work with their partners."

I run my fingers through my hair and think. "If it didn't work out, things could get weird."

"You're gone half the year, brother. If things get weird, you can go hang at one of your other homes for a while."

"True." I think about Vivien. "I *really* like her."

"Then go for it. You deserve to be happy, Carter. And from what the guys say, she's cool and *real*."

"Real?"

"Yeah, not Natalia. Thankfully." I hear her grumbling on the other end of the phone again.

None of my family liked Natalia. Not even my mom the one time she met at Christmas, and she loves everyone. *Everyone.*

"So, are you gonna go for it?"

"I'd like to," I say, distracted. "I'll think about it. Your advice helps though."

"Talk to her. Tell her how you feel. If she feels the same way, then bam, you've got your girl."

"Bam," I repeat absently.

"Okay. Gotta go. One of my newbies needs to be watched very closely. He's an accident waiting to happen."

"Right. Love you, sis."

"Love you too. Call again sometime. This was fun."

"I will."

We hang up, and I lean back in my office chair. I'll definitely talk to Vivien. Not yet. But soon.

CHAPTER TWENTY-SIX

VIVIEN

AND TO THINK, I was looking forward to the work. I had no idea he hired someone else to "spearhead" the foundation. If I'd thought for a second I was going to end up being the person who takes notes and fetches coffee and shit, I'd have thought twice about changing my life so dramatically. Carter should have been more forthcoming about my role in all this. Yes, we talked about the foundation. He was adamant that he didn't want to have any fancy gala fundraisers or anything that would thrust him into the spotlight. Hence my comment earlier, or the comment I tried to make about him not wanting to do that. Hell, I thought of the name that day in his studio. He loved hArt of the City Foundation. It made me happy to know I was helping get this going. Now, here I am, relegated to some kind of assistant. At least that's the way it seems.

I scoff. Who am I kidding? I don't know the first thing about this kind of work. Did I really think I would be running the operation? "Get over yourself, Vivien."

That reminds me. That Julia woman kept calling me Vivien. I should be upset with Carter about that, but why bother? I'm so effed up about my name, I'm starting to think I'm only making things worse. It certainly complicates things for people. Vivien is a much more professional-sounding name than Reggie. I should accept the fact that my dad named me Vivien Jayne Reginald. It's hard, though. He sort of screwed me up when he left. Not sort of. *He did.* One of these days, I'll need to deal with that. Just not today. Today, all I want to do is return to my apartment, change into my grubbies, and work in the studio for a while. It'll clear my head so I can think of happier things.

Like the fact that I met a guy at the mall. A very cute guy. A very *French* guy. He was working at one of the restaurants. When I stopped in to check it out, he greeted me at the door. *Jean-Claude.* That's his name. His accent was so sexy, it made me all fluttery. Here's what happened: I hadn't intended on eating anything at the mall, but I was hungry. Maybe my growling stomach was fate or something. I opened the door of Chez Bistro and was hit by an array of delicious smells. Before I could change my mind, a sexy-sounding voice behind me said, "*Bonjour, mademoiselle.*" I can't speak French, but I knew enough to recognize those words. He said, "Hi, young lady," or something like that. I smiled and turned to see a really cute guy.

"Hey," I said, pushing my short hair behind my ear. (Nervous habit.)

In a seriously hot accent, the cute guy smirked and said, "How can I help *vous*?"

I giggled like a freaking high school girl. "I, um, I was"—giggle—"just wondering if"—giggle—"there was a table available?" Yeah. So, that was like a slow-motion car accident. Sure, I've been known to giggle, but not like that. I looked around the place and saw it was practically empty. I went out on a limb and thought, yes, there's a table available.

"Vell, I shall introduce myself." He held out his hand. "Jean-Claude."

I held mine out to him in time for him to lift it to his lips. He kissed the top of my hand, and it tickled, which caused another giggle. "Vivien." What? I couldn't very well tell a cute guy from France my name was Reggie, could I?

"*Tres bon*, Vivien. Come. You must sit near *moi*."

I followed Jean-Claude through the restaurant, seizing the opportunity to check him out. I'd say he was close to my age, if I had to guess. We walked through the bar area where he gestured to one of the barstools. "*Voila*."

I climbed up and rested my elbows on the bar. He presented the menu to me, and I perused it, all the while watching him from the corner of my eye. When he returned, I ordered a side salad with French dressing (like I'd order anything else) and a glass of water.

"Oh, *non*. Drink. I vill buy. What do *vous* enjoy?"

"Okay." I nearly giggle again but save myself from further humiliation by clearing my throat. "Surprise me."

Jean-Claude winked at me as he made me a Gimlet. I've made those before. It's vodka, lime juice, and lime on the rocks.

"Refreshing for zee hot day."

"*Oooui*." God, I'm a dork. If you guessed that I giggled again, ding-ding-ding, you'd be a winner. I watched him work as I sipped my drink and nibbled on my salad. "So cute," I mumbled to myself. He's got dirty-blond hair that's cut short on the sides and long on the top. He had it slicked back in a pompadour style. His face was round, but not fat. On the contrary, he's actually kind of thin. He's definitely not muscle-bound like Carter. But who is? This guy is Carter's opposite. From the hair color and body type down to his fashion sense. They do have one thing in common: Jean-Claude's face is covered by a smattering of a beard. I wonder if he's just started growing it out. Carter gets that kind of beard by the end of the day.

I watched Jean-Claude work with the customers as I

finished my salad and drink. I love his name. So international. And he must make great tips. The guy smiles a lot. He's got a crooked little smile. *Swoon.*

When he checked on me at the end of the bar, he gave me that same smile. "Vivien. *Fini?*"

"Yes." Sadly. "Can I get my check?"

"*Non.* On zee house." He paused. "If you give *moi* zee telephone *numéro.*"

"You want my phone number?" I was giddy. Yay! He wants to date me. "Sure." He handed me his my phone. I typed my name and number into it and gave it back.

"Excellent, Vivien, I shall be in touch."

"Great. Good," I said sliding off the stool. My hobo bag dropped to the floor, so I bent to pick it up. When I stood up, I caught him looking at my ass. Ignoring that, I waved. "Talk to you soon?"

"Oui. Ce soir."

"Ce soir?"

"Oh, *fooff.* Tonight. I'll text tonight?"

"Great."

"Oui."

When I stepped out of the restaurant, I realized I was going to be late for my meeting with Carter. "Uber it is." It cost me more money, but I was home, or I should say, I was back to Carter's in no time. Just in time to meet frigging Julia.

MAKING myself a bowl of cereal for dinner, I decide to text Kai. He needs to know about my date.

Me: I met a cute guy today.

Kai: What? Does Carter have hot cousins or something.

Probably.

Me: No clue. I met him at the mall. He asked for my number. But, that's not the best part.

Kai: What's the best part?

Me: He's FRENCH!!! With a sexy accent and everything.

Kai: Wow, that's a lot of exclamation points, girl. French, huh? And you met him at the mall?

Me: He was a bartender at a restaurant. I stopped in for lunch.

Kai: Side salad and water?

Me: No.

Me: Yes.

Me: But he bought me a drink AND paid for my salad.

Kai: Chivalry ain't dead. Yippee.

Kai's sarcasm sort of stings.

Me: You aren't happy for me?

Kai: ****heavy sigh**** Of course I'm happy for you.

Me: Okay. Well, he's supposed to text me tonight. I'll let you know what he says.

Kai: Just send me screen shots, then it'll be like I'm right there with you.

Me: Sarcastic much?

Kai: I'm serious. It'll also let me gauge what he's like. You've got terrible taste in men.

Me: Do not.

Kai: Do too. Which reminds me, what's up with Richie Rich?

Me: You should talk.

Kai doesn't respond so I text again.

Me: Nothing. He hired someone to take over the foundation.

Kai: Huh? I thought you were going to do that.

Me: Me too. I guess I'm going to be her assistant or something. I don't know for sure. It's unclear what my role is in all that. I just hope it wasn't a waste of time to move up here.

Kai: Me too. I hope Carter Corcoran isn't playing you.

Me: Yeah. I don't think so, but I don't know. Okay. Let's think about my date with the French guy.

Kai: You've got a date?

Me: Not yet. But I will.

Kai: Ooh, I love this confidence. Go girl!!!

Me: Now who's using a lot of !!!'s.

Kai: Go make something out of clay. I've gotta go. Taking Kalani out for dinner.

Me: She's in town?

Kai: Long story, but she moved here. With me. **eye roll**

Kalani is Kai's baby sister. She's nineteen and very headstrong. (Don't say a word.) She was going to the University of Hawaii. I wonder what happened?

Me: Wow. That *is* news. You've got the space. Call me tomorrow and spill. I hope she's okay.

He's got plenty of room. Kai's got a three-bedroom condo with a view down Michigan Avenue. It's a sweet pad.

Kai: She's fine. No worries. I'll tell you all about it tomorrow.
Me: K. TTFN

I'm sitting by my phone, fidgeting with anticipation like a damn teenager. I can't even bring myself to go to the studio. I wonder how late Jean-Claude had to work? I look at the clock on my phone. It's after ten... not that late. I wish I'd gotten his number. I could text him——you know, tell him how nice it was to meet him.

"No, Vivien. Let him contact *you*." I flop on top of my bed. I need to be cool, calm, and collected. I should just get in my pj's and go to sleep. At my dresser, I search for jammies and end up organizing my socks. Anything to keep my mind off a certain Frenchman—like thinking about the day ahead.

Although, I've got nothing pressing to do in the morning. I can wake up whenever I want as long as it's in time for my lunch meeting. I'm dreading that. I'm not going to get along with Julia. I'm all too familiar with the Julia Mayfairs of the world. Girls like that have been looking down their noses at me since elementary school. She's prim and proper, not a wrinkle in her clothes or a hair out of place. In fact, it was wound up so tightly in a bun on the back of her pretty blonde head, it looked like it hurt. I'm sure she doesn't like me. I don't get why. Hell, she doesn't even know me.

When my phone dings, I yelp, literally, and launch myself on my bed to grab the phone on my nightstand. So much for calm and cool. Picking it up, I see a number I don't recognize.

Unknown Number: Hello, Vivien. This is Julia

Mayfield. Carter was nice enough to give me your number. I'd like to meet with you before lunch. Does that work for you?

I don't respond for a full five minutes.

Me: Okay. What time?
Julia: Let's meet bright and early, at eight? Can we meet in your guest house apartment?
Me: I guess.

I mean, WTF?

Julia: Excellent. Please have pad and pen ready. I've got quite a to-do list for you. LOL

LOL? Something should be funny to garner one of those.

Me: Sure thing.

I've got a better one than LOL... FML. Yeah, that's more like it.

CHAPTER TWENTY-SEVEN

VIVIEN

LOUD POUNDING on my front door wakes me. I roll over to check the time on my phone. Seven thirty. I know exactly who it is. "She said eight," I groan.

Slithering out of bed, I clomp to the front door. Opening it, I see a perfectly coifed Julia Mayfair in a black pencil skirt, white blouse, and black heels. Once again, her hair is pulled into a bun that looks almost painful. Her makeup is perfect, of course. She looks me over from head to toe, then at her watch. "I thought I told you I wanted to meet this morning."

"Eight. You said eight."

"Well, I'm always early. You need to anticipate that."

No, I don't. Who the hell does she think she is? It's too early to deal with this shit. "Come on in." I leave the door open and turn my back on her, making my way to the kitchen. I might as well be a good hostess. "Coffee?"

"No, thank you."

I turn to see her looking around my place. She picks up a magazine that was here when I moved in and drops it back down, then moves over to the small, round dining table and takes a seat. Reaching into her fancy leather briefcase, she removes a laptop, the same leather-bound notebook I used for notes yesterday, and her fancy pen. She sits clicking the pen repeatedly, annoyingly.

I feel myself grow agitated, but then think, *No. You need to give her a chance. Think of this as a learning experience.*

As the coffee brews, I grab a bowl from my drying rack and prepare to pour myself some Cap'n Crunch.

"Seriously?" She sounds exasperated.

"What?"

Tapping the pen on the table like a drumstick, she snaps, "You're taking your sweet time, aren't you? I'm ready to get started."

Jesus. FML. "Sorry, but you're early. If you wanted to start at seven thirty, you should have said seven thirty. It's common courtesy."

"Well," she grumbles. "Hurry up. I don't have all day." I turn to pour a coffee when she mumbles, "I knew this was a bad idea."

"Look." I turn to face her. "What is your problem? You barely know me, and you've got this opinion of me that isn't fair. I'm a hard worker. I have always worked my ass off. You have totally misread me."

"We'll see," she says, scooting closer to the table.

Blowing out a gust of air, I move to the table to sit in the chair opposite the Queen Bee. Placing the cup on the table, I wait for the high commander to begin.

"Where are your supplies?"

"Like?"

"Computer? Paper? Pen?"

I stand up and reach for my laptop. It's old, circa 2011, but it works okay. I set that on the table and walk to a box I haven't unpacked yet. Books, paper, you know, stuff from school. I dig around until I find a sketchbook with a few empty pages. Next, I dig down deep for a writing tool. I find a pink colored pencil. It's sharp. It'll do. Moving back to the table, I see she's been watching me.

"Are you going to change into something appropriate?"

God, she's driving me nuts. I want to shake her and tell her to loosen up. Sure, I'm not wearing a bra and I'm barely wearing clothes, since I wore a tank top and itty-bitty shorts to bed. But, whatever. "Nope. You show up early, you get what you get."

"Fine." She slams open her fancy notebook. "Ready?"

"Ready, Freddy." I want to laugh but better keep quiet. Her majesty is in a pissy mood.

"I've got a list of things I need you to do." She tears out a sheet of paper and pushes it over to me. I look down at it and frown. Jesus, if she already had the list written out, why'd I have to go in search of paper and pen? This woman is infuriating. It's okay, because the next thing I'm going to say is going to piss her off. I'm almost giddy about telling her. "Um, I don't have a car."

"You don't have a car?" She's practically vibrating. "How are you supposed to run errands for me if you don't have a car?"

I shrug. "The bus?"

"The bus," she squeaks. Slamming the notebook shut with a slap, she does the same thing with her laptop.

Damn, she's angry. "Look, Carter said I could borrow one of his cars. I'll do that. Okay?"

"Fine." She sucks in a deep breath and opens her stuff again. This woman is wound tighter than a duck's you-know-what. Oh, hell. I'm just going to say it. Ass. She's wound tighter than a duck's ass. "Do you think you can take care of numbers one through three by lunchtime?"

I look at her list.

1. Post office: 250 first class stamps—something artsy looking.

2. Office supply store: 250 9x12 envelopes, 500-box of letter-size security envelopes, printable address labels, carton of copy and print paper (10 reams per box), box of file folders (pack of 100), box of pens, box of pencils, sticky notes, five two-inch binders, clear tape, stapler, staples, and a large whiteboard with dry-erase markers.

3. Starbucks: Triple, Venti, Half Sweet, Non-Fat, Caramel Macchiato.

I stare at the list, wondering about several things simultaneously. One, how am I going to pay for all this, and two, What. The. Ever. Loving. Fuck? This entire thing is pissing me off beyond belief. I can't wait to call Kai, so I can vent like never before. I look up at her as she types something on her laptop. "How am I supposed to pay for all this?"

"Use your own money. When everything is settled, I'll have Carter reimburse you."

"Just the stuff from the office supply store is in the hundreds. I don't have that kind of cash."

She blinks at me like I'm from an alien planet and going to probe her. "This is ridiculous. She reaches into her fancy bag and pulls out an even fancier wallet. "Here." She tosses a credit card at me. "I want all the receipts, and buy nothing for yourself. This is all for the foundation."

Jesus, does she think I'm an idiot or what? "I would never—"

"Sure," she mutters.

"Is that all for now?" I've had enough. "If you want me to get all of this, I'd better get going." Anything to get her out of here.

"Yes. I'll stay here and work while you're gone."

"I'd prefer you didn't."

"Excuse me?" She looks affronted.

"This is my home. I—"

"This is *Carter's* home. My understanding is that you live rent-free while you help with this foundation. We'll be using your apartment as our base. I thought he talked to you about this?"

"Nope." He sure didn't. I feel my eyes burn. I recognize the feeling as tears and will them back. I refuse to show any emotion in front of this seriously infuriating woman, or Carter, who is now enemy number one.

"Well, I'll be here early and I'll stay late. You'll have to deal with it." As she's about to type something, she adds, "As a matter of fact, I'll need a copy of your key. Then I can come and go as needed."

Ignoring her request for a key to my home, I clap my hands together. "Right. Welp, I'm going to change."

"Business casual. You're representing Carter now."

What the hell is business casual? I sure as shit hope it's denim cut-offs, a tee, and flip-flops. If not? Oh, well. I march into my room and dress quickly. When I step back into the living room, she ignores me. I grab her credit card and slide it into my back pocket.

"You're not wearing that."

"Yes, I am."

Tossing her pen down on the table, she leans back in her chair and crosses her bony arms. "This will not work if you insist on being insubordinate."

Insubordinate? "What is this, the army?" I scoff.

"Something like that."

"I'll change before we meet for lunch. I'm going to be lugging a bunch of stuff around. I need to be comfortable."

She rolls her smoky eyes. "Do you have a printer?"

"No."

"Get one of those too. Laser printer. Buy extra cartridges as well."

I grab the list and am out the door before she can give me any other orders. I stomp up the steps to Carter's deck, enter the code, and walk right in without knocking.

Fuck that guy.

I stomp some more, right over to the row of car keys by the garage entrance. I search the keys for one that looks old and for a Nissan.

"What're you doing?"

His voice startles me and I jump. Turning my head, I glare up at him. And I remember the last thirty minutes of my life. Julia. He's the enemy. I need to remember that.

"Sorry, Viv. Didn't mean to spook you. But, what're you doing?

Controlling my irritation, I say, "I need to borrow your old car."

I feel his heat next to me and smell his soapy, musky scent. It's almost as good as the glasses. *Almost.* His muscular arm slides so close to my face, I feel his coarse arm hair brush past my cheek. "Here, just keep this set. I've got a spare here." He points to one of the other hooks.

"I don't want to use it all the time. I'm just running some errands today."

He looks down at me, causing me to look up at him. "Damn," I mumble. "Kryptonite."

"Huh?"

"You're wearing your glasses again." I sigh almost forgetting my sour mood. Almost.

"Studying my playbook."

"Right." I gulp, then take the keys from his hand. "Fine. I'll keep the spare set of keys, but I'm only using it for emergencies."

"Whatever you need, babe."

Babe. I love it when he calls me babe, even though I know it means absolutely nothing. It's the same as calling me dude, only not as annoying. *You're still pissed, Reggie. Don't forget.* "Okay, well, thanks, Carter. See you around." I wave as I open the door to the garage and gasp. "Holy-crapola, Carter."

Chuckling behind me, he leans in close to my ear. "I like cars."

"And motorcycles." The garage is massive. There are six cars parked in a row across four double garage doors. At the farthest end of the garage sits three motorcycles. They're all black and huge. Why does one guy need three of those? Hell, why does one guy need six cars?

Still close to my ear, he breathes, "I'll take you for a ride sometime."

I swallow hard and think about that double entendre. The only thing swirling in my head is the words, *I wish.* "Okay," I croak.

He's the enemy. I keep forgetting that.

Carter's arm moves out and around the doorway to my right. I watch as the third double garage door from us begins to open. I peer around the corner and see Carter's hand on one of the electric door controls. "There's an opener for the garage door on the visor. You've got the gate app. Just click it when you pull out. When you get home, you can park in the garage or take one of the outdoor spots closer to your place. Okay?"

"Yes. I got it."

I walk quickly to the car and pull the door open. Sliding in, I lean back and nearly fall flat. Carter has the seat as far back as it can go, and the back of the seat is in the reclining position.

"Sorry."

I flinch when I feel his palm on my thigh. Tingles again. *You're mad at him, Viv.*

"Forgot to move the seat up for you, shorty." He pulls a lever here and twists a knob there until I'm upright and close enough to the wheel to be able to drive, then pulls the seat belt out and drags it across my chest. "You've got some of my kryptonite too, Viv." Clicking my belt in place, he pulls his big body out of the car. "It's all filled up. I just had it serviced and detailed for you. I even had them add some girly smelling shit."

I suck in air. "Jasmine." Smiling up at him, I say, "Thanks, Carter." He's making it very hard to be angry with him. I reach for the door handle, forcing him to move back. I've got to get the hell out of here. I can't spend any more time with the Clark Kent of South Barrington. He's messing with my mojo. "See ya later." I pat the wheel. "I'll take good care of Alma."

Chuckling, he pats the roof of the car. "Sounds good. See ya. Drive safe."

I shut the door, turn the key, and listen to the old car purr to life. "Nice," I mutter. I could get used to having a car. Putting it in drive, I move cautiously out of the garage. It's been a while since I've driven, so I need to be careful. Especially since I'm parked between two fancy-schmancy cars. Putting door dings on those things would cost me a fortune.

Once outside, I navigate around the ugly fountain and down the driveway. Hitting the remote, I watch the gate open slowly. As soon as I'm to the street, I hit the blinker to enter traffic and I'm off. A trip that would normally take me over an hour on the bus takes me fifteen minutes in Alma. Having wheels is awesome.

CHAPTER TWENTY-EIGHT

CARTER

OUR LUNCH MEETING IS, in a word, tense. Julia doesn't seem to feel the need to acknowledge Vivien at all. She's been directing all of her information and questions to me. I keep looking in Viv's direction, but she's busy playing with her plate of grilled chicken and vegetables.

"Don't you like chicken?" I ask.

"Oh, yes. It's delicious," Julia answers, even though I was directing my question to Viv.

"Viv?"

"Huh?" She looks up like she hasn't heard a word.

"Don't you like chicken?" I grilled it after marinating it all night in my special citrus blend. It's juicy and delicious.

"Oh." She takes a tiny bite, nods, and then makes that yum sound. "It's good."

She's full of shit. "I can get you something else."

"Don't be absurd, Carter. She can eat what you've served her."

Why did Julia just sound a lot like an evil stepmother? Turning to Julia, I say, "If she doesn't like it, I'll get her something else. I don't make people eat things they don't enjoy, Julia."

"Very well." She sighs. "I'm not a big chicken fan."

I roll my eyes at her, then turn to Viv. "And you?"

"I love chicken, Carter. It's really delicious. I promise. I'm just not very hungry."

"Can you make me a salad?" Julia again.

"Let's finish this"—*fucking*—"meeting first. Shall we?"

Julia takes the lead again. "Of course. As I was saying—"

"Viv? What are your thoughts on all of this so far?"

She looks at Julia, then at me. "Why are you asking *me*?"

"Because I respect your opinion."

Viv scoffs. "Yeah, right."

I'm confused. What the hell is going on? Do the two women dislike each other? If that's the case, they'd better figure this out, because I'm leaving tomorrow for a bunch of team shit. If they claw each other's eyes out while I'm gone, this nonprofit will never get off the ground. "I'm leaving tomorrow for ten days. You'll both have all that time to figure things out."

"Well, before you go, I'll need a key to Vivien's apartment."

What? "Why?" I don't think Viv would like someone else having a key to her place. Would she?

"So we have a place to work."

"Just work in here. I'll be gone. Set up right here in the dining room. Okay?"

"Wonderful. Excellent." Julia seems especially happy about the new plan.

Why does Vivien look so relieved?

Something is going on with these two, but I don't have time to figure it out right now. Plus, I'm not sure I want to venture into that lady dynamic. I'll just let them sort it out. If there are still issues when I get back, I'll step in. I nod inwardly. It's a good plan. I'm not worried. They'll get along. They're professionals, after all.

As I clear the dishes, I hear the two women. "Vivien, we'll need to work late tonight. I've got another meeting this afternoon, so I'll meet you at your place around four."

"No can do. I've got a date tonight."

A date? I turn quickly at her words and drop a plate in the process. Pieces of porcelain end up all over the floor and counter.

"Are you okay?" Vivien asks from the doorway, her face showing real concern.

"Yeah." I look around me, assessing the damage.

Julia steps in. "Vivien, get a broom and clean that up."

I watch Vivien's face fall. "Sure. Carter? Where's a broom?"

What the fuck is going on? "I've got it."

"No. Where's the damn broom?" Vivien snaps.

"Pantry. To your left."

She opens the pantry door and steps inside. Returning, she has a broom and a dust pan in her hands. "You'll need to move so I can get to the broken pieces."

"Give me the damn broom, Vivien."

She stares at me with such intensity in her brown eyes, but there's sadness there too.

"Babe?" I say quietly. "I did this. I'll clean it up."

"Fine." She drops the broom and pan and steps out of the kitchen, around the breakfast bar, to the patio door. "I'm out of here." Her voice sounds shaky, upset.

"Viv?"

Ignoring me, she shuts the door behind her.

"Where'd she go?" Julia's standing in the doorway with hands on hips.

"Lay off, Julia."

"What?"

"I said lay off." I sweep up my mess and pour the pieces into the trash. "I think the meeting's over, don't you?" I hope to God she says yes.

"Of course. I know you're busy. Will you be checking in while you're away?"

"Doubtful, but I'll try." We've got a bunch of team shit next week, including some press junkets and other public appearances. It's mandatory fun; otherwise, I'd skip it.

"Very well. Have a good trip. I'm sure I'll get a great deal accomplished while you're gone."

"You mean you and Vivien?" Hopefully, the two will work out whatever issues they've obviously got going on here and become a well-oiled machine. A team.

"Sure. Of course. Vivien too."

Sweeping up another pan full of shards, I remember why I dropped the plate in the first place. *Vivien's got a date?* The thought of her going anywhere with anyone else puts me on edge. *What if I'm too late?*

CHAPTER TWENTY-NINE

VIVIEN

I DIDN'T GO HOME after my *wonderful* lunch meeting. I went to the studio. It's the one place I can get my feelings under control. Working with clay is liberating. Concentrating on the process of rolling a coil, scoring it, and brushing slip on it so it will stick to the piece before it is just the monotonous kind of task I need to find my center. It's going to take a lot of coils to shake off the day I've had, though.

I peek over at my clock and see it's three. My date with Jean-Claude is in four hours. I've got plenty of time to shower and change. Reaching into a bag of clay, I'm distracted as a beam of light gradually appears at the doorway. A large shadow steps over the threshold, and I immediately think it's Carter.

"How's my Viv?"

I squeal with happiness. "Kai? You came?"

"I did. Thought I'd surprise you. Luckily, the gate was open, otherwise... not much of a surprise, huh."

I wipe my hands on the towel next to my work area and run as fast as I can, throwing my body into his. Wrapping my arms around him, I press my face into his chest, and that's all it takes for the waterworks to start. Sobbing in my best friend's arms—

his big, strong, safe arms—feels so damn good. Normally, I don't let people see me cry, but I can't hold them back anymore. Kai won't judge me.

"Aw, baby girl. What's wrong?" he says so sweetly and softly.

"Ev-everything." I sob some more.

"Everything? I thought things were good?"

He rubs his big hand up and down my back, trying to calm me. "I thought you had a date with a gorgeous Frenchman."

I'd sent Kai a text telling him Jean-Claude finally texted me at two this morning. He had worked a double at the restaurant, opening and closing the place. He apologized multiple times, but I know what it's like to work in the restaurant biz. He promised to make it up to me tonight.

"I do have a date." I pull away from him, wiping the tears and snot from my face. "I'm excited. It's just been a stressful, shitty day."

He takes me by the hand and leads me over to two stools next to the table. Looking around the place, he whistles. "This is a damn fine studio space, girl."

"I know." I shudder, holding back another sob. "It's the bright spot to an otherwise bad decision."

Kai taps my chin with his finger. "Do I need to kick the ass of one large NFL player?"

That makes me laugh. Not that I doubt Kai would and could do it, but he's just not the type of person to turn to violence. "No. I'm fine. Just working for Julia Mayfair is intense. She's the most anal retentive, type-A personality in the world. She's wound tight." Returning to my clay, I add, "And she hates me."

"How could she hate you? Didn't you just meet?"

I shrug. What else is there to say? "Let's talk about something else. How's Kalani?"

"Heartbroken."

"Oh?" Last I heard, she was happy at the U of Hawaii. "What happened?"

"She fell in love with her Sociology professor. He didn't feel the same way."

"Oh, poor Kiki." That's Kai's nickname for his baby sister. "She's so gorgeous. The guy must be an idiot." Seriously, Kalani Apatu is stunning. She's short like me, but that's where the similarities end. She's got sleek, shiny dark hair that hits right above her ass and a body made for swimwear. If she weren't so incredibly sweet and kind, I'd hate her guts. Just kidding. No one could hate that girl.

"He's married," Kai mumbles.

"Oh, no! Did she know?"

"Apparently not. So she decided to move here and check into Loyola or one of the other universities in Chicago."

"That's a good plan. She'll be near her big brother." Kai dotes on and spoils her almost as much as their parents. She's a special young woman. "You should have brought her with you. I'd love to see her." It's been almost a year since her last visit.

"Nah, I wanted to see you. Besides, I can't stay long. I just wanted to get a look at this date of yours. Give him my seal of approval." Kai walks around the studio space. "You weren't kidding about this place, Viv. This is a ceramic artist's dream." He turns back to me. "You made the right decision coming up here. You just need to focus on this." He raises both arms, motioning toward the room. "Focus on this and not on the shit with the job. Take advantage of the time here to create new work, a new series. Think of the annoying boss lady as a means to an end. If you turn your focus to this, you won't mind that job so much, doll."

I listen and nod. He's absolutely right. I need to buck up and just do the job. I can come in here after a day with Julia and create. "You're right, Kai. Thinking about it that way makes it seem much less frustrating." I smile at my bestie and relax my tense shoulders.

"Now, tell me what you're wearing on this date."

We spend the next hour talking and laughing. I've missed my friend so much it's almost painful, but having him here today is just what I needed.

CHAPTER THIRTY

CARTER

I STEP CLOSE ENOUGH to the patio window that my breath hits it and look to my left, down toward Vivien's house and the studio. Checking my watch, I note the time. "Five forty-five. I wonder what she's up to?" I haven't seen her since the lunch meeting. I know that's only been a few hours, but since she left upset and angry, it's all I've been thinking about. That and her *date.*

Without thinking, I open the door and jog to the studio. I might as well check on her, get a look at her fucking date. Entering the space, I stop in my tracks. She's not alone.

"Hey, Kai. What's up, man?" *Wait! Maybe her date is with Kai.*

"Nothing. How's it hangin', big guy?" he says in a flirty tone.

I probably need to tell him I'll never play for the other team, but I suspect he already knows. "Good, man. How was your family trip?"

"Great. Saw lots of great art. You ever been to Europe?"

"Yeah, spent a summer there for a study-abroad program."

"Cool."

I nod. I guess that's the end of that conversation. I turn my attention to Reggie, hard at work on some abstract sculpture. She hasn't so much as glanced at me since I walked in. That's a bad sign.

"Hey, Vivien."

"Oh, hey, Carter."

She still hasn't looked up at me, so I force the issue. We need to get past whatever happened earlier today. "Whatcha making?"

"Nothing. Just messing around." She shrugs.

"Okay."

"*Welp*, I need to stop." She looks up at Kai. "I need to get ready."

"Ready?" I ask. "For what?" I'm just pretending I didn't overhear her earlier.

"She's got a date," Kai says, rolling his eyes.

"A date?" I feel my jaw tense and my brows furrow. "With whom?"

"Jean-Claude," Kai says in an extra-breathy voice. I guess he's trying to sound like Vivien.

"Who's Jean-Claude?"

Sighing, Viv wipes her hands on her apron. She finally looks at me, and I swear I can still see the hurt in her eyes. "Just a guy."

She pulls off her apron, and I have to swallow to prevent a moan. She's wearing a very tight, hot-pink tank top. I don't think she's got on a bra, since her nipples are poking out, but I can't be sure.

"You two macho men can hang here and play with clay while I go get ready." She walks around the table and into her apartment, shutting the door behind her.

"What the hell did you do, man?" Kai says, leaning against the big table, arms crossed over his wide chest.

"Huh? What're you talking about?"

"You did something. She can barely look at you."

"Nothing that I know of," I say defensively. I'm being completely honest.

Kai stares at me for a bit too long. "You did something. She was jabbering away until you walked in. The second she saw you, she clammed up. Whatever it was, it was not good, man. Do I need to kick your ass?"

I scoff. "Like you'd be able to."

"I'm a black belt."

Shit. "Nah, man. You don't need to kick my ass." If he's a black belt, he could probably do it.

"I think you did something, you and that woman you hired, but I'll let it slide for now."

"Gee, thanks," I mutter.

Changing the subject, Kai stands up, uncrossing his arms. "We'll talk about this after she leaves. In the meantime, show me your paintings."

"What? Now?"

"Now."

"Fine." I turn to the door and look back, nodding for him to follow me. "They're in the main house."

I lead the way back to the house and up into my painting room, then open the door and step inside, letting Kai walk past me. "Most of my paintings are in the closet."

Kai turns to me and smirks. "In the closet?" he snickers.

He opens the closet door and steps inside. I don't follow. And not because he's gay or anything. I'm nervous about what he's going to think or say about my work. When you show people your artwork, it's like revealing part of your soul, your secrets. It's intimidating and scary. It throws a door wide open to probable rejection.

He steps out of the closet holding the painting of Casey and the abstract painting, the one with Vivien's colors that I did the other day. He moves over to the easel by the window, setting the two paintings next to the landscape painting. I follow so I can hear the verdict.

"You ever take any classes?" he asks, staring at the three paintings.

"No. Well, yes, I took a high school art class with my girlfriend, but nothing after that."

"Hm, interesting," Kai says, tapping his finger on his chin. "Here's the thing. You can move forward in one of two ways."

I look over at him. "Okay."

"One. You could take some painting classes. Maybe a figure painting class or two," he says, pointing at Casey. "You've got a great sense of color." He points to the abstract painting. "On this abstract painting and your landscape here, your colors are bright and energetic. Playful." He points to Casey's portrait. "This one is full of emotion. The colors are dark and muted. Did she mean something to you?"

"She did. She was my high school girlfriend. Killed by a drunk driver."

"Oh, shit. That's sad, dude." He looks back at the painting. "You showed those feelings in this. The face is way out of proportion, but it doesn't matter. This painting is all about loss."

I nod. It was all about loss. I was fucked-up for a long time over losing Casey.

"So, your second option is to just keep painting. You've got some good things going on here. It's intuitive and interesting. It's already good. No classes needed." He looks back at me and blinks, thinking.

I remain silent.

"So, which is it? Do you want to improve on your figurative works or keep painting and learning as you go along?"

"I'd like to learn to draw and paint figures. I just haven't had the time to devote to classes since getting drafted." It's true. I'm fascinated by the famous figure paintings by people like Van Gogh.

"Cool. That's a good compromise. I can teach you some things for now. After you get more comfortable, you can think about a painting class or a life drawing class."

I nod in agreement.

"Grab a sketchbook and meet me back in the clay studio. I'll show you some stuff while I'm here."

"You want to work in the clay studio?"

"Well, no, not really. I want to get a look at this tool she's going out with," Kai says with an arched brow. "She's got terrible taste in men."

"Oh, yeah, right." That fucking date. The idea of Vivien going out with another guy is making me crazy.

After putting away my paintings and finding an empty sketchbook, I follow Kai back to the studio. I might as well learn what I can while he's here. As I pass through my kitchen, I grab a six-pack of Guinness from the fridge and a bag of chips from the pantry. I've no idea if Kai likes either of these things, but I'm hungry, and thinking about Reggie's date makes me want to drink.

"Ah, you've brought sustenance!" exclaims Kai as I walk in the door. "I want to order pizza, but you need to tell me where to order from around here."

"Sure thing. Lou Malnati's delivers. Their deep-dish pizzas are pretty good."

Kai checks out Lou Malnati's online menu, asking me what toppings I like. Once that's sorted, he calls the restaurant and orders a large deep dish, half with his toppings and half with mine. I jot my address down on a piece of paper for him to tell the delivery guy. "Tell them I'll leave the gate open and to come to the guest house." I listen as he repeats my information, then I sit at the worktable with my sketchbook and a pencil, ready for my lesson.

Kai grabs my sketchbook and opens to a clean page. "Let's start with the basics." He demonstrates how to draw a face in proportion using the width of one eye. "With the width of one eye, you can determine where the other eye goes, where the tip of the nose belongs, how far the bottom lip rests from the nose, and even how wide all of those things are in relation to the eye, and so on." I watch as Kai draws my face in a matter of minutes.

"Whoa, that looks just like me, man. I had no idea."

"It's harder than it looks at first, but once you get the hang of it, it's not bad." He turns to a blank page and scoots my sketchbook back. "Now you try. I'll be your model."

Shit. This makes me nervous. It's one of the reasons I've kept my art stuff so secret. While my family knows I like to paint, I've resisted showing them anything. I'm afraid they won't like it. So, having a guy I barely know sit here and watch me is unnerving. "I'll try."

Working slowly, Kai talks me through the process. I follow his step-by-step instructions mapping out all the important parts to his face. Once that's done, I focus on the angle of his almond eyes, the width of his nose, and the shape of his mouth. I'm stopped from finishing his right ear by a knock on the door.

"Pizza," exclaims Kai.

I jump up. "I'll get it." I jog to the door and pull it open, but it's not the pizza guy. It's a short, doughy-faced guy dressed in skinny jeans, a plaid shirt, an even plaider bow tie, and suspenders. Fucking hipster.

"Yeah?" I look to his left to see if maybe the pizza is out there somewhere. Nope.

"*Allo?* Iz Vivien *a la maison?*"

"Who're you?" And why in the ever-loving hell is *he* calling her Vivien?

"*Je suis* Jean-Claude." He holds out his tiny hand.

I have an uncontrollable urge to grab it and squeeze until he's forced to his knees. But I don't. Instead, I arch my brow at the little putz. I know something he doesn't. For starters, I know you should never trust a guy with two first names. I learned that the hard way in college when I caught my roommate, Mark-Paul fucking my on-again, off-again (after that it was permanently off-again) girlfriend. I turn my back to him and see Kai already knocking on the apartment door. When it opens, I see red.

Viv is wearing the shortest red dress in history. Okay, not the shortest dress, but it's pretty damn short. I can see at least half her thick thigh. Her skirt is all swirly too, so when she walks, it swings. As she gets closer, I let my eyes wander up from her legs to her chest. *Jesus.* The dress ties around her neck like that Marilyn Monroe dress, making her tits press together and leaving the most impressive cleavage I've ever seen. My fingers twitch just thinking about touching them, touching her. I growl inwardly, because she's showing enough cleavage to drive a man to drink. Why in the hell is she wearing that dress for this fuckwit?

"Ooh la la, Vivien. Tres belle."

I snort and roll my eyes. This idiot is so full of shit.

"*Merci*, Jean-Claude." She giggles.

The other thing I know about this guy? He's not French. If I had to guess, I'd say his real name *is* Claude, but that's it. He's as American as I am. But he's got Reggie convinced he's the real deal. Well, let me just take care of that problem right this minute. "Jean-Claude?"

"Oui?"

"Salut mec. Je sais que tu es plein de merde. Si vous ne dites pas la vérité à Vivien, je le ferai." (*Hey, dude. I know you're full of shit. If you don't tell Vivien the truth, I'll do it.*)

I watch the twit blink at me. His round cheeks blush. But

I've got to hand it to the guy, he's good. "Oh, you Americans. Tres drôle."

Yeah, he knows just enough French to hang himself. "Si vous ne confessez pas, je vais lui dire tout de suite. Tu m'entends? Vivien mérite mieux que toi." (*If you don't confess, I'm going to tell her right now. You hear me? Vivien deserves better than you.*)

"You know French?" squeaks Vivien.

"Oui, Vivien." I look back at Claude. "J'ai passé quatre ans de français et passé un été à Paris à ne parler que le français." Turning around to face her, I translate. "I've had four years of French in college and spent a summer in Paris speaking only French."

Jean-Claude sputters as his face flushes to a deep magenta.

"I don't think your Frenchman is actually French, babe."

She looks at Jean-Claude, then back at me. Her face has turned a bright shade of red as her eyes narrow into slits. "Is that true, Jean-Claude?"

He shrugs. "Chicks dig the accent."

She turns to me, the anger still on her face. "How did you know?"

"Instinct." I shrug. "And he was butchering the language like a tourist."

"Instinct?" she says bitterly. "Was it also your instinct to embarrass my date? To embarrass *me*?"

"Huh? No." *WTF?*

"Come on, Jean-Claude. If that's really your name. I didn't shave and luffa my entire body to stay home in front of the television."

She shaved? Everything?

"Sweet," says Claude.

"You're still going out with him?" I mean... seriously? This guy's a damn liar.

Reggie looks back at me as she reaches for dipshit's arm. Before they have time to get out the door, I want to emphasize the fact that this tool is a faker and a cheat, so I ask, "What's your real name?" I want to know even if Reggie doesn't.

He looks at Vivien, and his cheeks tint red. He should be embarrassed. "Jared Calvin. Call me JC."

"JC? Jared Calvin?"

"Yep."

"So, you're not French?" Viv's pink face has turned pale all of a sudden.

"Nope. Irish, actually."

"Oh." That's all she says before she walks out the door with JC trailing behind her like a puppy.

I turn and see Kai leaning on the table with a smirk on his face. Crossing his arms over his chest, he mutters, "Told ya."

"Told me what?"

"She's got shit taste in men."

"No shit. I never wanted to pummel a guy so much in my life. And I play professional football."

"I was right about you."

"Me?"

"Yeah. You've got it bad for Viv."

If he means I'm horny as fuck around her, then yes, he'd be right. Okay. I've got it bad for Vivien but I'm not about to admit it to him. "No, I don't."

"You do. I said so at Giordano's, but you denied it. Now I know for sure." Why does Kai have that smug-ass expression on his face?

I'm about to deny it again as a knock sounds on the door. "Pizza." Maybe he'll shut up and eat. I march to the door and open it wide.

The delivery guy peeks inside the room, then at me. "You order pizza?"

"Uh-huh." I reach out and take the pizza in one hand and slap a couple bills in his empty hand. "Thanks." I slam the door in the poor guy's face. I need to eat. My hunger and irritation with the entire conversation has made me ravenous.

"Dude, I paid for that with my card."

"Well, I guess that guy had a good night, then. Come on, let's eat." I growl.

I'm relieved Kai stops giving me his fucking advice. Until he says, "Word to the wise. You never want to embarrass Viv. Especially not in front of other people."

I sputter. "I wasn't trying to embarrass her. It was him. I knew he was faking it."

Tsking, Kai adds, "I know what you were doing and why you did it. I've just got to ask—"

"What?"

"When are you going to make your move, Carter?"

"My move?"

"When are you going to admit you've got a thing for her? You'd better work fast. She'll date that tool just to prove you wrong."

"No, she wouldn't." *Would she?*

Kai nods knowingly. "She would, and she will. The only way you're going to get her to forgive you is to force her hand."

"Force her hand?"

"Shit, Carter. I thought you had game with the ladies. Apparently, you don't."

"I've got game." I just don't when it comes to a woman like her. "Why did that asswipe get to call her Vivien?"

He shrugs, sipping his beer. "She's weird about her name, as you know. It's rooted in her hang-ups about her dad."

"Oh? What'd her dad do?"

"He's an actor, and he chose that over his kids."

"When? How old was she?"

"Thirteen." Taking a bite of pizza, he adds, "Warning. She doesn't like to talk about him."

"Okay." I nod. I need to know more, though. "Has he been in anything?"

"Yeah, he's been in a couple national commercials."

"She's seen them?"

"Yeah. She was embarrassed. For him, I think." Kai shrugs. "I don't know a lot about it. She's tight-lipped about her feelings on him, but if you ask me, her dad's a selfish prick. The sad thing is, she has all sorts of feelings about the guy. Bottom line though, she loves him more than anything. He left right at that age when a girl thinks their daddy can hang the moon."

"You've given this some thought."

"I love her."

With the bottle halfway to my mouth, I stop. "You love her?"

Nodding, Kai smiles. "I do. If I weren't into guys right now, I'd make my move. But Vivien Reginald is a forever kind of girl. I'm not ready for that." He arches his brow. "Not yet. So, if you're just hoping to fuck her and leave her, don't do it."

"Jesus. What kind of asshole do you take me for?" Probably the very kind I've been in the past. Look how I treated Natalia. What is it about this girl that makes me look at life differently?

"The player kind of asshole."

"I wouldn't do that to her. It doesn't matter. It's moot. She works for me. We're friends."

Kai chuckles, "Yeah, right."

He's starting to annoy me with all of his assumptions about me and the questions. "Are we done?" I nod down at my sketch-pad. "With the lesson?" I think the lesson ended up being about more than just art.

"Sure." He looks at his phone. "I think I'll head back to the city. I don't want to cramp Viv's style in case she wants to bring that guy home tonight."

I choke, spitting beer all over my drawing. "What? You think she's bringing that tool back home?" *To her bed?*

Kai throws his head back. Slapping his palm on my shoulder, he says, "I knew it. You've got it bad, man."

"Whatever." I turn to leave but turn back. "Will she bring him home with her?"

He shrugs. "She's had a long dry spell. Who knows?"

I move to the door.

"You could hang out in here, listen for her to come home—"

"No." *Yes. I'd love to do that. I could pretend to make more cereal bowls.* "Maybe." I release a feral growl, thinking about Vivien with JC.

"You're picturing her with that guy, aren't you?"

"No."

"Liar."

"Whatever. I'm going home. Safe travels."

"See you, man."

"Kai?"

"Yeah?"

"Give me your phone."

"Ooh, are we exchanging numbers?" Kai coos.

"Viv wants you to have the app to open the big gate. So you can visit whenever."

"Cool. Give me your number too."

I arch my brow.

"Just in case."

Nodding, I download the app, enter the access information, and then add my phone number to his contacts. "There you go, man."

"Great," he says, looking down at his phone. "She'll be all right, Carter."

"I hope so." I really hope so.

I walk out the door with my sketchbook in one hand and what's left of the beers in the other. Maybe if I get drunk, I won't think about Vivien and the hipster.

———

I TRIED to sit in my living room and watch television for several hours after Kai left, but I kept walking out to the deck and checking for lights at Viv's. I must have walked in and out of my house twenty times. I finally gave up, and now I'm in the studio, trying to center my damn clay on the wheel. A thought occurs to me: I may be too strong for this. I think my strength is working against me right now. I mean, petite Vivien can do it so easily. Maybe I'm just too forceful?

With renewed determination, I scrape off the sloppy, wet clay and grab some new out of the bag. I wedge it like she taught me and return to the potter's wheel. Dropping the clay ball onto the wheel, I lean down and say, "Now, you listen here, you big glob of clay. You will center for me, and it will be amazing. You hear me?" I try one more time and fail. The clay slides all over the bat as it spins out of control. I'm only able to keep the ball of clay from sliding onto the floor with sheer will. When I decide that tonight is just not my night, I flop the gooey, wet ball into the bag of clay, seal it tight, and clean up my mess.

"Now what do I do?" I peer at the time on my phone. Not quite eleven. "She must be having a good time."

I need to stop talking to myself. I think I'm on my way to crazy-town.

CHAPTER THIRTY-ONE

VIVIEN

WE'RE quiet on the drive to the restaurant. It could be because we're nervous or because of the bad start to the date, but my money's on the fact his car is louder than a Metallica concert. I think a new muffler is in order for his little piece of shit car. At a stoplight, it's quiet enough for me to ask, "So, Jean-Claude, er, I mean JC, has this fake accent of yours worked on a lot of women?"

He shrugs. "Sometimes, yeah. I do it at work, for customers, you know? It's exhausting sometimes. I knew I wouldn't be able to keep it up forever, but I saw you and thought you were sort of pretty for a fuller-figured girl, and you seemed to like the accent. I had to try."

"Oh." *Sort* of pretty? *Full-figured?* Hm, I guess it's not the worst thing anyone has ever said to me. "Why do you do it?"

"Tips, mostly. They go up a lot when I use an accent. It makes it more authentic. But I'm a theater major, so the practice helps me with my classes."

Oh, hell no. A theater major? I promised myself I'd never date anyone who did any kind of acting. "And everyone at work just goes along with it?"

"Sure. Why not?"

"I don't know. It seems..."

"What? It seems what?" he says defensively.

"It seems sort of unseemly."

"Unseemly? What does that even mean?"

"You want the definition of unseemly?"

He nods.

I blink at him. He needs me to explain the word? "It means improper or inappropriate."

"Geez, Vivien. You're not my mom."

Damn, I wish I'd never told him my real name now. It sounds wrong coming from him. "Actually, my name is Reggie. Would you mind calling me that instead?"

"Reggie? That's a guy's name."

I squeeze my eyes shut as I slowly breathe in and out. How can this date get any worse? Time to make some shit up. "Oh, you know. I just think Vivien sounds like an old lady name." I faux giggle. "Reggie sounds more hip."

"Well, that's true. I can see that. Plus, you've got really short hair."

Jesus. This guy is a frigging idiot. "Yeah, there's that." I'm done with this conversation. It is what it is. Jared is a fraud, yes. He's dumb too, for sure. But I still like him. He's sort of funny. No, I don't *like* him, *like* him. But maybe he could be a friend. Only time will tell. Sure, I think he's misguided and naïve, but it's not my place to set him straight. "So, let's go somewhere fun. Where there's music and lots of people."

"Oh, you don't want to go out to dinner?"

"Nah. Let's relax and have some fun." I need that more than anything right now. Life has gotten too serious lately.

"Cool. I know just the place."

Before I can brace myself, JC plants his foot on the gas pedal, doing a U-turn in the middle of the intersection. I guess we're going the other way. We end up in front of a place called Shirley's Piano Bar. I groan. I hate shit like this. He's going to make me sing. I know it. Or worse, Mr. Theater Major will sing enough for both of us. I look down at myself and groan again. Why did I bother dressing up for this guy? I wore a sexy dress. And heels. What a waste. My feet are already killing me.

Jared parks and jumps out to wait curbside for me to step out. "You're gonna love this place, Reg."

I don't even bother correcting him on my name. Anything but Vivien works, honestly.

He holds his hand out to me but instead of grasping it, I hold on to his elbow. I get no reaction. He must not care either way as he leads me into the space. The second we're inside, there's a loud "Jared!" being shouted all around the place.

Awesome. He's a regular. And popular. Maybe it won't be so bad.

––––––––

IT'S WORSE.

Jared isn't *just* a theater major. He's a *musical* theater major. That means he sang every single song, sometimes getting up on the small stage with the piano player, and one time he even crawled on top of the piano to belt out "Defying Gravity" from *Wicked.* When he stood on top of the baby grand to belt out the high part, I knew I'd finally made it.

To hell.

I'd plummeted straight to hell.

But that's not all. He didn't just sing a lot. He drank a lot. So much so I called him a cab and, with some help from his friends at the piano bar, got him into said cab and off to his house. At least I hope it was his house. It was the address on his license. A giggle escapes me thinking about JC waking up in the wrong place. God, I'm diabolical. I stop giggling as soon as I remember the date from hell.

"When will I ever learn?" Yeah, I'm talking to myself about my taste in men. First Carter, now that guy. JC. I'll give him one thing. The guy can sing show tunes like nobody's business. I could see him onstage in an off-off-off-Broadway production of *Cats* or whatever. I wish him luck. "Break a leg," I mutter as I hit the button on my phone app to call for an Uber.

With my key in hand, I unlock the deadbolt and push it open and then drag my tired ass into my house. All I want to do is eat a bowl of the Cap'n, take a long shower, and fall into bed. The second I cross the threshold, I know I'm not alone. "Shit." *Is there an intruder?* My place is dark except for the flickering light of the television that leaves the room aglow. I know I didn't leave it on. Stepping into the room, I see the silhouette of a man lying on the sofa. A big man. Kai? I thought he said he was going back to the city. I step closer and see it's the other big man in my life. Carter's in my place, watching television? It's irritating. I don't go to his house and crash. Carter and I will need to have a *chat*. Like the ones my mom likes. A serious one.

I snap on the lamp on the side table, and what I see before me makes my blood run cold. "You ate my cereal?" I screech.

My box of Cap'n Crunch is on the coffee table, on its side. I had just enough left for tonight and tomorrow. There's a bowl with milk remains at the bottom and a spoon off to the side. *Oh, hell no!* I step close to him, finding he's fast asleep. Damn, he's pretty when he's sleeping. It's a shame I'm going to bloody his lip for this.

Leaning down close to his ear, I shout, "Carter!"

He startles, moving so fast I don't see the back of his hand coming toward me until it connects with the side of my face. The force of it propels me backward. I land on my back on top of the coffee table, causing a chain reaction. Milk, bowl, spoon, and the Cap'n fly every which way. I feel moisture all over me and know it's the milk. At least I hope it's the milk. Maybe it's blood? The left side of my face hurts like a son of a bitch.

"Shit. Viv?" I blink up to see Carter, concern all over his face. "What are you doing?"

"Huh?"

"Shit, woman. Never wake a guy up like that."

I place my palm on my hot cheek. "Well, I'm so fucking sorry." I feel the heat of the tears on my cheeks before I know they're coming.

"Oh, shit, Vivien. I didn't mean..."

I look to my left and see the cereal box. "Y-y-you ate my c-c-cereal."

"You're more concerned with that than your face?"

"It's my only food, you ass. God, I'm so sick of people treating me like shit." Carter's got his hand out to help me up, but I slap it away, instead opting to roll off the table and onto my knees. Using my hands, I pull myself up to my feet.

"It was on the counter. I didn't realize it was all you had. Viv?"

I'm not listening to him. I've had it. Gathering myself somewhat, I wipe my cheek and wince. Damn, it hurts. "Is this my apartment?"

"Yes. You know it is."

"Then you need to respect my privacy."

"It was getting late. I was worried about you. I wanted to be sure you got home okay."

"You ate my food." I look up at the kitchen and see an empty jug of milk. I whimper at the sight. More tears fall. "You d-d-drank my milk?"

"I needed it for the cereal."

That's it. I press my hands over my eyes and bawl. My shoulders shake as torrents of moisture fall from my eyes.

"Vivien, I'm sorry. If I'd known…."

Okay, that pisses me off. I lower my hands slowly. Sucking in air, I say, "Why would you need to know? This is *my* apartment. Not yours. Why would I need to tell you"—I lean into him and shout this last part—"Not. To. Eat. *My.* Food?" God that felt good.

"Viv."

"Go. Please just go. I'm tired. I've had a bad day." Shit, a bad year. A bad *ten* years, come to think.

"I'm sorry, babe. I'll replace the cereal and milk."

"Just go."

Without another word, he turns and leaves. When I hear the door click shut, I look at the mess on the floor but decide ignore it for now. Stepping over the upturned bowl, I march to the bathroom, strip, and step into the shower. Turning on all three showerheads, I let the hot water cool me down before scrubbing off the scent of the date from hell. Wrapping myself in a towel, I walk to the bed, drop the towel, and crawl under the covers. I'm asleep before I have time to think.

———

SUNSHINE BLINDS me as my eyes flutter open. I roll over and wince. My body hurts everywhere. Especially my left cheek. I place my hand over it, finding it feels swollen.

"What time is it?" I have to think for a second to remember what happened.

I remain in bed a while longer, thinking. I need to talk to Carter. I feel hypocritical about the cereal thing last night, since I am living here for free. But we need to talk. A chill runs over my body. I realize I must have kicked my blanket off in the night, and I'm naked. Grabbing the towel from the night before off the floor, I wrap it around me and step out to the kitchen.

"Coffee," I utter like a zombie.

When I catch a glimpse of my breakfast bar, I blink. "What the hell?"

The entire counter, about three feet by five feet, is covered entirely by boxes of cereal. There's got to be fifty boxes. I step closer and see the majority of them are traditional Cap'n Crunch, my favorite, but there's also peanut butter flavor and berry flavor. In the mix is a selection of Fruity O's, Frosted Flakes, Life, and a few others.

I giggle at the sight of it all. *God, he's such a dork.*

Rounding the bar, I pull open the fridge and see two gallons of milk. Not only that, there's luncheon meat, cheese, lettuce, tomatoes, and a bunch of other veggies. I'm not a super big fan of veggies, but it's good to have some on hand. Opening my cupboards, I see they're filled with soup, more canned vegetables, fruit packs, apple sauce, pasta and sauce, and assorted crackers, chips, and bread.

"Wow." I've never had this much food in my entire life. I should feel guilty about all of this. I hate when people spend money on me, but I'm going to accept this gift. He owes me after last night. I turn back to the breakfast bar to see a note.

Reggie,

I'm very sorry I ate your food and imposed on your space. I was just there to make sure you got home safely from your date. I got hungry as I waited though, so I ate your food. It won't happen again. I hope this will tide you over until you can get to the store .

Your humble servant,

Carter

P.S. There's an ice pack in the freezer. Your face looked really swollen this morning.

I blink at his note. "This morning?" I blink some more. "He saw my cheek *this* morning?" How did he see my face? He had to have come into the bedroom. "No." I was naked. I feel my face heat to about a million degrees Fahrenheit. I should be angry that he came back into my apartment. I should march right over to his house and read him the riot act. But I can't. Instead, I'm hoping I'll never see him again. "Shit, I'll never be able to look him in the eyes again." *Never*.

CHAPTER THIRTY-TWO

CARTER

WHERE DO I START? Should I start with the fact that I know I shouldn't have gone back into her place without her permission? I knocked. Twice. When she didn't answer, I let myself in. But in my defense, I had perishables. They needed to be refrigerated. Then I checked on her. I was already inside her apartment. I was already in trouble, and I was concerned about her face. Why wouldn't I check on her? I feel like a complete asshole about that. Shit, she startled me, and now she looks like she went fifteen rounds with Ali.

When I stepped into her bedroom, I nearly stroked out. There she was. Vivien Reginald, sound asleep and completely nude on her bed, looking like a goddess. I was frozen to the spot, just inside her bedroom door. The sun was shining through her window, casting a ray of light across her belly. Her left hip hung over the bed. One arm was draped over her hip, barely covering her pussy. The other arm was straight out to her side. Her breasts, Jesus, her breasts. They were natural, teardrop shaped and exquisitely tipped with nipples and areolas the perfect shade of pink. Her nipples themselves were pebbled. She was probably chilled. I should have covered her, but that would be a goddamn travesty. I stared for a minute, wishing I had my paints and a canvas with me.

My dick was hard, making me feel like a fucking pervert, but I was there to check on her face. When I finally looked, I felt a mixture of horror and humor. The side of her face was swollen and bruising had started. That was the horror part. The fact that her mouth was open slightly and she was snoring was the funny part. Honestly, the woman was so beautiful that, snoring aside, all I wanted to do was paint her. I wanted to fuck her too, but the artist in me was enamored with the way she lay on her bed. Maybe someday I'll get to paint her like that, except she'll be in *my* bed instead of this one.

In any case, I left her a note. I knew I should have left off the part about seeing her face because she'll no doubt conclude that I saw her in all her naked glory, but it feels wrong to pretend I didn't. She needs to know I was there. I smirk. Part of me wants to see what she'll do after she reads the note. I imagine her storming over to my place, hands on full hips, telling me off. I won't argue.

I wait for what seems like hours, even though it's just past nine. My flight leaves at four today, so I want to clear the air with her before I have to head to the airport. I've done every-thing I could to keep myself busy until she wakes up. I've finished my workout, packed my carry-on, and showered. I've eaten and checked my messages. Surely, she's up by now. Should I go over there? Like a lightbulb over my head, an aha moment sends me walking to the studio. I can work on a bowl. She'll hear me and come into the studio.

Once I'm in the work space, the smell of clay hits me. I feel a rush of adrenaline. Oil paint gives me the same sensation. Just the scent of it makes me want to pick up a brush. I stand at the table, facing her door, wedging clay. Maybe I should drop a tool on the ground or something. She'll hear me then. Nah, I'd better play it cool.

Clay wedged, I grab a bowl for water, a sponge, and the tools Vivien showed me how to use that first night. I work to center the clay, but no matter how many times I try, I can't get it. It's goddamn frustrating. I throw the glob of clay down, rinse off my hands, and march to her door as I dry my hands on my sweats.

I bang on the door. "Vivien, I need help." I hear movement and then nothing. "Viv? I hear you. I know you're in there."

The door opens slowly, revealing Vivien's bruised cheek and eyes that appear to be angry slits, though her voice says otherwise. "Yes?"

"You got a minute? I can't get this thing centered."

"Um, well..."

She's not going to do it. I misjudged her reaction to my note. She's obviously uncomfortable with me knowing. Or maybe I'm assuming too much. I need to clear the air so things aren't fucked-up between us. "May I come in? For a minute?"

She hesitates, but then opens the door. "Sure."

I step inside, and for the first time since meeting her, I feel nervous. I expected to see the angry, sexy Vivien. Not this one. This one is defeated, embarrassed. "Vivien?"

"Come on in. I'm watching the happy fantastic fun hour."

"Huh?"

"*The Price Is Right*. That's what we always called the show growing up."

"Oh, I see." Walking over to the sofa, I ask casually, "So, how was your date last night?" *Please say it sucked, please say it—*

"Don't ask."

Hell, yeah! It sucked. "Okay, I won't." I cheer inwardly.

She sits down on the sofa, bringing her feet up beneath her pretty bottom.

I plop down next to her. "Listen."

She holds her hand up. "Not yet. They're playing Plinko."

I look at the television and see a contestant standing above a giant board with the word Plinko written on top. The guy sets a flat silver disk at the top of the board and lets it go. I watch it bounce around, getting bumped left and right as it hits nail things sticking out, and then falls to the slot labeled zero dollars.

Vivien moans, "Bummer."

At the base of the board, there are slots with various money amounts from one hundred to ten thousand dollars listed inside. I watch the guy release another disk, holding my breath. Damn, this is kind of exciting. When it lands on one thousand, I make a yipping kind of sound.

She looks over at me with an arched brow.

"What? It's exciting."

"He's got one more disk."

We both watch as he drops the final piece. It seems to take an hour, but when it reaches the bottom, it looks like it will fall into another zero slot and then somehow redirects and lands in the ten-grand spot.

I clap and whoop. "Awesome."

She turns and gives me the first smile of the morning. Wincing, she touches her cheek.

"Did you ice it?"

Her face flushes red in seconds as she nods. "About that."

I don't give her a chance to chastise me. I'll just confess my sins. "Listen, I'm sorry. I shouldn't have gone into your bedroom."

"No, you shouldn't. I'm really embarrassed. Did you see... everything?"

"No." She was lying down so no, I didn't get to see *all* of her.

Her shoulders fall in relief as she looks down at her hands.

"But what I *did* see was beautiful, Vivien. I wanted to paint you."

She glances up at me, startled. "Oh, wow. Thank you," she whispers. She looks back up at the television, and her mood rapidly changes. Her hands fly up to cover her eyes. "Oh, fuck. Can this day get any more embarrassing?"

I look up at a commercial for erectile dysfunction. "Hey, no worries on my end. No need to feel embarrassed."

"No, ass." She points to the TV. "My dad."

Not wanting to give away my knowledge of her deadbeat dad, I play along. "I don't need to know about his erectile dys—"

"No. Carter." She points again. "That guy right there. On that commercial. *Is* my dad."

I turn back to the television to see a good-looking older man, a silver fox, talking about his problems in the sack. His arm is around a woman about his age. At the end, they're both in a bathtub out by a lake. "Serious?" I don't want to let on that I know about him, because I want to see how much she'll tell me.

"Serious. He left us to pursue his 'passion.'" She uses air quotes. "He said he couldn't be a father *and* an actor. He chose the latter."

"He left you? How old were you?"

"Thirteen."

"Does he live around here?"

"No. I think he's in New York."

"You think?"

She shrugs. "Last I heard, he was trying to make it on Broadway. I don't really talk to him. My sister does. She was too young to remember."

"Oh, I see. I'm sorry, Vivien."

Sighing, she leans her head back on the sofa, all the while nibbling on that damn lip piercing. A man could lose his mind watching her do that for too long. Peeking over at me, she adds, "At least you didn't see the one about opioid constipation. That one was *really* embarrassing."

I chuckle. "I bet." I reach over and squeeze her knee. "Sorry about your dad, Viv."

"Me too, Carter. Me too."

CHAPTER THIRTY-THREE

VIVIEN

I CAN'T BELIEVE I told Carter about my dad. The only other person who knows about my daddy drama is Kai. With my head in my hands, I mutter, "Why, why, why?"

It's probably because I was feeling particularly defeated and vulnerable. When Dad's face appeared on the television, I needed to talk about it. In the past, I've been alone when his commercials have popped up. I was certainly relieved Carter didn't ask a bunch of questions afterward. What else can I say? *Yeah, so anyway, Carter, my dad just threw me away like last week's trash.* Nope. Not gonna feel sorry for myself. It was ten plus years ago, for crying out loud.

Carter left right after all of that, saying he had to get ready for his flight. I haven't moved my ass off the couch since. Perhaps he wanted to hightail it out of here because of my depressing story. I don't blame him. I'm just big ole Debbie Downer today.

Flopping down so I'm now lying on the couch, I grumble, "God, I'm exhausted." I'm emotionally and physically wiped out. The last two years are finally catching up to me thanks to full-time school, working three jobs, my thesis show, and the paper I turned in the day before I graduated. All of that has taken a toll on my body. Right now, all I want to do is sleep for days.

Alas, that's not possible. I look up at the clock. It's five after one in the afternoon. It dawns on me that Julia hasn't shown up. What if she's sitting in Carter's dining room, waiting on me? I roll off the couch in search of my phone. The last time I saw it, it was in my purse. "Now, where's my purse?" Seeing a flash of red next to the side chair, I reach down. "Gotcha."

Looking at my phone, I see I've got at least one voice message from my mom and several texts. I'd silenced it on my date last night, so it's no wonder I didn't hear it dinging. I play Mom's message first.

"Honey, this is your mom. Just checking in. I'd like to plan that visit soon. Looking at my calendar, I've got an opening this Saturday. I'll bring my lasagna. I know you love it. You make the salad. Deal? I'm going to plan on it, but call me to confirm. I miss you, honey. I can't wait to see you."

I open my message app and decide to reply to Mom with a text. I'm not in the mood to chat this morning.

Me: Got your message. Saturday sounds great. How does six sound? I'll have the gate open for you. Just drive around the ugly fountain and park next to the silver Nissan. I'll be watching for you.

I see the dots moving around. Mom's typing a reply, but all I get is the thumbs-up emoji. I laugh. And she said she couldn't do "the texting."

Next, I read Kai's text sent last night.

Kai: I'm home safe. Call me tomorrow and tell me all about your date. XOXO

Julia's is next. She sent hers at six this morning. "Get a life, woman."

Julia: I've got meetings all day today. Be ready to work
at seven tomorrow. We'll meet in Carter's dining room.
Dress professionally. In the meantime, work on the logo.
I want to see it in the morning.

That text makes me smile. What? I actually get to do something I enjoy? Yippee! I turn in search of my laptop. Spying it on my table, I grab it and return to the couch. Luckily, I still have all my Adobe software from my undergrad design classes. The versions are super old, but they'll work.

The day flies by as I work for several hours on two logos. One's a smaller version made with a heart shaped palette and brush for letterhead, and the other one for print advertisements with the entire name, hArt of the City Foundation. I used blues and oranges for the color scheme—Bears colors. I hope he likes it. When I'm finished, I smile from ear to ear. I'm proud of what I've made. What is it about being creative that makes my mind and body hum? More than anything, I love making art.

Saving everything, I want to send the files off to Julia so she can see I was actually working today. I message her, asking for her email address. She replies immediately, so I send her my files. I stare at my computer, waiting for a reply, an acknowledgment, something, but nothing comes. I guess no news is good news. They must have been acceptable.

———

WHILE CARTER IS AWAY, I work with Julia from seven thirty most mornings until five. My mornings with her start with creating my to-do list, then I work the entire day getting what I can completed. A good result of all this running around is that I now know my way around South Barrington, Barrington, Schaumburg, and several other suburbs as well as Chicago. I've been to catering companies and bakeries for menus and samples for Julia to try. I've collected catalogs, more office supplies, and stamps. I know her favorite coffee from Starbucks, her favorite salad from Panera (the Seasonal Green Salad, hold the dressing), and I know exactly how to order her favorite sandwich from Potbelly. It's the Clubby with no bacon, no mayo, no ranch, and no cheese. **eye roll** *I mean. Why bother?* God forbid I screw up an order. I've had to go right back and make them redo it twice.

At the crack of dawn on day seven, I lumber to the kitchen, moaning, "Coffee. Cereal." It's all I need. Once I've got the pot brewing, I grab an extra-large cereal bowl and fill it with Fruity O's. My second favorite. When I lift the milk carton, it's light. Too light. "Shit." I'm out of milk. I could run to the store. *Or...* "I could see if Carter has any."

Slipping on a pair of flip-flops, I look down at myself. I'm wearing my favorite Pony tee with a pair of cut-off sweats. One leg is longer than the other, but I don't care. I pull the door open and walk to the patio steps. The only sounds I hear are my feet flopping. It's hard not to since everything is so quiet. Tranquil. At his back door, I enter his code without even an eye roll this morning. I'm over it. After it beeps, I pull open the door and step in. There are no lights on, but thanks to the wall of windows, sunlight illuminates the entire space and I can see my way to his kitchen. Rounding the corner, I nearly run into her. I squeal out my shock as a short, auburn-haired woman drops whatever she's holding and screams, "Jesus!"

"Shit!" I shout right back. "Who are you?" No doubt she's one of Carter's women. I quickly look at her in her entirety and wonder if it's possible. She's nothing like Natalia. As a matter of fact, she's even more Natalia's opposite than I am.

She's short, like I said. If she's five-feet-two, I'd be surprised. Not only that, she's curvy. *Very* curvy. Her boobs are even bigger than mine. I can't help noticing, since she's wearing jeans and a tight gray tee that says Flynn Construction on the front. She's got tons of red hair piled on top of her head and huge eyes that are a shade I've never seen before. They're golden, like a sunflower. Her face is round, with a tiny nose and freckles sprinkled over the top. She's really beautiful.

"Um, may I ask? Who are you?" I say, trying not to be rude.

Bending down to pick up the grocery bags she dropped, she mutters, "Well, I think I know who you are. Reggie?"

"Yes, I'm Reggie. Are you one of Carter's women?"

Pulling up to her full height, the redhead smiles. Then she throws her head back and laughs a really awesome laugh. It's warm and natural.

Setting the bags on the counter, she responds, "Well, I'm his sister, so I guess it makes me one of his 'women.'" She air quotes. See, for some reason it works for her.

"Kennedy?"

She reaches one hand out for me to shake. I slide my palm in hers as she squeezes. Hard. My hand is in a tiny vise.

"Wow, you've got quite a handshake," I mutter in pain.

"Yours is good too. You can tell a lot about a person from their handshake."

"Oh, okay." I have no idea what she means. We stare at each other for a few seconds. "I came to borrow some milk." I feel like I'm intruding. I just need to see if he's got any milk and then I'll skedaddle. I can't just do that and leave, though. It'd be rude. So I look at the grocery bags covering the counter. "Can I help you?"

"Nah, my husband is bringing the rest in from the truck."

"The rest?"

"The rest of the party shit. We're having my parents' anniversary party here next weekend, so we brought everything we'll need, since Carter's gone."

"Oh."

"You didn't know about the party? He said he was going to invite you."

"Oh, not yet." *He talked to his sister about inviting me?*

"You live here too. Of course you're invited."

Oh, that makes sense. More sense than me thinking he wanted me there for other reasons.

She reaches into a bag, pulling out five or six packages of hot dog buns. "I have it on good authority that you're cool. I hope you can come."

"Oh, well, he—"

"Shit, girl. You're invited. It's just a pool party-slash-barbeque-slash-keg. Nothing fancy."

"If you're sure."

"Positive. Great. It'll be nice getting to know you. My brothers said you were funny."

"Oh, well. I try," I say, shrugging.

When the door slams, I turn to the garage entrance as a gorgeous redheaded man holding a large box heads our way. He's massive. Not as muscle-bound as Carter, but just as tall. I swear, I've never seen this many beautiful people in one family in my life.

"Where do you want it, babe?"

Kennedy snickers and points to the only empty spot on the counter. "Reggie, this is my husband, Ernie."

I hold my hand out to shake his.

He grabs it and squeezes. Hard.

Damn, these people and their handshakes. "Nice meeting you."

"You too. You're coming to the party, right? Johnson and Clinton said you'd be the life of the party."

"Oh, I don't know about that. But I'll plan on being there." I wonder if I could invite Kai?

"Cool." He turns to his wife. Bending almost in half, he gives her a gentle kiss on the lips. "There's one more box of shit, babe. I'll be right back."

When he turns to leave, I watch Kennedy as she checks out her husband's backside.

Giggling, I say, "Do you think he'd mind if I borrowed some milk? I can't have cereal without milk."

"Hell, no. Help yourself. God, Carter *must* be in love with you. Cereal is his main food group."

I blush. "No. He's not. But I can appreciate a fellow sugary-cereal connoisseur." She steps out of the way of the fridge as I open it. He's got a half gallon of whole milk. "Thanks. I'll pay him back before he gets home."

"No worries. He won't be home for several days. It'll go bad if someone doesn't drink it."

That's true.

I step out of the kitchen and turn back to her. "Nice meeting you, Kennedy."

"You too. See you Saturday, hopefully."

"Same here."

I walk quickly out the door, resetting the alarm to the back door, heading straight to my place. I need to eat and drink some coffee or this day will never get off the ground.

CHAPTER THIRTY-FOUR

CARTER

I WAS able to catch a nonstop early morning flight out of Newark International. Our meetings and media shit were over, so I changed my ticket to get home in time to help set up for the party tomorrow. It's my folks' thirtieth wedding anniversary. It seems impossible that a couple could be together that long, but they've done it and they've done it with love, friendship, and a ton of patience. They're definitely an example I hope to live up to one day. The one bit of advice they've repeated to all of us is that you should marry your friend, not your lover. I never understood what they meant until I met Casey.

Edward picked me up at O'Hare and is now driving me straight home. I'm exhausted, but there's no rest for me until tonight. First order of business? See how Julia and Viv are doing. I hope they've accomplished a lot. I haven't had a chance to check in with them this last week, but I have confidence in them.

Pulling through the gate, Edward rounds the curve, and I gaze at the fountain. "Hey, Ed?"

"Yes, sir."

"What are your thoughts on the fountain?"

He chuckles. "Well, sir, I think it's butt ugly."

I throw my head back and laugh. "I feel the same."

"Perhaps you could hire your young artist friend to create something new?"

Smiling, I say, "That's an amazing idea. I just might do that." Ed and I chatted about Vivien in the car on the way to the airport. Edward thinks Vivien is a "very special young lady." Of course I agreed and told him how talented she is.

Pulling to a stop in front of my home, he opens his door to step out. "Let me get your bag."

"No need. Stay put. I'll grab it. Just pop the trunk." Opening my door, I turn to him. "Thanks, Ed. See you in a few weeks." When he takes me back to the airport for yet another set of team meetings and events.

Entering my home feels wonderful. I'm a homebody, and being away for long spans of time gets to me. I leave my duffle by the front door, and when I find my way to the dining room, I stare in disbelief. What was once my dining room is now more like a war room. There are papers everywhere. A large white-board is resting on the sideboard, against the wall with lists of things to do. Several items are crossed off the list, but I don't get the chance to read them before Julia spots me.

"Carter!" she exclaims. Rushing toward me, she reaches out and takes both my hands in hers.

I stiffen at her a little too familiar greeting. Patting one of her shoulders mechanically, I gently push her away from me. I spy Vivien, the only person I wish had run to me, sitting on the floor on the other side of the table, doing something with small index cards.

"Hey, Viv." I smile at her but get a weak smile in return.

"Welcome home, Carter." Her voice is soft and, if I know her at all, I'd say it sounded sad or maybe defeated. She's probably just tired.

The tension in the room remains, so I clap my hands together in the hopes it'll stop. "What have you ladies accomplished while I was gone?"

"Well," starts Julia, "I've done so much."

There she goes, talking like she's doing this on her own. I don't reply, deciding to hear the rest.

"I've scheduled interviews on most of the Chicago morning talk shows starting in September to discuss your foundation. You'll be interviewed by the *Tribune and* the *Sun Times* that same month. I've contacted a number of outside contractors to help with the gala."

"Wait. Gala?"

Beaming, she hops up and down on her toes. "Yes. I've secured the ballroom at the Cultural Center downtown. No easy feat, let me tell you." She winks. "It's the perfect venue to launch the Carter Corcoran Foundation for the Arts. I planned it for your week off during the football season."

I blink, then look over at Vivien, who is staring at Julia with her mouth agape.

"What did you call the foundation?"

My question was directed at Vivien, but she remains mute.

Julia titters. "The Carter Corcoran Foundation for the Arts. It's perfect. Here." She turns her computer around. "Check out your logo."

I lean forward and lower my head to see the images on her laptop. It's a black logo made up of my initials, CC. The two Cs are overlapping and one is backward, surrounded by a circle so it looks a lot like the Chanel logo. The words Arts and Foundation are above and below the Cs, making it appear more like a formal seal and nothing like what Vivien and I talked about.

I look over at Vivien, who hasn't moved a muscle since Julia started talking. Not one muscle. Crossing my arms over my chest, I do my best to rein in my anger. "Vivien? What the hell?"

She's pulled from her fog at my words. "What the hell what?" She stands from her spot on the floor and walks to stare down at the laptop. She's wearing a dress. A pretty navy blue dress that looks demure, conservative with its high neckline and short sleeves. She's beautiful, yes, but she looks more like a Julia than a Vivien right now.

Shaking my head slightly, I need to get back on track. Back to this mess. "The fuck is that?" I point at the computer. "This is nothing like we discussed. Nothing. And I told you specifically that I didn't want my name anywhere in the name of the foundation. I told you that, Vivien. I think I was pretty damn clear." God, I'm fucking pissed right now.

Turning around slowly, I see her eyes are wet.

Oh, great. She's turning on the waterworks, but I'm not going to fall for it. "I'm so fucking disappointed in you. I leave for week, and you decide to change everything about my vision for this thing. Hell, I told you specifically that I didn't want a gala, and I definitely don't want to go on any fucking talk shows. This *isn't* about me. This is about the kids and the teachers. You *knew* this."

Without a word, she steps around me and out the dining room entrance and, moments later, out the patio door. Turning to Julia, I say, "What the fuck just happened?"

She shrugs and turns to gather up papers.

That's it?

"I need to run, Carter. I've got some, er, things to do this afternoon."

I watch her cram her shit into her leather bag. It's like she can't get out of here fast enough. I'm expecting her to say more, but when she says nothing, I walk away from her. I need to shower and get my shit together. In my bedroom, I strip out of my jeans and dress shirt, leaving me in only dark blue boxer briefs. As I'm about to enter my bathroom, my bedroom door flies open to a panting Vivien Reginald.

God, she's gorgeous.

Viv's holding a laptop open in her arms as she stomps into my room. Shoving the thing in my face, she says, "Here, asshole."

I look down at the logo we discussed, a heart shaped palette, and smile when I see the blue and orange. The name *hArt of the City Foundation* is in the same Bears colors and an artistic font.

Looking up at Vivien, I ask, "Why didn't you use these?"

"Are you fucking kidding me right now? I sent her these files. She must have hired someone else, because she said nothing to me." She's practically spitting. "Why would you think I had a say in any of this shit? I'm just a glorified assistant to her highness down there. All I've done for two weeks is run errands for that woman." She's pointing out my door. "I've driven ten thousand miles in your car doing shit for this foundation like getting coffee and salads for Queenie." She turns to leave. "And for the record, I"—she points to her chest—"am the one who arranged for your frigging interviews and practically had to prostitute myself to get that goddamn ballroom at the Cultural Center for your bye week. Per *her* orders. I knew you would be pissed, but *you* hired her. *You* deal with it. She barely speaks to *me* unless it's to berate me or boss me around." She stomps to the door but turns back to say one more thing. "Oh, and one more thing." She pauses. "I quit."

"Wait!" I shout, reaching her before she has a chance to run. Placing my palm on her upper arm, I ask, "Why would Julia be in charge? She's merely the consultant. You're in charge."

Scoffing, she says, "You're joking, right? She's been in charge from the beginning. Remember our lunch meeting?"

Okay, so that explains the tension that day. Why did I not see what was happening? "You should have said something."

She rolls her eyes so hard it looks painful. "What was I to think? When we talked about this, from the beginning you said you wanted me to 'spearhead' your foundation. I had no idea you were going to hire a consultant. You didn't say one fucking word to me. She just appeared that day in your house." She rubs her palms over her face, groaning. "You watched her talk down to me, Carter. You watched her demand I eat what I was served and clean up your fucking broken plate. Did you not think that was strange? I mean, if I was in charge, didn't you ask yourself, 'Gee, why is Julia talking to Vivien like she works for her?' Huh?" She pulls her arm away from my hand. "You suck, Carter. I'm so pissed at you right now, all I want to do is punch you in your goddamn pretty face."

"Do it."

I think I surprise her, because she halts all movement. "Yeah?"

"Yeah. Do it. Except don't break your hand. You need it for clay."

She rears her fist back and stops, frozen in time. Her angry face has morphed into something else. It's fallen, and moisture is gathering in the corners of her eyes as she lowers her raised fist to her side.

"Babe, I'm sorry."

"You're sorry?" she says, sniffling. "You're sorry you let her treat me like shit or you're sorry you were too self-absorbed to see it?"

I reach out and stroke her soft cheek with my finger, wiping away a tear. Softly, I say, "Both. But why didn't you say anything? I thought we were better than that."

She hasn't moved. She's letting me touch her, and I've never felt so unsure in my life. I'm half expecting her to bolt. "Carter," she croaks. "I work for you."

"Not anymore." I chuckle.

"No." She releases a laugh. "Not anymore. I'm going to let you deal with the high priestess."

"Forgive me?"

She looks away, moving back like she's about to leave. Is that a no? I'm not giving up. I'm sincere here. I made way too many assumptions. Stepping closer to her, I slide my finger under her chin, encouraging her to look up at me. "Viv?"

She's biting on that fucking lip ring like she's nervous.

Fuck. I want that thing in my mouth. "Babe," I whisper.

I slide my palm around her neck as I lean down to kiss her, but I stop. I want to be sure she wants this too. She looks into my eyes, and hers crinkle at the corners. Smiling eyes. I touch her lips softly as she slides her hands over my shoulders and around my neck. A tingle rolls down my arms and back as she touches me. Jesus, this girl gives me chills.

She opens her mouth slightly, and I take it as a sign. I pull her to me until nothing can come between us. No light, no air. The kiss becomes intense fast. I can't get enough of her mouth. I suckle on that fucking ring and swipe my tongue over it until my tongue is back inside her mouth. I'm so fucking hard I feel like I could come from her kiss alone.

Reaching down, I place one hand on each luscious ass cheek and lift. She makes a sweet sound of surprise. She pulls back slightly, but only enough to kiss my face and around to my ear. When she bites on my lobe, I fucking growl. I love that shit.

"Yeah, put your teeth on me, Vivien."

She listens, nibbling on the column of my neck as I walk us over to my bed. Setting her on the mattress, I pull back just enough so I can look at her. I want her skin on mine.

"Take your dress off, baby." I want to see her.

She's hesitant. Nervous? But she does it, slowly. When the bottom edge of her dress passes above her breasts, I stop breathing momentarily. Yeah, I saw her tits that day she was naked in her bed. But seeing her like this, practically nude with only a sexy white lace bra and tiny panties, is the most breathtaking thing I've ever seen. I'm in love. No joke. I'm. In. Fucking. Love. And not just with her tits. Her face is so soft she looks coy, vulnerable.

"Vivien? If we start this, I won't be able to stop."

She nods, but I'm not sure she understands what I'm saying. I'm not just talking about today.

I move over her, kissing her lips again. This time slowly. I swipe my tongue on her piercing and kiss my way down her neck. With my hand, I gently push her back to the bed. My mouth moves over her collarbone. I run my tongue over the top of her chest, between her breasts as my hands move up from her waist to her tits. I feel them, skim my fingers over the lace. Feeling her nipples peak, I bring my fingers to the edge of the bra and tug pulling the nearly see-through covering down, revealing my prize.

Lowering my head, I use my tongue to tease her left breast. She moans, which signals I'm doing something she likes. Sliding as much of the tip in my mouth as I can, I suckle until she's writhing. Damn, so responsive. I move to the other side and repeat. I could spend hours on her tits alone, but there's so much more to explore with Vivien Reginald. Kissing the tip of each breast softly, I let my eyes move down over her soft tummy. I place my nose close to her skin to breathe her in. I smell her arousal. Now, I want to feel it, see it. I place my hand on her panties and look up at her. I need a sign, a signal, letting me know this is okay.

She nods.

I smile as I use my fingertips to slide her panties down. She lifts her hips to help me. I move unhurriedly. I want this reveal to be one I remember for the rest of my life. I've seen plenty of naked women. Most of them were a lot like Natalia. I don't remember the last time I was with someone with a body like this. Like sin.

When the white lace slides over her wide hips, I keep moving them down. When I get a glimpse of her hair, I rest my nose there and smell again. So fucking sweet. When I can't wait any longer, I drag the panties down the rest of the way and off. *Finally*. I stand up and take a step back. I need to look at her in her entirety. This is what I pictured that day. The image I had of her in *my* bed.

"Jesus, Vivien. You're so fucking beautiful."

I sense hesitation, and a blush has swept across her face. Her hand moves to cover her pussy.

"No."

She stops her hand from moving any further.

"Scoot back, honey. Spread your legs for me."

She does so, hesitantly. With her head on my pillow, she brings her legs up and opens them, and it's like a flower blooming. I can't help noticing how wet she is and it's making my dick painfully hard. I place my hand on my cock and rub up and down, trying to give him some relief. This is taking every bit of restraint I've got. I'd love to rip off my briefs and fuck her into oblivion. But not today. Hell, I fantasized about her—jacked off to thoughts of this body in the shower but I honestly didn't even think we'd ever get to this point. I imagined if we decided to take it to the next level, we'd just talk and hopefully touch and kiss. This is so much better.

Keeping my boxer briefs on, I place one knee on the bed and then the other. Moving between her legs, I peek down again. "This okay, Viv?"

"Yes," she whispers.

I start at her foot and let my hands roam over her ankle, leg, up her soft thigh. "So soft," I mutter as I do the same to her other leg. Using my palms, I press her legs open further.

She seems uncomfortable, so I check again. "Baby, if this is too much, too fast, just tell me."

"No. It's good. It's just been a while since..."

"Shh, I've got you." Besides, I don't want to hear one fucking thing about her last time.

I bring my hands up to her center and slide one finger through her wetness. She moans as my thumb brushes her clit. I do that again several more times, then stop to investigate the rest of her. No worries. I'll get back to that soon.

Using my thumbs, I open her further so I can see her, see everything. She's fucking perfect. Pink, wet, and so damn pretty. Moving closer, I place my elbows between her thighs and nudge her open more so I can fit my wide shoulders between her legs. I use my nose to bump her clit, making her moan again. Swiping my tongue from bottom to top, it's my turn to moan. So sweet. I hurriedly lick her again and feel a franticness come through me. Like I can't get enough of her, like I've got to have it all. I work quickly, suckling, biting, eating.

Vivien is squirming and muttering, but I'm too focused on what I'm doing to figure out what she's saying. When her hand slides onto the top of my head and her nails drag across my scalp, I moan. It feels so good. So good I come. Just like that, I come. Right in my underwear like a damn teenager. Should I be embarrassed? Maybe. But, I'm not going there. It couldn't be helped because when you're pleasuring the sexiest woman on the planet and she makes the most erotic sounds I've ever heard, it happens. Deal with it.

Releasing a low moan into her pussy as I do, I feel her fluttering beneath my tongue. Sliding a finger inside, I feel her squeeze me tightly as she comes down from her orgasm. I lick her several more times, taking in her essence.

Pushing myself back up on my knees, I look down at her, relaxed and sated. I thought she was beautiful before, but nothing has ever looked this perfect. I move up above her again and kiss her tenderly, whispering, "You're so fucking beautiful, Vivien."

She blushes again but smiles. "You are too, Carter."

I slide off the bed and step quickly into the bathroom to clean myself up. I'm in a hurry because half of me is worried she's going to be gone by the time I get back to the bed. In my room, I smile when I see she's still there. Moving closer, I ask, "Can we lay in bed for a while?" I don't want to spook her, but I also don't want her to think this was a one-time thing. This is all happening so fast.

"Sure." She scoots over to make room for me.

I slide in behind her and pull her into me so we're spooning. I reach down and bring the blanket over the top of us and wrap my arm over and around her. She's so soft. I nuzzle her neck, kissing the side of it and whisper to her, telling her how sweet, how special she is. I'm asleep in minutes, but before I'm out, I get an overwhelming sense of something I'm not sure I can explain. Something I haven't felt for years.

I'm calm.

I'm satisfied.

I'm home.

CHAPTER THIRTY-FIVE

VIVIEN

I'M WRAPPED IN WARMTH, so comfortable I almost don't notice something prodding me in the ass. That's not so comfortable until I realize what it is. And who it is. *It's surreal. I'm in bed with Carter.* This is major.

How did this even happen? One minute I was telling him off; the next, he was kissing me. I've no idea what to think about any of it. Kai told me he thought Carter had a thing for me, but I didn't believe him. Even now I'm not so sure. We should probably talk. Yes. We should definitely have a serious chat, but right now I just want to enjoy being held tight in big, thick arms. I'm not sure I could even talk if I wanted to, which I don't. Not right now.

I wiggle my bottom to see if I can get his big thingy to a more comfortable location. When it moves to that spot between my cheeks, I sigh. That is until I feel his hips move against me. I want to moan. This man excites me. I move back into him because, damn it, I can't help it.

"Vivien," he says huskily. "You'd better stop moving."

"Why?" I nearly whine. "I don't want to," I say in a slightly hoarse voice as I push my ass back again.

Growling like an animal, he rolls me onto my back and, before I can blink, Carter is above me. It happens so fast. How'd he do that? His lips are on mine before I can utter a word. His tongue sinks deep into my mouth, meeting mine along the way. God, the man can kiss. I wrap my arms around his shoulders and slide them down his huge arms. Next, I move them over his chest and skim his nipples with my fingers, pinching them.

Carter pulls away from me right at that moment. His eyes are so dark they're dilated. His breathing has turned to pants. "I want to be deep inside you so badly, Viv."

I want that too. "What's stopping you?" I mean, I'm naked. He's nearly naked. *Hey! Why isn't he naked?* Time to remedy that. I reach down and run my palm over his erection and feel faint. He's ginormous. I wondered about that the first night we met but did my best not to think about it after that. It was pointless to wonder. But now, with my hand wrapped, or nearly wrapped, around him, I now know for sure. He's definitely in proportion.

"Vivien?"

I look up into his eyes and whisper apprehensively, "I want you too, Carter."

"Fuck," he grumbles as he jumps off the bed.

For a second, I think he's leaving. But it's not the case. I watch as he slides his boxer briefs down his thick thighs, over his legs and feet, and kicks them away. When he turns and bends down to his jeans, I think I come a tiny bit. That ass is perfect, round, perky. In a word, it's remarkable. When he stands back up, he's got a shiny gold package in his hand.

I move myself to a seated position, so I can watch him. When he hands me the condom package, I open it with my teeth. His eyes grow round as he growls again. Placing the condom over the head while his hand reaches out and brushes over the tip of my right breast, I shiver. I roll it down slowly, watching my hand as I go. Is it possible to have a pretty dick? I never thought so, but Carter Corcoran has a beautiful dick. Trust me. When he's fully sheathed, I look up. His breathing is labored, and his eyes are gazing into mine.

"You sure, Viv?"

I love how he asks me every step of the way. It makes me feel more confident that what we're doing here is right.

"I'm sure." I lie back on the bed, but he reaches out his hand. I place mine in his.

He tugs me up again. I don't know what he's doing. I've only ever done this stuff missionary position, so I follow his lead. He steps to the end of the bed and sits on a padded bench like the one in my room. The one I thought was used for putting on socks. Only now I can see just how versatile it can be. I stare down at his face and let my eyes wander downward. He's magnificent. I'd love to sculpt him. His chest is hard and perfectly formed. There's a small tattoo over the center of it. I caught a glimpse of it that shirtless day in his kitchen, but now that I'm closer I can see it's one word. A name? I lean down and read *Casey*. It says Casey. The sight of it causes a wave of emotion to wash over me. This man is so sweet, so kind to remember her that way. I brush my thumb over the word but get distracted by his abs. Geez, I thought those things were mythical, only ever seen on the covers of romance novels. Kai's got a great body, but he doesn't have those. I drag my eyes down to his erection that has got to be eight inches long or more. Again. Mythical. It's never going to fit.

Still holding my hand, he pulls me until I'm between his open legs. Without a word, his hands slide up to my breasts. He kneads them with his big paws, pinches, and then uses his mouth like before. It feels amazing. So much so, my hips move back and forth on their own. God, I'm so wet. His hands leave my chest, and I feel them slide over my ribs to my lower back, then to my ass.

Squeezing my cheeks, he pulls me closer. "Straddle me."

Damn, he's so bossy. I look down at his massive thighs and wonder if it's possible to do this. Placing one knee on his right side, I push up and do the same on the left. I'm split so wide apart it hurts a little, but when he slides his hands from my ass to my lady parts, I forget about any pain. His fingers are fluttering around my center, opening me up further. I moan and feel myself press down onto his hands. I've never felt this needy before.

I scoot closer to him until my center is directly above his, then look down at him nervously.

"You okay, honey?" he asks in a husky voice.

"You're never going to fit."

He chuckles, and I'm a goner. "We'll fit."

I nod and start to lower myself as he leans back against the bed, giving me more room. When his tip is nestled into me, I stiffen. I mean, this is it. I'm about to screw Carter Corcoran. Right or wrong, I'm about to do it.

With his hand on my waist now, he urges me down. I squeeze my eyes shut as he fills my core. Using my body weight and the strength of his hands, I'm able to move all the way down until he's completely seated inside. It's intense. He's big. Very big. But it feels so damn good. I finally open my eyes to see Carter wincing.

"Oh, shit. Am I hurting you?" I try to scramble up and off, but he holds me in place.

"No, Jesus, Viv. It's amazing. You're so fucking tight. Just give me a second."

"Oh." Okay. I watch him doing practiced breathing like he's in labor. I'd love to laugh at this, but he's concentrating so hard I don't want to mess it up.

"Okay. Now slide up, slowly."

I use the strength of my knees to slide back up until he's at my entrance again.

"Now down."

I do as he says over and over again until it's a much faster pace. God, it feels so good.

"Faster," he mutters.

With the help of his arms and hands, I'm practically bouncing on top of him. I'd be embarrassed if I had room for any other feelings besides utter and complete euphoria.

"Oh, Carter. Yes. Carter. I'm almost there. Don't stop."

"Get there, Viv. Get there."

One or two more thrusts and I'm there. So *very* there. "Ahh, Carter." I come so hard I see stars.

He presses up into me one more time, and his moan is so loud, the room vibrates with the sound. When he opens his eyes, he blinks up at me. Our eyes meet, and I watch as his lips gradually widen into the most breathtaking smile I've ever seen. His dimple appears, and I watch as a slight pink color tints his cheeks. Is he blushing?

"That felt fucking good, Vivien. The best."

I look down at him and feel my own heated cheeks. I smile. "It was."

I feel his hands pressing up, and I know he wants me to get up. I move slowly and wince at the pain. My knees and my lady bits are all tender. But well worth it.

"Let's go take a shower," he says, standing up, my hand in his.

I nod and follow him. I've never had a shower with a guy before. I've never felt confident enough or comfortable enough with any of my past partners, all three of them, to do anything like this. But now I do, and I know this'll be fun because I'm doing it with Carter. My friend and now my lover.

CHAPTER THIRTY-SIX

CARTER

"I'VE NEVER BEEN CLEANER after doing so many dirty things." Vivien giggles as I dry her body for her.

She already helped me, so it's only fair I return the favor. I could look at her body all day long. It's so soft and round. She's got a real body, and couple that with everything else that's real about her, and I've found myself a keeper.

"Damn, I'm starving. I haven't eaten since the flight. What about you?"

Her stomach rumbles.

I bend and kiss her belly button. "Time to feed my woman." Walking nude into the bedroom, I search my dresser for some athletic shorts. Grabbing clean boxers, I cover my lower half as I watch Vivien slip her dress back on. When I see she's going without her bra and panties, I almost drag her back to bed. Knowing she's got nothing on underneath the dress is going to drive me insane.

Taking her hand in mine, I lead her out of my bedroom and down the stairs to the kitchen. "Sit down. Let me cook something up." I open the fridge and peer inside. "What sounds good, honey?"

She doesn't respond.

I turn and look at her. She's nibbling on her lip ring. Why? "Vivien? What's wrong?"

"Nothing."

"You're chewing on that lip ring of yours. That means something's up."

Her eyes are big and round, like I just shared something surprising with her. She has to know she nips at that thing when she's feeling uneasy. Right?

The moment is interrupted by a knock on the front door. We turn to each other. "It's probably one of my brothers." I lean out the doorway and yell, "It's open."

The door opens, and Johnson steps inside. "Hey, we're here to set up for the party."

"We?"

"Clinton, Kennedy, Ernie, and me."

Shit. I'm not ready to do this shit right now. Johnson looks at Vivien. "Hey, Reggie. How's it going, gorgeous?"

Okay, he needs to knock that shit off. She smiles at him, then starts on that damn piercing again. What's happening?

Johnson looks from Viv to me. "Why are you both wet?"

Vivien coughs and looks at the floor.

"We're not wet."

"Your hair is wet. So is hers. Did you guys go for a swim?"

"Yes. We went for a swim." I'm not ready for everyone to know yet, especially with a house full of a hundred and fifty people. Not yet.

I look at Vivien, expecting her to smile at my response, but that's not the look I'm getting. Her lips have formed a straight line. Something in the past five minutes has removed her smile and the sparkle in her eyes. There's no time to analyze what that all means as the front door opens and the rest of my siblings pour in laughing and talking.

"Hey, guys." I walk around the island to hug my sister. "Kenny. Let me introduce you to Vivien."

"We've met."

"Oh? When?"

"When Ern and I dropped off party supplies. She popped in to borrow some milk."

"Oh, that's cool. I told her she had free rein."

"I bet you did," Johnson whispers, looking down at me. "You and I both know you weren't in the pool just now."

I shrug. "I've no idea what you're talking about."

"Suit yourself." He shrugs as he opens my refrigerator. "Got any beer?"

Ignoring Johnson, I watch as Clinton plops his ass on the sectional, reaching for the remote and flipping channels while Kennedy and Ernie sort through supplies in the kitchen.

"Listen up." Kennedy claps to get everyone's attention. "Now, here's the drill. I've typed up honey-do lists for each of you guys for today. Be sure to mark off each task as you've completed them."

She hands me mine, and I read the first item: *Make sure grill is ready. Need propane?* I look up at her. "The grill gas line is tied to the house. I never need to go get gas."

"Well, la-tee-da, fancy man."

I smirk, then look at the list again. *Sweep deck, wipe down tables. Make sure you let your people know when the party starts.*

"Oh, man. I've got to set up all the tables again? That job sucks," Clinton whines as he reads his list.

"Sorry, baby brother. Low man on the totem pole and all that," Johnson mutters.

"That's not fair. What's on Ernie's list? To kiss your ass all day?" Clinton is only teasing, but he'd better watch it.

"As a matter of fact," Kennedy says, looking at her husband, "He's my assistant. Aren't you, honey?"

"Sure am," Ernie says with his mouth full of something.

Is that potato salad he's holding? I love potato salad. I walk over and grab the large bowl from him. "I'm starving." Pulling the fork from his hand, I dig in.

"I bet you are, Romeo," Ernie says only loud enough for me to hear.

"Johnson," I growl.

"What?" he says with an innocent pout. "All I meant was—"

"Never mind," I mumble.

Kennedy claps her hands together again. It's rather annoying. "All right, ladies. Enough chitchat. Let's get this show on the road. We've got two hours of daylight. Let's go, let's go, let's go."

Now do you see how she became foreman on commercial job sites? She gets shit done.

When I search the room for Vivien, she's nowhere to be found. "Yo, anyone see where Vivien went?"

"Who's Vivien?"

"Reggie, Clinton. Vivien is her real name."

"Wow, she's definitely a Vivien. Sexy name for a sexy girl."

"Knock it off." I punch my little bro in the arm, not hard, but hard enough for him to know I meant what I said.

"Shit, dude. That hurt. What's the big deal? You sleeping with her now or something?"

"No. Don't be ridiculous." I don't want them to know. Not yet. Not until I tell Vivien how I feel and know if she feels the same.

I walk past him in time to see Vivien's back. She's walking at a fast clip right toward the patio door. I'm getting tired of seeing the back of her as she leaves.

CHAPTER THIRTY-SEVEN

VIVIEN

I CAN'T GET out of Carter's house fast enough. My thoughts and emotions are all over the board. First Johnson's questions, then Clinton's offhand remark, all rebuffed by Carter. He had the nerve to say a relationship between us would be "ridiculous." I guess that's true. I thought so from the beginning but was stupid enough to believe that what we just did up in his bedroom meant something to him. It certainly meant something to me. Shit, I can't believe I let that happen. No, I know why I let it happen. I needed it.

Scrounging around in my kitchen, I search for something to eat. I'm not in the mood for cereal. Yeah, I know. It seems impossible to me too. I discover a box of microwave popcorn in one of my cupboards. It must have been something Carter bought for me that morning after he knocked me on my ass. It wasn't a big deal. Nothing broke, and it healed fairly quickly. I had some great foundation that covered it enough to hide it from Julia.

And speaking of Julia. What a nightmare. I really ended up hating the woman's guts by the end of the ten days. The way I got through each day was picturing all the ways I could maim her. No, now don't go getting all stressy about that. I'm nonviolent, all talk and no action.

My phone dings. I'm tempted to ignore it, but I'd better look in case it's something important. I see Carter's name illuminated on my screen.

"Goody." I don't want to talk to him, but I'll read his text message.

Carter: Where'd you go?
Me: Home
Carter: Why?
Me: Hungry and tired.
Carter: Come back. We're ordering pizza.
Me: ...

I can't believe I'm about to say this, but...

Me: Don't be "ridiculous."
Carter: ...

I wait for him to respond. He's a smart guy, he'll get it. I wait, staring at the three dots vibrating on the screen indicating he's typing. I wait another few minutes but eventually drop the phone on the counter. I'm not going to stand here and—

The knock sounds on my door. "Crap." I know it's him. "It's open."

He steps in, wearing the shorts from earlier but he's finally put a shirt on. A Bears tee, of course. "Viv?"

I roll my eyes and look up at the ceiling. I spy a cobweb and shiver, hoping it's not attached to anything with eight creepy, crawly legs. I need to clean. When his palms come to rest on my waist, I look at him. "What?" Yeah, I'm miffed.

"The only reason I said that shit was because they won't let it rest if I admit we're together. I wanted to talk to you first. We were so busy doing other things, we didn't talk about what we were doing."

"Okay. What *are* we doing?" I'm still miffed.

"Let's sit down. Let's talk."

I flop onto the couch unceremoniously. My skirt flips up, and I quickly smooth it back down. I don't know why I bother. The man just had me naked for the last several hours. He's rubbing his palms up and down his thighs. *Is he nervous?*

"Vivien?"

"Uh-huh." I'm mesmerized by the man.

Reaching for my hands, he pulls them and me closer. "I wanted to talk to you. You know, before we, uh—"

"You mean before we had sex earlier?"

"Yes. As you know, one thing led to another, and there wasn't a lot of talking."

"That's true." He *is* nervous. It's so cute.

"I planned to talk to you. To tell you how I felt about you. To explain my intentions."

I blink at the big man in front of me. I know my mouth is hanging open by the breeze on my teeth. "Your intentions?"

"Yes. My intentions. Anyway..." Carter stands up and walks to the chair across from my spot. Sitting back down, he continues. "I've been waiting, in part because you were working for me and I didn't feel comfortable crossing over that line. When I was away, I decided I couldn't wait any longer."

"You did?"

"Yes."

"But you didn't even text me."

Carter runs his nervous hands through his hair. "I'm confused about you." He chuckles. "Hell, I even talked to Kennedy about you."

"You did? What'd she tell you to do?"

"She told me to go for it."

"Well." I laugh. "You certainly did that earlier."

"I did," he smiles. It's a little smug. "So, tell me, Viv." He scoots closer to me. "Do you feel the same? I mean, I'm hoping you have similar feelings. About me. Do you?"

Do I have feelings for Carter? Of course I've got feelings for Carter. "Well..."

"Don't leave me hangin', woman."

"I've had the hots for you since the first second I laid eyes on you."

He chuckles, and you know what that does to me. "Oh yeah? Were you hoping I was actually propositioning you that night?"

"Hell, yeah. I wanted to climb you like a damn tree." I giggle, but I'm stopped mid-giggle by a kiss. It's not like any of the other kisses. It's deep and hurried. I kiss him back, matching his fervor.

"I've wanted you for so long, Viv. God, I can barely get a night's sleep thinking about your body and your soft skin. I want you in my bed every night. I want to wake up to you every morning. I imagine us making plans, traveling, and making art together."

"Wow, you've really thought about all that, with me?"

"And more." He leans down and kisses me tenderly this time. "Do you want to try? With me?"

"I do. I'm just not sure I'll be any good at it. My feelings about relationships are a bit skewed." Thanks to my dad. "But I want to try."

"So, we're doing this?" His smile is so broad and happy, and I'm the reason for that smile.

"Yeah, we're doing this."

"Fuck yeah!" Carter reaches down and wraps his big hands around my waist, lifting me up until I'm over his shoulder.

I scream in surprise. "What the hell? I'm too heavy. Put me down."

"To the bedroom!" he shouts like some kind of warrior. "It's time we consummate this new relationship."

Wow, I'm in a relationship with Carter Corcoran. I feel like I should know more about him. "What's your middle name?" I'm upside down, my face looking directly at his ass. It's a good place to be.

"Franklin."

"As in Franklin Delano Roosevelt?"

"No, as in Franklin Corcoran, my grandfather, but that works too."

"Good to know."

"Yours is Jayne."

How'd he...?

"They said it at your commencement. Why Jayne?"

"Mansfield. You know, the actress."

"I do. She was beautiful."

"She was."

Stopping in my bedroom, he lifts me off his shoulder and sets me down gently. "She doesn't hold a candle to you, Vivien."

"Oh, thank you." I know I'm pink from embarrassment and probably shouldn't believe him, but I do.

CHAPTER THIRTY-EIGHT

CARTER

"SHE DOESN'T HOLD a candle to you, Vivien."

"Thank you, Carter."

No more talking. I reach down and slide my hands under her dress, slipping it up and off before she has time to think. "Lay down, Viv."

Sitting on the bed, she scoots to the middle and lies back. The sight of her spread out on her bed is doing things to me. *She's mine.* I run my palm over my dick, trying to calm the ache behind the fabric of my shorts. I'm afraid to take everything off for fear this will be over before we start like earlier.

I lean down, crawling to the center of the bed until I'm directly above those magnificent breasts. I swipe my tongue over one pert little nipple, already hard and pebbled, my tongue only increasing its arousal. I move to the other breast as Vivien arches her back.

Damn, she's sexy when she wants me. Hell, she's sexy when she doesn't.

I move back to her other breast and suckle that one. With my right hand, I hold the other and squeeze it gently. I pluck at her nipple like I'm playing an instrument. She's making amazing noises, moans, and sighs. It's music. Sexy Vivien music. I pinch the free nipple, and she gasps.

"Too much?" I say, looking up at her.

"No," she says. "Don't stop."

Oh, I won't. I change to the other side and repeat. By now she's literally writhing on the bed. Moving down, I slide my fingernails down her rib cage, past the dip in her waist, then down to her pussy. I don't know where to start. I look up at her face. Her pretty brown eyes are hooded. "What do you want, Vivien?"

"You," she says in a husky whisper.

See? So damn sexy. "Where? Where do you want me?"

"Inside," she says, running her hands over her breasts. She pinches her own nipples, and I'm a goner.

Moving over her, I kiss and lick my way up over her chest. I nip at her shoulder, then below her ear. She's moaning again. I look down into her eyes and smile.

Her smile in return is hesitant and sweet.

"We're doing this?" I ask softly.

"We're doing this."

I place myself at her center and press inside slowly. Her legs wrap around me to pull me in even closer, deeper.

"You feel so fucking good, honey."

"You do too, Carter."

Hesitating, I realize I didn't suit up. "I'm not wearing a rubber."

"On the pill, and I haven't had sex in a long, long time, so please don't stop."

"I'm clean. I've never gone without. Team docs check us regularly."

"Fine. Good. Now move." She sounds bossy. "Please?" Now that sounded like begging.

I can't disappoint her. I pull out halfway and press back in slowly. She's wet and so damn tight. A man could lose his mind with a woman who feels this good.

I can tell she wants to say something, so I stop. "What? Tell me what you want. I can't read your mind, and I want this to be good for you."

"Okay." She blinks. "Harder. Faster."

Oh, fuck yes. "No problem." I lean down and kiss her, my tongue delving into her mouth to tangle with hers. I pull almost all the way out and thrust back in, sucking on her lip ring as I go. I pull out again and pump into her faster. Each time is faster, harder. Just like she asked. I'm kissing her and touching her, and it's frantic. My focus is on everything. When she starts the dirty talking, I almost lose it.

"God, yes, Carter. Fuck me hard. You're so big. Don't stop. Please."

I reach down and run my middle finger over her hard clit, circling around and around. Her words start to jumble. I'd laugh if I didn't have to focus on not coming like a teenager.

"Don't. Yeah. Jesus. Fuck me. Oh, shit. I love—"

Love? Did she say love?

"I love it. Don't ever stop, Carter."

Oh, well, damn.

I rub her harder and pinch her hard nub, which puts her over the edge. She moans my name as I continue to thrust into her. I stop, pulling out.

I place my hands on her hips and encourage her to roll over. "On your tummy, babe."

She rolls over slowly, then pushes herself up to her knees.

"Perfect." I look down at one luscious ass. Running my palm over her right cheek, I mumble, "Open your legs."

She does as I ask. Lining myself up, I press inside and moan so loudly, it echoes. "Holy shit, Viv. You feel so good."

"Carter," she gasps. "Oh, God... Don't stop."

One of these days we'll make love. Not tonight. I've been waiting too long to go slow. I grab her hips and plunge in as deep as I can.

She screams.

"Am I hurting you?"

"No!" she shouts, sounding angry. "Do it again, Carter."

I chuckle at her demands but do as my woman asks. I'm able to go only a few more minutes until I throw my head back and release myself inside her. Panting, I lean down over her back and kiss her at the spot where her spine meets her neck. Such a pretty neck. I wrap my arms around her and pull her down onto the bed so we're spooning again.

Whispering into her pretty ear, I say, "We're doing this." It's not a question. It's a statement.

"Yes," she says sleepily. "We're doing this."

"Viv?" I whisper.

"Yeah?"

"Tomorrow. Come to the party with me?" I sit up and look down at her face. "As my date."

"We're really doing this."

"We are. You can invite Kai up, if you'd like. I bet you miss him."

Rolling over to face me, she smiles but her eyes are sad. "I do miss him. Can I invite his little sister too? I think Clinton should meet her."

"Uh-oh. Are you playing matchmaker?"

"Maybe." She runs her palm over my scruffy cheek. I love her touch. "She's gorgeous. He won't mind the introduction, believe me."

"She can't be prettier than you." I kiss her nose.

Scoffing, she says, "She's way prettier." Placing her finger over her mouth, she adds, "I'm glad you think I'm pretty, Carter, but there are people out there better-looking than me."

I run my hand over her hip, past her waist, to her breast. I slide my palm across the tip. "No way. No one prettier."

CHAPTER THIRTY-NINE

VIVIEN

ONE O'CLOCK. The party is in full swing, and I've yet to get the nerve up to join the fun. Carter offered to walk me over, but I told him I wanted to wait for Kai and Kalani. They're running late. Apparently, Kai needed new swim trunks. The man is from Hawaii. He's got swim trunks galore, but Kalani confessed that he wanted new ones before he meets the "Corcoran hotties."

I peek out the window one more time and nearly jump out of my skin when a tall Hawaiian walks past. Opening the door before they can knock, I startle Kai right back. On his left stands Kalani in a pretty pink and orange swimsuit cover-up. I push past my bestie to wrap Kiki up in my arms.

"It's so good to see you, and I'm so glad you're going to be living here." Leaning back, I see a smiling Kiki. "We'll have to go out sometime."

"I'd like that, Viv." She turns to face Carter's backyard. "This is a huge party. I didn't expect it."

"Me neither." The good thing is there are so many people, no one will know or care that I'm wandering around. "You look cute, Kiki. I love your cover-up."

"Thanks. We just picked it up."

I look up at her brother expectantly.

"Where's your suit, Viv?" Kai asks.

"Um, I lost it?" I chuckle, because Kai will know I'm fibbing. "I didn't have time to get a new one." Even though I've got some money now. I was just starting to get bi-monthly checks, then I quit. It reminds me I need to look for a new job.

"That's what I thought."

"What did you think?"

"Don't be mad."

"Why would I be mad?"

From behind his back, Kai pulls a bag. A shopping bag with Nordstrom printed on the side. "I had a feeling you didn't have a swimsuit, so I got this for you."

"Kai. No."

"Consider it an early birthday present."

"Kai, no. Why?"

"Because you deserve an early birthday present. Now, stop arguing and go put it on."

Taking the bag from him, I peer inside and then reach in and pull out a dark blue sheer dress.

"Cover-up." Kai smiles.

Laying that over my shoulder, I grasp the swimsuit. It's navy blue with small white polka dots. Setting the bag down, I hold up the suit from the top. It's cute. A one-piece with ruching around the middle and a halter neck. There are supportive cups for the top and underwire.

"It's called a Miracle Suit."

"It'd have to be to fit me. This thing looks tiny."

"It's a sixteen. The whole purpose of it is to pull you in tightly, especially around the middle, to give you a super sexy silhouette."

I arch my brow, wondering how my best friend knows so much about it. He shrugs. "The clerk told me."

"Go try it on, Viv." It's Kiki's turn to nudge me along.

"Fine." I turn, leaving the empty bag at Kai's feet.

In the bathroom, I pull off my dress, bra, and undies and stare at myself in the mirror. With one deep breath for courage, I step into the leg openings in the swimsuit and start the long trek up my body. Like my old suit, this one stops midthigh. "Kai says it's a sixteen. That's my size. It should fit." Grasping the sides, I pull up and up and up until it's covering my chest. I'm overflowing a little bit, but not bad. Tucking the girls in a little, I tie it around my neck, smiling the entire time. "Damn, girl. You look good." That's me. Talking to me.

And I do look good. It *is* a miracle suit. Turning in the mirror, I get a look at my butt. The suit does a great job lifting and supporting that part of me too, all while looking kind of chic. With the dotted fabric, the ruching in the middle, and the halter top, I sort of look like a pin-up girl.

Out in my living room, I walk out with hands on my waist. "It fits!" I'm so damned excited.

"Holy shit, Viv." Kai's mouth is hanging open.

Kiki's giving me a toothy smile. "You look so good." She bobs up and down, clapping. "Sexy, Viv."

"I feel sort of sexy." It could be from the suit or it could be from recent events with a certain big man, or maybe both.

"Let's party," Kai shouts.

I'm ready except I need the cover-up. Returning to the bathroom, I slip on the sheer navy cover-up. It has long, flowing sleeves, but it's cut to fit closer to my body. The front is shorter than the back and there are pockets on either side. Taking one last look at myself, I run my fingers through my hair and dab on some lip gloss. I feel pretty. I really do.

"Let's go!" My turn to shout.

Kai holds the door for us, and as I pass him, I step up on my tiptoes to kiss him on the cheek. "Thank you, Kai. It's perfect. I feel good in it."

"You look good in it. I'm not surprised. I've got great taste."

"You do. You picked me to be your best friend."

———

WALKING OVER TO THE POOL, the first person I see is Clinton. "Hey, Veggie."

Okay, that one is new. "Veggie?"

"I combined Vivien and Reggie. Since I'm not sure which name to call you, I've dubbed thee Veggie."

"Awesome." Laughing, I move aside to introduce Kai and Kalani. "Guys, this is Carter's baby brother, Clinton."

Kai shakes his hand. "Hey, Clinton." There's a lilt to his voice. I've noticed him do that when he's a little nervous. It also means he thinks Clinton is adorbs, which he is.

"Nice to meet you." Clinton turns to Kalani. "And you too."

"Same," she says with a smile but not much else. It's weird. I thought for sure they'd fall all over each other. They'd look perfect together, and their babies would be so damn cute.

"Reggie? Are you going to introduce me?" Johnson says shyly.

"Johnson, this is my best friend, Kai Apatu, and his sister Kalani."

"Kalani," he says softly, moving past his brother to stand in front of her, his hand outstretched toward her. "Johnson."

When she places hers in his, they both stand frozen, staring at each other. I want to interrupt them, break the stare, but I think I picked the wrong brother for Kalani.

"Call me Kiki."

"Kiki," Johnson repeats softly.

Awwwwkward. They're just standing there holding hands, gazing at one another.

"Welp!" I turn to Kai. "Let's leave these two to get to know one another and grab a beer." I also want to find Carter.

Chuckling, Kai moves around his statue-like sister. "Good plan."

Once we're far enough away, I say, "I thought for sure she and Clinton would hit it off."

"She's got a thing for blond guys."

"It looks like he's got a thing right back."

"It does, and I'm not sure how I feel about it. What do you know about him?"

"Not much. He's sweet. And single."

"To you he's sweet. And single is good." He sighs. "Oh, hell. I'm not going to get involved."

I snort because Kai is nothing if not *involved*. "Good plan, Kai, baby." Stepping on the stairs, I turn to Kai. "Food and drinks are up here."

The second my feet hit the top of the deck, I hear my name.

"Reggie!" shouts someone.

I look around the deck but don't recognize anyone.

"Reggie!" I follow the sound of the voice. It's below me. I peek over the edge of the deck and see Clinton now floating in the pool on a blow-up raft, beer in hand.

"Yeah?"

"Grab me another beer and join me in the pool. The water's great!" he yells, holding up his can.

"Jesus, Clinton. She's not a bartender," Kennedy says, appearing next to me.

"Actually, I was a bartender." I giggle and lift my hand for a firm shake. I know she's into that. But instead, she wraps her arms around me and hugs.

"I'm glad you made it. I've been looking all over for you."

"Oh, well, I had to wait on my friends to arrive. Kennedy, meet Kai Apatu."

Shaking his hand, she smiles. "Wow, you're really good-looking."

"You are too, beautiful."

Interrupting, I ask Kennedy, "Have you seen Carter?"

"In the house. He was talking to his ex."

"Natalia's here?"

Kennedy nods, "Perhaps talking is the wrong word. Yelling. He was yelling at Natalia. You should go find him, get him out here where the fun people are."

I arch my brow. "I'll do my best. Let me go find him. Come on, Kai, let's grab you a drink."

"Right behind ya, Viv."

CHAPTER FORTY

"NATALIA, you weren't invited. You need to go."

"But why?"

God, I hate when she whines. "Because we're not together and this is about my parents, not about you." *And my folks don't like you.*

"I know, but—"

Now she sounds pathetic. "Just go home."

Her eyes start to water, and I roll my eyes. "I'm not doing this with you, Natalia."

"But I won't cause any problems."

Yes, you will. She won't be able to help herself. "Why would you want to be at a party for people you don't like to celebrate an anniversary you don't care about?"

She's about to answer when something behind me grabs her attention.

Natalia sneers, "Jesus. Doesn't she have a life?"

I turn in time to see Vivien walk through the doorway with Kai in tow. She looks amazing. I'm not surprised she can make a one-piece swimsuit look like that. I'm just glad she's partially covered up. She's for my eyes only.

Natalia's eyes have left Vivien and are now on Kai. "You're shitting me?"

"What?" asks Vivien.

"You landed *that* guy?" she says, rudely pointing at Kai. "What is going on? This can't be happening. There's no way in fuck that a fat cow like you got a guy like that. You must have a magic pussy."

I hear a gasp. "Mom?" Shit, she shouldn't have to listen to this bullshit.

"I'm sorry. I'm interrupting."

"No, Natalia was just leaving. Isn't that right?"

"Fuck you, Carter."

My mom has her palm resting over her heart. She's distressed, and I don't blame her. My mom knows people cuss, but Natalia was plain vulgar. She's not used to that kind of vitriol. I look down at Vivien, not knowing what to expect, but she's glaring at Natalia now.

"Look, Natalia," Vivien says in her own defense, "I'm okay with you not liking me, because I don't like you either. You're mean and bitter, which makes you ugly."

"I'm not ugly."

"Inside you are. You're rotting inside like a bad piece of fruit."

"Again with the food. Don't you ever think of anything else?"

Vivien looks up at me and shrugs. She's not making much headway with this, but I need to let her say her piece.

"Natalia, I may be fat, but at least I'm nice, and there's more to life than skinny."

"That's because you've never seen how the other half lives."

"Yeah, well, I get to eat French fries and ice cream."

"I see that."

I reach out, touching her arm. "Viv, you tried. You said what you needed to say. Now it's on her."

"Don't talk about me like I'm not here!" Natalia stomps her foot like a petulant child.

"Dear?" Oh, shit, my mom's jumping into this shitstorm. "Natalia, dear. Please leave my party. This is about my husband and me, and I'd prefer to leave the drama at the door. Thank you for coming. Please show yourself out."

"Fine," Natalia sputters. "Carter, this isn't over."

Yeah, it is, but I remain quiet. If I say more, this will never end. Natalia stalks away in a huff. When the front door slams, I release the tension in my shoulders. "Ladies. Kai. I'm very sorry for that."

"Not your fault, honey," Mom says patting my hand. "Now, introduce me to your new girlfriend. I've heard a lot about her."

After introductions, I lead Kai out to the kitchen showing him where the beer and mixers are kept. Checking on Mom and Vivien moments later, I hear them laughing like old friends. Shit, who knew seeing that happen would make me feel like I'm the fucking happiest man in the world? Sure, Mom loves everyone, except Natalia, but having her and Viv really like each other is more important than I even realized. I hear Mom tell Vivien a story about me when I was young. It's an embarrassing story, but I don't mind her hearing those. I want her to know all my stories, good and bad, and I want to hear hers.

After grabbing drinks for Kai and Vivien, I take her by the hand and lead her through the throng of people, introducing her as my girlfriend to each and every person. My father is particularly smitten with her. I think he wanted to keep her next to him for the remainder of the party, but Kai and his sister are her guests, so we found them and hung with them most of the time. Viv was right, Kalani is very pretty, but nothing compared to my girl.

When the crowd starts to thin, Vivien excuses herself to walk Kai and Kalani to their car. I follow along, as does Johnson. I'm not sure what's happening with Johnson and Kai's sister, but there's definitely something. I've never seen my brother so quiet. He's barely spoken a word to any of us today. All he's done is stand near Kalani. He spent a lot of time gazing at her and listening to her. I'm not sure if you grasp the significance of this or not, so I'll try to put this into context. Johnson is the oldest sibling. He's a damn bossy know-it-all, which means at no time does Johnson ever stop talking, at least normally. Until Kalani.

CHAPTER FORTY-ONE

WALKING down the sidewalk away from Carter's pool area, Kai, Kalani, Johnson, Carter, and I are all laughing and talking. My hand is in Carter's, and I don't remember a time when I felt this happy and part of something like a family. So, it's no surprise that my momentary sense of family would come crashing down in mere seconds when I see a man walking toward me. He's wearing a pink polo shirt and khaki shorts. I feel like I've seen him before. Taking three more steps, it hits me like a goddamn Mack truck.

"Daddy?"

The man with the graying temples who I've only seen on television lately turns to me. "Reggie?"

Reggie? He called me Reggie? Since when does my dad *ever* call me Reggie? *He* calls me Vivien. "It's Vivien," I squeak. "You always called me Vivien."

I feel a big hand wrap around my upper arm, but I pull away from the touch. I'm not sure if it was Kai or Carter. No matter, I can't deal with anyone's touch right now. Not even theirs.

"I know. Your sister said..."

I don't hear any more words, because my focus has switched to the young woman standing behind him. A young woman holding a child. I'd guess the baby is about a year old. I recognize her. I've seen her before. In the photos of me as a baby. She looks just like me.

I look at the woman then. She's not much older than I am. If she's twenty-six, I'd be shocked.

My eyes turn back to my dad. "Who is that?" I ask, pointing at the child.

"Reggie, this is Meryl. Your half sister."

My sister? I've got another sister? One named after Meryl Streep, no doubt.

I blink at him, then at her, then at the woman staring in the direction of Carter, Johnson, and Kai with a gleam in her eyes.

Pointing rudely at the woman, I ask, "Who's that?"

"My wife, Kelsey."

"Your wife? Kelsey?" I squeak as I force myself to swallow. "Your daughter? Meryl?" I glare at him, hoarsely asking, "You have *another* family?"

He smiles like he's proud. Proud of his new, better family. "I do."

I'm totally shocked. Gobsmacked. When Mom came over, bringing dinner and my little sister along, I wasn't especially thrilled to see Grace, since we're like oil and water. It was then Mom told me Dad was coming into town sometime this summer. He's visited Chicago a few times since he left and always asks her to let us all know. Well, she did, only she neglected to tell me about Daddy's new and improved family. The Reginalds 2.0. Maybe she didn't know.

"When did you get married?"

"Right before Meryl was born," Kelsey answers. "We were sorry to hear you couldn't make the wedding with the other two."

"I didn't know." Wait. *What?* I feel my face turn scalding hot. "Who else was there?"

"Grace and Dean made it. Dean was my best man."

Dean? My brother Dean was *in* the wedding? The same Dean who put Dad's face on the bulletin board in the garage and spent months throwing darts at it? Hell, he threw a hatchet once after a particularly bad day. He hates Dad with a passion.

"Grace was one of my bridesmaids," Kelsey says, gazing at her baby, then back at Carter and the other guys. She's fluttering her eyelashes at them, and it makes me want to poke her eyes out.

Mine.

Instead, I blink and blink and blink. What the ever-loving fuck is going on here? "Daddy." I blink again and swallow. "I didn't know about any of this. No one told me any of this."

"They didn't? I was sure Gracie would tell you."

She should have. She was in my home less than a week ago. "Why didn't *you* tell me, Dad?" My shock is gone now. Anger is what is left in me. I'm so pissed and hurt by all of this.

"Well, I knew you were still upset with me." He shrugs like it was my bad. "Grace thought it'd be better coming from her."

"From *her?*" My hands are in tight fists at my side. My face is probably magenta, and my heart is beating so hard I'm sure it's going to jump out of my chest any second. My breathing is now labored, and I'm not sure what to do first. I could either punch him in the face and then yell at him, or I could yell first. Yeah, I'll do that. I lean forward so I'm only five or six inches from his face. "No one bothered to tell me, *Dad*, that you've replaced me with another kid." Not even Mom. She had to know. I'm not surprised about Grace though. She's always thought Dad deserved our acquiescence, and I never gave it. I point at the baby. "Nobody told me you've replaced all of us with another family."

I lean in a bit more and lower my voice. "I distinctly remember you telling us you had to choose between your career and a family. You chose the career. Remember?"

He nods slowly.

I step back because I suddenly need space from him. "No one bothered to tell me any of this, and yet here you are on my doorstep. How did you find me?"

"Your sister told me."

"Grace gave you my address?" I'm going to kill my sister.

He nods again. "She said you were living in a mansion with a wealthy professional athlete. I thought I'd stop by and introduce myself."

I told her none of that, only Carter's name. She must have googled him.

"So, you're here to what? Meet the famous athlete?"

"Well, and to see you too, of course."

Of course he's here to meet the famous person. I'm just his link to the man himself. But I'm not going to give him the opportunity. "Well, I'm afraid he's fucking busy, Dad."

I see Kelsey from the corner of her eye cover Meryl's ears. I turn to her. "Seriously?" I look at her. "I'm her fucking sister. She might as well get fucking used to my fucking language, *Kelsey*."

Just as I turn back to Dad, I see Carter approaching. As he nears me, I feel the uncontrollable need to run to him and hide beneath his shirt, for him to take me away from all of this. Why not run to him? Once he's close enough, I launch myself into his open arms. Wrapping my arms around him, I press my face into his chest. "Take me away from here, Carter. Please?" I say with a shaky voice.

I feel myself being lifted. Carter's got one arm around my back and the other beneath my knees. I wrap my arms around his neck and let him take me away. I'm not sure where he's going until I smell clay. We're in the studio, but he's moving through it to my apartment. Once inside, he walks to my bedroom and sets me on top of the covers. Leaning down, he kisses me tenderly. Kneeling, he pulls off my flip-flops. "Lie down. I'll be right back."

CHAPTER FORTY-TWO

CARTER

SHE TOLD me to take her away, so that's what I'm going to do. When I step out of Viv's house, Kai, Kalani, and Johnson are all waiting on the sidewalk. "How is she?"

"Upset."

"I don't blame her," Kalani says, an expression of shock on her face. "What father does that to his daughter?"

Kai answers, "A selfish, callous asshole."

Kai's right. If I hadn't seen that for myself, I wouldn't have believed it. "Is he gone?"

Johnson finally speaks. "Fuck yes, he's gone. I escorted them out to their car as soon as you carried Viv away."

Kalani gives Johnson a beaming smile, and he returns the gesture. Shit. There's something going on there. She's so damn young. My brother's close to twenty-nine. If she's twenty, I'd be shocked. That's quite an age difference.

"Good riddance." Kai is angry. Furious.

"I'm going to take Vivien down to my place in the city. She needs to get out of here for a while."

"I agree. Where's your place?"

I give Kai the address, and I'm not surprised to hear his condo is only blocks from mine.

"Once she's up to it, let's all go out."

Kalani turns to Johnson. "Do you live in the city too?"

"I do." He smiles and stares at her.

Isn't he going to tell her where he lives? He's got it bad for this girl. I've never seen him like this. The guy is a player. He knows how to reel in the ladies. But this girl? I think he's in over his head.

I'll tell her. "He lives in Lincoln Park."

"Oh, that's not far." The girl is trying, but Johnson's giving her nothing.

"Yo! Johnson. You want to meet up with us in the city later this week?" Only if Viv's up to it.

"Yeah. That'd be great."

Has he seriously lost his shit here? I need to get a move on, so I slap my brother on his shoulder. "You two should exchange numbers so you can set everything up."

"Yeah?" Johnson says, blinking at me.

"Yes." I walk toward my house. "I'll talk to you guys in a day or two."

Racing up the steps, I enter my place and see my sister, Ernie, Mom, Dad, and Clinton cleaning up. "Hey guys, sorry. Just leave that. I'll hire someone to—" I hesitate. "I need to take off." They all look at me, concern washing over their faces. "It's a long story, but Vivien's estranged dad just showed up here unannounced. With a new family. She's upset."

"Oh, the poor dear," coos my mom.

"I'm taking her to my condo downtown. We'll be there for a few days. We'll stop by one day. Sound good?"

"Of course, of course. Come for dinner and don't worry about the house. We've got this. We'll lock up too."

"Go spend time with your sweet girl." That's my dad. Told you he was smitten.

"Great. Thanks." I kiss my mom's cheek. "I'll call you."

After taking the steps two at a time, I change into jeans and a T-shirt and grab my leather jacket from my closet. Sliding on some leather boots, I check my wallet to make sure I've got everything I'll need. I jog back down the steps, past Kai and the other two, back into Viv's house. In her bedroom, Vivien is sitting in the same spot where I left her. She's chewing on her lip ring, staring into space. "Babe? I need you to change into some pants and something warm on top."

"Warm?"

"Warm, and some boots."

I open her closet door and step inside. She doesn't have much. Grabbing a pair of jeans and a flannel shirt, I walk back to her. "Stand up. Let me help you change."

"No. I can do it." She takes her clothes, tossing them on the bed. "Those jeans are too tight."

I'd like to see that.

Walking into her closet, she returns with some of those black legging things and a long-sleeved blouse in one hand and some short black boots in her other. I watch her pull off the swimsuit cover-up and stare. "You look so gorgeous in that suit."

"Thanks. Kai bought it for me."

WTF? Kai bought her a swimsuit? I should punch the ass in his face for that, but I can't fault his taste. He knew what would look good on her, and he was right.

"Better back up. This thing is holding in everything."

Wait? Was she just dissing herself? Well, screw that. I step closer to help her untie the top from the back of her neck. Next, I watch her push the suit down over her breasts and look down as she shimmies her behind out the rest of the way. I could watch her make that move all day, every day.

"There." She releases a breath.

I sit on the bench at the end of her bed and marvel at her as she finds panties and slides on a lace bra I want to take right off of her. She dresses in her leggings and top, then stands before me.

"Now what?"

"Pack a small bag for a few days. You know, with a toothbrush, stuff like that."

"Pack a bag?"

"We're going to my place in the city for a couple of days. We'll meet up with Kai and Kalani for dinner later this week."

"Oh, that sounds fun." She wraps her arms around my neck, leans down, and kisses me. "Thank you, Carter."

"You're welcome. Grab a few things. Don't bother with sleepwear." I wiggle my eyebrows suggestively, which makes her laugh. Mission accomplished.

She takes twenty more minutes to fill a small duffle, asking questions occasionally, like, "Should I bring a dress?"

"Sure, babe."

"Shorts?"

"If you want."

"Hair dryer?"

"Nah, I've got one." *I think.* "Do you have a jacket? Denim or leather?"

"Leather?" She steps back into her closet, returning with an old bomber jacket. "Grandpa's."

"Perfect."

I pick up her bag, tossing it over my shoulder. Kissing her hastily, I take her hand in mine and lead her out through the living room, where she picks up her slouchy purse thing.

In my garage, I lead her to the bikes. She stops dead in her tracks. "A motorcycle?"

"Sure. I thought we'd take the bike down into the city. That's why I had you wear warmer clothes."

"You want me to ride on that thing?"

"You'll be fine. This one has a touring saddle with a back, so it'll be safe and comfortable for you to ride. Just hang on to me." I kiss her nose. "I'll keep you safe." Pulling out my keys, I open the trunk that houses two helmets. "For you, milady." Handing her one and setting mine on the seat, I place her small duffle in their place. Locking the trunk back up, I help her with her helmet, making sure it's snug and buckled correctly. Safety first. "You want it tight, but not too tight. This one also has a sun shield that pulls down." I slide a visor down over her eyes.

I slide mine on and throw my leg over the seat. I hold my hand out to her. "Put your foot on the rest there and throw your leg over." She steps on the peg and teeters. I get a good grip on her arm. "I've got you."

"Hey, I can hear you through the helmet."

"We've got internal speakers and a mic so we can talk as we ride."

"They think of everything."

"They do. Come on. Hop on."

She places her hand on my shoulder as she swings her leg over the seat of the massive bike. She slides into place snugly against my back. I reach back and take her hand, bringing it around my waist. I do the same with the other hand. I feel her body pressed to mine and do my best to will my dick to behave. "Stay close, out of the wind. Keep your feet on your foot pegs. I don't want your legs to touch the hot bike. Hold on tight. When I lean, you lean the same way. Got it?"

"Yes. Got it. God, I'm so nervous," she says through the mic.

The engine comes to life, and I feel vibrations everywhere. I walk the bike backward and straighten it, facing the open garage door. "Ready?"

"No. Yes." She giggles.

See? I knew getting on the bike would take her mind off the shitstorm from earlier.

With a rev of the engine, we lurch forward and zip out of the garage, almost past the ugly fountain—which reminds me. I stop the bike. "Could you design me a new fountain?"

"A fountain?"

"Yeah, like one of your pieces from the show."

"I've never designed a fountain before." Her voice is lilting, excited. "I'd have to research it."

"Is that a yes?"

"Definitely. It's a yes." She squeezes me around the waist.

I pat her hand. "Good. Because that thing is butt ugly."

"It certainly is."

Restarting the bike, we make our way out of the gate and onto the road. Speeding down I-90, I feel the air whipping past us and the rumble of the bike below us. It's liberating. At least *I* think it is. "How're you doing back there?"

"Good." She giggles as I pass car after car on the toll road.

"You like it?" I ask.

"Yeah. This is amazing."

"It is. I always feel so free out on my bike." That's exactly the right word. Free.

"This would be fun to take on a road trip. The seat's really comfortable."

"This is a touring bike. It's made for road trips. I'm happy you like it. It's one of my favorite things to do." I chuckle into the microphone. Damn, I'm happy.

The ride is over before I know it. I pull up to my building and drive around to the underground parking entrance. Parking in one of my three designated parking spots, I say, "You hop off first."

"I think my legs are numb," she says, laughing. Holding on

to my shoulder, she stands on the peg and slides her leg over the seat to the ground. She's about to lose her balance, but I grab her hand in time.

"Whoa, Viv."

"Thanks." She pulls the helmet off and then runs her fingers through her hair. She needn't worry. Tousled and flushed is a good look on her.

———

HITTING THE ELEVATOR BUTTON, I step close to Vivien. "So you liked the ride?"

Clearing her throat, she nods. "Yeah. It was fun."

"Good. I'm glad. I love taking it out and about. It's more fun with someone else though."

"I can see that. You'd have no one to talk to in your fancy helmets."

"True. Did you know you can make a call with them too? They've got Bluetooth."

"No way."

"Way."

The elevator doors swing open to the forty-second floor of the high-rise condominium I bought with part of my signing bonus when I was first drafted. It seemed like a sound investment since the building was still under construction at the time. The location is perfect on East Waterside. I loved the layout of the place with its open floor plan, three bedrooms and three baths, plus a study. It's industrial looking, but the interior designers they had on staff did a nice job softening that part up for me. I like a warm home, not one made of cold stone and metals. While many of the others have concrete floors, mine are hardwood. Most of the kitchens are black and silver, sleek. My cabinets are mahogany, and my counter is natural stone. I've got a view of Navy Pier and Lake Michigan from my huge living room windows and a narrow patio that extends the length of the entertaining space. It's a great condo. I just prefer country life.

"So, are you hungry? I can order from the restaurant down on the street level."

"Oh, okay." Vivien hasn't said much since she walked into my place. "I could eat."

"Do you like it?"

She turns to me. "Who wouldn't like this place, Carter? It's amazing."

"It's all right." I shrug. "I like the quiet of the other house, but this is a nice change of pace."

"I bet. The best of both worlds."

I watch her walk to the window and stare out at the water. "This view is incredible."

I step up behind her, getting close enough to wrap my arms around her. It feels so good. So right. "It is. I've painted the view a couple of times. Once on a sunny day; once with ominous clouds just out there," I say, pointing to our right.

Turning her head to look up at me, she says, "I'd like to see those."

"They're at the other house. I'll show you sometime." I hold her tighter. I want her to know I'm here for her. "How are you? About earlier?" I'm afraid to mention anything specific.

Sighing, she relaxes into my body. "I'll be fine, Carter. It was just a shock. I'm angry as hell at my brother and sister. I choose to withhold judgment on my mom's role in all this, because something tells me she has no idea he was going to show up today."

"Do you think she knew he was remarried?" I ask kissing the top of her head.

"Probably. But, who knows? My sister has been playing this fucked-up game with all of us."

She stops there. I get the feeling she's done talking about it for now. "You thirsty?"

"God, yes."

I step away from her, moving to the kitchen, and get us both a bottled water. "Here you go."

She takes it from me and gulps down half the bottle.

I laugh, "You *were* thirsty."

"Told ya. Now, you promised me food."

I laugh again. "Just tell me what you're hungry for, and I'll get it."

She gives me a smoldering look. Stepping around the island, she stands next to me and places her palm on my ass. "First, a burger and fries. Then, you."

"I know just the place," I blurt. "They'll deliver in less than thirty minutes."

We spend a few minutes sitting on the large, modern sofa, just looking out the window at the view. With my arm around her and her head on my shoulder, I play with her hair. It's damn short but it suits her. Plus it's as silky and soft as the rest of her. When she looks up at me, I do the natural thing, I meet her lips with mine for a slow, seductive kiss.

It turns heated in no time. I reach around her and place my palms on her ass, lifting her until she's on my lap. I take the zipper of her jacket between my fingers and move it down slowly until it's open enough for me to slide my hand inside. Cupping her breast, I lean up and kiss her again spending time on her piercing. Damn, I love that thing.

While I do that, Viv unzips her coat the rest of the way and it's on the floor before I know it. Next, the pretty blouse hits the floor. With the bra the only thing left on top, I look it over and find a front latch. I'm familiar with those. I set to work unleashing her from the confines of the dastardly torture device.

"Finally," I sigh.

My mouth finds its mark in seconds. I lick and suck and lick some more. She arches her back as I support her with my hands. I'd love a picture of her like this. Better yet, a painting. I could do an entire series of nude paintings of Vivien Jayne Reginald.

I'm trying to reach into her leggings when the doorbell sounds. "Damn." That was faster than thirty minutes.

"You go get the door. I'll meet you in the bedroom," she says in a deeper than normal voice.

"Great idea." I pull my wallet out of my pocket as I practically sprint to the door. Opening it, I take the bag and pay the delivery woman, giving her a generous tip, of course.

Racing to the bedroom, I stop at the doorway and take in the sight before me. Nude from the waist up, Viv's sitting in the middle of my bed, legs crossed in front of her, hands resting back on the bed. It's like a siren's call. It makes it very hard for me to focus on the food and not on her glorious tits. At the bed, I set the food down and watch as Viv reaches into the bag. Peering inside, she gasps. "Geesh, how many did you order? I'm not *that* hungry." Reaching in she retrieves a fry or two.

On my own, I can eat three double burgers if I've had a hard workout so I always order extra.

I stare at her as she bites into a golden potato. Handing me back the bag, she moans as she chews. Holy fuck. She's even sexy when she eats. "So good. Thank you."

I love her moans. But now's not the time. "Water? Soda? Beer?"

"Sure. Another bottle of water, please."

I return with two more waters. Slipping off my shoes, I pull off my jeans so I'm wearing only my tee and boxer briefs, then climb onto the bed with her. "Shall we watch something?"

"Sure." She hits the remote and scrolls through some of my DVR, then stops on something and giggles. "My goodness, you sure do like porn."

I look up and see the list of movies I've rented and purchased in the past. I feel my cheeks heat up. Shit. I'm embarrassed. Shrugging, I confess, "I like porn."

She uses the buttons on my remote to look through the list. "You don't have any anime porn."

"Anime porn? As in cartoon porn?"

"Yeah. It's super-duper dirty."

"Super-*duper* dirty?"

"Can we get YouTube on this fancy television?"

I reach for the remote and go to the Smart TV menu. Handing her back the remote, she searches the web for the thing she was looking for. When she finds it, she hits Play.

I blink a few times to make sure I'm seeing what I'm seeing. "Holy shit."

"Told ya."

It is *super-fucking-duper dirty*. It's about a girl auditioning to be a porn star. "Jesus." It's dirtier than any porn I've ever seen.

I look over at Vivien and see her squirming around on the bed. "That turn you on?" I know I'm turned on. My dick was getting hard just being next to her, but seeing this and then her, I've tented my boxers completely.

Vivien slides over in bed and lays her head on my shoulder. "It's hot, right?"

"Uh, yeah." I watch as two animated men approach the girl and do shit to her that a live actress could never do.

I'm stroking Viv's back. "Would you ever do the human equivalent of that?" I point to the screen.

"Maybe." She pauses, then gasps. "But don't even *think* about putting something like that in me!"

I chuckle until I feel her hand slide over my belly, to the waistband of my shorts. "Babe?"

"Yes?" she replies as she slides her fingers beneath the elastic band.

When her hand meets my dick, I nearly jolt out of my spot. "Viv," I breathe heavily.

"Push your boxers down, Carter."

You don't have to ask me twice. I slide them down to midthigh and watch my cock pop free. She wastes no time wrapping her small hand around me, then pumps up and down, squeezing just the right amount, all while watching the movie.

"Wow, she's limber," mumbles Vivien.

"She sure is." I'm not really concentrating on the movie, but I can't help noticing that when the animated woman goes down on one man, Vivien follows suit.

I suck in a breath as she licks the head of my cock. Moaning and panting, I'm able to choke out, "Vivien, you don't have to."

She gives me an odd look. "Well, duh. I want to. It turns me on to hear you make all those sexy noises."

"It does?"

"Hell, yeah." She moves closer to my dick and licks me from base to tip.

My voice is strained, but I'm able to say, "Okay. If you insist." I look down at her seminude body and wish the leggings were off too. "Take off the rest of your clothes."

"I will if you will."

I yank off my tee and kick off my boxers. See? I'm a team player. "Perfect. Now suck my cock, honey."

"Dirty boy," she breathes as she puts me in her mouth, sucking on the head. "Mm."

Holy fuck. She's good at this. So fucking good. I slide my hand down her back, over that beautiful ass of hers, and through her slit. She's sopping wet. She likes this. I swirl my finger around until I find her clit and rub that as she sucks me like a goddess. My personal fucking goddess. I can tell she's getting close just by the way she's sucking my cock. Excitedly is probably the best word. That and she's moving her ass right along with my fingers, helping herself along.

I want to see what's happening on the video, but my eyes are riveted to Vivien. My hips are moving in time with hers, but I'm trying not to shove myself into her mouth. It's a lot to take in and I don't want her hating this. "So close, baby. Don't stop."

"Mm, mmm."

With one of my thick fingers inside of her, I pump in the same rhythm and until I feel her begin to squeeze me. It's all it takes for me to start to lose it. "Okay. Okay. Stop. Stop. Viv."

She pulls her mouth away and pumps me with both hands until I burst. I come so hard I feel like my soul is emptying from me.

"Holy shit, Viv. You're good at that."

"Yeah?" She looks surprised. "I'm glad you liked it. You're my first, but I've watched a lot of porn and Kai gave me tips, so—"

"What? Kai? You and Kai?"

"No, he gave me tips. You know. It wasn't a hands-on lesson." She slaps my thigh and laughs.

I look surprised, but inside I'm doing a happy dance. I'm her first. "I couldn't tell. That was the best one I've ever had." I use my hand to cup her cheek. "Thank you."

I sigh because I'm relaxed and tired. "Let me get cleaned up, then we can relax and watch another movie."

"A porno?"

"No." I laugh. "Not unless you want to."

"I'm ready to watch something else. Do you have any popcorn?"

"I don't know. You can check the kitchen."

"Do you have something I could put on?"

"Third drawer down in the dresser is the T-shirt drawer."

I roll out of bed and step into the bathroom, turn on the shower, and step under the spray. In minutes, I'm out again and drying off. I walk into my bedroom naked and make eye contact with Vivien.

"I could so get used to this," she says, staring at me.

"Good."

"I mean, watching you walk out of the bathroom like that should be its very own porno."

I chuckle. "As long as you're my costar."

She blushes, and it's beautiful. Vivien is beautiful all the time, but seeing her lying on my bed in one of my beloved Bears shirts with a bowl of popcorn in her lap is the real deal.

When my phone chimes, I pick it up and read the text. "So, we should probably talk about Julia."

She releases a groan like a wounded animal. "Why?"

"Because you aren't quitting the foundation. We're restructuring."

"Does she know?"

"Yes. I talked to her on the phone this morning before the party. She misunderstood the hierarchy."

Vivien scoffs. "You mean the one where she's the boss of me?"

"Yeah. That's the one. I take complete blame for that. She's used to running the show, and I didn't really clarify your role. Now she understands that you are equal partners."

"Forgive me, but I have a hard time believing she won't revert back to the queenie status the minute your back is turned."

"If that happens, babe, tell me. I'll nip it in the bud."

"Fine."

"Good. She's coming by tomorrow afternoon."

Vivien grumbles, "Tomorrow?"

"Tomorrow afternoon." I lean down and kiss her lips to seal the deal. "So what movie did you choose?"

"I should make you watch *The Notebook* for making me work for her again."

"*With* her. Not *for* her."

I get a hard eye roll as I try to take the remote. "We're watching *Titanic*."

"*Titanic?*"

"Well, not *TITanic*." she snickers. "I want the one with Kate and Leonardo."

I arch my brow as I reach for the remote. "Smartass. Don't underestimate the cinematic brilliance that is *TITanic*." I look over at her. "When you're ready, I'll reenact my favorite scene from the movie."

She throws her head back and laughs. "Can't wait, lover boy."

"Okay, let's see if we can rent it." I scroll through my subscription movie channels and spot it. "There it is."

The movie is killer. I've always been fascinated by the story of the *Titanic*. I look over at Vivien and decide to share a story with her.

"Once when I was young, the Museum of Science and Industry in Chicago had a *Titanic* exhibition with relics from the ship. The cool part was, when you entered the exhibit, they gave you a card with a name and the number and location of your room on the ship. As you exited, there was a large board of names of those who died. I checked the board and discovered that my name, the person I represented in the exhibit, had stayed in the third-class part of the ship and perished when the ship went down. It made it real. I'll never forget that."

"Wow. I think I'd like to see the relics. I'm not sure I'd want to know my fate."

"You hungry?"

"A little. Do you have any cereal?"

I give her a shocked expression. Hand over my heart, I say, "You wound me. How can you even ask that question?" I jump out of bed and head toward my kitchen with Viv in tow. Opening the pantry door, I step aside so she can look inside.

She laughs. "Your entire pantry is filled with cereal."

"And?"

"And you haven't even been here! Do you have fresh milk?"

"Sure do. The condo has a concierge who'll arrange for grocery delivery, cleaning services, stuff like that."

"In that case, I'd like some Cap'n Crunch, if you've got it."

"Absolutely, I've got the Cap'n. Regular, Peanut Butter, or Berries?"

Tapping her chin, she thinks. "You know, I haven't had Berries for quite some time. Let's try that."

CHAPTER FORTY-THREE

I'M EXAMINING the complicated digital controller for Carter's shower when I hear voices. Tugging at the bottom of my tee to make sure it's covering everything since I haven't yet replaced my undies, I move to the door. The voices are getting louder. Not because of my proximity to them but because they're more heated, for sure.

Moving down the short hallway, I'm able to see one person. Natalia. *What is she doing here?* Whatever she's doing, she's standing next to a large suitcase, dressed to the nines again. This time, she's in an electric-blue miniskirt and black tank top that probably cost more than all of my tank tops combined. Her heels are black and sky high.

"I'll ask you one more time," Natalia spits. "Who the fuck are you?"

The other woman answers, "None of your business. Who are you?"

I recognize the other voice. It's Julia. I thought Carter said she'd be here this afternoon, but it's just after ten now. I lean forward to get a look at her. Wow, they're twinsies. Julia's wearing a tiny skirt as well, but she's paired it with a more conservative white top, and her skirt is gray. She looks good in white.

"I *live* here," snaps Natalia.

"You live here?"

"Yes, I'm with Carter."

"*You're* with Carter?" I watch her put her hands on her hips. "He's never mentioned you. I'd know if he was seeing someone. We've got a connection."

"What is wrong with you? Stop repeating everything I say. What is so hard for you to understand? I'm. With. Carter!"

Not sure what to do, I opt for entering the room. They might as well know they're not alone and that *I'm* the one with Carter, not them. It's a brave move on my part, but I'm feeling courageous these days. I step into the room, catching Julia's eye first.

"Vivien?"

"I..."

"Did you crash here last night?" She thrusts her hands on her hips hard. "Carter won't like that. This isn't a place for you to just hang out because he feels sorry for you and gave you a pathetic job on his foundation."

Wow, that's a lot of words. Hateful words.

It's Natalia's turn. "What are you doing here? Is Carter here?"

"He's—" I don't know where he is. He must have gone out or something. I woke up and he was gone.

"And why are you wearing his shirt?" Natalia has moved closer to me. "He'll kill you for wearing one of his precious Bears shirts."

She reaches for it with her long pointy nails and grasps the collar, scratching my neck.

"Ouch. Fuck, that hurt." That's gonna leave a mark. A big one.

Ignoring me, she yanks on the neck of the tee harder this time. I lurch forward, but I catch myself from falling. I turn to get away from her but she grasps the back of the tee, yanking it up above my head, scratching me again. I'm in the most awkward position, with my eyes covered and arms sort of caught up in the shirt. I'm stuck. I can't go forward and definitely not back so I do the only thing I can think of, I drop to my knees and attempt to pull the shirt back down but she's not having it.

"No! Take it off!" she screams.

I think she's lost her damn mind. Wrapping my arms over my chest, I hold on tight to the shirt. Yes, they can both see my back and my bare ass, but I refuse to let her strip me naked. I squeeze my eyes shut, wishing Carter were here. *Where is Carter?*

"Take it off, you fat bitch." She continues to yank on the shirt. Natalia has seriously gone crazy.

"No," I say quietly.

"Lady, leave her alone. She works for him." Julia's now moved into the fray. "But not for long, after he finds out she's crashing at his place like this."

Natalia takes a moment to address Julia. "This is none of your business. I bet he's fucking her. Can you believe it? She's so fat and ugly."

Julia scoffs. "They're not sleeping together. He wouldn't. A guy like that wouldn't date her."

They seem distracted, so I'm about to make a run for it when a deep voice from somewhere in the room shouts, "What the fuck is going on?"

I'm suddenly released from Natalia's grip which causes me to fall forward. I catch myself with my hands.

Carter drops a white bag on the floor and rushes to me. Getting down on his knees next to me, he asks, "Vivien? Are you okay?"

"No," I mumble, pretty sure I'm bleeding from Natalia's talons.

"What the ever-loving fuck? Who did this to your back?"

I look up at him, then at Natalia. Pushing the shirt back down, I sit back on my butt and reach for my neck, feeling wetness. "Natalia."

He bends down to look at my neck. "What the fuck?" he says with such intensity that the room goes completely silent. He points to my neck, looking at Natalia. "You did this?"

Defiantly, she crosses her arms. "She was wearing one of your shirts. I was trying to get it back for you."

"She assaulted her, Carter." Julia points at Natalia. "I watched her."

Carter looks at her. "You witnessed this?"

"I tried to stop her."

No, not really. I look over at Carter and shake my head slightly. I hope it's enough, because I don't feel like saying it out loud. *Both of these women are devils.*

Carter leans closer to speak into my ear. "Do you want me to call the police? She assaulted you. You can press charges."

The last thing I want is to press charges. I should, though. She deserves it, but with someone like Carter, you know, in the news, he'd get dragged into this. I don't want or need the drama. I shake my head. "No."

He looks up at Natalia. "You're lucky she doesn't want to press charges. But I do. You entered my home without permission."

Natalia rolls her eyes like she can't believe how absurd Carter's words are. "You gave me a key, Carter."

"My attorney retrieved that key, I believe. I informed building security that you're no longer allowed up to my place. How did you get in?"

She crosses her arms over her chest and juts her hip out, not saying a word.

"You made a copy of the key." Carter isn't asking. He figured it out. Holding his hand out, he places his palm flat out in front of her. "Give it to me."

"No." She's so damn defiant.

"Fine. I'll have the locks changed this afternoon. How did you get past the concierge?"

Natalia says nothing. She doesn't have to. I'm sure all she had to do was smile and flirt with whoever is working today. Men are stupid.

"This is ridiculous, Carter. You're never here."

"It's my home in the city. It's for my use, not yours."

"But *she* stayed here?" she spits as she points to me.

"She's here with me. We're together now. She can be here whenever she wishes, or anywhere, wearing anything of mine. And it's none of your business. It was already none of your business when I told you weeks ago that I didn't want to see you anymore."

"*She's* with you?" This time it's Julia. "Seriously? But we had a connection." The tone of her voice is so high, it's penetrating into my brain.

He places his warm palm gently on my lower back. "Seriously." He looks at me, then back at her. "You want to know what else I'm serious about?"

"What?"

"I'm serious about firing you."

Sweet! Ding dong, Julia's gone.

"B-but...," she says, shocked.

"It's not working out. Vivien and I will work on this together."

"You have no idea what you're doing." Julia is pointing at me now. "She—"

Carter nips it in the bud. "We'll figure it out. Some of the guys have done it before; they'll help us."

I love how he keeps saying "we" and "us." I smile up at him, then at the two angry women.

Carter points to the door. "It's time for you ladies to go."

"But, Carter," they both whine.

"You're lucky there aren't police here for this, Natalia. Go before we change our minds."

"Fine. Fuck you both." She looks at Julia. "Fuck you too."

Julia takes the high road and turns to leave. "I'll send you my bill."

"Fine. My attorney will look it over and be in touch."

"What?" Julia sounds shocked again.

"Julia, be sure you bill me for your own work, not for Vivien's."

"Fine!" She stomps to the door.

I watch her disappear through the door and listen for it to slam, then commend her for not lashing out at the last minute.

Carter turns to Natalia. "As for you, my attorney will be in touch. You really will pay for her medical bills. Plus, I think she's entitled to some additional compensation. You know, for pain and suffering."

"You won't get a cent from me, Carter."

"Not me. Vivien."

"Especially not *her*." She rolls her giant suitcase to the door and slams it on her way out.

I look over at him. "Jesus, you sure can pick 'em."

"They picked me. I picked *you*. So, yeah, I *can* pick 'em." He stands up holding out his hand for me. I take it, and he helps me up. He gently pulls the T-shirt up over my head. "Let's check out these scratches."

"Wow, you really don't want anyone wearing your Bears shirts, do you?"

"You can wear my Bears shirts anytime you want. Hell, I prefer it. If you weren't bleeding all over this one, I'd tell you to wear it back to bed so I can fuck you in it."

"Oh."

"But since you are bleeding all over it, I want to see if we really do need to head to the doctor."

"I'm fine."

"Let me be the judge. I've been scratched up plenty, so I'll know what should be tended to by a professional."

"I don't have insurance."

"No worries."

"Carter, I am worried. It's expensive."

"Stop. This is my fault. I should have had the locks changed two months ago."

"True." I smile, then wince when he touches the area around the scratches on my neck. Those are deep, I can tell.

"The neck is the worst. It's still bleeding. I don't think you need stitches, but you may need antibiotics."

"Okay."

"Let's clean you up, and we'll go to urgent care."

I sigh and nod. There's no reason to argue. I don't want to get an infection, and knowing Natalia, she's crawling with bad germs. "What did you ever see in her?" I look up at him as he arches a brow. "Wait, don't answer that."

"I will answer it." He reaches down for the shirt. "First, come in the bathroom so I can clean the wounds."

I follow him as he answers the first question. "When we first met, she was nice. She laughed at my jokes. She was beautiful and, yes, vapid. It's what I liked back then." Patting my bottom, he nudges me until I'm in front of him. "Hop up on the counter."

I scoot my ass up onto the edge, and he helps me the rest of the way until I'm seated. He moves his big body between my legs and uses his finger to lift my chin. Kissing me softly, he pulls back and inspects my neck. It's sort of strange that I'm completely naked and he's completely dressed in his workout clothes, but I don't care right now.

He places a clean washcloth beneath the faucet and then gently dabs at the wounds. With a gruff voice, he says. "This one is deep but not as bad as I first thought." He shakes his head and sighs. "I'm sorry she hurt you, baby."

"It's not your fault."

"It is."

"Okay, maybe it is. You need to change all of your locks and passcodes. That woman can't take a hint." I laugh but I meant what I said.

His face takes on a whole different expression. Sadness. Guilt.

I place my palm on his scruffy chin. "I was kidding, Carter. It's not your fault."

He nudges his chin into my hand like a cat, making me smile. "You like that?" I ask.

"I like everything you do. I especially like your touch."

"Me too."

Leaning forward so that his forehead is against mine, he sighs again. "I'm falling for you, Viv."

"Falling for me?"

"Falling. I could love you so easily."

"Me too, Carter. But it scares me."

Kissing my nose, he smiles. "I know. I'll be gentle."

"Promise?"

"Promise."

He pushes some of my hair behind my ear. "So, we're doing this?"

I smile back and kiss his nose. "We're doing this."

His palm slides behind my neck to hold me in place for the sweetest, deepest kiss of my entire life.

I was wrong. I'm not falling. I already fell.

CHAPTER FORTY-FOUR

MY GIRL IS brave as fuck. Not only did she need a shot of antibiotics, but she couldn't remember the last tetanus shot she had, so she endured one of those too. Plus, the doc had to clean out her neck wound, which looked painful as hell.

At home, I slipped a clean Bears T-shirt over her head and tucked her into bed with the television remote. "Oh, I forgot. Hang on." I leave the bedroom to retrieve the white bag still on the floor. Back in the bedroom, I continue. "I bought you donuts this morning. Do you like donuts?"

"Of course." She smirks. "Who doesn't? What kind?"

"Well, I bought a couple glazed, a chocolate-iced cake donut, and a few filled things."

"What's your favorite?" she asks, reaching for the bag.

"Everything," I say with a chuckle. "You?"

"I love glazed donuts. The chocolate one sounds good too." I hand her one of each along with a napkin. She starts with the glazed biting into the soft pastry. "So," she says with her mouth full, "where were you?"

"I went for a run, got my girl donuts, and this." I hold up a key. "It's the key for this place. I figured you'd want to go see Kai while we're down here. The concierge knows to let you pass. Make sure you've got an ID the first time though, especially after that shit this morning. The locks will get changed today. I'll have a new key to you later this afternoon. In the meantime, I'm going to ask him to ID everyone who wants up here."

"Good idea. You've surrounded yourself with some crazies."

"Oh?"

She nods, biting into her donut. "Mm, so good."

Christ, I've got it bad. Watching her eat a damn donut even makes me hard.

CHAPTER FORTY-FIVE

VIVIEN

"WE WATCHED ANIME PORN."

Kai nearly chokes on his popcorn at my confession. "No way. Which video?"

Kai and I have spent a night or two in the past watching cartoon porn. We have to mute the sound because he hates the high-pitched voices of the animated characters. They are pretty annoying. "The one where the girl auditioning to be a porn star."

He chokes again. "Christ, Viv. That one was nasty with a capital *N*."

"I know. He loved it." I giggle, sipping my wine.

Carter dropped me off at Kai's with a promise to pick me up for dinner. We napped for about an hour today after the drama at his place and a couple of hours at urgent care. The rest made a world of difference. After I explained my wounds, a furious Kai gave Carter permission to pick me up after he and I had some alone time. Geesh, alpha males.

"Did he talk about all the things he wanted to do to you while he watched it?" Kai says, moving closer and dropping his voice for effect. He's such a pervert.

"No. He couldn't talk."

Kai chokes again. "Why not?!"

"I was giving him head."

Kai falls back onto the sofa and throws his hand over his face. "That's it. I'm dead. You slay me, girl." Sitting back up, he looks at me like he doesn't recognize me. "What a lucky bastard."

"Me?" *Yeah, I know.*

"No, him. I hope he knows what he's got in you."

I throw a pillow at him.

"Hey, I'm not just talking about the blowie. I'm talking about everything. You're the entire package, Viv. You're a unicorn."

I throw another pillow at him. "Shut up!" I know I'm red from embarrassment. He's got to stop complimenting me. Besides, I'm not the unicorn. Carter is.

Kai moves over to sit right next to me. "Seriously. You do know how amazing you are? What a catch you are?"

I look into Kai's dark eyes. "Stop. I mean it. I'm nothing special." I sip my wine. "But he did tell me I gave him the best head of his life."

"No doubt. Did you do what I suggested?"

One time when we were drinking cosmos, I asked him to give me tips on BJs. "I may have, yes."

"Of course you did, dirty girl." He sips his drink and winks at me. "I give great head."

"So, what's up with Johnson and your sister?"

"No idea. She's pretty tight-lipped. I did catch her whispering and giggling on the phone last night. I'm assuming it was Johnson on the other end."

"Can't you ask her?"

"Not yet, but you know I will, Viv. You *know* I will."

"I do indeed. You're the nosiest person I've ever met."

"Damn straight." He sips his drink and winks.

I bust out laughing. God, I love this man.

———

CARTER PICKS me up at six sharp, freshly showered, in a snug pair of jeans that show everyone how amazing his body is. Couple that with the tight black tee he's topped it off with, and he's a muscly package created to make us all drool. After he and Kai do that man-shake-and-back-pat thing they like to do, I make my way to the door.

At the door, Carter whispers, "I brought my bike."

"Oh, goodie!" I squeal. I love the bike. "Let's go for a ride along the lake."

"You got a sweatshirt? It'll be chilly on the bike."

I look back at Kai. "Can I borrow—"

"Closet."

I speed walk back to his room to his walk-in closet. It's so organized it makes me giddy. Kai keeps his closet so tidy, he should be on one of the HGTV shows. Hell, it's even color coded. I go to his sweatshirt section and pull out the first one. I stare down at it and smile. Slipping it on over my head it's so long, it falls to my knees. I walk back out to the room and up to Carter with a smirk on my face.

"Nice sweatshirt, Viv."

"Thanks," Kai replies. "I got some free tickets to a game. Thought I'd better wear Bears colors, man."

"It's perfect. Now, let's go cruise town."

"Bye, Kai."

Carter chuckles as he holds the front door for me.

"Make good choices, honey pie," Kai says in a high-pitched voice.

As soon as Carter pulls the door shut, I lean up and kiss his lips. "I like you a lot, Carter Corcoran."

He gives me a million-watt smile. "I like you more, Vivien Reginald."

"Not possible," I mumble as we walk to the elevator.

"Let's call it even."

"Sounds good."

CHAPTER FORTY-SIX

CARTER

WE'RE WALKING BACK into the lobby of my building, my arm wrapped around Viv's shoulders, and I've never been happier in my life.

She laughed and chatted the entire ride down Lake Shore Drive on the back of my bike. We parked at a perfect spot, Promontory Point, with the best views of the city and the lake. I turned around, straddling my bike the other way, and we kissed and whispered and kissed some more. I swear I feel like a teenager with this girl, and it's only been a couple of days. We ate at a food truck that served tacos and found a spot in the sand to eat. It was, hands down, the best date I've ever been on, and it all just happened spontaneously.

"What do you want to do now, babe?" I ask as we step off the elevator on my floor.

"Wanna watch a movie?" Vivien suggests as I unlock the door.

I stop mid-key-turn and look back. "What kind of movie?"

She slaps me on my arm and giggles. "I'm pretty tired. Maybe just something with a lot of car chases and things blowing up."

I throw my head back and squeeze my eyes shut. "How could you be any more perfect? The next thing you're going to tell me is that you like video games."

"I *love* video games!" she squeals excitedly. "Do you have some? I didn't see any gaming consoles anywhere. Not that I was snooping, I wasn't. I didn't."

I watch her blush and decide to stop her before she turns and runs. "No problem. They're disguised. I'll show you, but let's stick with a movie tonight. Sound good?" I touch her cheek with my palm. "And you can snoop all you like. I've got nothing to hide. I mean, shit, you already raided my porn stash."

She throws her head back and laughs. It's a beautiful sound.

"Let's make some popcorn," I say.

"What about ice cream?"

"Got it. Vanilla *and* chocolate."

Running her hand down my bare arm, she repeats my earlier sentiment. "How could *you* be any more perfect?" I love it when she touches me.

"I've got all the Bourne movies. You like those?" I ask, stepping into the living room.

"I love Jason Bourne," she coos. "He's hot."

Maybe that one is a bad idea.

"But you're way hotter," Viv adds.

She just made my dick hard. "Bourne it is, then."

We work together in the kitchen making popcorn. I grab two bottles of water while she takes the bowl. We've changed into our pajamas, me in a Bears tee and sleep pants and Vivien in just an old University of Illinois shirt. I'm not sure I'll be able to concentrate on the movie, knowing what lies beneath that shirt of hers, but I'll give it my best shot.

Once the movie starts, Vivien curls up to my side, absently running her hand over my chest and stomach. I place my hand over hers and hold it still. She's got no idea what she does to me.

I need to distract her for a little bit. "So, now that I've fired Julia, do you think you can take over the job?"

She stiffens against me. "Carter, she literally had me running errands from morning until night. I have no idea what she did."

Pausing the movie, I turn in my seat to face her. "I've got a serious question for you, Vivien."

"Okay." Her lips turn down and she bites on her lip ring.

"Here's the serious question. Will you come with me?"

She jerks her head around to look at me. "What?"

"I said, will you come with me? To New York. Well, technically it's New Jersey, but you can see New York from my condo."

"You want me to move with you? I—"

"You what?"

"I... I don't know. It seems so big."

"Well, they do call it the Big Apple."

She slaps my arm. "You know what I mean. Living together?"

"You lived with me before."

"I lived near you, not *with* you, Carter."

"Think of the art we can check out." I pull her closer. "I leave next week. That gives you time to think about it. Preseason football starts next month. When that happens, I'll be in New Jersey for weeks at a time."

"For how long?"

Even though the only light in the place is coming off the TV, I can still see her nibbling on her lip ring. God, I want to bite that thing. "For the season. Then we can come back home in the off-season."

"Can I think about it?"

"Of course. Talk it over with Kai. I don't want you to do it if you're not comfortable with the idea. I'm in this for the long haul, Viv. If you don't want to go this season or if you want to come out later on, I'm fine with it either way. But I want you there. I want you with me from now on."

"Oh."

"Think about it. We'll talk when you've decided."

She nods and cuddles up to me. I wrap my arm around her and pull her close, hitting Play on the movie. We sit snuggled up to each other, and it's bliss.

CHAPTER FORTY-SEVEN

VIVIEN

"KAI," I whisper into the phone.

"Why are you whispering?"

"Carter's in the shower. I need to tell you something, but I've gotta make this fast."

"What?" he whispers back.

"He wants me to go to New York with him."

"*Whahhhh?*" Kai says in his Scooby-Doo voice. It makes me laugh every time. "Serious?"

"Serious."

"When did he ask?"

"Last night."

"And you said yes, right?"

"No. Not yet."

"What's the holdup, woman?"

"It's big."

"It's big, but you should go. You've got nothing holding you here, well, except me, and I'll be here. If it doesn't work out, you've got a home here with me."

"God!" I rub my eyes with the palms of my hands. "It's such a huge step. I barely know the man."

"But you're in love with him." It wasn't a question. He knows me that well.

Pulling my hands away from my face, I confess, "I think I am."

"Then go for it, honey. You're young and beautiful; he's young and beautiful. And rich." He mumbles the last part.

"I don't care about his money."

"That's what makes you a unicorn. You've got great tits and you couldn't give two shits about his money."

I reach for another pillow, holding it over my mouth so I can scream into it without alarming Carter.

I really want to go with him. I've never been to New York, or I guess, to New Jersey. The farthest east I've been is to Columbus, Ohio, for a high school band competition. Yeah, I was a band nerd. Bass clarinet, baby.

"I'll think about it."

"Just. Say. Yes. You know you're going to, so just do it."

"I'll think about it." He's right. I'm going to say yes. How could I not?

———

CARTER STEPS out of the bathroom wearing only a towel and his glasses. "Carter, you're killing me here."

"Kryptonite?"

"Kryptonite."

"I've got the cure," he says huskily. Marching right to the bed to stand in front of me, he leans down for a passionate kiss.

Moving my head back so I can look into his eyes, I say, "I talked to Kai."

"About?"

"About New Jersey." I can't seem to say, *About moving with my brand-spanking-new boyfriend to another state.* (Ooh, I said spanking.)

"What'd he say?"

"He thinks I should try it."

"Try it? He thinks you should come with me and see how it goes?"

"No, that's not what he meant. It's not what I mean." I pull away from him a little further, leaning back to look at more of his face. "You know I'm scared."

"I do. And I get why."

"Okay. Well, here's what I propose."

"I'm listening."

"I think I should go with you."

His delight is obvious as he reaches for me, grinning ear to ear.

I put my hand up to stop him. "But I need you to be patient with me. I may need space. And if I need to come back and hang with Kai for a week or something, you need to let me. I will do my best not to freak out and bolt, but I'm a runner. So, I'm going to try really hard to tell you when things are bothering me or worrying me or if I feel hurt."

He's nodding, but he looks worried.

"And I need for you to do the same with me. If we aren't able to talk it out, like I do with Kai, then this"—I point back and forth between us—"will never work."

"Communication."

"Exactly. And patience."

"And space?"

"Yes, and space when it's needed." I nod. "And one more thing."

"One more thing?"

"I have to find a job."

"No. You don't."

"I do. I can't let you pay for everything. Besides, my student loans will be due in a couple months."

"Fine. But if you must work, it will be running my foundation."

"Carter..."

"No. Give me a little time once we get to Jersey. I'm going to talk to a couple of guys on the team. They'll help us get it started again."

"We'll see." I slide my hand into the top edge of his little towel and tug.

"Just give me two weeks after we get there. If we haven't figured out what to do, then we can revisit this. Remember, I want to commission a new fountain from you. If the foundation is on hold, you can work on that."

"I don't feel right taking money for that."

He gapes at me. "You can't be serious."

"Well—"

"If someone else hired you, would you take money for your work?"

"Of course."

"I rest my case."

"Okay."

"Now, let's seal the deal."

"With sexy times?" I ask with a smile.

"With *very* sexy times." When he places a knee onto the bed, his towel catches beneath. As he crawls toward me, it falls completely off. We're done talking.

CHAPTER FORTY-EIGHT

"I'VE NEVER BEEN on a plane before, Carter, let alone first class." God, I'm so excited. I've been excited ever since the night I told him I'd come with him. I've been vacillating between nerves over making such a giant relationship leap and total excitement thinking about said giant relationship leap. That, and seeing all the museums and galleries firsthand, the ones that house all the famous works in my art history books. And so much more.

"I think you'll like it, babe. The seats are bigger, more comfortable. We can watch movies or television. They'll get you champagne or anything you want. Plus, the food isn't terrible. It's awesome."

"How long is the flight?" I ask, fidgeting nervously in a chair in the first-class lounge.

"It's nonstop to Newark, so it only takes a couple of hours."

Once we're seated on the plane, I run my hands over the plush seats. "Wow, this is nice. The seats are so comfy. I bet you'd hate flying in the way, way back, huh? The seats look half this size back there." I'm just rambling now.

But he smiles down at me. "Yeah. I'm too big for those puny

seats back there. It's a perk of playing in the NFL that I really appreciate."

"There are things about being a wealthy, foxy athlete that you don't appreciate?" He's surprised me. How could he not appreciate everything?

He smirks. "Foxy?" Chuckling, he adds, "I don't like the publicity. Fans are okay if we're winning, but in New York, if you're losing, the fans are brutal. It sucks."

"I could see that." No, I can't. I'm just commiserating with him. My mind is all over the place with my decision to move, so I've been doing my best to keep busy. Carter and I packed up my measly belongings and shipped them to his place in Weehawken, New Jersey. I left my sculptures back at the studio, although I shipped one as inspiration for the fountain. I guess he didn't need to ship anything since he's got yet another condo there.

I'm just snapping on my seat belt when I hear Carter laugh.

"What's so funny?"

He holds up his phone. "Ben has been dealing with Julia Mayfair."

"Ben? Who's Ben?"

"My agent and attorney."

"He's your fixer?" I chuckle.

"In a way, yeah."

"So, what does fancy-pants Mayfair want?"

"About a hundred grand."

My eyes bug out of my head as I stare at Carter. "No fucking way."

"Way."

"She's completely insane."

"She's threatening to go to the press. She's conjured up some sexual harassment bullshit."

"Sexual harassment?!" I squeak. "You never touched her."

"She was referring to you, whom she named as her employee."

"I only got one paycheck, and it was from you."

"True, but she hired some high-powered attorney and they're trying whatever they can to fight the NDA."

"Nondisclosure agreement? She signed one of those?"

"You bet. It's watertight. If she goes to the press, she'll have to pay me a lot more than a hundred grand."

"So, what is your fixer going to do?"

"If she pursues this, we'll file suit."

"A lawsuit? For what?"

"Mainly underperformance and unmet project goals. Then there's overspending. She sent me a bill for twenty grand for office supplies."

"Twenty thousand dollars?" I say too loudly, but there's no way. "Carter, I've got all the receipts, or photos of all the receipts. She sent me to get everything."

"You took pictures?" he looks surprised.

"Well, I tend to lose receipts, so I always snap a pic of them."

"Good to know. Send me those, would you?"

"I will."

"Appreciate you trying to help, Viv." Turning back to his phone, he types.

"No problem, babe. Glad to help." I pat his hand.

He stops typing and looks over at me. "I like it when you call me that."

"What? Babe?"

He nods. "A lot." He looks back over my shoulder, then up toward the front. "Ever heard of the mile-high club?"

"Yes. And we're not doing it. We'll get caught, and it'll be all over the sports stations and then I'll be on television wearing this old T-shirt"—I point to my favorite Pony shirt—"and no makeup and it'll be humiliating. Kai won't speak to me again because of how hideous I looked on national television and... well, no. Just no."

Carter chuckles. "You're hilarious, Viv."

"I know. I'm the funny fat girl."

He growls. Loudly. Then leans down until he's an inch from my face. "I never want to hear you disparage yourself like that again. You're perfect. Fucking gorgeous. I love every goddamn curve on your body. Do you get me?"

"Carter. Chill out," I say, smiling. Yeah, I get him, and I love him for it. *Wait? Love? Shit. I'm so screwed.*

I pull my phone out of my hobo bag to check my messages. Mom has messaged me a lot this week, especially since I may have mentioned that I was going to be in New Jersey for a few months. I wanted her to know because she's a worrier, but my fear is that she'll tell my sister, who will turn around and tell my dad, so I was intentionally vague about the details. I should have known that wouldn't fly with Mom. Not surprisingly, I have a message from her. I tap the icon and read:

Mom: I wish you would call me. I want to hear more about why you'll be in New Jersey "for a few months." I will not lie though, honey. It concerns me that you're just up and leaving Chicago. I haven't even talked to you since we had dinner.

Yeah, I'm a shitty daughter. But it makes me wonder. Does she know Dad stopped by Carter's place? Did he say anything to my sister about the confrontation? I'd call my sister if I ever wanted to speak to her again, which I don't, in case you were curious.

Me: I'll call you when I get settled in Jersey, no later than tomorrow night. I promise. I'll explain everything.

Okay, not *everything*. There are just some things we shouldn't tell our moms. I snicker at my own thoughts.

"Sir? Miss? You'll need to put your phones on airplane mode soon," the air host says to us nicely.

I bet he's only being nice because we're in the fancy seats. But I do as I'm told. Putting my phone back, I look up at Carter as I wrap my arms around myself and whimper, "I'm so frigging nervous."

Carter lifts the armrest between us and stretches his arm around my shoulder, nudging me closer to his big body. I scoot as far as my seat belt will let me.

"Put your head on my shoulder. We'll snuggle until we're in the air."

"Snuggle." I giggle as I do what he says. Who'd pass up a chance to cozy up to Carter Corcoran? Not *this* girl.

"You laughing at my use of the word snuggle?"

"Nah. You just make me happy." I press myself into him and breathe in his scent. He smells delicious. So delicious I want to lick him. I place my hand on his hard stomach and absently rub him there. He grasps my hand and holds it in his.

Whispering into the top of my head, he says, "If you keep doing that, the mile-high club is the least of your worries."

I giggle again and squeeze his hand. "Duly noted, big guy."

"HOLY SHIT, Carter. Another condo with amazing views?" I say, standing at the wall of windows in the living room. His place in Weehawken, New Jersey, is even nicer than the one in

Chicago. It overlooks the Hudson River with views of the Manhattan skyline that are postcard perfect.

"I don't own this one. I'm leasing it from a former teammate. He's playing for the Texans now, but he didn't want to sell this place."

"I don't blame him." The sky is dark, and the lights from New York are sparkling over the water. I'm speechless.

"Tax write-off," Carter mumbles as he sets my carry-on bag down.

"Smart financial move, Carter." I wink. Hell, I know nothing about smart financial moves. But I know what a tax write-off is.

"Come on. Let me show you around."

I follow my man back the way we came in, to find the master bedroom with a huge attached bath. It looks like a spa. There's a shower large enough for us to share, and same with the bathtub. It's then it hits me. I'm living with Carter Corcoran. A shiver runs down my arms, so I rub them to force the feeling away.

"You cold, Viv?"

"No, just excited." And I am excited.

He leans down and kisses me. It's a soft, sweet kiss that I wish would go on longer. "Welcome to your home away from home, babe."

"Thanks." I smile up at him, staring into his pretty green eyes.

His eyes smile back at me. He's happy too.

"Come on. Let me show you the rest."

Taking my hand in his, he shows me the laundry closet just outside our bedroom and a second bedroom with an attached bathroom. Next, he stops in front of a door next to the bedroom but doesn't turn the knob. "This is a surprise. For both of us."

"Oh?"

He pushes the door open to a large room that was probably a bedroom but is now a fully functioning studio space. My eyes feel huge in my head, and my gasp is loud. "Carter! You didn't tell me you had a studio here!"

I walk toward a large table that's ideal for hand-building clay. A tall shelf behind the table holds several boxes of clay, tools, and glazes. I'm sure there's a mini supply of everything I'll need. It seems the man took notice of the things I used when I worked.

He moves to the closet door and opens it. I peer inside. What used to be a closet now holds a small kiln.

"Is that legal?" I know kilns can be housed in smaller spaces now, but I'd hate for him to burn down his friend's condo.

"After I checked with my friend who owns the place, I had it installed by an electrician and inspected by the local fire department. The walls and ceiling are all concrete so it's safe. Plus, when we move, we can take it with us."

We? I love how he includes me. "When did you do all this?"

"After you said yes to coming out here with me, I got on it."

I feel my eyes burn. I'm so at a loss for words. I don't want him to see me cry, but I give myself up when I inadvertently sniffle.

"Baby." He moves to face me. "What's wrong? I thought you'd like this."

Looking into his eyes again, I let out a big ole sob. Wrapping my arms around his neck, I pull myself into him, blubbering, "I l-love it, Carter. You're so g-good to me." I sniffle. "I don't deserve it. I haven't given you anything."

I sob again into his shoulder, feeling mine shake until his big arms wrap around me, pulling me in closer and then up into the air. I feel us moving and hold on tight to Carter's neck as his hands hold me up by my big bottom.

"Shh, Vivien."

I can't shush. I'm overwhelmed with emotions. I'm tired too, but it's 99 percent emotion. Carter carries me out of the studio and into the living room. Still holding me, he sits on the couch. With his hands under my arms, he lifts me until I'm straddling his lap. I bite my bottom lip, worrying. I bet I'm crushing him, but his hands are secured to my backside. He uses them to nudge me further onto his lap.

Looking at him again, I wipe my cheeks with my hands. "Sorry," I mutter. I'm so embarrassed.

"There's no need to be sorry, Viv." He pushes my hair away from my face. "I'm glad you like the studio. I want you to be happy here, and I know you need to create to be happy. It's why I've set up my easel in there as well. I can paint or make a boring tile with you." He chuckles. "It's for both of us."

"Oh, okay."

"But mostly for you."

"You're always doing nice things for me." I sniffle again. "I just take, take, take."

He chuckles softly. "You gave me a chance."

Scoffing at that silly statement, I roll my eyes. "Who wouldn't? Look at you."

"You moved here on less than a month's notice so I wouldn't be without you."

I roll my eyes again, and it hurts a little. I need to stop rolling my eyes. "It's not the same thing."

"I think it is. You never ask for anything from me, so it makes it fun to give. I love making you happy, Vivien. It makes me happy."

"I'd love to make you happy too, but I can't afford to buy you things."

"I don't need *things*." He cups my cheek with his palm. "I've got *things*. What I need is my best friend, who also happens to be my sexy girlfriend, by my side."

"I'm here. I want to be here with you," I whisper.

"I know. What else can a guy ask for, huh? You're with me. You're my partner. I'm going to rely on you to be there to console me when I limp home after a terrible loss." He lifts his brows up and down. "And to celebrate our victories with me and the team. Not to mention the boring events we'll have to attend."

Oh, wait a second. I didn't think of that. I'll have to meet some of the people on his team. Events? "The team? Events?"

"Yeah. The team, the WAGs, and events."

"The WAGs?" Whatever that is, it doesn't sound good.

"It's what we call the wives and girlfriends of the players and coaches. You'll meet some nice women. Some not so nice. You'll sit with them at games. They do fundraising events for special causes throughout the season. Stuff like that."

I must look stricken, because suddenly Carter looks worried. "It'll be okay, Viv. Everyone is very nice."

"Carter?"

"Yeah?" he replies hesitantly.

"I'm not WAG material. I'm so very anti-WAG. I'm going to embarrass you." I start to sob again, and I don't know why. "I'm terrible in social situations. I get nervous, but it comes across as surly and antisocial."

"Vivien, please don't cry, honey." He wraps his big arms around me and pulls me close. "You won't embarrass me. I'm proud you're on my arm. You're beautiful, smart, talented. What man wouldn't want that at a fancy event?"

I yank my head back and stare at him. "I don't have anything to wear to a fancy event. All I have are old tees and jeans." Fresh tears stream down my face.

"I thought of that. You're going shopping with a friend of mine."

Flopping my head back, I blink up at the high ceilings. I give up. I can't not go shopping. It will mean him spending more money on me, and I wish it was at least with him instead of a stranger. "I'd rather go shopping with you. What if I pick something terrible?"

"You won't pick something terrible. I want you to wear what you like to wear. Don't choose something just because you think it's something one of the other WAGs would wear. I'm with *you*, Vivien. I lo—like you exactly as you are."

"I want to go shopping with you." I touch his scruffy, bearded face.

"How 'bout this. You go shopping tomorrow with my friend Ken for a dress for this first event, and I'll take you shopping next week."

"Ken?"

"Yeah, he's my stylist."

I give a startled laugh. "You've got a stylist?"

"We all do."

"But all you wear are sweats and tees."

"I know. But he gets me stuff for events like the one this Friday. It's a big dance thing in the city. Formal."

"Formal?" *Oh, crapola. This is going to suck balls.*

"Yes. Formal."

I stare at my man. "You waited to tell me all this until you got me in your lair, didn't you?"

"I sure did. If I'd told you in Chicago, you'd still be there."

"Damn straight." I slap his arm. "You tricky dick."

Snickering, Carter pats my butt. "Feel better?"

"I do. After hearing about all this stuff I've got to do for you, I'm thinking you owe me."

"Ooh, do I owe you sexual favors?"

I feel him growing hard beneath my ass. "Yes, but first food. Then sexy times."

"Food? I can handle that. Let's make it quick. Sexy times sound so much better."

He slides me off his lap and races into the kitchen. Opening the fridge, he yells to me in the living room, "Want a sandwich?"

"Sure." I follow him into the large kitchen.

"Turkey, ham, or roast beef?"

"Turkey, please."

He hands me a sandwich that's already made and wrapped in plastic.

"You have ready-made sandwiches in your fridge?"

"Always. I have someone who comes in and stocks my fridge while I'm here."

"Wow."

"Eat up. Sexy times await."

I comply, and it is everything I could have hoped for with this amazing man.

CHAPTER FORTY-NINE

CARTER

"EVERYTHING HURTS," I moan in the huge open shower in the locker room of the NY Giants practice facility. My arms, legs, back, abs, head, and, shit, even my eyelids hurt like a bitch.

"It's because you're a pansy ass," says my teammate and friend, Ollie V.

"Am not," I grumble. "I worked out hard in the off-season. Maybe I'm getting too old."

"Right." He starts to step out of the shower room. "You're not old, man. But the longer you play the game, the harder it is to get your body back to playing form."

He should know, he's been in the league for seventeen years. I don't know how he's done it. He's on the D-line with me, but his job is to tackle as many members of the opposing team as he can so I can get to the player with the ball or the quarterback, whichever comes first.

Turning off the water in the shower, I grab a couple towels on my way out to the locker room.

"You ready for tonight?" Ollie asks as he dresses in our regular streetwear of sweats and a tee.

"Yeah. I'm bringing Vivien with me. You'll get to meet her."

I'm excited the two will meet. He'll love her, and I hope she likes him too.

"Can't wait."

"Are you bringing your wifey?"

He's been married for twenty-plus years to Danelle, since his senior year in high school. They've got four kids, two in college, one left in high school, and his oldest, Cameron, is a rookie outside linebacker for the Cardinals. He's proud as hell of his kids and his wife. Don't let his grumbling fool you.

"Of course, man. She lives for this shit. She's probably been at the beauty shop all day getting a new weave or something." He chuckles. "Costs me a damn fortune."

"Well, I can't wait to see Vivien. I've never seen her in anything formal." It's true: I'm pretty stoked to see her. I don't care what she's wearing. I know she'll be beautiful. I just hope she's having a good time today. She went with Ken to get all styled and made up courtesy of Ken and his army of fashion and beauty minions.

I look up at the clock. "Shit. I've got an appointment for a haircut myself." I quickly dress in a clean tee and sweats and slip on my Vans. "See you tonight, Ollie."

"Sure thing," he says, gathering up his workout bag.

I race out to my car and jump in. Arriving at the place where I'm supposed to go, Ken's orders, I'm only a few minutes late. Miraculously, I find a place to park and jog into the shop for my appointment with Sebastian, Ken's go-to hairstylist.

By the time Sebastian is done, he's cut two inches off my hair, shaved off my beard, tried to wax my eyebrows (hell, no!), and given me a facial that included a seaweed mask the shade of baby-poo green. It felt disgusting but, honestly, my face feels softer. Who knew?

"You look fabulous, Carter."

"Thanks. Uh. Good job."

"Come back soon, will you? It's rare I get to work on someone so beautiful."

I look around the salon, and all I see are beautiful people. I shrug. "Yeah. Sometime. Ken's taken care of the bill, yeah?"

"Yes. Now go," he says giving me that shooing motion with his hands. "You're going to be late."

He's right. I'm late.

————

I'M WAITING in the lobby at my condo for Vivien to arrive, adjusting my tie nervously. Ken assured me she'd be ready to go by five since the event is in Manhattan and we'll need extra time to get there. But Ken sent a text ten minutes ago telling me they're running late and to meet them down here. I adjust my tie again, a nervous habit when I'm dressed like a penguin. I check my watch again and brush off invisible lint from my black tuxedo sleeve. I hear the door open and look up. It's Ken, and I'm disappointed. But then I remember she's with him. I lean to my right to peer around him, and when I glimpse her, my breath stops. I almost can't catch it again.

She steps into the entry shyly. It's fucking adorable, but I can't speak. Vivien is, without a doubt, the most beautiful woman I've ever seen. She's wearing a floor-length dress, black with see-through lace. The part beneath the black lace resembles the color of her pale skin. It's fitted at the waist and flows out from there in a soft cloud. But the best part of the dress is the top. It plunges down the front, all the way to the waist. It's not slutty-looking because she's contained in the dress perfectly and there's a piece of fabric holding the dress in place over her chest that you don't notice until you get close.

She approaches me hesitantly. "Do you like it?"

"Jesus, Vivien." I step to her and place a hand on each of her bare arms. "You look incredible. How do you feel? Do you like it?" I want to be sure she's happy.

"Yeah, I do. I've never felt prettier, like a stupid princess." She looks up at me and gives me a big gorgeous smile. "I like how you just reacted to me. You made me feel pretty with just a look."

"I won't be the only one, Viv. I'll need to stand guard and keep those assholes away from you." I know I sound hard-nosed, but what I just said? All true.

Ignoring my jealous rant, she says, "Before we go, we need to take a picture together and send it to Kai."

"Ken, will you take our picture?" I say, turning to him but not taking my eyes off Vivien.

"Of course." He pulls his phone out of his pocket and steps back. Before he snaps the picture, he says, "You two look amazing together."

"Thanks," we say simultaneously.

Ken clicks two photos and promises to send them to both of our phones, then shoos us out of the lobby.

I take Viv's elbow and lead her out to the limo. Yeah, I hired a limo. I'd like to have a drink or two tonight, and I won't if I'm driving. Besides, it's fitting for a princess to have a carriage.

"I like your hair," I say, reaching out to touch it. But I stop midway, knowing how women get if you try to touch their hair on nights like these.

"You can touch it," she says with a smile. "There's a ton of hairspray in there, so beware. It feels like cardboard."

I still don't want to touch it. It looks impeccably styled, and Ken would kill me if I messed it up. "Did you color it?"

"Yes. Ken thought the platinum blonde was too brassy, so he toned it down to this. It's more golden."

"You got it cut?"

She arches a brow. "Do I look like a boy again?"

I nearly choke. "Fuck, no!" Her hair is shorter than it was the night I met her, with the longer front ending at about her chin. She looks like a modern-day pixie. "You look sexy as hell, babe." I stare at her face, unable to get over how large her eyes appear and how full her lips are with the deep red lipstick. It's then I notice she's not wearing her lip ring. I reach out and touch below her lip. "No lip ring?"

"No," she says with a scowl. "Ken told me it looked 'garish' with the dress." She used air quotes and stink eyes.

"You can put it back in if you want, Viv. It's your choice."

"No." She brushes her skirt absently with both hands. "He's right. I'll put it back in tomorrow. No biggy." Sizing me up, she changes the subject. "You cut yours too." She runs her fingertips over my chin. "And you shaved."

"Do you like it?"

"I do. But I liked the beard too. You always look good."

She hasn't stopped touching me, and it's making my dick hard.

I take a second to peek down her dress but am disappointed when everything seems locked down tight. Shame.

I grasp her hand from my face and kiss her palm. "I'm so glad you're here with me."

CHAPTER FIFTY

I CAN'T BELIEVE how it feels to be dressed up like this, accompanied by a man who looks this good. It's surreal. We've been walking around the huge ballroom for over an hour. His palm hasn't left my lower back for longer than it takes to shake hands with people. He keeps running his thumb back and forth, sending tingles right up my spine, into my hair, then back down to my lady land. I'd tell him to stop but if I do, he will.

I've met so many famous people tonight. Hell, just the entrance to this place was like a Hollywood premier. There wasn't a red carpet, per se—it was New York Giants blue—but it was a long carpet like the ones you see in the magazines. Each player had to walk across it for pictures and interviews. Carter held my hand the entire time, introducing me as his girlfriend. I didn't have to say a word. I merely smiled and nodded when people said hello to me.

I've got to admit, so far, it hasn't been terrible. That's probably thanks more to Carter never leaving my side than to the event itself. As for the event, it's a little boring so far, but we're still at the cocktail hour. I've been nursing the same glass of champagne for the last half hour. I figured it was best if I only had a couple of drinks tonight. I haven't eaten all day, so I'm afraid I'll get tipsy and make a huge fool of myself. No, thanks.

As I listen to some old guy drone on and on about Carter's stats, I take a moment to scan the room. I get halfway around when I see someone I was hoping to never see again. Natalia. I use my elbow to nudge Carter as discreetly as possible. He feels me and looks down, then whispers, "Just one sec, babe." As soon as the old guy stops talking, Carter makes his move. "If you'll excuse us, I need to grab a drink before they call us for dinner."

Ooh, dinner. I'm starving.

The old guy says, "Nice to see you, Carter. Nice to meet you, Vivien."

"You too," I say with a smile. After we're far enough away, I whisper, "Who was that?"

"John Mara."

I shrug. Never heard of him.

"The owner of the team."

"Oh, wow."

"Do you know Rooney Mara? She's an actress."

"I've heard of her." I think she was in *The Girl with the Dragon Tattoo.*

"He's her uncle. She's here somewhere."

"Oh, wow. That's cool." I loved the book and the movie.

We stop in line at the bar. "So, why did you elbow me?"

"Oh, shit. I forgot. Natalia's here."

"Fuck. Where?"

We both look around the room, but I spot her first. "She's over by John Mara."

He looks over in that direction and cusses again. "She's with Nelson."

"Who's Nelson?"

"Rookie QB."

"Quarterback?"

"Yeah. I wonder how she sunk her claws into him."

I wince when he says "her claws." I've felt those. They hurt.

"I'm sorry." He looks at my neck. It's healing nicely and, thanks to the makeup Ken used, you can't even see them tonight.

"No worries. I know what you meant."

"We need to ignore her, okay?"

I nod. "No problem." I definitely do not want to talk to her. A fresh drink is in order. Maybe I'll forget my plan to sip my wine and drink up. I'm not sure I can deal with her tonight.

Carter gets a glass of golden liquid and gets me a fresh glass of champagne. It tastes way better when it's cold. He leads me to our table, a giant round one that looks to seat eight. Carter places his hand on my back and leads me to the only person seated at our table. "Hey, man. Let me introduce you to Vivien." He steps aside so I can move in front of him. "Viv, this guy here is my oldest friend, Ollie V."

"Olive?" *That's a weird name for a guy.*

He chuckles and gets to his feet, and I have to crane my neck in order to see him as he rises. He's even taller than Carter. "Olivier is my real name. Only this jackass calls me Ollie V." He extends his hand, and I place mine in his. Bending, he kisses the top of my hand. "The pleasure is all mine, Miss Vivien. Carter has talked nonstop about you. He wasn't wrong, darlin', you're a beauty."

"Who's a beauty?" The words come from a tall woman as she moves up next to Olivier.

"You are, darlin' wife." He leans down and kisses her cheek. "Danelle, meet Vivien. Carter's girl."

"Well, aren't you lovely." Danelle steps around her husband, past Carter, and straight to me. She wraps her arms around me and squeezes. "Finally, Carter. A girl with real curves."

I blush at her words. I know what she's actually saying. Fat.

A fat girl. I guess Danelle gets it. She and I are about the same size, only hers seems to be settled in her bottom and mine in my top.

"I've been telling him to stop picking those scarecrows with no personality for years now." Danelle's eyes get huge. "Oops, speak of the devil."

I direct my eyes where she's looking and watch as Natalia steps up to the table trailed by a tall blond man.

"Well, isn't this cozy?" she says snidely.

Leaning down, Carter whispers in my ear, "Do you want to find a different table?"

I shake my head. We were assigned this table, and it'd be weird to make someone else switch with us. It'd be a whole thing. "No, I'll sit by Danelle."

"Good plan." We swap places so I can sit between Danelle and Carter. Natalia sits down between Carter and the quarterback. I've forgotten his name already.

"Vivien?"

Oh, great. Here we go. Natalia's got something to say.

"Yes?" I reply as calmly as possible.

"You look lovely tonight."

Okay. If I'm not mistaken, that was a compliment. "Thank you."

"Did you order it from the internet?"

I blink at her. *What a strange question.* "No."

"Hm, weird."

"What's weird?"

"Well, most stores in the city don't carry your size. I figured you'd have to order it from Amazon's plus-size department."

I turn three shades of red, starting with magenta.

"Natalia," growls Carter. "Don't start."

"What? It was a serious question. I was just curious how she was able to find a dress in her size in the city."

I'm not going to let it bother me. When Danelle pats my leg, I look over at her.

She gives me a warm smile and another pat. Leaning down, she whispers in my ear but not very quietly, so Natalia can hear her. "She's a fucking bitch, girl. Jealous as hell. Don't listen."

"Fuck you, Danelle," Natalia spits.

Ollie stands up so fast his seat falls backward and points to Natalia. "Not one more word. Do not talk to my wife like that, and same goes for Carter's girl. I will have your ass kicked out of this party and any future Giants parties for eternity." He looks at the quarterback. "Word to the wise, rookie. This girl is toxic. Do not bring her to any other functions, or the D-line will make an example of you at practice. You get me?"

The rookie nods but doesn't say a word. Natalia's face is pink. I'd tell you it was with embarrassment, but that's not what it is. She's seriously pissed but does an excellent job of keeping it under control. Slapping her napkin in her lap, she reaches for her glass of wine, takes one sip, leans in, and spits it out, at me. Some of it lands on my plate, some on my chest, but the majority hits my face.

"Oh, forgive me. I couldn't help myself. This wine is terrible."

I've got makeup on, a lot of makeup, more makeup than I've ever worn in my life, and I need to be sure it's not running all over my face. I leap to my feet. "I'm going to the ladies' room." Sliding between our chairs, I step toward the bathrooms. I pass Carter's chair and nearly round the table when I feel my foot catch on something. I lurch forward so fast I can't catch myself. I hit the terrazzo floor hard, hands first. It's not wise to put your hands out first when you're falling, but it beats falling face-first. I hear something snap before the pain strikes. But when it does, it hits hard.

"Oh, motherfucker!" I shout. Rolling onto my back, I

attempt to sit up while clutching my wrist to my chest and doing my best not to vomit. "Oh, shit. It hurts." Tears fill my eyes, because the pain is unbearable.

Carter rushes to kneel at my side, looking panicked. "Viv?"

"I think it's broken." I know it's broken. My right hand is turned at a very unnatural angle. It's grotesque, and it's making me sick. I feel myself turn clammy and hot.

"Christ, you're turning white. Lay down, Vivien." He looks up and shouts, "Ollie, get Doc Sorenson." Looking back at me, he says, "Lie back." Placing his hand behind my head, he scoots his legs beneath my head so it's got a place to rest. "Lie back, baby. Doc Sorenson's our team doctor. He'll know what to do."

"Okay," I say weakly. "I feel like I'm gonna be sick, Carter."

"Breath slowly, in and out. Concentrate on my face, angel."

"Jesus, could you two be any more disgusting?" spits Natalia.

"You should go," says the quarterback.

What's his name? Nelson?

"Excuse me?" Natalia hisses, glaring at her date.

"I saw you trip her," he says loudly.

Carter growls as Ollie returns with the doctor. He's down on the floor with me before I can blink. "What happened, honey?"

"Fell."

"Tripped," mutters the QB.

"Tripped?" It's Ollie's turn to ask.

"She tripped her. I saw it," says the rookie QB.

Ollie turns to her just as the doctor attempts to touch my wrist.

I squeal in pain. "It hurts," I whimper.

"I'm afraid it's broken, honey." He looks over at Carter. "Call 911. I don't have my bag with me tonight, and the paramedics have emergency splints on hand. We need to get this stabilized and some painkillers going. Setting this will be rough on her."

"I'm on it." Ollie's got his phone out before the doctor's even done talking.

"Sit tight, sweetheart. We'll get you taken care of as soon as possible."

As we sit on the floor, I watch two security guards approach the table. "Someone called security?"

"Please escort her out," Danelle says, pointing to Natalia. "She's responsible for this poor child's injury."

"Are you pressing charges?" one of the big guards asks me.

I start to shake my head, but Carter interrupts. "Yes."

"What?" screeches Natalia like an injured owl.

"Then we'll need to get the cops in here. We can't touch her. They'll need to file the report."

"Well, I'm not going to stay here for this!" Natalia says, stomping past me.

"You'll sit your ass right back down," Ollie says with the phone to his ear again. "I've got the cops on the way."

"You can't be serious, Carter. It was an accident," whines Natalia.

God, her voice is grating.

Carter looks at the quarterback, and I follow his gaze.

"Carter, she did it on purpose. She had to work to get her foot out there." He swallows so hard that his Adam's apple bobs. "I didn't even invite her. She invited herself when my date cancelled at the last minute."

Something tells me the date was a friend of Natalia's. It all makes sense. Now, if the pain in my arm would just calm down, I might survive this. God, it hurts.

Nelson isn't finished. "She made us sit here. Our table was supposed to be over there"—he points to the front of the room —"but she switched the tags around on the seating chart."

The only thing good about the current drama is that it has taken my mind off my wrist. But only for a second. Fortunately, it takes the paramedics no more than fifteen minutes to arrive. It's amazing they're so fast, considering the size of the city and number of accidents that occur daily. They've got to be busy with serious stuff. No matter. The first thing they do is inject me with happy juice. In seconds, the pain has ebbed somewhat and I'm smiling at everyone.

"This shit is awesome. Can I get more?"

Everyone is chuckling, even the paramedics. "Maybe another time, ma'am."

"*Ma'am?* Geez, guys. I'm not my mom."

They all laugh again.

"Yes, ma'am."

"You all suck," I grumble, then I giggle as they help me onto the gurney.

They ask me to lie down as they cover me with a white sheet. As they're rolling me out, the huge crowd in the ballroom claps. Carter chuckles, and I stare at him, perplexed.

"They always clap when they wheel a guy off the field."

"Oh." I blink. "Oh! It's like I was injured playing football. I get it." *Funny.* I giggle again and can't seem to stop. Well, until I'm in the emergency room at the hospital and they decide it's time to set my wrist. That's when the fucking fun really begins. It's also when my hatred for Natalia takes on a whole new dimension. "The next time I see her fucking face, Carter, I'm going to punch it. With brass knuckles."

He chuckles, but then stops when he sees how serious I am. "I mean it. I'm tired of bitches like her pushing me around. Not to mention she ruined my makeup and probably my new, beautiful, perfect dress," I growl. "She's going down, Carter. Don't try to stop me either."

"Wouldn't think of it, babe. Have at it."

"Yeah, well…" I've calmed slightly. "She'd better watch out."

"Duly noted, beautiful. Duly noted." He runs his hand over my cheek, into my hair, and it feels good. So, so good. I think the new pain meds have taken over, and I'm suddenly sleepy. "Wake me up when they come to put a cast on. I want a pink one, Carter. Make sure they put on a pink cast."

"I will, Viv."

"No! Purple! I want purple. Pink is pretty but purple is *purple*. You know what I mean?" I don't hear him respond because my eyes close, and I can't force them open no matter how hard I try.

CHAPTER FIFTY-ONE

I COULD KILL Natalia with my bare hands, but I won't. I'm letting the team handle it. There were other witnesses besides the rookie who saw her do it. They've got a legal team that rivals the best firm in the country. They said they'd take care of it since it happened at a Giants function and so my name isn't dragged through the proverbial public relations shitstorm. They're doing it for me and for Vivien, and I appreciate their assistance.

Viv's been asleep off and on for twenty-four hours thanks to the strong pain meds the hospital sent home with her. It makes her a little loopy, but I'd rather have a loopy girl than one in pain. My poor Viv. I heard her wrist snap when she fell. It was loud as fuck, echoing in the huge open space of the ballroom. That hurts. I know. I've broken a bone or two.

The worst part for Viv is that it's her right hand. She won't be able to work with clay for a while. The doc says she'll need to wear the cast for six to eight weeks. Not a purple one, not yet. They put her in a temporary splint until the swelling goes down. She'll get her purple cast next week. By then, she may want a different color. I'm somewhat anxious to see what she ends up with; maybe Bears orange. I could suggest that.

I don't think she realizes the extent of the damage. Don't get me wrong: she'll heal. But she'll be forced to do other things for a while. This could be a good time to get Olivier and Danelle over to help us navigate this foundation shit. They started one many years ago, so they know the basics. I'll call them once Vivien is back on level ground. In the meantime, I need to get lunch prepared. I should be at practice, but Coach gave me the day off to be home with Vivien. Tomorrow, Ken will be here to hang out with her and Danelle the day after, so we're covered there.

Reaching into the fridge, I pull out fresh produce to make us a side salad. I've also cooked up some ground turkey burgers. I hope she likes ground turkey. I didn't want to wake her up to ask. She needs her rest. When the food is ready, I grab her plate and bowl and make my way into our bedroom. She's sound asleep, facedown, with her wrist propped up on a pillow.

"Vivien?" I set her food on the nightstand and touch her shoulder. "Viv?"

"No, I'm tired," she groans.

"I know, but you need to eat so you can take another happy pill." That's what she calls the pain meds. She seems to like them, but I won't let her take them for long. They're addictive. I've seen the havoc they've caused former players and friends. Not good. But she needs them for a day or two.

"Fine." She rolls gingerly onto her back. "I hurt everywhere," she whines.

"I know." I reach down to adjust the pillows so she's sitting up. "Move up to a seated position."

Mumbling and groaning, she complies.

I grab the lap desk I use to study my playbook in bed and

adjust it over her lap. Placing the burger down in front of her, I watch her expression.

"What's this?"

"Turkey burger. There's cheese, tomato, and lettuce on there. Do you want ketchup? Anything else?"

"Ketchup would be good. Thanks, Carter."

I place the salad next, and she smiles. "Is that ranch dressing?"

"Yeah. I know you like that."

"I do. Yum."

"Be right back." I return with the ketchup and sit next to her as she tries the burger. "Good?"

"Yeah. But where's your food?"

"Oh, I was going to eat at the table."

"Well, shoot. Help me up so I can eat with you."

"Not today. I want you to stay put. I'll go get mine and eat in here, then."

"Okay." She takes another bite of her burger and smiles. "Really yummy. Thanks."

"Good." I jog back out to the kitchen and grab my plate of two burgers and a salad bowl double the size of hers. What? I'm a growing boy. I need the protein.

On the bed next to her, I eat my salad first. I always eat my salad first. It seems strange to eat it during or after. Once that's finished, I set the plate with my burgers on my lap and bite into the first one. Damn, so good. I wolf down the first burger and have started on the second when I feel her eyes on me. I look over, and sure enough, she's staring.

"What? Do I have mustard on my face or something?" I wipe my mouth with the back of my hand and stare at her.

"I love you, Carter."

All I can do is stare. And stare some more. It's taking me a minute to get my bearings. In that time, her face, which started off unsure, has settled into more of a frown. Before she gets the wrong idea, I set my burger down, place the plate on the nightstand, and turn to face her. I move in close so she can see my face clearly. "I love you too, Vivien. So much."

She beams and nods. "Good." Biting into her burger, I smile back as we continue eating like nothing just happened.

"So, I've got good news."

"Oh, yeah?" she replies, nibbling on her food.

"You remember Ben?"

"Your fixer?"

I laugh. "Yeah, my fixer. He got Julia to settle."

"Settle?"

"Yep."

"You're not going to tell me how much, are you?"

"Nope."

"It's not a hundred thousand dollars, is it?"

"Nope." We threatened to tell our own story to the press if she talked. Our story would ruin her business. Hers would only tarnish my reputation, but Ben felt I'd be able to regroup after the foundation was off the ground. "Nothing close to that." I smile at Viv. "And your photos of all the receipts helped a lot. She padded her expenses."

"Uh-huh. Figures." Vivien rolls her eyes. "She only deserves enough for two weeks work."

"I agree." Patting her knee, we finish our meal in near silence. I finish all of mine, but she's still got half her sandwich left.

"I'm full. Thanks, Carter."

"No problem." I pick up my plate and bowl and stack hers on top. "I'll get your pill."

"Can we wait on that? I feel okay. I'd rather get up and move around some. Maybe we could watch a movie."

"I can set us up in the bedroom."

"Nah, living room. I want to see the view."

I take our plates to the kitchen and watch her as she moves out to the couch. I grab several pillows and my soft throw from the bed, getting her comfortable on the couch while also making sure her wrist stays elevated, then take her ice pack to refill it. I've been monitoring her since we got home from the hospital. The swelling has to go down before they'll put a cast on it. Filling the pack with fresh ice, I return and set it on her wrist.

"So, what do you feel like watching?"

She looks over at me. "You're going to hate me."

"Never."

"What do you want to watch?"

CARTER IS PERFECT. No, now don't roll your eyes at that. I know he's not *perfect* perfect, but he's pretty close. He treats me like his queen, and I'm working hard to reciprocate. I'm so used to being alone and taking care of myself, it's not natural for me to just flip a switch. So, every day I try to do something nice for him.

Take today, for example. At last I'm getting my cast on, and I'm choosing Bears orange as the color. He didn't ask me to do it, but I know how much he loves his precious Bears, so I'm going to surprise him with that choice. See? Baby steps. After that, I will give him the best blowjob of his life. In his car. Well, I'll suggest it. If he opts to wait until we get home, I'm okay with that too.

———

NOW I'VE GOT a brand-new hard cast over my wrist, and I went one better on the color. It's wrapped in Bears orange *and* blue. He smiled the entire time they wrapped me up. When it was done, I asked, "You like it?"

He shrugs. "It's not purple."

I blink at him confused.

"Because purple is just *so* purple." He shrugs.

He'd told me I said that the night in the ER. I was totally out of it. I flip him the bird with my good hand. "Should I ask them to change it, then?"

He stands up quickly and walks toward me. "No way. I love the colors." Leaning down, he kisses me softly. "Ready to go home?"

I know he's got to get back to practice. Heck, he's still sweaty from the morning session. He looks smokin' hot even after working out. "Sure."

He opens my car door for me to slip inside. We're parked in an end spot in the parking garage attached to the giant medical plaza where my appointment was. It's nice and dark in the cavernous building. It's perfect, so I look to our right and left to make sure there are no other people around. When I see no one, I decide to risk it. When he slides in, he leans to press the start button, but I place my hand on his. "Thank you for taking care of me."

"You're welcome." He smiles and attempts to start the car again.

"I'd like to do something for you," I whisper, never letting my eyes leave his face.

"You don't have—"

I place my left hand over his dick and move it up and down slowly. "I know I don't have to."

"Viv?"

I move my left hand into the elastic band of his shorts, finding him immediately hard. "No boxers?"

"Mm, um, no?"

"Naughty boy." I feel him get even harder with those words.

"Fuck, Viv." With my bum hand, I push up the center console and move toward him. "Viv. I just worked out."

It doesn't bother me. It undoubtedly should, but it doesn't. "Help me with your shorts, Carter."

He lifts his hips and pushes his shorts down just far enough for his dick to pop free.

"You sure about this, Vivien?" He's practically panting. It's been almost a week since we last touched each other. I'm just as turned on as he is. "Your hand. Does it hurt?"

See? He's worried about my hand. "I'm not going to use my hand."

He groans loudly and lays his head back against the headrest. "You're going to kill me, woman."

I ignore him so I can concentrate on my task. I run my nose along him and note that he smells good. Really good. I slide my tongue up the side of his shaft and use my left hand to follow my tongue up, placing pressure on that thick vein.

"Fuck, Viv."

I repeat that since he seems to like it. When I get to the top, I swipe my tongue around the head, all while making a yummy sound. Sliding my mouth over him, I make that sound again. God, this man is amazing. Delicious.

"Vivien," he moans.

I love his sexy sounds. Scooting closer, I take him as far into my mouth as I can. I'm nowhere near a deep throat kind of person. Not yet, anyway. I do my best to get deep without, I suck and lick, swirling my tongue over the head again. I feel his hand on the top of my head and instantly soak my panties. I moan on him and place my hand on his. I want him to take control.

He mutters, "Jesus, woman. You're so fucking perfect," as he gently presses down on the top of my head.

I don't want him to be gentle. Not really. I let him guide me down and press up, sucking and licking as I go. I use my left hand at the base of his shaft to move along with my mouth. His hips have started moving up and down with me, and his hand is pressing slightly harder and faster. He's close, urging me on. I speed up to match his frantic pace, adding more suction as I go. I'm getting so excited myself, when he slides the hand that was on my head down into my leggings and panties, I come the minute his finger touches my clit. I moan loudly over him, and it's all it takes. He's moaning and pumping into my mouth as he comes.

"Shit. Sorry. I should have warned you."

I pull away from him and blink. I can't look at him. I haven't swallowed yet, and I don't want him to see my mind whirling. Before I know it, he's got his shirt off, holding it in front of me. I grab it and place it over my mouth. As discreetly as possible, I use the shirt to... you know. I move it to a clean spot and wipe him off.

I feel his finger under my chin. He's nudging it up so I'll look at him. When I do, he appears serious. Really serious. It makes me worry.

"Hands down, Viv. That was the best, hottest, fucking blowjob I've ever had. I will dream about it for the rest of my life."

I blush. I know I do. I feel the heat on my cheeks, but smile through it. "I'm glad."

"Tonight, I return the favor," he says matter-of-factly.

It's my turn to look serious. "That's not why I did it. You don't have to pay me back."

Sliding his thumb over my lip ring, he says softly, "I want to. I miss tasting you, being inside you."

"Oh." *Well, in that case.* "Me too."

"But only if you feel up to it. I know your wrist still hurts."

"Not that much," I say, holding up my Bears arm.

He chuckles as he slides his shorts up over his hips. "I need to get back. Is Danelle stopping over today?"

She nods. "She and I are working on your foundation stuff. She really knows what she's doing. Maybe you should hire her?" He gives me the side-eye, so I know that makes him cranky. "Just sayin'."

"It's you and me." Smirking, he adds, "Mostly you."

"I get that." He's going to be too busy for the next six months. This is on me.

"Which reminds me. I need your bank information."

"Why?"

"To pay you." He taps the steering wheel with both hands impatiently. "And if you say no, I'm going to spank that bottom tonight."

I should say no. I'm curious about the spanking, but I can't. I need money. I'll work my ass off to earn it too. "Fine."

"Fine? That's it? You're not going to throw a fit about wanting to be independent?"

"You're paying me for a job. A job I will work hard at. So, no, I'm okay with *earning* the money. I just don't like the idea of being a kept woman, sugar daddy." She winks.

"Fair enough." He looks at me. "But let me just say, I was hoping I could spank you later."

"Me too," I mutter.

"I heard that."

"Good." I look over at him. "Tonight. Spank me."

"Christ." He runs his hands through his hair as his shorts start to tent.

"Spank me." I giggle as I watch them tent more.

"You're a cruel woman, Vivien."

"Sorry. I'm naughty. You should spank me."

He chuckles, but his laughter doesn't stop him from growing harder. "Oh, I'm going to spank you."

CHAPTER FIFTY-THREE

CARTER

THE SECOND we're back in the condo, I grab her by the waist and carry her into the living room. Setting her down behind the couch, I growl. "Turn around. Bend over the back of the couch."

"Now?" she squeaks. "You're doing this now?"

"Yes, damn it. My dick is so fucking hard. I'll never be able to practice if I know you're home wet and waiting for the spanking you've asked for." Literally.

I watch as she tentatively bends over the back of the couch, then lean over her back and place a pillow under her cast. "If it hurts, tell me. I'll stop."

"Okay."

I push down her shorts and panties, revealing her creamy white, round ass, and run my palm over both cheeks. Her skin is so fucking soft. Moving my hand back, I swat at her right cheek. It immediately turns a light shade of pink. I should be turned the fuck on by the sight, but the only thing going through my head is that I hurt her. She made a whimpering sound when I slapped her bottom, and I hated it, even if it did sound like a turned-on kind of whimper. I can't do it to her. I rub my palm over the area to ease the redness.

Choosing to skip the spanking portion of the afternoon, I slide my finger through her center and growl, "You're fucking soaked."

"Mm-hmm."

I slide my thick finger into her, pumping in and out. My dick is hard as a rock. Looking down at her, I feel precome drip out at the sight of her magenta ass. Pulling my finger out, I push my shorts down. "This is going to be hard and fast." I'm not going to last.

I place myself at her entrance and thrust inside.

"Oh, God," she gasps. "Yes. Fuck me hard, Carter."

I pull out and plunge back in, holding on to her hips as I go. This is going to be punishing. I don't want to hurt her, but this is fucking hot as hell. I can't help myself. I spread my legs to get better balance, and I fuck her so hard my vision blurs.

"Yes!" she screams. "Don't stop, baby. So close."

I fucking love it when she calls me that. I do as she asks, slamming into her a few more times until I feel her squeeze my dick so hard I come on the spot. We're loud. I know we are. Luckily, the walls around this place are thick.

I slump over her back and kiss her neck. "You're the hottest fuck, Viv."

"You too, Carter," she says panting.

I kiss down her spine as I pull out. Watching myself drip from her, I wish, for the first time in my adult life, that my woman wasn't on birth control. I want to place my hand over her entrance and hold myself inside her until she's pregnant with my kid. Fuck. I want Vivien to be the mother of my kids. This shit is getting real.

Stepping back, I reach out and pull her up. "You okay?" I seriously went for it. It was a pounding.

"Yeah." She's still breathing heavily, her face pink from exertion. "It was hot."

"It was." I bend to kiss her lips and stay there, smiling at her like an idiot. "Now that's what we call a quickie." I bend the rest of the way to pick up her shorts and pull mine back up. "Here you go, milady."

"Thanks." She kisses my cheek and heads to our bedroom. "You'd better get to practice. I'm going to cook tonight, so I don't want you to be late."

"You're cooking?" I'm following her into the bedroom. I mean, she's naked from the waist down. What else can a man do?

"I can cook." She mumbles something else I can't quite make out.

"All right, I need to go. I'll text you when I know when we'll be done."

"Sounds good," she yells from the bathroom. "Have a good practice. Don't get hurt."

"I won't."

I grab my keys and wallet and head out. I'm an hour later than I said I'd be. I'll just blame it on the clinic. It'll be fine.

———

FINE WASN'T the right word. Torture is more like it. Coach was so pissed I was late that he made the entire D-line run, not jog, an extra thirty minutes on the treadmill. It was ridiculous. We're adults. We should be past the point where coaches punish us collectively. Right?

It pissed the guys off, and I'm pretty sure they knew I was fucking around, literally. They aren't talking to me at the moment, but I'll smooth things over—starting with Ollie V, on the treadmill next to me.

"Sorry, man."

He gives me a dirty side-eye. "Uh-huh." He's running a fast

clip but breathing normally. The guy is fit for an old man. "You get some?"

I look back at him and smirk. "Twice."

He chuckles. "Well, you were due, huh? She probably hasn't felt up to it since your bitch of an ex maimed her."

The truth is, Ollie hates Natalia. Always has, ever since Natalia said some pretty shitty things to Danelle. I get it. Oh, wait! I know how to get on his good side. "Viv told me the next time she sees Natalia, she's going to punch her in the face."

Ollie chuckles again.

"With brass knuckles."

That did it. Ollie throws his head back and laughs hard. "Well, shit, man. You're off the hook. Tell your girl I'll hold the bitch down for her." He turns to the row of guys all running. "He's off the hook, fellas. He promises never to fuck us over again." He turns back to me. "Right, brother?"

"Right," I say loud enough for everyone to hear. "Never again."

The rest of the defense grumbles and mumbles. Some nod while others just give me dirty looks.

"Hit the showers, assholes," one of the assistants yells into the workout room.

Thank fuck. The first thing I do once I'm at my locker is text Viv.

Me: Showering. Be home in forty-five.

Viv: Okay. Drive safe, babe ;)

CHAPTER FIFTY-FOUR

VIVIEN

OKAY. Confession. I can't cook. I can make a mean bowl of cereal, and sure, I flipped some pancakes at the Palace Grill whenever we were super rushed, but the batter was already made and the grill was already set at the right temperature. All I had to do was ladle out the batter and watch it cook for three minutes, then flip. That's it.

So, tonight I'm trying to impress my man with my *skeeels* in the kitchen. Nonexistent "skeeels" apparently, because I'm failing. I know he eats a lot of protein and veggies, so I thought, *stir-fry! How hard could it be?* And I didn't have to go to the store because his fridge was already stocked with fresh veggies and chicken breast.

"Shit!" I shout while trying to avoid the splattering of hot oil. It hit my good hand twice and my face one other time. "Why are you doing that?" I shout at the electric wok I found in Carter's cupboard. Hell, I even watched a bunch of YouTube videos about this. I tap the wooden spoon I found with the wok against the edge for emphasis as I talk to the pan again. "You aren't supposed to hurt me, you bastard."

When I hear the front door slam, I get myself under control and go down the hall to meet him.

"Honey, you're home." I get up on my tiptoes and kiss him. "Go get changed. Dinner's almost ready." Is it me, or did I just sound like a '50s housewife? Yeah, I thought so.

I turn to go back to the kitchen, but he grabs my arm and pulls me into him. Sliding his palm behind my neck, he kisses me. I press into him and get into the kiss. I could so get used to waiting for him to come home every night. I wrap my arms around him, wooden spoon still in hand, and press my chest into his. It's then I smell it—the burning!

"Oh, fuck!" I pull out of his arms and race to the kitchen. Smoke's everywhere. At that moment, the most horrendous horn sounds.

"Fire alarm!" yells Carter over the sound. He gets to the wok and unplugs it from the wall, flinching as hot oil hits him on the arm.

"Come on. Let's go." He grabs the hand still holding the spoon and pulls me down the hallway and out the door. "The fire alarms are all connected. We need to go downstairs."

I head straight for the elevator, but he grabs my arm. "Stairs, babe."

"Oh. Right." On the way down, we're met by other residents, all bitching and complaining about the alarm. *Please don't tell them it was me, Carter.* By the time we're on the main level, the fire trucks are there. Carter approaches them, and I watch them talking and nodding. He hands them a set of keys as they enter the building.

I peer around and see a lot of unhappy people. *Sorry.* I want to say it out loud, but I can't. I feel like such an idiot. I'm never cooking again. Well, I'd cook mac 'n' cheese. I can cook that. And hot dogs. I'm good with hot dogs. But anything that requires hot oil and watching YouTube, no thanks. Oh, and brownies. I can bake a mean pan of brownies as long as it's from a box. I should have just made that.

"Stick with what you know, Vivien," I mumble to myself.

Carter pulls me close. "No harm, babe. It's all going to be okay." He pats my ass with his big palm. "So, you ever use a wok before?"

"No."

"Tricky. Woks are tricky."

"Apparently."

I feel his body shake. When I look up, I see he's attempting to keep himself from laughing, but it's no use.

"Just go ahead and get it over with. Laugh, for Christ's sake."

So, he does. Loudly. People are watching, and I think it's helping lighten their moods because they're starting to smile. Well, everyone but one guy. He's still pissed. Oh, well. Can't be helped.

When the fire crew comes back out, one of them walks toward us while the other one yells "All clear."

As people make their way back inside, our fire guy says, "You've got some smoke damage but nothing else." He looks down at me because he's almost as tall as my fella. In a thick Jersey accent, he says, "Maybe no more wok, huh?"

"No more wok." I lift my good hand and hold up three fingers. "Scout's honor."

"Good, glad to hear it. Have a good night, folks."

"Thanks, man," Carter says, doing that man handshake, backslap thing.

Do they know each other? "So," I say with a sigh. "Wanna order pizza?"

"Yeah, sweetness. I wanna order pizza."

I clean up the kitchen while we wait for our food to be delivered. Luckily, it only took a good scrubbing to get the char off of the kitchen counter and cupboards. Once the pizza arrives, we get cozy on the sofa. Before he can turn on the television, I say, "I got an email from my dad today."

He stops chewing and looks at me. "Oh? What'd he say?"

"He said he heard I was in New York."

"From your mom?"

"In a roundabout way. She almost certainly told my sister." I shrug. "Who else would tell him? My sister seems to enjoy my pain. I don't know why Mom felt she needed to tell Grace."

"Maybe she's worried about you, Vivien. It's what moms do. Shit, mine emails me daily."

"She does?"

He nods, smiling. "So does my dad. My brothers and Kennedy text a lot." He pushes my bangs out of my face. "What did you say to him?"

"Nothing at first. I waited an hour before I got the nerve to respond." I set my plate down on the coffee table. "He wants to meet for lunch."

"Lunch? When?"

"Tomorrow."

"Where?"

"Delmonico's."

"Delmonico's?" Carter repeats, perplexed. "That place is pretty fancy. It's a New York City institution."

"I've heard of it, so it must be." I laugh. I hate fancy places. Well, at least I've got clothes to wear. Ken set me up with a few outfits that will work for luncheons. His words. Not mine. "Should I go?"

Carter sets his plate next to mine and pulls me onto his lap. "That's up to you. The only thing I worry about is him upsetting you. He's not the most sensitive person I've ever met."

"Well, I was thinking," I say, running my finger over the collar of his tee, "that maybe he regretted everything that happened at the party. That he's remorseful. His email sounded sincere." I want him to be remorseful and sincere. Something other than the egocentric, egomaniacal father he was that day. "Let me read his message to you." I pull the phone out of my bra. What? It stays put in there. I tap on the buttons until I get to my email messages, then read, "Hello, beautiful girl. I heard you were in New York. That's exciting to hear. I'm writing because I'm hoping I'll get to see you. I'd like to take you to lunch at a wonderful place called Delmonico's. I understand if you don't want to, but if you want to bring your young man, that's okay too. Let me know if you're free tomorrow. I hope to see you soon, Vivien. Love, Dad."

I look up at Carter and see his furrowed brow. "What?"

"Nothing. I'm glad he reached out to you. I just don't want you to get hurt again."

"I won't. I'm prepared for the worst." I brush imaginary lint from my shorts. "Can you come with me?"

"So, you already told him yes?"

I nod.

He releases a deep sigh. "I can't. Not tomorrow."

I start to scoot off his lap, but he stops me as I say, "It's okay. I figured out the bus route, and it's not that far."

"No buses, Vivien. I'll hire a car."

"No. That's expensive."

"Not really. Plus, it'll wait for you and bring you back. It's well worth it to know you're safe. You're not familiar with the area yet. I'll be able to focus on practice if I know you're being driven."

Wow, he's trying hard to get me to take the car. He pulled out all the excuses. "Sure. That's cool. I'm supposed to meet him at two thirty."

"Lunch at two thirty? That's late."

I shrug. "It's fine with me."

"I'll get a car set to pick you up at one thirty. That'll give you plenty of time to get there."

I give him a quick kiss on the cheek and slide off his lap, picking up my plate in the process. I'm suddenly starving. "Thanks, Carter," I say with a mouthful of vegetable pizza.

"No problem." He sounds cranky now.

I hope he's not angry I'm going out on my own tomorrow. Nah, he wouldn't be. He's just a little worried? He's not the only one.

CHAPTER FIFTY-FIVE

CARTER

I'M off my game today, can't seem to focus. I hate the idea of Vivien meeting her father alone. She's not familiar with the city, and I don't trust him. Not in the least. Something isn't sitting right with me about this whole deal. Sure, maybe he did realize he was a prick to her, but what if he didn't? All I can picture in my head is Vivien upset and flying back to Chicago to be comforted by Kai. I want to comfort her. *I'm* her man.

I look at the clock on the scoreboard above me, seeing it's just after one o'clock. "If I leave practice now, I could be showered and changed and at Delmonico's in time for lunch."

"Who're you talking to, crazy?"

"Shut up, Jordan." God, I hate that guy. He's always mouthing off. He's a defensive back who thinks he's a Hall of Fame contender his second year in the league. He's a blowhard.

"Can't help crazy," he says, running past me.

I lose track of the play and end up flat on my back, then wince as I attempt to get back up.

"Where's your head at today, Carter?" screams my coach.

"Not on this," I mutter.

"If you can't concentrate, maybe you should take the afternoon off?"

"Okay. Sure." I start to jog off the field toward the locker room.

"Carter!" Coach yells even louder. "Get your ass back on the field."

Fuck. I thought he was serious. "Coach?"

"What?" he replies, but he's not looking at me. He's watching the play on the field.

"I need to go."

Now he's looking at me. "Again? If you leave, your line is going to hate you."

"Why?"

"Because they're going to run."

"Come on, man. It's serious. I wouldn't ask if it wasn't, and you know it." I've got my hands on my hips. "Let's make a deal."

"What kind of deal?"

"I'll not miss another practice or meeting for the rest of the year."

He arches an eye at me.

"And I'll donate ten grand to your favorite charity."

"Fuck. Fine. Go."

I turn again to leave.

"But I want a check for St. Jude's on my desk tomorrow."

"Sure. Fine. But are you gonna make them run?"

"Fuck, yeah. They're running. Partly because of you, but mostly because your entire line has their heads up their asses today. You get to run tomorrow, twice as long."

"Fine. Whatever." The guys are going to kick my ass, but I need to do this. I jog off the field, helmet in hand.

———

TRAFFIC'S A NIGHTMARE. I was able to shower and dress and get out the door fast, but by the time I got on the 495 to get to the city, I knew I'd never make it. "Summer road construction," I grumble. I've been on the road for twenty minutes and haven't even made it to the Weehawken exit.

Resting my head against the back of my seat, I'm tempted to call and let her know I'm on my way, but what if I don't make it? This traffic shit in Jersey and New York can be unpredictable. No. I'm not going to call her.

Another ten minutes pass, and I peer up ahead and see movement. "Finally." I put my car in drive and lean forward, waiting for a chance to move. When I hear a bell chime, I look down at my gas gauge. "Fuck." I'm almost on empty. I won't be able to pull off until this traffic gets moving. Only a few more minutes, and we all start inching along. Another twenty and I'm able to get to an exit with a gas station.

Filling up as fast as the stupid fuel pump will go, I get back onto the 495 and make it through the Lincoln Tunnel. The traffic is moving okay now as I note the time, almost two o'clock. In the city, it's slow going as well, but by the time I take Eleventh Street and merge onto West Street, the traffic is flying. Parking is another issue, but I get lucky when I see they've got valet parking.

Pulling up to the restaurant, I toss my keys to the attendant and thank him. Jogging to the door, I'm met with people exiting. They all look like they're going to a garden party in their suits and dresses. I look down at myself. I'm not dressed for this. I'm wearing a white New York Giants workout shirt in that moisture wicking fabric. It's new, but it's still a workout shirt. I'm also wearing standard-issue Giants sweats and sports sandals all emblazoned with the team logo. I look stupid, to be honest. Oh well, it can't be helped now.

Opening the door, I get a whiff of food. Jesus, it smells good.

I ate with the team earlier, but I'm hungry again. Maybe I'll be able to eat lunch while I'm here. I step up to the hostess and smile, giving her my smirk for added insurance.

She looks me up and down and, when she sees my face, smiles brightly. "How may I help you?"

"I'm supposed to be here for lunch. I'm late." It's just after three, but I made it.

"What's the name on the reservation, sir?"

What is the name? I'll just give the last name and see if that works. "Reginald?"

She peers down at her book and nods. "Right this way." She picks up a large, black, leather-bound menu and steps in front of me.

I follow her into the dining area, around some glass and wooden shelves topped with mirrors, and through a maze of tables. I hear murmurs of recognition as I walk through. It's not surprising. I'm like a giant walking, talking billboard for the team with all of my gear on. From the corner of my eye, I spot a famous New York comedian I've seen in countless movies. I've met him at a couple of Giants functions. He's a favorite of mine. I make eye contact with him and give him a chin lift. He gives one back.

Rounding a corner, I note another section of built-in shelves with glass doors that house expensive whiskeys. Damn, I could use a drink right about now. My nerves are getting the best of me. Eventually, we reach a tiny table in the back of the restaurant, near the kitchen entrance, where my girl is seated with her dad.

Stepping up to the table, I look at her and I know, from the tight expression on her pretty face, that I did the right thing. Her face appears to be carved from granite. "Vivien?"

She looks up at me and blinks.

"You okay?"

She gives her head a slight shake but then smiles up at me. "I thought you had practice."

I don't get to answer her before her dad stands up and loudly declares, "Son, you made it! I was hoping I'd see you."

He was hoping he'd see *me*? Oh, shit. I get it now. And I'm going to kill the fucker.

CHAPTER FIFTY-SIX

VIVIEN

I SHOULD NEVER HAVE COME. My gut told me to stay home, but my heart hoped. When I arrived, my dad was already at the table. As the hostess brought me over, Dad saw me, then looked around me like I wasn't there. "Where's Carter?"

"At practice."

"Oh." He looks dejected. "I should have thought of that," he mutters under his breath.

Why? Why should he have thought of that?

"Perhaps dinner would have been better for him." He's not asking. It seems like he's just making a mental note.

With no hug or kiss on the cheek from Dad, I pull out my own chair and sit down. We're seated at a tiny table in the farthest part of the restaurant, next to the kitchen doors. It's noisy, and when my chair gets thwacked with the swinging door, I know I'm in the worst seat in the place. Well, I take that back. The worst seat would be near the restrooms, so I guess this is better.

It's surprisingly busy for two thirty in the afternoon. This place *must* be an institution, and apparently a celebrity hot spot, because I just saw a famous comedian and an actress I know I've seen on a primetime show. It's no wonder my dad wanted to come here. He wants to be seen. I squeeze my eyes shut, and it hits me. He wanted Carter here—to be seen with Carter.

"How are you, Dad?"

"Good," he says, sipping his water. "But not as good as you, apparently."

"What does that mean?"

I haven't moved from my initial position since sitting down. My hands are in my lap, grasping at the skirt of my new dress. A dress I picked out (with Ken's approval) to replace my favorite flowered dress a la the 1970s. He calls it a "day dress." The pattern on this dress is similar to my old one, with a black background and large colorful flowers all over it. The collar isn't white and it's sleeveless instead of long-sleeved, but there is a cool trim detail that I love. The other difference between my two flowered dresses? The price. My old dress cost me $3.50 at a thrift store. This one was closer to $350.00. Ridiculous, I know. Ken assured me this was the going price for fashion these days, plus he insisted Carter gave him an unlimited budget for my new wardrobe. I'll pay him back with the money he's paying me to create the new fountain and for working on the hArt of the City Foundation. But the dress is cute, and I feel pretty in it, although I don't know why I went to such trouble. I even took out my lip ring again. All for this?

My mind returns to the table and to Dad as he talks. "It means I saw you."

I lost track of the conversation. "Saw me? Where?" *If he saw me, why didn't he say hello?*

"In the paper and on television."

I blink at him. "You saw me on television?" *When was I on TV?*

"You were at a gala or some such with Carter Corcoran last week, right? Since then, you've been all over the New York papers as 'Carter Corcoran's New Love Interest.'" He uses air quotes. Do I even need to comment on my father using air quotes? No? Good.

"I don't understand. Why would I be in the paper for that?"

Dad winks at me and nods. It's weird. I don't like it. I like what he says next even less. "You're a sly one, Reggie."

I squeeze my eyes shut again. I hate that name. I'm Vivien. "Sly? How?"

"Landing yourself a famous boyfriend." He winks, and it makes me shiver.

"I didn't *land* him, Dad. I met him. I liked him. He liked me. There's nothing dubious there."

"But, my dear, you're famous now."

"I'm not. I—"

"You really need to go with it. You could make a name for yourself. Get invited to all the best parties and events." Chuckling, he adds, "And you can bring your old man with you."

Oh, so I was right. This is all about him and his fucking career. I feel my body turn ice-cold. It's a strange physiological reaction, but I can't help that. I want to stand up. I want to run. But all I do is sit there and listen.

"So, here." He slides a card to the center of the table just as our waiter approaches.

I lean over to read the black script on the small rectangle as he orders.

"I'll have a glass of house white and the classic burger." Leaning over, he smiles at me. "You wouldn't mind picking up the check would you, Reggie? Now that you've snagged a rich man, you can afford to treat your old man. Am I right?"

"No." I mean, why would I think my father would invite me to lunch and then pay? The fact he would assume I'd use Carter is offensive, but what's the point of saying anything? I'm suddenly exhausted.

"And for you, miss."

"Water is fine. House salad with ranch, please." I hand him my menu.

"Good idea, honey, eating a salad. Although I'd skip the ranch dressing. Perhaps vinegar and oil? You could stand to lose some weight if you're going to be photographed. You looked so-so in the pictures I saw, but the weight is going to have to come off or they'll make fun of you."

So-so? What the fuck is he talking about? I keep my mouth shut because he seems to be on a roll.

He pushes the business card the rest of the way. "This is my agent. Give him a call. He'll get you all sorted out. He can line up a nutritionist for you and a personal trainer. Also, a stylist wouldn't hurt. That dress is..." He makes a face like he just smelled something bad.

My dress is what? Adorable? Amazing? God, this man is infuriating, and he's my father.

"So, how did you meet Carter?"

"At a"—I can't tell him I met him at an art show, can I?—"club."

"A club? In Chicago?"

Duh, where else? "Yes."

"Which one?"

"Chrome." It's the only club I know, and that's only thanks to Kai.

"Was he with other famous athletes?"

I shrug. "I don't know."

"What was the big party like here in New York? Were there other famous people?"

"Rooney Mara." There were others, but she's the only one I remember.

"Oh my God. Did you talk to her?" Dad's leaning over the table so far, I fear he may end up in my lap.

"No." *I didn't have time because I fell and broke my hand, so I was busy being carted off by paramedics, but thanks for asking.*

"Seriously?" He looks angry. "You had an opportunity to meet someone as famous as she is, and you didn't? Shame on you."

Why would he be angry? Shame on me? This is a nightmare. When our food is finally served, I stare down at my tiny plate of salad. I've got no appetite but pick up my fork and move it around my plate, bumping my tomato and cucumber around. I look up at him and see he's taken a big bite of his burger. He smiles at me as he chews. I know he's got more questions.

Swallowing, he leans in again, conspiratorially. "Have you considered getting pregnant?"

I drop my fork and stare at him. "What the hell are you talking about, Dad?"

"You know? To secure him."

"You mean, trap him?" I clench my teeth, and my hands are in fists on the table. I'm rigid as a stone. Just then I hear an angel.

"Vivien?"

I look up and see him. Carter. And it's the best thing I've ever seen.

"You okay, Viv?"

I shake my head slightly and give him a smile. "I thought you had practice."

I don't get a chance to hear him answer because my dad has jumped up in front of Carter. His hand is outstretched as he announces loud enough for all to hear, "Son, you made it. I was hoping I'd see you."

Carter looks confused, but only for a second. I watch as the realization hits him. My dad only wanted to see him, or better yet, he wants to *be seen* with Carter and me, so he can talk about his famous daughter and her even more famous boyfriend.

I nod slightly when Carter and I make eye contact. I'm still reeling since Dad suggested I get knocked up so I can trap him. The thought sickens me. Not the thought of having a baby with Carter. That thought is a nice one. It's the thought that I'd even consider trapping my sweet man.

My feeling is this: If we end up together, good. If we don't, it wasn't meant to be and he was meant for someone else while I was meant for a shitload of cats in an efficiency apartment in Chicago. Truth.

CHAPTER FIFTY-SEVEN

CARTER

I CAN TELL by the look on her face that she wants to make a run for it. I've seen it one too many times since I've known her, and that's only been a few months. "Vivien? You ready to go? We've got that thing."

"Oh, what thing?" her dad says, still holding my hand tight like I'm his lifeline.

Think fast, Carter. "For her hand. She needs to see a physical therapist. Her appointment is uptown."

"Oh?" He looks down at her, then at her hand like he's just noticing her blue-and-orange-striped cast. "You hurt yourself?" He turns back to me like he's sharing some special tip on my girl. "She was always very clumsy. I thought she'd grown out of it."

Like he'd know what she did or didn't grow out of, having been gone for ten years. "What would you—"

"Okay!" She jumps to her feet and steps up to both of us. "Dad, we need to go. I can't be late for my appointment, and Carter has to get back to practice. Right, dear?"

Dear? I want to chuckle, but from the look on her face, I'd better not laugh at anything for the foreseeable future. "Right."

"Well, dang. I was hoping to get to know you, son."

"Another time?" *Like never.*

"Sure. Sure." He looks sad, but I refuse to feel sorry for the man.

As we depart, he grasps Viv's upper arm. "Honey?"

"Yes?" She sounds almost hopeful.

"Our bill?"

"Oh," she chokes. "Right."

Reaching into her purse, she retrieves her wallet. Grasping her hand, I pull her along. "I'll take care of the bill up front, Mr. Reginald."

"Oh, how nice of you. Thank you so much, son," James Reginald simpers.

"No problem."

I guide Vivien through the tables and stop at the hostess station. Pulling out my wallet, I toss the woman at the front a hundred-dollar bill. "That's for their lunch. Under Reginald." I start to leave but stop, "Oh, and please be sure the server gets the rest."

"Of course, sir. I'll take care of it."

I don't reply. Instead, I get her out the door as fast as I can. The moment we're outside, I wrap my arm around her waist and walk her down the sidewalk about halfway to the corner, spotting an alley. Leading her just inside the mouth of the opening, I press her to the wall and kiss her. I kiss her hard and long. "I love you. Don't leave me."

She blinks up at me, dazed, like she wasn't really paying attention. "Why would I leave you?"

"Because I can feel your urge to run vibrating through your body, babe."

"That's not what it is." She sighs sadly. "I'm just angry with myself."

"At yourself? Why?" *Why in the fuck would she be angry at anyone but him?*

"Because I'm so stupid." I see her eyes fill with moisture. "I thought he wanted to see *me*," she says, placing her palm over her heart. "You know, to make up for the day at your house and for the time we lost. But he saw us in the paper and on TV at that team gala. He thinks I'm famous or something."

She looks down at her feet like she's embarrassed. "I don't even know that man back there. He's not the dad I remember, the one I loved so damn much." Sniffling, she lays her head on my chest. "Thank you so much for coming. I was just frozen there."

I rub my palm up and down her back. "I've got you."

"I know." She looks up at me, tears stuck in her eyelashes. "And I've got you too, Carter. There wasn't a second back there where I wanted to run away from you. In fact, the only thing I wanted was to run *to* you as soon as possible."

I pull her close. "I'm glad. I'd have had to chase you back to Chicago, and I'm already in the doghouse with Coach and my defensive line."

"What?" she squeaks. Pushing me away slightly, she looks into my eyes with a horrified expression. "You're in trouble? Carter! Why?"

"Because I left practice early." She tries to pull further away, but I hold her in place. "Look, I'd run forever to be there for you. I was worried your dad was going to do exactly what he did back there, and I couldn't risk losing you. I pictured you taking the hired car right to the airport." I snort, but it's not a laugh. "I couldn't focus on practice anyway. All I could see was you."

"Oh, Carter," she says softly. Placing her palm on my cheek, she looks into my eyes. "I love you so much. If it makes you feel better, I'll jog with you."

Now I laugh. "Okay. I should warn you though, it'll be five miles, at least."

"Oh, well, um, can I walk instead?" She smiles, and it's beautiful.

"Sure. You can walk alongside me. I hope you always will."

She looks surprised at my statement, but it's true. "I'm in this for the long haul, Viv. I hope you are too."

"I am. Definitely."

I take her hand and draw her out of the alley. It's a disgusting place for a conversation. "I like your dress. It reminds me of the one you wore the day you graduated."

"You remember that dress?"

"Oh, yeah. It's the day I realized I wanted you."

"Seriously? Why?"

"That dress was hella short, babe. It was hot." I look down at her new dress. "For the record, I like the old one more."

She laughs. "Figures."

"Let's go home so I can see what you've got on under that little thing."

"Who says I've got anything on under my dress?"

"Oh, you little tease." I pinch her bottom and then run my palm over it to see if I can feel panty lines. I can. "I feel them—you're not going commando."

"Nope. Never in a dress."

"Never say never. Maybe we should go out on a date and you can wear a dress without 'em?"

"You've got a one-track mind."

I shrug. "You're hot. Deal with it." I laugh.

She laughs too, then remains quiet until we get back to the valet. I look around, making sure her dad isn't standing out front. She's doing the same thing. I hand the kid my valet ticket, and he runs off down the street.

"Do I really have a physical therapy appointment? Because I don't remember the doctor saying anything about it."

"Nah. I was just trying to come up with something."

"Good move."

I watch as the kid tears down the street in my black BMW i8 Batwing Roadster. If he wrecks it, I'm going to be pissed. Lucky for him, he doesn't. Pulling up in front of Delmonico's, he swings both doors up and open.

"Is this your car?"

Oh, I forgot. She hasn't seen this one yet. "Yeah. You like it?"

"It's cool," she says, shrugging. "Impractical, but cool."

"Noted. Now hop in, princess."

She slips into the car and waits for me. I hand the kid a twenty and slide in beside her.

"I can't believe you fit in here, but it's surprisingly roomy."

I nod as I touch the button to shut the doors. "Seat belt."

She moves that into place and snaps it closed. "Ready for liftoff, sir," she giggles.

Just as I'm about to pull away, I see something from the corner of my eye. It's James Reginald stepping out of the restaurant. He's got his phone to his ear, chatting away.

"I loved him so much." She looks at me, her eyes rimmed red. "I still do. I know it's stupid."

"No, he's your dad. Of course you still love him."

"But he only loves himself."

"It seems that way, sweetheart. But I'm sure he loves you too. He just can't see the forest for the trees. The trees in that analogy, by the way, are his career."

She arches her brow at me. "You don't think I would have figured out the symbolism of the trees?"

"I just—"

"I'll have you know I graduated magna cum laude from Loyola. I get symbolism."

"Really? So did I."

"You graduated magna cum laude? I know you didn't go to Loyola."

"Well, summa cum laude from U of Illinois."

"Wow, not only did I land me a hottie, but he's smart too." She runs her palm up and down my arm. "I'm one lucky girl."

"You sure are." I wink at her.

"Oh, I probably shouldn't tell you this, but Dad thought I should get knocked up so I can trap you," she says, rolling her eyes.

At a stoplight, I turn to look at her. "I like the sound of the first part. And you can't trap someone who wants to be caught."

Blinking at me, I see her eyes turn glassy.

"Don't cry, babe. It breaks my heart."

"You want to have a baby with me?"

"Bab*ies*. Plural. Lots and lots of babies."

"Lots? Like how many is that?" She's not on the verge of tears anymore. She crosses her arms, ready for negotiations.

"Ten?" I chuckle.

"Ten?" she shrieks. "No way. Birthing a giant Carter baby is gonna sting. How 'bout one?"

"Five?"

"Three."

"Deal."

She nods. "Deal."

"Let's start today."

"Carter, no. It can take months, a year even, to get pregnant after you go off the shot."

"You checked?"

"Yeah, when I was nineteen and got my first one. I did my research."

"When was your last shot?" She's got my interest piqued.

"God," she says as she lays her head back. "Are we really talking about this?"

"We really are." The light finally changes to green, and I move down West Street.

"Fine. I'm due to get another one in a couple of weeks. I need to make an appointment."

I reach out and place my hand over one of her fists, then wiggle my fingers in between her clenched hand. "Don't."

"Don't?"

"No." I can't believe I'm suggesting this, but it makes sense. I'm really into this, and I know she is too.

"Carter, we've got two weeks. I need to think about it, and we need to talk more about it. Today was emotional. I don't want to make this decision just because we're both still sort of charged from lunch with my dad."

"That makes sense." I squeeze her hand. "You think. I'll think. Then we'll talk."

"Good." She looks out the window at the view of the city. "Is there a drive-through anywhere? I'm starving."

"A drive-through? In Manhattan?"

"Yeah. In Manhattan." Vivien rolls her eyes like I'm stupid. "There's no real estate for drive-throughs in this city?"

"We'll be in Jersey in less than thirty. There are a million places there. Can you wait?"

"I can wait. It'll give me time to think about what I want to eat." She hums quietly, then says, "You do realize you paid a hundred bucks for a side salad?"

"It's okay. I paid ten grand so I could leave practice early."

"Carter!" she shouts. "Why? God, you're such an idiot."

"For you? Yes, I'm a blubbering fool."

"Well, as long as it's for me." She flutters her eyelashes at me, teasingly. "Seriously, Carter. Stop spending money on me. If we're going to have ten kids, we need to save, save, save."

I feel my chest rumble with laughter before the sound makes it out. "Princess. I'll start being much wiser with the fifteen million I'll make this year."

"What?" she screams. "You're going to make fifteen... million... dollars?"

"Before taxes. Taxes kill me." And they do.

"Jesus," she mutters. "No wonder you throw it around like it's confetti." She crosses her arms over her chest like she's pissed.

"You angry about the money, Viv?"

"Yes. Stupid athletes."

Smiling, I shake my head. "You're going to have to accept the fact that I've got money, honey." That right there is why I'm positive I picked the right girl. Well, besides the fact that she's beautiful and super talented. Oh, and she's got great tits, but it's mainly because she likes me for me and not for my money.

"Whatevs," she grumbles. "This foundation of yours is going to be huge. You need to give back, *son.*"

"I plan to."

"Good." She nods as though she's just forced me into giving up money.

Whatever helps her sleep at night. I reach out and pat her knee. "I still want a nice nest egg for Carter Jr., Cathy, Christine, Caitlyn, Caleb, Christopher, Connor, Claire, Chloe, and Vlad."

She's giggling hysterically. "First of all..." She's trying to talk through her laughter. "You can't have a Christine and a Christopher. They'll both be called Chris." Wiping happy tears from her eyes, she adds, "And Vlad? You give me one *V* name, and that's what I get? He sounds like a vampire."

"If the shoe fits. You do like to bite."

Her face gets serious. "I do. And I'll bite you harder next time just for naming our kid Vlad. Besides, if I've got to push out some ginormous future football players, I think I should get to name them."

"No way. I want to name them."

"Fine. We'll do it together. But one thing is certain."

"What's that, Viv?"

"There will be no *Vlad* in our family."

"We'll see."

She harrumphs. "No, dork. *You'll* see."

EPILOGUE
VIVIEN & CARTER

FIVE MONTHS Later

FIRST OFF, I haven't seen or heard from my dad in five months. I've had the urge to email him once or twice, but then I remember how I felt the last two times I saw him and decide it's best to let sleeping dogs lie, for now, at least. Besides, I'm happy. *Really* happy.

Carter's football team is doing so-so this year. He doesn't think they'll make the playoffs, unfortunately. There've been a lot of changes since last season and, according to Carter, there have been growing pains. I've been to all the home games so far, and two away games. His entire family flew in for the first home game, as did my mom and Kalani. I wasn't surprised to see her, but Carter was. Johnson never left her side the entire weekend. I think it's getting real serious, real fast, but I guess I know how that happens. When you know, you know.

They all stayed in Carter's condo building in one of the rentable condos. It was cool that his family had an opportunity to meet my mom and she got to meet Carter. I was a little concerned she would read him the riot act, but the second she saw him, she blushed and became really shy. Once he introduced himself, there was no turning back. She is totally enamored with him. No surprise. Like anyone could dislike the man. Mom became fast friends with Carter's mom too. I have a feeling they'll see each other when they get back home.

Mom was reluctant to leave, actually. She liked New Jersey and loved New York. I also think she wanted to reach out to my dad, but after I told her about my last two meetings with him, she didn't press the subject.

After she left, Carter asked, "Do you think your mom likes me, Viv?"

I replied, "I think she loved you, Carter. Mom can't believe I finally landed a man."

He laughed.

"Let alone a catch like you." I kissed his scruffy cheek.

"She's nice," he's saying in my ear now.

"She is. She thought you were nice too."

"It's nice to be nice, Vivien."

eye roll "Whatever Mr. I'm Searching for Compliments. If you don't behave, I'm not going to let you keep reading over my shoulder."

So, anyway, back to our story. Kai flew in for one of the later home games and ended up meeting Ken. I'm not sure if sparks flew, but they're still talking to each other, so who knows?

"They sure did look cute together, didn't they, Carter?"

"Adorbs."

(I'm ignoring that comment even though it was hilarious.) At the games, I've been sitting with the WAGs, but mainly with Danelle. Mostly, they're all nice. The wives don't really afford the girlfriends much notice. I guess they figure until we've got rings on our fingers, we're not permanent fixtures. I get that. It's gotten better since Carter did in fact put a ring on my finger. That's right, ladies and gents: Carter proposed. It was exceptionally romantic and sweet. I'll tell you about that in a second. First, I want to tell you about the best part of the entire thing. The ring.

Now, I know you're probably shocked that I'm excited about my huge blingy ring, except it's not—huge and blingy, that is. What's amazing about it is that he designed it himself.

"That is pretty amazing."

"Yes, you got another compliment, dear."

The ring is so unique and beautiful and thoughtful. It's got no jewels on it, planned so clay won't get stuck in and around a stone. See? Thoughtful. Plus, he said, and I quote, "I never want you to take it off." He's a territorial guy. Anyway, it's a platinum band covered in carved letters, numbers, and symbols that he says represent *us*. We're having a matching band made for him to wear so we'll be twinsies.

The design on the ring includes a six and a nine for his jersey number and for, well, other things we like. There's an apple for our time in New York, the letter C that he says stands for Carter and Chicago, and a V for Vlad. Just kidding. It's for my name. There are also several small flowers. He says they represent the dress I wore the day he decided I would be his. And there are three overlapping hearts inside the band with room for nine more.

Why three hearts instead of two, you ask? Well, if you guessed it's because we're expecting a baby, you're correct! The only people who know are Kai and Danelle, so don't tell anyone. I want to wait a few more weeks before we tell our parents to make sure everything is okay. We'll be home soon for Thanksgiving, and I'm sure my brother and sister will be home as well, so they'll all find out at the same time. I'm not looking forward to seeing them, but I need to get past my anger. It's not good for me, or us.

I'm excited to tell Mom about the pregnancy. Right now, I'm six weeks along and feel like dog poo. I know *some* women (Danelle) have had perfect pregnancies. But not this girl. Luckily, I'm close to home and the toilet every day as I work on the hART of the City Foundation. I've reached the point where I need to hire more people, but I think I'm going to wait until we get back to Chicago for the off-season so we can start this thing at home.

Carter agrees. Besides, his contract is up this year, and he's hoping his agent can get him home to his beloved Bears. We're crossing our fingers for that. Don't get me wrong: living in New Jersey, so close to New York, has been wonderful. We get out as much as we can. For example, we've seen two plays, one musical (much to Carter's chagrin), attended three opening receptions for some very prominent visual artists, and visited countless museums and galleries. It's been inspiring. So much so that I've been busy with some of my own work. I've finished the maquette, or small model, for his fountain design. Carter got his hands dirty on that project too, literally, so we're calling it a collaborative design. We worked well together. I've got an idea rolling around in my head for us to do more of these together. Commissions we could do for free or in a nonprofit capacity for the foundation. I need to let that idea steep for a while, plus I'll need to talk to my fella about it too.

After my cast came off, I enjoyed having the time to actually create things again. Not only that, my work has changed, evolved. While my previous work was all abstract and sort of jagged and rough in texture, these are all smooth and organic. I'm blaming it on my pregnancy hormones making me change directions. Making me soft. It could also be because I'm happy and in love too. All of those things have aided in changing my work from angry-looking to tranquil. It's not a bad thing. Not at all.

"Hey, Viv. When are you going to tell them about my proposal? I worked hard planning that damn thing."

"Getting to that, Carter. And stop reading over my shoulder. It's annoying." I feel his arm slide around me and his big hand come to rest on my stomach. I'm not showing yet, but it's just a matter of time.

So, about his proposal. It was just as unique as the ring.

"Damn straight," he mutters in my ear. "And it didn't cost me a penny either."

I scoff. "The *proposal* was free."

"Okay, I may have paid off her student loans as a wedding gift, but she didn't know about that until after the proposal. In our bedroom. She was *very* grateful. That's all I'll say."

I laugh as I slap Carter on the arm to get him back on track. "Focus."

"Fine. So, yeah, I'm pretty sure you wouldn't have said yes if I'd hired a plane to drag a banner across the sky like Deacon did for his girl. Am I right?"

Deacon is a guy on his team. "No. It's true. I would have said no." Not really. Of course I would have said yes. Who would say no to this man?

This is what happened... Carter told me we had a couples retreat to attend during the Giants' bye week. It was intended to be a team-building thing. That's all true. The team wanted everyone to bond. Makes sense. They did it all in the Hamptons. *Fancy-schmancy.* We all stayed in a huge mansion on the water with its own private beach. The first team-building exercise was a scavenger hunt. Carter and I were teamed up with

Ollie and Danelle. To win, we had to find all the things on the list and get back to the campfire on the beach first. On the list were things like a flower, something from nature that makes a noise, something fuzzy, a four-leaf clover (that took a good hour), a perfect marshmallow roasting stick, a flat rock, something alive, and we had to get a picture of all four of us hugging a stranger (that was weird). When we made it back to the campsite, we discovered we were in first place, but apparently we still had one more thing to do.

It was then the team-building organizer gave us our final task. All four of us had to make a dance video to a song of our choice. Carter insisted on picking the song, so we let him. We only had a couple of minutes to get ready, so we stood in a line and waited for the music to start. God, I was so nervous. I am not a good dancer, and the fact that it was going to be forever saved as an mp4 video... ugh. Anyway, when they hit Play, I recognized the song right away. It was Bruno Mars's "Marry Me."

"Oh, shoot, Carter. I'm getting all teary-eyed again."

"Don't cry, Viv. Keep going with the story. It's a good one."

Anyway, the song began and the four of us started dancing. Ollie and Danelle were amazing together. It was like they'd rehearsed it. Carter did some moves that I'm not going to describe. Well, okay, there were some hip thrusts and biting of his bottom lip that was, well, in a word? Embarrassing. For Carter.

"Funny, babe. I dance like no one is watching."

Slapping his leg, I say, "Don't make me laugh. This is serious."

As the music played and we danced like idiots, I started seeing members of the team and the WAGs all step out onto the beach from every direction. It was like they were hiding out, waiting to watch us make fools of ourselves. So, I tried to jab Carter in the chest to point at all the people, but he wasn't next to me. I stopped dancing and looked over to see him kneeling in the sand. I did the normal things people do when stuff like this happens. I threw my hands over my mouth and starting bawling immediately.

"Then I popped open the box and said, 'Vivien Reginald. Please don't embarrass me in front of the offensive line. They aren't called *offensive* for nothing. Marry me.'"

"No, you didn't, dork." I'm laughing because he's funny. Wrong, but funny. "No, you said, and I quote, 'Vivien Reginald, you are the most breathtaking creature I've ever lain eyes upon. 'Tis nary another who can top your awesomeness. Put me out of my misery, young lass, and marry me.'"

Uh-oh. Carter's laughing now.

"'Tis nary? You know I'd never say 'tis nary." He's flopped on his back laughing his butt off.

I guess he doesn't remember it the same way I do. I shrug. "Oh well. As long as the results were the same."

"True dat, woman." He hasn't stopped laughing.

I'll give him a minute.

Or forever.

Yeah, I'll give him forever.

Want to start at the beginning? Check out the first book in the Flynn Series to get to know more about Hank, Mick, David, Ernie, and Ed.

Meet the Flynns.

Sure, they're alpha-holes but you can't help loving them. Mostly.

SOPHIE KINCAID FACES age thirty knowing she'll never have her own happily-ever-after. But, when she meets Henry Flynn, she finds herself dreaming of the tall, broad, and hot-as-sin Chicago police officer.

Henry "Hank" Flynn is a foul-mouthed detective who knows all there is to know about solving crimes. He has no interest in finding a woman unless it's for one night in his bed. That is until he's drawn to a little beauty named Sophie.

When Sophie's tenant is murdered, Henry finds himself on the case with a need to solve one murder and prevent another. Keeping Sophie safe and in his arms is his number one priority even when she doesn't think she needs saving. Sophie doesn't believe a man like Henry Flynn would want her; Henry believes fate has brought them together. Fingers crossed fate wins because who doesn't love a happy ending?

Hopeful Romantic (Coming soon.)

Thanks to Margie Dill (Coming soon.)

ACKNOWLEDGMENTS

Thank you to everyone from Hot Tree Editing for editing this book from start to finish.

And an extra special thank you to Becky Johnson at Hot Tree Promotions for your advice, expertise, and positivity.

And to my beta readers. Your feedback and patience is essential to this process. Thank you!

And to my mom who is the wind beneath my wings. Literally.

ABOUT THE AUTHOR

Kayt grew up in the midwest surrounded by a loving family which included three brothers, one sister, and parents who always fostered her creative side.

Kayt wrote her first book when she couldn't find a story about a certain type of a woman and a specific kind of man. She called it *Game Changer* and it couldn't have been a more appropriate title. It changed her life in many ways.

Her goal, as a writer, is to write stories that relate to all of us, to make readers laugh and maybe cry sometimes. Kayt hopes her readers can escape into a fantasy, one that's actually possible. Sure, some of the stories are dubbed "Insta-love" but that's okay. She fell in love with her husband pretty damn fast and with her daughter the second I saw her. So, it's a thing, I swear.

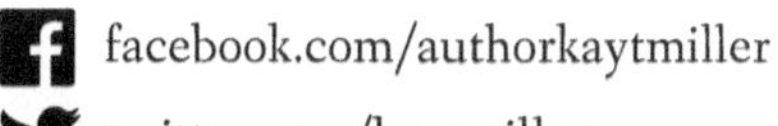 facebook.com/authorkaytmiller

twitter.com/kaytmiller1

 instagram.com/kaytmiller1

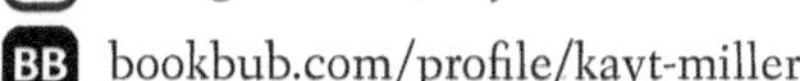 bookbub.com/profile/kayt-miller

THANK YOU!

Thank you so much for reading! When I start a story, it begins with an outline, notes, and lots of crazy thoughts running through my head. When I actually start writing, the characters take over, leading me through the story like they're holding my hand—guiding me. The process is exciting and cathartic. With that said, I hope you enjoy the story.

If you did, please go to my website, www.kaytmiller.com, and join my newsletter so you can be the first to know what's coming up next. And...

Please, leave a review!

Chapter 1

Happy Frigging New Year

"Yo! Mac. Hottie at three o'clock," my best friend says as she approaches me.

Looking to my right, I scan the crowd. "I don't see any hotties."

"No, I said *three* o'clock," Lauren clarified, annoyed. "Don't make me point. It's bad manners."

"I know. I looked at three o'clock and saw only Father Time." Seriously, there's a guy dressed up as Father Time. Ah, New Year's Eve in Chicago. It brings out the crazies.

"No, dork, *my* three o'clock."

"That would be my *nine* o'clock, not my three o'clock."

"Crap, girl, just look to the right."

"Wait, my right or your right?" Lauren can be so confusing.

"Jesus, now he's gone. You missed him. He was your dream man."

"Ooh, you mean he looked like Jason Momoa?" I look frantically around the room.

"What? No. Jason Momoa is your dream man?"

"Uh... yeah. After *Game of Thrones*, he's *everyone's* dream man. Ooh, did you know he's the new *Aquaman*? He was perfect for that part. The man is a god."

"Well, this guy was hot, and he was actually *here*," Lauren says, rolling her eyes. Even at the best of times, the girl barely puts up with me. She continues, "He's got blond hair, and he had that faux-hawk fade haircut that's so in right now. Plus, he had on nerd glasses."

"Holy shite. I love me some faux-hawk. Add the nerd spectacles, and I can feel it in my pantaloons, *giiirrrl*. Gimme. Where is he?"

Lauren giggles. "God, you're such a dork. Spectacles? Pantaloons? Where do you come up with that stuff?"

"I read a lot of Regency-era romances."

"You mean Regency erotica. You're a pervert," she deadpans.

I let out a surprised giggle. *Lauren, Lauren, Lauren.* "It's not erotica. It's *romance*. Sure, there are some naughty little debutantes types in the books and even some wicked rakes, but it's all in good fun."

"Whatevs. I'm going back to Blake. He'll be lost without me."

I snort, rather unattractively, I'm sure. But the truth is, she's right. Blake is her husband of almost a year, and he would literally be lost without her. I'm not sure the man can choose his own clothes, to be honest. I think she chooses his outfit for the next day and sets it all out before they go to bed. It works for them, and I guess there's nothing wrong with it. He adores her and she him, no matter how creepy their love seems to me.

Now that I'm on my own again, I decide to move around the

ballroom with eyes peeled for the mysterious "hottie at three o'clock." While I do, I do my best to put this into perspective. Even if I find him, Mr. Hottie would not be interested in me. There's nothing extraordinary about MacKenzie Blue Parker. I'm just your average woman with an average face and a larger-than-average ass, but who *does* have an interesting middle name.

"Thank you, Mom," I say softly, looking up toward heaven. I'm not sure why she used a color for my middle name. When I asked Pops about it, he just said she was whimsical. I love that he used that word to describe my mom. I don't remember a lot about her, but I do remember that she was pretty and lots of fun.

I squeeze through the throng, turning my body this way and that, saying "excuse me," "pardon me," and "oh, I'm sorry my ass knocked your drink out of your hand." After all that, I'm grumpy, my feet hurt, my head hurts, and I'm still hungry even after nibbling on the delightful spread they've got here. I'm trying to look on the bright side but *ugh*, New Year's Eve sucks.

Are you wondering why my feelings about such an optimistic holiday have taken a nose dive? Personal history. Yep, personal history tells me New Year's Eve is a night filled with loneliness, sore feet, and worst of all, shattered expectations. I'm referring specifically to the promised kiss at midnight that never seems to happen—at least not for me. *Why did I let Lauren talk me into coming to this fancy-schmancy party tonight?* Oh, I remember. It's because I'm a sucker for my best friend's charms. I'm a grown-ass woman. You'd think I could turn her down, but Lauren Jacobs-Warner practically guaranteed that I'd have the time of my life tonight *and* I'd get a kiss at midnight.

I don't know why I let her do this to me time and time again. Yeah, my dress is fabulous. I actually feel sort of pretty in it. Pretty but pained. I've been thrust into fashion purgatory with four-inch heels and a too-tight Spanx undergarment. Ugh. I seriously think the people that invented Spanx are sadists—not to mention strange. I mean, who says "undergarment"? No offense, Spanx Incorporated, or whatever you call your business.

To be honest, I'd rather be home watching Netflix and eating junk food. That's my usual activity on holidays like this one, but my best friend sweet-talked me into this. I told her I didn't have the appropriate clothes for this part. I even modeled my best outfit, a pair of black leggings and sparkly top. But that wouldn't do for my friend, the little socialite. So she gave me a dress, an old one of hers that she "didn't really like." I don't believe her for a second. I mean, how could she not *love* this dress? This dress is *Ah. Maze. Ing.*

Imagine a dress that Audrey Hepburn might wear in *Breakfast at Tiffany's*. It's black with a delicate lace overlay. Beneath the lace overlay is a satin dress with a sweetheart bodice. The lace top has a boat neck that is open to my shoulder. Simply put, it's spectacular. Itchy, but spectacular. Oh, and it's got pockets. It's perfection. It has three-quarter sleeves and a flirty skirt that's lined with tulle so that it flares out at the waist and stops right above my knee in a 1950s style. It's a flattering silhouette, because it hides my larger-than-average rump. The truth is, that's the only reason this dress fits me, because Lauren's got a perfect bod. She's five-feet-eight with an hourglass figure in perfect proportion. I'd be jealous if I didn't adore her. But I do, so I'm not.

To ensure I'd attend this little shindig, Lauren even provided me with a date—her cousin, Frederick. He's not really my type, though. Not that I have a type. I haven't even had an actual boyfriend, per se, so maybe *type* is the wrong word. I have book boyfriends, sure. Television and movie boyfriends, of course, but nothing in the flesh. Yeah, so *type* is the wrong word. Perhaps I should just say he's not my dream man. He's short, only an inch or two taller than my five-feet-five-inches. He's also a tad doughy. I know that's not at all nice to say since I'm a bit doughy myself. But he's got a paunch on him like a sixty-year-old man, and he's only in his thirties. He's a little too young to have the dad bod, if you ask me.

Too judgy? If so, I'm sorry. I'm sure Freddy is a great guy.

He seems nice enough, though. I've met him at a couple of the Jacobses' family gatherings. The Jacobses are rich as Croesus. That's what Pops used to call rich people. It fits. He's rolling in it. So, this is more *his* kind of party, not mine. Lauren means well—she really does. But I'm so *not* this girl. I'm a starving artist. Figuratively. Not literally. No, *literally*, I live off of forty-cent packages of ramen noodles and macaroni and cheese in the blue box, so, no, I've got lots of carb-induced meat on my bones.

Case in point. Right this minute I'm surrounded by hundreds of rich people, famous people, important people, and politicians. I think I saw the governor a few minutes ago. We're in a huge ballroom in one of the five-star hotels in downtown Chicago. The ballroom is practically the size of a football field. Above me are the most spectacular chandeliers I've ever seen. They're enormous and appear to be dripping with jewels. The way they glitter and sparkle makes the entire space feel like a scene from a fairy tale. Because I'm no princess, and this place is so beyond anything I've ever seen, it makes me feel self-conscious.

Everyone is dressed in tuxedos and beautiful gowns or cocktail dresses like mine. Thankfully, I don't look completely out of place here. Waiters and waitresses dressed in penguin suits are walking around with trays of finger foods and flutes of champagne. There's a relatively large orchestra sitting off in the far corner near the huge dance floor. Several couples are already out there cutting a rug; not the kind of dancing I'm used to. This is fancy, grown-up, ballroom dancing, not the grind-your-ass-into-the-guy-behind-you dancing that I've done at clubs. No matter, I won't be dancing tonight unless I want to make a complete fool of myself.

As my eyes scan the room, I notice the long table filled with endless amounts of food and delectable-looking desserts, and my stomach rumbles. *Of course, I'm hungry.* In the center of the table is a giant ice sculpture of a swan. If it were sitting on the floor, it would probably stand taller than me. The swan's neck is bent down as though it's ready to take a bite out of all of the deliciousness below it. The main bar is nearby, while other smaller bar stations are located throughout the ballroom. Deciding a drink is in order, I cross my fingers that it's an open bar. I brought a little money with me, but I'd rather save that in case I need a taxi home.

Walking to the bar, I look to my right and spot Lauren standing with her husband, Blake. I recognize the people they're with as old family friends. I scan the other way in search of my "date." *Now, where did he go?* I spot him standing near the bar with a group of guys. They're in a small circle, and each man has his phone in his hands, texting.

I walk toward Frederick in the hopes that he'll be fun tonight. He hasn't proven to be much of a date thus far, but he *is* doing me a favor, I guess. I'm sure Lauren had to coerce him into bringing me. I move to stand next to him and wait for him to notice me. Should I tap him on the shoulder so he knows I'm here? Do I stand and wait for Frederick to ask me to dance or if I'd like a drink? I decide to do my best to be a good date. I wait. And wait. And wait. Nearly ten minutes pass, and Frederick does nothing but text and talk to his buddies. None of the guys even look at me. It's annoying. What? *Am I hideous?* I don't think I'm that tragic-looking. I've got cool hair that's naturally reddish-auburn and cut bluntly just past my shoulders. I've also got the ends tipped with blue tonight, like my middle name. It's only temporary color, but I'm an artist; we artists need to have funky hair at special events. It's the law. I giggle, which draws several pairs of eyes to me. Oh, *now* Frederick notices me.

"You okay?" he asks. He doesn't make eye contact with me, and before I can respond, he's back to his phone. I hear him mutter to his buddies, "Chick is weird." The men chuckle at that little slight, and that's it? That's all I get? Whatever.

"Asshole," I grumble as I start to move around the room again. I can keep *myself* entertained. I'm used to doing things alone. That's probably why I hate stuff like this. I'm much better on my own, in my own world, in my own head. There's nothing wrong with being alone. It's being lonely that sucks.